PRAISE FOR BARBARA NICKLESS

Gone to Darkness

"A gritty, hard-boiled crime novel with breathless action and deep, sturdy characters. Detective Sydney Parnell and her partner, Clyde, a police dog, are a tantalizing duo, and the story's narrative and dialogue are authentic and witty and demand compulsive reading. *Gone to Darkness* is everything you want in thriller fiction."

—Robert Dugoni, #1 *Wall Street Journal* bestselling author of the Tracy Crosswhite series

"Nobody does atmosphere better than Barbara Nickless. With deft strokes, she draws impending doom within bleak settings and then colors them with vivid action and brilliant characters, both human and canine. *Gone to Darkness* is mystery and suspense writing at its best!"

—Margaret Mizushima, award-winning author of the Timber Creek K-9 Mysteries

"Barb Nickless's *Gone to Darkness* is another stellar entry in the Sydney Rose Parnell series. Even though she's now a Denver police detective, Sydney and Clyde catch a case involving trains, a unique milieu that Nickless masterfully evokes. Readers who enjoy an atmospheric setting, a kick-ass yet vulnerable heroine, solid police procedurals, fast-paced yet lyrical writing, and/or the closeness of a human-dog partnership should immediately buy or borrow every book in this series. (I stop short of suggesting stealing a copy, but if that's your only option . . .)"

—Laura DiSilverio, award-winning and nationally bestselling author of *The Reckoning Stones*

"Barbara Nickless creates characters who matter—to each other and to the reader, who is fortunate to journey with them. With *Gone to Darkness*, Nickless expertly crafts a dark tale brightened with heart, humor, and humanity. It's a tightly woven, always escalating, keeps-you-up-past-your-bedtime novel. And Sydney Parnell is my favorite kind of detective: a relentless empath on a mission to solve herself as well as the crime, navigating her demons to ensure justice for the victims of evil."

—Matt Goldman, Emmy Award winner and *New York Times* bestselling author of the Nils Shapiro series

"In the fourth episode of her popular, bestselling Sydney Rose Parnell series, award-winning thriller writer and fan favorite Barbara Nickless leaves no doubt that she's on the fast track to A-list stardom. In *Gone to Darkness*, the action never slows, and the suspense ratchets up in every chapter of this delightfully twisted and energetic page-turning thriller from the mind of a budding superstar!"

—*Mysterious Book Report*

Ambush

"A nail-biter with some wicked twists . . . Fast-paced and nonstop . . . Sydney is fleshed out, flawed, gritty, and kick-ass and you can't help but root for her. Nickless leaves you satisfied and smiling—something that doesn't happen too often in this genre!"

—Bookish Biker

"*Ambush* has plenty of action and intrigue. There are shoot-outs and kidnappings. There are cover-ups and conspiracies. At the center of it all is a flawed heroine who will do whatever it takes to set things right."

—BVS Reviews

"*Ambush* takes off on page one like a Marine F/A-18 Super Hornet under full military power from the flight deck . . . and never lets the reader down."

—*Mysterious Book Report*

"*Ambush* truly kicks butt and takes names, crackling with tension from page one with a plot as sharp as broken glass. Barbara Nickless is a superb writer."

—Steve Berry, #1 internationally bestselling author

"*Ambush* is modern mystery with its foot on the gas. Barbara Nickless's writing—at turns blazing, aching, stark, and gorgeous—propels this story at a breathless pace until its sublime conclusion. In Sydney Parnell, Nickless has masterfully crafted a heroine who, with all her internal and external scars, compels the reader to simultaneously root for and forgive her. A truly standout novel."

—Carter Wilson, *USA Today* bestselling author of *Mister Tender's Girl*

"Exceptional . . . Nickless raises the stakes and expands the canvas of a blisteringly original series. A wholly satisfying roller coaster of a thriller that features one of the genre's most truly original heroes."

—Jon Land, *USA Today* bestselling author

"*Ambush* . . . makes you laugh and cry as the pages fly by."

—Tim Tigner, internationally bestselling author

Dead Stop

"The twists and turns . . . are first-rate. Barbara Nickless has brought forth a worthy heroine in Sydney Parnell."

—BVS Reviews

Blood on the Tracks

A *SUSPENSE MAGAZINE* BEST OF 2016 BOOKS SELECTION: DEBUT

"A stunner of a thriller. From the first page to the last, *Blood on the Tracks* weaves a spell that only a natural storyteller can master. And a guarantee: you'll fall in love with one of the best characters to come along in modern thriller fiction, Sydney Rose Parnell."

—Jeffery Deaver, internationally bestselling author

"Beautifully written and heartbreakingly intense, this terrific and original debut is unforgettable. Please do not miss *Blood on the Tracks*. It fearlessly explores our darkest and most vulnerable places—and is devastatingly good. Barbara Nickless is a star."

—Hank Phillippi Ryan, Anthony, Agatha, and Mary Higgins Clark Award–winning author of *Say No More*

"Both evocative and self-assured, Barbara Nickless's debut novel is an outstanding, hard-hitting story so gritty and real, you feel it in your teeth. Do yourself a favor and give this bright talent a read."

—John Hart, multiple Edgar Award winner and *New York Times* bestselling author of *Redemption Road*

"Fast-paced and intense, *Blood on the Tracks* is an absorbing thriller that is both beautifully written and absolutely unique in character and setting. Barbara Nickless has written a twisting, tortured novel that speaks with brutal honesty of the lingering traumas of war, including and especially those wounds we cannot see. I fell hard for Parnell and her four-legged partner and can't wait to read more."

—Vicki Pettersson, *New York Times* and *USA Today* bestselling author of *Swerve*

"The aptly titled *Blood on the Tracks* offers a fresh and starkly original take on the mystery genre. Barbara Nickless has fashioned a beautifully drawn hero in take-charge, take-no-prisoners Sydney Parnell, former Marine and now a railway cop battling a deadly gang as she investigates their purported connection to a recent murder. Nickless proves a master of both form and function in establishing herself every bit the equal of Nevada Barr and Linda Fairstein. A major debut that is not to be missed."

—Jon Land, *USA Today* bestselling author

"*Blood on the Tracks* is a bullet train of action. It's one part mystery and two parts thriller with a compelling protagonist leading the charge toward a knockout finish. The internal demons of one Sydney Rose Parnell are as gripping as the external monster she's chasing around Colorado. You will long remember this spectacular debut novel."

—Mark Stevens, author of the award-winning Allison Coil Mystery series

"Nickless captures you from the first sentence. Her series features Sydney Rose Parnell, a young woman haunted by the ghosts of her past. In *Blood on the Tracks*, she doggedly pursues a killer, seeking truth even in the face of her own destruction—the true mark of a heroine. Skilled in evoking emotion from the reader, Nickless is a master of the craft, a writer to keep your eyes on."

—Chris Goff, author of *Dark Waters*

"Barbara Nickless's *Blood on the Tracks* is raw and authentic, plunging readers into the fascinating world of tough railroad cop Special Agent Sydney Rose Parnell and her Malinois sidekick, Clyde. Haunted by her military service in Iraq, Sydney Rose is brought in by the Denver Major Crimes unit to help solve a particularly brutal murder, leading her into a snake pit of hate and betrayal. Meticulously plotted and intelligently written, *Blood on the Tracks* is a superb debut novel."

—M. L. Rowland, author of the Search and Rescue Mystery novels

"*Blood on the Tracks* is a must-read debut. A suspenseful crime thriller with propulsive action, masterful writing, and a tough-as-nails cop, Sydney Rose Parnell. Readers will want more."

—Robert K. Tanenbaum, *New York Times* bestselling author of the Butch Karp and Marlene Ciampi legal thrillers

"Nickless's writing admirably captures the fallout from a war where even survivors are trapped, forever reliving their trauma."

—*Kirkus Reviews*

"Part mystery, part antiwar story, Nickless's engrossing first novel, a series launch, introduces Sydney Rose Parnell . . . Nickless skillfully explores the dehumanizing effects resulting from the unspeakable cruelties of wartime as well as the part played by the loyalty soldiers owe to family and each other under stressful circumstances."

—*Publishers Weekly*

"An interesting tale . . . The fast pace will leave you finished in no time. Nickless seamlessly ties everything together with a shocking ending."

—RT Book Reviews

"If you enjoy suspense and thrillers, then you will [want] *Blood on the Tracks* for your library. Full of the suspense that holds you on the edge of your seat, it's also replete with acts of bravery, moments of hope, and a host of feelings that keep the story's intensity level high. This would be a great work for a book club or reading group with a great deal of information that would create robust dialogue and debate."

—Blog Critics

"In *Blood on the Tracks*, Barbara Nickless delivers a thriller with the force of a speeding locomotive and the subtlety of a surgeon's knife. Sydney and Clyde are both great characters with flaws and virtues to see them through a plot thick with menace. One for contemporary thriller lovers everywhere."

—Authorlink

"*Blood on the Tracks* is a superb story that rises above the genre of mystery . . . It is a first-class read."

—*Denver Post*

AT FIRST LIGHT

ALSO BY BARBARA NICKLESS

Blood on the Tracks

Dead Stop

Ambush

Gone to Darkness

AT
FIRST
LIGHT

BARBARA
NICKLESS

Text copyright © 2021 by Barbara Nickless
All rights reserved.

Published by Thomas & Mercer, Seattle

www.apub.com

Amazon, the Amazon logo, and Thomas & Mercer are trademarks of Amazon.com, Inc., or its affiliates.

ISBN-13: 9781542026413
ISBN-10: 1542026415

Cover design by M. S. Corley

Printed in the United States of America

To my ghosts, which are many

PREFACE: A LOVE LETTER TO CHICAGO

The city of Chicago sounded its siren call for me long ago. A too-short visit only cemented my love for this bustling, brazen, brilliant city built on a swamp. A place where the lake and the rivers keep trying to take back what was once theirs—and where the people of Chicago refuse to cede more than a few basements or an underpass or the occasional tunnel. Where corruption rubs up against idealism, where neighborhoods shift and gentrify and shift again.

My plan, when I began writing *At First Light*, was to return to Chicago and stay with family on an extended sabbatical. I wanted to begin like a tourist and then take a deeper dive into the city's architecture, its culture, and especially its people.

Then came the 2020 pandemic. And everything changed. The citizens of Chicago—like so many Americans—suffered terribly. And I remained in Colorado.

I considered shifting Evan and Addie to another city. But nothing about that felt right. So I persisted. And as I struggled to get to know the city from a distance, what I learned is that Chicagoans are among the most generous people you'll meet. From detectives to bookstore owners to attorneys and beyond—when I asked for help, people gave generously of their time and knowledge.

For a list of some of the people who helped, please read the acknowledgments in the back. And for the many, many other resources I used while writing this book—both for Chicago and for other aspects of the story—please visit my website at www.barbaranickless.com.

Finally, for everything about Chicago that I got wrong, I offer a heartfelt apology. I confess to altering certain locations such as Washington Park to suit the needs of this story. And to being deliberately vague about the location of Evan's home. If you notice errors, I'd love to hear from you so that I get it right on Evan's next adventure.

Barbara Nickless
March 2020

ONE

Excerpt from *The Narratives of Serial Killers*
Semiotician: Evan Wilding, PhD, SSA, IASS
Proceedings of the International Conference on Semiotics

Every murderer creates his own story.

This story may be simple or elaborate, coherent or deeply fragmented.

Serial murderers often leave signs and symbols at the crime scene—messages for the police to decipher. Notes, maps, images. The posing of the body, a unique modus operandi. The killer is the riddler extraordinaire, and his narrative—the story he wishes to tell—is the enigma he presents to the detective.

Someone—perhaps Nietzsche—once said that those seen dancing were thought insane by those who could not hear the music.

Our job is to find the killer's music.

THE VIKING POET

Listen!

I am the wolf who walks your nights. The horror who haunts your days. Hear me—I am the soldier who slays the sinners.

Come, sinner, you who violate the Law. Walk with me.

Am I not fair company?

We will spend tonight together. And if you cannot answer my riddle, then I will—I must!—finish Odin's work. When it is over, I'll send birds to guide you from this world into another, as custom demands. Birds whose presence in Chicago defiles nature. Then I'll scatter runes to tell the world of your sins.

Remember: fate goes ever as it must.

And I am your fate.

ᚷ

I speak my words aloud then, satisfied; cap my pen; and close the journal. It's evening. The sun, Sunna, riding in her chariot, nears the far horizon. All around, shadows gather.

I look past the translations of *Beowulf* stacked on my desk. Past the knife. I pick up the framed photo of Alex and touch a finger to the glass.

A sound. Outside, a murmuration of starlings flurries past the windows. I stand and, still holding Alex's photograph, I cross the room to stand in the dying light. I wonder what soul the birds accompany tonight.

Who came for you, Alex, when you lay broken deep in the earth? Who carried your soul to the underworld?

My fingers tremble on the picture frame.

The last rays disappear. Red still burns in the western sky, but overhead, a scattering of stars appears in the darkening vault, jewels on a diamond broker's velvet cloth.

I replace Alex's photo on the desk, then drop to the floor and knock out a series of push-ups, lunges, squats, and planks. I work until my breath comes hard and sweat sheets from my naked skin.

To calm my mind. To prepare for what is to come.

Then I shower and dress, draw on my coat, slip my cell phone and car keys into a pocket.

My work is nearly done. Not much longer now before the businessman's soul journeys on and I turn my attention to the next sinner.

For there is always another sinner.

Chapter 1

A bitter mid-November night slouched off to make room for a grim day that no one considered an improvement.

The wind off Lake Michigan rattled awnings and swept rain and trash along the streets and pressed dank fingers against the exposed necks of the locals—paper delivery boys, taxi drivers, cops—who stomped their feet and adjusted their scarves and dreamed of tropical beaches and sun-warmed skin.

Near a forlorn section of the Calumet River, Detective Adrianne "Addie" Bisset stared at the body of a man murdered more than once. By her count, he'd received three fatal wounds, and although all were cruel, she couldn't be sure which injury had served as the actual coup de grâce. It was the detective's macabre game—had it been the slashed throat, the tightened noose, or the bone-crushing blow to the head?

The body lay curled on its side, half in, half out of the water; the murky slosh of the Calumet broke and swirled around the dead man's legs, which were held in place by wooden stakes. She noted the victim's bound hands. His nakedness. The injuries to his face she hoped were postmortem. The man's wounds spoke of ritualistic violence. The carved sticks arranged around his head suggested a dark magic.

Addie's fingers rose to touch the cross around her neck, and she found it oddly reassuring that after four years of seeing almost everything one human could do to another, death could still leave her shaken.

She checked the time on her phone: 6:50 a.m. The machinery of homicide investigation—what Addie thought of as the three-ring circus in blue—was about to begin. In an hour, this haunted place of wind and water and the cries of birds would be carefully orchestrated pandemonium.

First things first. She crooked a finger at the uniform who'd called in the body.

"Find Dr. Evan Wilding," she said. "He's probably off in a park or reserve somewhere in the city, hunting with his hawk. Start with Washington Park near the university and use mounted patrol to track him down. Here's his cell number"—she ripped a sheet from her notebook and jotted numbers on the paper—"but he probably won't answer. When patrol finds him, tell him I need him ASAP. Tell him we've got one of the weird ones."

The young cop squinted at her from beneath his cap with its blue-and-white-checkered tartan. His cheeks and ears were red in the cold. "Is Dr. Wilding the one they call the Sparrow?"

"That's him."

"The dwarf, right? I read about some case he solved. He's a forensic semio . . . semioti . . ." The officer's voice trailed off into a linguistic thicket.

"Forensic semiotician." Addie turned her attention and her phone back toward the corpse. She snapped a photo. "And he prefers to be called a person with dwarfism. Or better yet, call him by his name."

The cop persisted. "But what is that exactly? A forensic semiotician?"

Another snap. The corpse seemed to lunge in the phone's flash. "It's someone who studies the signs left by a killer. Any rituals the killer performs or writing he leaves at the scene."

"Signs, ma'am?"

She turned to face him. The officer looked barely old enough to vote. His eyes were locked on some distant point high above the body. Maybe this was his first.

"Signs. Why don't you ask him when you find him?" She made a shooing gesture. "Now go. And don't let him put you off. I bloody well want him here."

"Yes, ma'am." The patrolman spared a glance for the body, then headed up the hill toward his blue-and-white unit parked on the dirt road behind Addie's SUV. His shoes squelched in the mud along the path he'd taped off from the rest of the crime scene.

Addie turned back to the corpse. She had learned to say *bloody well* from the very British Evan. The phrase had served her well ever since she'd given up swearing for Lent one year and decided she liked being the cop who didn't curse.

Always the rebel.

A witch's gale scattered wavelets across the river, carrying the bite from Lake Michigan, the punch of it like a cuff from a bear. The body's lower half swayed in the reeds. Only the fact that it had been staked down kept the river from tugging it into deeper water.

Far away, lights gleamed on the Chicago skyline, illuminating the Willis and Tribune Towers, the rippling visage of the Aqua Tower, and the square-shouldered, no-nonsense rise of the John Hancock Building. The Mag Mile Lights Festival was only a week away. Thanksgiving a few days after that.

A holiday this man would never again celebrate.

"I'm sorry for what's happened to you," she said to the corpse.

The body stirred as if still capable of hearing and understanding. As if it longed to rise out of the dark water and take in the glittering lights with her, imagine feast-laden tables and crackling fires, plump turkeys and tart cranberries and the velvet smoothness of all things pumpkin, finally raising a boisterous toast with family and friends: *Here's to a good year!*

Addie touched the cross around her neck again and kept taking photos.

CHAPTER 2

Twelve miles away as the crow flies, Dr. Evan Wilding also stared at death, albeit through binoculars. In this case, the victim in question was a rock dove.

The once-fine specimen of bird lay breast up in the rain-sodden field, its blue-gray feathers a lighter wash against the autumn gold. Evan's goshawk watched it from the ground ten feet away, her damp wings spread in a show of bewildered aggression at this bird that refused to flee.

Evan lowered his binoculars and hurried as well as he could across the misty pasture, his pants soaked with rain, water beading off his hat. Part of him was worried that the rock dove had been poisoned—toxic bait that Ginny might tear and swallow. Another part of him was distressed by Ginny's predicament—a hawk on the ground was an awkward creature, stumpy-legged, slow-moving, displaced from its normal arena of air and space.

Out of the sky, she fared little better than he.

Ginny cocked her head at his approach, her yellow eyes fierce, her mouth open in unhappy confusion. He wriggled a bit of raw meat in his gloved left hand and whistled.

She shifted on her yellow-scaled legs and glared.

"Come on, Ginny. Be a love." His breath hung in a cloud.

Falconry was a humbling art. Hawks were not domestic—they were sharp-taloned, razor-beaked, feathery tufts of wildness that condescended now and again to perch upon an offered fist. While his love for the young Ginny had been instant and all-consuming, hers for him was a slow-blooming affair, a bond built on the steady accretion of trust.

That, and a regular supply of raw meat.

He glanced at his watch as the minutes ticked by.

Some days, he wondered if he wouldn't have been better off with a dog that came when he called and gave him the utter adoration and obedience he surely deserved. A creature who would boost his ego rather than flatten it.

Today was shaping up to be one of those days.

"Ginny, you are being completely wretched."

He wriggled the bait again. After a long hesitation in which the hawk appeared to cycle from being his partner to wild beast and back again, she flapped heavily into the air and landed on his glove, tearing greedily at the bit of flesh.

"That's my fine lady."

Evan leaned over the lifeless rock dove. *Columba livia*, aka pigeon, aka flying rat. Its plump breast had been cleaved nearly in half by a sharp tool. The blood on its dark-gray breast and iridescent green neck feathers shone bright red in the light rain.

Nothing natural in this small death. But definitely not poison.

He straightened to his full height of four foot five. Doing so didn't give him much of a vantage from this small, low-lying field. Close by and around him in all directions, woods glowed in the rain as if lit from within. Dark firs and nearly naked white ash and elm trees stabbed the low dome of the sky. A narrow gap in the woods revealed the placid waters of the park's lagoon. In the far distance, traffic growled as the city grumbled to life.

Closer by, the trees shone wetly—silent sentinels.

Evan looked again at the pigeon. Its feathers trembled in the drizzle, giving it false life.

Unease touched a cool hand to the back of his neck.

He had been granted special dispensation to fly Ginny at Washington Park during off hours. It was good exercise, and park officials appreciated Ginny's efforts to winnow the city's overpopulation of pigeons. Though the battle to keep the city's buildings, statues, and sidewalks clean of droppings was an unending task, Evan was—as far as he knew—the only one sanctioned to pursue pigeons in this particular park.

His mind ran down the possibilities of who might toss knives at nesting birds.

A hunter. But then why leave the carcass?

Perhaps someone with a hatred of pigeons and a concurrent desire to improve their knife-throwing skills.

Or, possibly, a madman.

Evan's imagination was vast, and admittedly sometimes encouraged by his fondness for drink. Thinking outside the box was what he was paid to do. But his flights of fancy were generally limited to the speculation required when deciphering ancient scripts or decoding the rants of murderers and terrorists. He was not known for seeing madmen behind every bush, even when his work often brought him into their realm.

The second option, he decided. The knife-wielding hater of pigeons. Once again, he felt a sense of disquiet as he took in the silent woods. The park was now officially open, and soon joggers and walkers would descend upon the trails. But for the moment, he and Ginny were quite alone.

Or so he hoped.

"Home we go, Ginny," he said. "We'll call in and report this on our way."

But Ginny had seemingly forgotten the pigeon, and her gaze had gone elsewhere. Leaves rustling nearby suggested a mouse or a squirrel burrowing to escape the hawk, and her golden eyes blazed with eagerness for the hunt.

"Not now," he warned.

He reached toward his bag for her hood.

As if she sensed his intent, Ginny pushed off from his fist, yanking her jesses free from his surprised grip and disappearing into the thicket with the sepia flick of feathers.

"God's wounds," he muttered, watching as she vanished into the trees. "I'm getting a dog!" he called after her.

He pulled out his phone, noticed that he'd missed a great many calls, then pulled up the GPS tracking app. Ginny was headed due north, which would take her over the playgrounds and softball fields. Which would, fortunately, be empty right now. It was always an awkward moment when your hawk hazed young children.

From far away, someone shouted, "Professor Wilding! Are you here?"

He squinted east, into the rising light. He could just make out the navy uniforms and bright-blue helmets of Chicago's mounted police.

Police.

That didn't bode well.

But at least he was no longer alone in the woods with a pigeon slayer.

He looked at the missed calls. Six showed an unknown number. Nine were from a homicide detective, Addie Bisset. The best detective on the force in his opinion. Certainly the bravest. A woman with a fine mind and rarified taste who loved his cooking and his library equally.

Given all this, she was, naturally, his best friend.

Still, dear friend or no, she didn't generally call him nine times in the early hours of a workday.

"Professor Wilding!" came the voice again, young and male.

The clouds parted, washing the scene with pearl as a man and a woman on horseback drew close. The officer in front raised his cupped hands to his mouth. "Doctor Wild—"

"I'm right here," Evan said.

The man dropped his gaze and gaped at Evan.

"Professor Wilding, I presume," he said.

"The same," Evan said.

The officers closed the gap. Now Evan could see the names stenciled on their coats. Officers Blakesley and Osborn. His mind went automatically to the etymology of their names. Blakesley was the name of a village in Northern England. The name Osborn was also Anglo-Saxon and meant *divine bear*.

"Damn easy to miss," said the man. Officer Blakesley. He was big, with neatly trimmed blond hair and a ruddy complexion that now deepened with a flush. "What I mean is, with the fog, you came out of nowhere."

"I'm short is what you meant," Evan said. "It's all right to speak the truth."

The second officer urged her horse closer. "Detective Bisset has asked for you, sir. Patrol tried calling."

"I don't check my phone when I'm hunting," Evan said.

"Hunting?" She frowned.

"With Ginny." Evan enjoyed a brief moment of being the one with the knowledge instead of standing on the other side. "And speaking of hunting, someone has been murdering pigeons."

"We get that a lot," Blakesley said.

"With knives?" Evan moved aside so they could see the pigeon's tattered body.

Osborn leaned forward in her saddle. "Shit."

Evan's brain cataloged the word. *Shit. From the Old English word* scitte, *meaning* purging *or* diarrhea. *Taboo after the sixteenth century and censored from the works of James Joyce and Hemingway. Modern derivations include* shitload—*a great many;* shit-faced—*drunk; and of course* shitticism, *from Robert Frost's description of scatological writing.*

Thus was the curse of being a semiotician. No word too common to avoid scrutiny.

"Did you see anyone?" Blakesley asked.

"Not a soul." Evan glanced up, looking beyond their shoulders. "Ah, here she is."

Both officers flinched as Ginny came in from the north, swooping low over their heads. Talons outstretched, she slammed onto her master's gloved fist. Osborn's horse skittered sideways. Blakesley kept his roan in firm check.

Ginny fluffed herself, then settled. Her lids lowered halfway, a sign of contentment. A few drops of blood marred the white feathers of her breast.

Blakesley smiled. "A goshawk, isn't she? A friend of mine use to fly them. She's a beauty."

"She's enormous." Osborn's voice sounded both admiring and annoyed. She coughed as if to cover up her annoyance. "I saw your talk a few months back on the origins of human sacrifice in Mesoamerica, sir. At Cobb Hall."

"You're a student?"

"Date night. His pick. He didn't last for date number two, but your talk was fascinating."

"I'm glad you enjoyed it," Evan said.

"I've attended all your public lectures ever since." Her eyes lit with enthusiasm. "Next month's is about the petroglyphs of the Ancestral Puebloans, right?"

Evan nodded. The upside to being a semiotician was that you occasionally attracted enthusiasts.

But Blakesley laughed. "God, Sal, you're such a nerd."

"And you, Ed, are a bonehead," she said, apparently unoffended.

Evan ran a hand along Ginny's feathers. She ignored him and eyed the cops with a wild gleam in her golden eyes. "No eating public servants," he whispered. More loudly he said, "So where is Addie—Detective Bisset?"

"She's where the Calumet joins the Little Calumet." Blakesley tipped his head south. "A mile or so from the recycling plant. There's a patrol car waiting nearby to drive you there."

Evan opened his mouth to protest. He had work to do. His ongoing attempt to decode the Minoan script of the Phaistos Disc. His semiotics class this afternoon at the University of Chicago, where he taught. A meeting with a classics professor to discuss early Cretan hieroglyphs and another with the head of the humanities department to review his planned sabbatical.

Appointments arranged for weeks. Everything planned to a T. Only a rigorous schedule gave Evan any hope of achieving his goals, which were many.

"Sir?" Osborn asked. "Are you coming?" It didn't sound like a question.

Planned to a T. He leaned his head forward until it touched Ginny's. "She said she needed me?"

"That's right, sir. She said we weren't to take no for an answer."

"Well, then." He let out a breath and simultaneously let go of his plans for the day, his hopes for progress on the endless stream of undeciphered mysteries. "I'll follow patrol there. I doubt his car is equipped to carry a hawk."

"Yes, sir."

The officers turned their horses. He trudged after them, Ginny complacent on his glove. Post-hunt, she'd let the wildness go out of her.

He needed to do the same.

CHAPTER 3

Addie shoved her numb hands into the pockets of her parka.

Around her, radios hissed, a woman from Forensic Services took photos, and someone else worked on a series of sketches. Other techs walked up and down on the road above, searching for evidence. The crime scene had come alive. On her orders, everyone except the techs kept well clear of the corpse, waiting for the medical examiner and Evan. Her partner, Patrick McBrady, had arrived ten minutes ago and stood with his butcher's arms folded over the broad expanse of his chest, chatting with another tech, Justin Wao, about the new pizzeria in Jefferson Park. How they diced anchovies straight into the cheese so that eating a slice was like sticking your head right down into the fishy netherworld of Lake Michigan.

"Sounds fuckin' awful," Patrick said. "But it works somehow. You know?"

Kind of like the Chicago PD, she thought.

"It's the Irish in you." Wao wrinkled his nose. "You guys'll eat anything. I mean, *haggis?* I wouldn't touch that for love or money."

"Haggis is Scottish, not Irish," Patrick said. "And anyway, aren't you from Cambodia or something? Don't you guys eat monkey brains?"

"Fuck you," Wao said amiably.

Addie snugged her Chicago Bears beanie lower over her ears as rain drizzled over the scene. It promised to be a Monday in the worst sense of the word. The call to the scene had come as she lay spooned against the warm and deliciously hunky body of her latest romantic interest—Clayton L. Hamden, attorney to the stars. Or at least attorney to the Cook County political body. Their plan, just as soon as they'd dragged themselves out of bed, had been to enjoy breakfast and a run through the park near his condo with maybe a few minutes to play in the shower before they departed for their respective offices and began the week in a suitably satiated manner.

Someone had once told Addie that she went through men the way a rat terrier chewed through vermin—quickly and with ruthless efficiency. But Clay felt different. Never mind that they all felt different until, without warning, they felt like all the others. Maybe Clay wouldn't be just a few weeks' fling. Maybe he'd be something more. Her cousin had called the night before with the news that yesterday's horoscope had guaranteed Addie's life was about to undergo a dramatic change.

The body, she was sure, didn't count as dramatic change. It was the department's six hundredth homicide of the year and the twenty-sixth for her and her partner. Murder as usual.

Even if it was unquestionably the weirdest body they'd had.

Patrick wandered back over to stand beside her on the low ridge, one hand curled around a cup of coffee from a nearby gas station where they probably pulled their water straight from the Calumet. She curled her lip. The tech was right. Detective Patrick McBrady would put anything in his body. Not for the first time, she observed that her partner was the color and size of a slab of beef. His broad face and thinning hair shone red, like a can of tinned meat; his wide eyes Frank Sinatra blue; his generous nose a map of broken capillaries. Classic old-school Irish cop, a stereotype Patrick played to the max. In his immense paws, the twenty-four-ounce cup looked like it had been filched from a child's tea set.

"You catch the game yesterday?" he asked.

She shook her head. Clayton wasn't a native Chicagoan, and in his opinion, the Bears were worthless, unable to scare up a good quarterback and thus perennial losers at America's favorite sport. So far, this obvious lack of faith and foresight was the only mark against him.

"You missed the Bears against the Vikings?" Patrick's eyes flicked toward her. "Whoever he is, it must be serious."

She pushed up her beanie with her middle finger.

"Ha!" He was gleeful. "Definitely serious. But the asshole doesn't like football. Did you run 'im?"

"You only *think* you're funny, Paddy Wagon."

The nickname made him laugh, as if he hadn't heard it a thousand times. But no way was Addie going to share her love life with her partner. She trusted him every day with her back. She'd pick him as her partner over just about anyone on the planet when it came to drug dens and dark alleys. But not with her private romances. That was when Patrick got all fatherly and tried to give her advice. If her own daddy wasn't allowed to comment, she sure as hell wasn't going to let "Father" Patrick McBrady throw in his two cents.

She used a tissue to dab the end of her nose—which ran whenever the weather turned cold—and huddled into her coat.

The rising sun rippled over the city. It spotlighted the tops of the trees and danced a line across the water. It didn't reach the corpse. Addie noted for the fiftieth time the braided noose pulled tight around the swollen neck. Just below the rope, the throat had been slit ear to ear. And the back of the head was staved.

"Three in one," Patrick said. "Why, you think?"

"I'm thinking it was part of a ritual. What's also odd is the way the killer made sure the victim couldn't move —presumably *after* death."

Patrick furrowed his brow. "Maybe he didn't want the body floating away."

"Or maybe he was afraid it would get up and come after him," she said, unable to resist baiting her superstitious partner. "Haunt him forever."

He took the bait. "True that. It's an eerie setting to serve as a man's final resting place."

"Dirty, you mean. Polluted. The water just about glows."

"Nah. It's more than that." Patrick shoved his hand in his left pocket. She knew he kept his father's World War II pocket shrine there. Joseph holding the baby Jesus.

"Oooooohhh." Addie moaned like a ghost.

This was a routine between them. Addie teased her partner for being superstitious, and he acted more gullible than he was, pretending to cringe at every black cat and broken mirror.

But this morning, Patrick gave a mournful shake of his head. "All the people used to work around here in the factories, and now they and their kin are nothing but ghosts. Either because they were forced out and had to leave their hearts and homes behind. Or because they died here, probably of hopelessness."

"Got up on the wrong side of the bed this morning, did you?"

"Maybe." Patrick frowned, a deep crease in his weather-worn face, and shook off his mood. "God, it's cold. Should have worn my thermals." He nodded toward the crime-scene techs. "At least we ain't those poor bastards in the water."

Three techs waded through the knee-high shallows—one scooping a net to sieve for evidence while two others pushed poles into the mud to erect a tarp over the corpse, protecting it against the prying eyes of riverside strollers or passing fishermen.

And news helicopters. This was the kind of body the media loved.

Patrick aimed his cup back toward the path that led down from the road. "Bastard covered his tracks."

Addie followed his gaze toward where the mud had been raked over, presumably by the killer. Outside of the scoured section and the area taped off by the patrol cop and now used by the rest of the crime-scene crew, the muddy path that led down from the road was filled with footprints. The techs had roped it off in the hopes they'd get something from it, but she wasn't holding her breath. Kayakers, fishermen, day hikers—despite the pollution, they all used this area. At night, other sorts came out.

"No car," Patrick said. "If our guy drove down here to score something, how'd he get here?"

"Maybe he picked up his killer and they came here together for whatever business they had in mind."

"Or the killer picked him up. You think our victim walked down to the river on his own?"

"He looks like he weighs a couple hundred pounds. A big man for someone to carry or drag."

"Maybe the dogs'll be able to tell us." Patrick tipped back his head and got the final dregs of his coffee before crumpling the empty cup. "Whaddaya make of all those sticks?"

Long wooden slats had been pressed horizontally into the mud and arranged around the head of the corpse like the rays of the sun. The killer—or someone—had carved each stick with a sharp instrument, etching tiny lines that looked like letters in an unknown alphabet.

She said as much, about the writing, and Patrick nodded. "That why you called your friend?"

"That, and the posing of the body."

Patrick stuck a cigarette in his mouth but didn't light it. He'd given up smoking three months earlier but said he still liked the feel of the cig in his mouth. "So is the little guy coming or what?"

"It took them a while to find the *professor*. He should be here any minute."

One of the techs screamed and leapt out of the water.

"Get it away!" she shrieked, barreling up the hill toward them.

An immense brown-and-black snake slithered out of the water after her. Thick of body and several feet in length, the reptile coiled up against the dead man's spine. It raised its head and regarded everyone with unblinking eyes.

"Mary Mother of God," Patrick said.

"Shit," threw in Wao. "That's a water moccasin."

"Kill it!" someone shouted.

But Addie yanked off her gloves, snatched up one of the poles meant for the tarp, and hurried down to the water. Sensing her approach, the snake moved to wriggle under the corpse, but she pressed the end of the pole gently against the reptile, holding it in place. With her other hand, she grabbed the snake near the middle of its body, pulled it away from the corpse, and tossed it into the water.

"Northern water snake," she said to the tech as she walked by. "It might have bitten you, but it's not poisonous."

The tech was bent over as if she might lose her breakfast.

"Not here," Addie warned.

"It's barely forty degrees," Wao said. "The hell is a snake doing here?"

"Snakes brumate," Addie said. "A form of hibernation. But they're not in a deep sleep. Likely either we or the killer disturbed its den."

"It's a bad sign," Patrick said.

"It's a water snake," Addie snapped.

"Serpents mean treachery, you know. I'm telling you, there's something bad about this case."

She couldn't tell if he was kidding. "Bad for the victim, you mean."

"Bad for all of us."

She laughed, loudly enough that some of the techs turned to see what was so amusing. "So now we're going to solve crimes using signs and augurs?"

"That's your friend's job. But still . . ." He gave her a look filled with admiration. "I had no idea you were a snake handler."

"Four older brothers." She shrugged. "Learning about reptiles was a form of survival." Not to mention staying calm around bats, mice, spiders, and scorpions. She'd learned to remain chill around pretty much every kind of beastie. Except rats. Show her so much as a picture of a rat and she'd go find a nice bed to hide under.

Unless that's where the rats hid, too.

The tech straightened and approached, her gold-and-green Kente cloth headband bright in the morning's gloom. Her brown skin held a grayish cast.

"Poisonous or not," she said, "I am *not* going back in the water unless you get me a boat. But I found this at the same time that bit of nasty showed up. It was near the victim's feet."

She held out her net. Inside was a waterlogged wallet.

Addie snapped on latex gloves, fished out the wallet, and opened it. She listed the contents out loud to Patrick. "A Chicago driver's license, an American Express card, and a Visa Platinum. A Costco card, ten identical but almost illegible business cards"—she squinted—"for a jewelry store on Michigan Avenue, and another card for Sugar Hill Ministries with the name James Talfour, Caring Ministries Associate and an address in Georgia. There's also a plastic punch card for a cupcake shop. Sixty-two dollars in twenties and ones." She studied the face staring back at her from the license. A Black man with a neat goatee and a confident expression. The resemblance to the corpse was not straightforward, given the positioning and condition of the body, but it was there nonetheless. "James Talfour, age forty-two. Address in the Gold Coast area. North State Parkway. The name on the DL matches the one on the business cards."

"If we're looking at Talfour, he didn't get this way from a robbery," Patrick said, stating the obvious because it was his job to do so—no theoretical stone unturned. "Why take the man's wallet and then just toss it nearby?"

"You're seriously wondering about the wallet? Why strangle a guy, then cut his throat and break his skull? Why make him a halo and scratch funny little lines into it?"

Patrick shot her a knowing grin. "Didn't get any this morning, did you? Maybe your new guy doesn't like *any* kind of ball sports."

"If you want me in a good mood, next time bring me a doughnut." She was still going through the waterlogged wallet. "Could be Talfour tossed his wallet into the river himself. Or maybe he dropped it when he was taking a walk. There's also an access card for a health club. Lakeshore Sports and Fitness in Lincoln Park. This guy was doing well for himself."

Patrick snorted. "A walk? Like maybe an evening stroll? You think that's what brought a North Shore guy down here? More likely drugs. Or prostitution."

"He was a minister," Addie protested.

"And your point?"

"Right. I'll check with vice."

"This place looks pretty good for either a quick one up against the pier or a needle in the arm."

Addie nodded. "Let's say he meets someone down here. They do their business, then the hooker-slash-drug-dealer strikes while Talfour is floating in a post-injection or post-coitus state of bliss."

"Like a praying mantis."

"What?"

"The females eat the heads of the males after they copulate." Patrick nodded wisely. "I saw it on a nature show."

"You tell your wife that?"

He shrugged trucker's shoulders under his leather jacket. "Why would I give her ideas?"

Patrick talked the talk. But Addie knew he and Mary were deeply in love. They'd met in a pub in West Clare when Patrick was reacquainting himself with his Irish roots. A lifelong bachelor, Patrick had fallen hard. He'd brought Mary back across the ocean with him, along with a tendency to *talk Irish*, as he put it.

After five years, the pair was as goofy as newlyweds around each other.

Addie sighed. True love. It was possible.

She placed the wallet and its contents into a bag and signed it back over to the tech. She was trying to ignore an uncomfortable tingling that had started in her gut and spread outward like an electrical storm. A wealthy, successful man brought down in the prime of life. It gave her a miserable thought: cases like this one—grisly, weird, important— could build a cop's career.

She scowled. Maybe Clayton, lawyer to the rich and famous, was rubbing off on her.

A horn sounded on the road above them, and suddenly everyone around was standing a little taller, shoulders thrown back another inch.

Her scowl deepened. "The brass."

"Maybe you shoulda held on to the snake," Patrick said.

An officer raised his voice—"Good morning, sir"—and a moment later, Lieutenant Criver appeared at the top of the rise. Tall and fit, dark-haired and seamlessly tanned, Criver loomed on the horizon with his military-square shoulders and an imposing glint in his steel-blue eyes. Superman in a navy-blue suit.

The lieutenant had moved here from Texas, bringing with him Sergeant Billings, her and Patrick's immediate boss. Billings stood at Criver's right elbow, pale and hairless. Like a ghoul.

Addie hadn't thought badly of Thomas Criver at first. Like everyone else, she'd been drawn to his charisma and his man-of-the-people persona. She liked the way he cursed like a street cop and downed doughnuts while going out with his men on patrol. He soothed the brass, swapped stories with his subordinates, and looked reassuringly manly and capable at press conferences. Addie had celebrated along with everyone else—it seemed they finally had a cop's cop in charge of their unit, a man who would fight both with them and for them.

Then, slowly, she'd realized that this lieutenant who would fight for his men would *only* fight for his *men*. He wasn't a misogynist, per se. Nor did he feel threatened by women. He simply believed women were not as capable. He no doubt found it sad. Regretful, even. But facts were facts.

Now Criver had a potentially big case, and Addie was his primary.

Things should get interesting.

On the windswept river shore, the lieutenant's gaze slid past her and landed on the victim. He pressed a finger to his dimpled chin. "James Talfour. I know that name. Didn't he serve on the board for some big charity? Something about helping Black kids?"

"We'll look into that, sir," Patrick said. "You hear anything about him being a minister?"

"No." It was Billings, who scratched his own chin, sharp as a boat's keel, and said, "I know him. Owned a jewelry shop. Finer Things. This, sir, is a guy who could hustle."

Criver glanced at Billings, like a rhino suddenly aware of the tickbird on his back. "You knew him personally?"

"Not personally, sir. No. But I've been in his store. Black guy in those fancy shops. Had to check him out. He was a gouger." He gave an emphatic shake of his head. "Wanted twelve thousand for a tennis bracelet."

Criver whistled. Even Addie found her thoughts momentarily diverted from Billings's racism by the prospect of spending twice what she'd paid for her car on a trinket for her wrist.

Criver's gaze skipped over Addie and zeroed in on Patrick. "What do we know?"

While Addie fumed, Patrick shuffled his feet and filled the lieutenant in. He finished with, "We're bringing in an expert on these sorts of cases. A professor from the university."

Criver's expression shifted from chilly to polar. "What is this going to cost the department?"

"We've used Dr. Wilding before," Addie said. "It's always been approved. From the top."

"Intellectual types, I've come to learn, are rarely worth their egos or their fees. Outside of court, anyway."

Billings nodded. "I know what you mean, sir. Know-it-alls. Eggheads and brainiacs."

"Well, sir." Patrick scratched behind his ear with a thick forefinger. "The dead guy won't mind. We'll keep the professor on a tight leash if that'll help."

Addie looked down the hill to hide her smile at Patrick's defiance.

From up above came the crunch of tires on gravel and an engine shutting off, then a door opening and closing. A swell of murmurs went through the gathered officers like leaves chased by the wind.

This happened whenever Evan showed up.

Addie spun around. "There he is."

CHAPTER 4

She met Evan at the top of the rise. He stood next to his truck, tapping something into his phone, apparently oblivious to the openmouthed stares. It was a routine she'd seen him use a dozen times—a ruse, actually. He went through this charade of checking his phone to give people time to recapture their equilibrium before they had to meet his eyes.

The pretense would break her heart except that she knew Dr. Evan Aiden Wilding—professor of semiotics, linguistics, and paleography at the U of C, world-renowned interpreter for government agencies of the writings and symbols left by killers and terrorists and madmen—would deck her if he saw even a hint of pity in her eyes.

Once the nearby cops finished with their double takes, they pulled back, as if Evan might be contagious.

"Troglodytes," she muttered. More loudly she said, "Dr. Wilding."

Evan lowered his phone, looked up into her eyes, and smiled from beneath the hood of his olive-green parka. She took him in as she always did. Vivid green eyes set in squint lines; thick, curly brown hair; a Van Dyke beard; and a face as quirkily handsome as a character actor's—the one who played the brilliant Cyrano to the movie idol's De Neuvillette.

The top of his head came exactly to her sternum. If they'd been lovers, he would have fit neatly under her chin. A thought she'd pushed out of her mind more than once.

No wonder people called him the Sparrow. Although he insisted the nickname came not from his size but from the idea that seeing a sparrow means a secret will soon be uncovered. A don at Oxford had gifted him with the title when, as an undergraduate, Evan bested twenty-three of the country's best semioticians to crack a code the government was proposing to use on one of its top-secret projects. Evan had needed two days. His nearest competitor took an additional six hours and seven minutes.

Addie knew about this because she'd researched Evan when they were on the way to becoming friends. This was after she'd skidded on her heels and all but fallen into his arms at an art exhibit. *And* spilled both their drinks. Despite the casualties—a pink Cosmo, a Manhattan, and her dignity—Evan had laughed until she couldn't help but join in.

A good start to any friendship.

Addie admittedly thought of Evan as a freak, but not in a way that had anything to do with his height. The guy had attended Oxford at age eleven, graduated with two PhDs at seventeen, then gone off to do good deeds in foreign lands for a few years before settling in the States and making a name for himself as a forensic semiotician.

A *brainiac* indeed. She was glad he was on their side.

She offered her hand, indicating they were meeting here as two professionals rather than old friends, setting a precedent for the officers around her. "Thank you for coming."

He shook her hand. "Of course."

She led him around a gaggle of officers and past the lieutenant's black Suburban, heading down the road to a vantage point she'd picked out earlier—she wanted to give him a chance to take in the scene before he had to deal with the crowd. Automatically, she matched her pace to his.

Behind them, she heard whispers.

"Who's the midget?"

"They call him the Sparrow. Supposed to be some kind of expert."

"On what? Hobbits?"

Addie's shoulders came up, and she half turned. Evan touched her lightly on the arm.

"Save it for something worthwhile," he said.

He was right, of course. He always was.

She waited until they were out of earshot. "Anyway, I'm sorry to drag you in, but I meant what I said. Thanks for coming."

"Did I have a choice?" he asked mildly.

"One of these days, I'm going to just issue a warrant."

"Two brawny officers on their fearless steeds—I thought you had."

She narrowed her eyes at him. "Is that bird shit on your coat? And mud on your knees. You look like the proverbial cat draggings. Were you *crawling* through the woods?"

He brushed at the mud on his pants. "You *do* care. And here I thought you loved me only for my mind."

She cut to the right and up a secondary ridge that rose above the water. "Who says I love you at all?"

"I'm crushed."

"Good." She stopped at the crest of the hill where the wind blew unfettered. "Now that we've reestablished my authority, why don't you take a look at the scene and tell me you're not interested."

The ridge gave them the highest nearby vantage point to look out over the corpse and the riverbank and the dark emerald water rippling outward beyond the dead man. She knew Evan liked to start with the big picture. A murderer's choice of locale—for the death or to dump a body—was the first step that led Evan into the dark maze of the killer's mind.

He called it the tug on the thread that would ultimately lead to the minotaur.

He asked, "Do you know the victim's name?"

"We haven't turned the body yet, but based on a wallet found nearby, he's a middle-aged Black businessman from the North Shore named James Talfour."

"Okay," he said.

She stepped back, giving him room.

✗

Evan drew in a deep breath and turned slowly in place, absorbing 360 degrees of the Chicago horizon. He took note of the slow current of the Calumet rolling by beneath a light mist. The muddy, beaten-down path through the weeds that provided access from the road to the shore. His eyes tracked the narrow, unpaved lane east, back toward the abandoned gas station he'd driven by moments earlier, the place choked with weeds and saplings and littered with roach clips, shreds of tinfoil, and used needles.

The killer could have arrived at this spot from the road or by water. Either way, he hadn't simply stumbled upon Talfour's final resting place. He'd been here before. He'd placed his victim in this swampy location with deliberate care.

Evan brought his gaze back to where he'd started and zeroed in on the body. From this vantage, James Talfour was little more than a vague shape huddled on the ground, his mud-spattered body curled into a fetal position among the reeds and partially concealed by the tarp rattling overhead.

"He's nude," Evan said.

"As the day he was born."

"And is that a noose around his neck?" he asked.

"He was garroted, had his throat slit and his skull bashed in."

"A triple death," Evan said. "Three is a number that carries significance in many religions and cultures."

"A religious killing?"

"Impossible to say right now. The killer was very thorough."

She nodded. "But the victim's face is tranquil. As if he'd just gone off to sleep. He might have been drugged."

"Are his hands bound?"

"With rope. And there are stakes, pinning him down. Also bits of grass on his skin, as if he'd been dragged into place."

"So he didn't arrive here by boat."

"Doesn't appear so. The killer raked over any drag marks or footprints. Although with so many prints, I don't know why he bothered."

Evan turned his gaze on Addie, but he wasn't seeing her. To himself, he murmured words about men with silvery hair who lay, rotting and foul, in dark water.

"What are you talking about?"

"The author and scholar J. R. R. Tolkien—it's something he said about bogs. Who called it in?"

The wind flapped her coat open, and she zipped it shut. "A kayaker found the body this morning at four a.m."

"A kayaker was out on the river three hours before sunrise?" He shuddered. "It would have been in the teens then."

"You're a wuss, my friend."

"Unequivocally."

"Anyway, we're checking him out. The guy says he goes out every morning before work. Wears a neoprene suit and uses a headlamp. He's got a spotlight on his kayak. He heard something on the shore as he was paddling by, like something heavy sloshing in the reeds. When he shone his light over, the beam picked out the body."

"James Talfour." Evan mulled the name. "Why is that familiar?"

"He's a big name on some charity board, apparently." She filled him in on what else they knew about the victim.

"And how long has the body been here?" he asked.

"The coroner is on the way, but I'd guess Talfour has been dead fewer than five or six hours."

"Tell me about the sticks around his head."

She frowned. "That's your job, isn't it?"

"Well, yes. Wood, of course, signifies primordial matter. The Greek *hyle*. In India, *materia prima*—the universal substance. Wood, in turn, comes from trees—the living example of the universe's constant regeneration. The symbolism of the halo is probably obvious. A characteristic of Christian saints stolen outright from the Roman emperors. Given how violently many of those saints died, the halo might tie in with the three forms of death our victim suffered."

She laughed. "Let's hear it for eggheads."

He arched an eyebrow. "It's good of you to keep me humble. It's also entirely possible the killer was unaware of the significance of wood outside of the most obvious religious aspect. Perhaps he simply hates Catholics." He looked up at her. "Or saints. And of course, you have the significance of a noose around the neck of a Black man. It's a sad and terrible crime, but not outside the bounds of what your own profiler must see from time to time. What made you call me?"

He didn't bother adding what she already knew. That he wanted out of the forensics business. That he had too much other work to do. That he preferred to avoid dead bodies unless they were at least several centuries old. A month after they met, he'd told her he didn't understand her fascination with the dead. She'd countered by telling him he was the guy who spoke twelve dead languages.

"They aren't just sticks," Addie said. "There are weird markings on them. Like some kind of writing."

He could almost feel his own ears prick. With some guys, it was boobs or butts that got their motor running. With him, it was writing.

Actually, with him it was all three. It was a wonder he hadn't become a tattooist instead of a semiotician.

She grinned. "I've got you now, don't I?"

He sniffed. "Possibly."

"You ready for a closer look?"

"Lead on, Macduff."

"Just steer clear of Lieutenant Criver. The guy with the tan and the million-dollar suit. He's not big on academic types. Same with Sergeant Billings. The oily sidekick."

Evan raised a brow, and she shot him a warning glance.

"Don't you dare bait them," she said.

"I'm shocked you think I would."

They jogged down the hill and returned along the road before cutting down the lower rise. Patrick was busy with one of the techs, but when they tried to skirt the lieutenant, he stepped into their path.

"This is our specialist?" he asked, his eyes narrow.

Addie said, "Lieutenant Criver, this is Professor Evan Wilding. An expert on the signs and writings left by killers. He was responsible for the capture and conviction of the Copper Hills Killer last year."

"I see." Criver pressed two fingers to his chin. "The Copper Hills Killer was caught based on a series of texts, as I recall. Rather straightforward. This case seems likely to be much more complex."

Evan wasn't fond of having his bona fides questioned. Especially by anti-intellectuals. "I'll scrutinize the premises and of course the *corporis*," he said. "If, upon examination, I have nothing to contribute that would provide succor to your brilliant detectives as they labor steadfastly to resolve this most dastardly of crimes, I'll retreat to my ivory tower and voilà! *Et erit ex capillum tuum.*"

"What?"

"I'll be out of your hair."

Criver's lips thinned. "A lot of brain in that body, huh?"

Addie clamped a hand on Evan's shoulder. "Let's take a look at that *corporis*, shall we?"

He felt the lieutenant's gaze on him and Addie as they continued down the hill toward the body. When he glanced back, the lieutenant was heading toward the Suburban, trailed by Sergeant Billings.

Addie whirled on Evan. "I told you not to cross him. I need you on this case."

"Me? He loved me."

"Of course he did. About as much as he'd love a hemorrhoid."

"Are you suggesting that I'm a pain in his ass? I thought that was *your* job."

"No worries on that regard," she said darkly. "There's plenty of room in there for us both."

CHAPTER 5

Evan smiled when he saw Patrick leave the tech he was chatting with and make a beeline for him and Addie. He always appreciated the older cop's Irish humor.

"Thanks for coming," Patrick said to Evan.

"It's good to see you again, Detective."

They shook hands; then Evan plowed on, half stepping, half sliding down the bank in his trainers.

He should have kept his wellies on.

"Is it all right if I approach the body?" He tossed the words over his shoulder.

"Knock yourself out," Addie said.

"Just stay outside the tape," Patrick added.

Evan approached the corpse. Distantly, traffic came as a faint whoosh, like a far-off river. Closer by, a flock of starlings scolded from the branches of a cottonwood tree, and the water of the Calumet sloshed in desultory fashion against the shore, wavelets lapping at the dead man.

Evan had long ago trained himself to approach a murder victim as a puzzle. A locked box that needed the right key so that he could reveal the motivation behind the crime and lay bare the killer's secrets. A killer who posed a body, who left behind carefully arranged signifiers and symbols, had not killed in haste. Nor had he chosen his victim casually. The victim offered the killer something. Satisfaction. Revenge. The fulfillment of a sexual urge. Perhaps even, in the killer's twisted mind, a form of redemption.

Now Evan set aside the identity and likely suffering of the actual man who lay before him. The body on the ground transformed in his mind from a successful businessman—a once living, breathing human being with hopes and dreams and ambitions and a family—into a message.

What had the killer wanted to say by murdering this man in this way?

Who was the message meant for?

And what unintended messages had been left behind—messages that might prove to be the killer's Achilles' heel?

A sudden gust of wind tugged back his hood, and mist gathered on his exposed skin. Absently, Evan pulled his hood back up and cinched it as he took in the things Addie had already told him about what had been done to the victim. Then he focused on what she'd left out.

The right side of the victim's head had been shaved—the top of the skull still carried an inch of graying Afro. Cuts on the skin indicated the shaving had been done quickly, perhaps with a knife. Only after the body had been moved would they be able to see if both sides of the head were shaved.

In the eerily peaceful face, the left eye was closed. The right eye had been removed, perhaps with the same knife used to shave the scalp. Bruises showed on the rest of the face, darker patches on dark skin. The lower lip had been split from a blow.

In addition to the stake through the right thigh, smaller stakes had been hammered through Talfour's left forearm and another through his torso, just below the rib cage.

"Interesting," Evan murmured.

He removed his worn leather journal and a pen from an inside pocket of his coat and, turning so that his body shielded the paper, he sketched the victim, holding the paper down against the wind. As his hand moved over the paper and a form began to take shape, something familiar rose from the page into his fingertips.

A memory. He had seen a body like this one before. Long ago. His pen stuttered to a stop, and he closed his eyes, chasing the recollection.

"What's he doing?" Patrick asked.

Evan startled. His eyes popped open.

"Hush," Addie scolded Patrick.

But now Evan had it. Talfour had been posed to resemble a European bog body—the corpse of someone buried in peat during the Iron Age and slowly mummified by bog acids, much the way fruit is pickled in brine. Talfour, of course, wasn't mummified. But everything else about him recalled those ancient burials.

That settled, Evan allowed himself to focus on the wooden halo around the victim's head. He pulled out his reading glasses and took a cautious step closer to the corpse, mindful of the crime tape. Mud sucked at his trainers. Something stirred in the water nearby while tatters of mist hovered over the river like a fraying shawl. All about in the air was the dank, dark smell of the Calumet.

Arranged around the victim's head were eighteen unstained pine slats, roughly sawed, each ten inches long and two inches wide. The slats had been arranged in nine rows—two slats per row—so that they formed a twenty-inch-long radius around the victim's head. Each slat bore thirty or forty tiny, skillfully etched symbols.

Nine rows, Evan mused. Many cultures considered the number nine significant. There were the Greeks' nine Muses and the nine days and nights required for an anvil falling from Olympus to reach earth. The nine gates that once protected the Chinese imperial throne. The Aztecs' nine gods of darkness.

Writers, too, loved the number nine. The nine circles of hell in Dante's *Divine Comedy*. Tolkien's nine rings and nine wraiths in The Lord of the Rings. More recently, the nine regions of Westeros in George R. R. Martin's epic A Song of Ice and Fire.

But Evan was thinking primarily of the Norse god Odin and his association with the number nine. Odin—who prized wisdom—had hung himself from the tree of life for nine days until his sacrifice revealed the secret of the runes.

ODIN, Evan wrote in his journal and circled the name.

Because he'd realized immediately that the strange markings on the wooden slats were runes. The long-ago script once used by Germanic cultures reaching from Greenland all the way through the empires of Islam to the Greek Isles.

That was to say, Vikings.

He smoothed his beard.

Vikings were, if rather unfairly, best known for their brutal killing of Christian monks and the pillaging of their monasteries.

James Talfour had once been a minister.

Was that why the killer had chosen to leave his message in runic script?

The answer, he could hope, lay in whatever message the runes would impart once transliterated into the English alphabet.

As he copied the runes into his notebook, he recalled his long-ago study of the runic script. He'd taken a class as an undergraduate at Oxford. The course had been so drearily dull that it had all but killed his nascent interest in Old Nordic cultures. It took a certain talent to suck the life out of the gateway to a fascinating era in history. But Professor Nigel Cook had very nearly succeeded.

What Evan did remember was a scattering of facts. One, that there were four main types of rune-rows, or alphabets. Two, each character in a rune-row had a corresponding and meaningful word attached to it, such as *monster* for the *pursiaz* rune and *man* for *mannaz*. And finally, modern cultures often ascribed mystical attributes to the runes—a quality not much supported by the historical record despite the fact that the word *rune* came from the Old English *rūn*, meaning *secret* or *mystery*.

A mystery indeed, Evan thought.

Professor Nigel Cook had assigned endless pages of runes for his students to use in a two-step process of interpretation known as transliteration—going from runes to Latin letters—followed by translation of the words into modern English. Getting through the drudgery had required Evan to consume copious amounts of mead, supplied by his older classmates. Looking back through the resulting alcoholic haze, Evan now had only a faint memory of how the rune-rows and the Latin alphabet matched. Or the places where they didn't.

He finished jotting down the runes and removed his glasses. He pinched the bridge of his nose. He'd need to brush up on his *futhorc*, the English version of the runic alphabet. For he could tell that much—some of the letters the killer had etched on the wood came from the lesser-used English runic alphabet.

"Futhorc," he said out loud, as if the corpse could answer. "What made the killer choose that alphabet?"

Behind him, Addie said, "What are you talking about?"

Chicago dropped into place around him like a curtain falling. He straightened and tucked away his glasses.

"They're runes," he said. "From the Anglo-Saxon or English version of the rune-row."

"Rune-row?"

"Or alphabet, if you prefer."

The mud squelched as she moved closer. "Runes. You mean like those stones for telling the future?"

He shook his head. "Not exactly."

But she plowed on. "Now that you say it, I did think they looked familiar. My cousin sent me a set of rune stones a couple years ago. Aren't they some sort of pagan magic?"

"It's too soon to know if the killer intended anything mystical," Evan said. "Runes, in and of themselves, aren't magical any more than, say, the Latin or Greek alphabets."

Her eyebrows winged together. "I thought runes *were* mystical symbols. They're just letters?"

"I wouldn't say *just.*" As Addie and Patrick drew closer, Evan warmed to his audience. "Runic writing was invented hundreds of years ago. There are various theories about how it originated, whether it descended from archaic Greek writing or the Etruscan alphabet. But it was most commonly used to inscribe names and prayers on coins and monuments and important objects like jewelry and weapons. This particular version of the runic alphabet, what we see in front of us, was used by the Anglo-Saxons who invaded England in the fifth century."

Addie's eyes glowed. "What you're saying is, this is actual writing we're looking at."

Patrick grinned. "The killer left us a message."

"It's actual writing, yes," Evan said. "But I can't yet tell you if the letters form meaningful words."

"Oh, come on, Evan." Addie kicked at the mud. "Give us some idea."

"I'm not a runologist. I'll need time to transliterate the letters. And despite what some people claim, it's not a straightforward process."

"You said Anglo-Saxons," Patrick said. "Isn't that a fancy way of saying Vikings?"

"It's more complicated than that. But for our purposes, yes."

"If that's the case"—Addie pointed at the body—"is this how the Vikings buried their dead?"

"Not at all. The presentation of the body doesn't fit with the runes. I'm uncertain what to make of this."

"I thought you were the expert," Patrick said.

"Not at making snap decisions."

Patrick tapped a finger to the side of his nose. "So you haven't seen anything like this before?"

"Certainly not runic inscriptions on a halo around a dead man. As for the positioning of the corpse . . . well." He wasn't ready to share his bog body theory. Not without doing some research. "If you will send me pictures of the body and close-ups of the runes, that would be helpful." He glanced at his watch. "I need to go to my office and confirm a few things. Can you give me a couple hours?"

Addie sighed. "Sure."

Evan saw the disappointment in her eyes. "It's a couple hours, Addie."

"Sure," she said again, uncheered.

The three of them walked toward the ridge.

Lieutenant Criver stood at the top of the rise, Sergeant Billings nearby.

"So, Professor?" Criver called down. With the fog lifting, his voice echoed sharply over the water. "What do you make of it?"

Evan paused and shook his head. "I'm not prepared to discuss my thoughts quite yet, other than to say that our killer has a strong narrative impulse. Which should prove helpful."

"Narrative impulse?" Criver tilted his head. "What does that mean?"

"Some killers want to explain their crimes. To document them. They're compelled to tell their story."

"Hmm," Criver said.

"Consider the Zodiac Killer," Evan said. "Or even better, H. H. Holmes. He of the so-called Murder Castle. In 1895, Holmes confessed to killing twenty-seven people. He described his murders for the newspapers, including the infamous line, 'I was born with the devil in me. I could not help the fact that I was a murderer, no more than the poet can help the inspiration to sing.'"

The lieutenant's scowl melted into a carefully neutral expression that showed only the faintest suggestion that he was pleased. *He's hooked*, Evan thought. *He wants this to be something big.*

"You're suggesting that we have a modern-day H. H. Holmes operating here?" the lieutenant asked. "All that writing—is it a poem?"

"The writing is certainly suggestive of a confession," Evan said. "As to whether or not it's poetry, I can't tell you anything more at this point."

"How long did it take you to find the Copper Hills murderer?"

"A week," Evan admitted.

"I see." Lieutenant Criver's voice turned sharp. "Well, take your time, *Professor*. It's only a murder."

"I'm sorry." Evan squinted up at the lieutenant through the fine mist. "I was under the impression you wanted things done correctly. I am happy to offer idle speculation, if that's your preference. Quick and cheap, as it were."

Patrick made a sound that might have been a strangled laugh. Criver's carefully neutral expression cracked to reveal a flash of anger.

"You're a bit full of yourself for a man who can't qualify to ride the roller coasters at Disneyland."

Evan heard Addie suck in air, but he offered a mild smile. "A man in your position should know the importance of accuracy. At fifty-three inches, I am eminently qualified to ride anything I choose."

"Is that so?" Criver studied Evan as if taking the linguist's measure, then spun on his heel and strode off toward his vehicle. Billings rewarded Evan with a threatening sneer before he oozed after his boss.

Addie whirled on Evan.

"Not smart," she hissed. "He'll kick you off this investigation so fast, you'll think you're on a rocket. And then where will Patrick and I be?"

"I'm sorry." Evan spread his hands. "I feel it's my duty to educate."

Patrick tugged an ear. "In the lieutenant's case, that might be like trying to teach a pig to sing. It's pointless—"

"And . . ."—she cringed as Criver's car door slammed—"it has very much annoyed the pig."

CHAPTER 6

Evan's office in the Harper Memorial Library at the University of Chicago was his home away from home. The elegantly imposing building both inspired and comforted him, with its vaulted ceilings and coats of arms, its west tower modeled after the secularism of King's College at Cambridge, while its Byzantine-styled east tower drew inspiration from Christ Church at Oxford. Built in 1912, the immense library suggested the realms of both the divine and the secular.

Evan's gothic-style fourth-floor office suite, complete with bathroom and kitchenette, could be reached by the stairs, but he felt he could be forgiven for preferring the elevator. It was a question both of expediency and the desire to avoid getting run over during the stampede between class periods.

He let himself into his office and closed the door behind him. The traffic gods had been kind today, and he'd managed to get Ginny home and make it here in record time. Ignoring the immense windows that overlooked the quad—a tempting view every time he entered the office—he shrugged out of his parka, hung it on a peg near the door, and headed across the glossy wooden floors with their scattered Tuareg, Berber, and Persian rugs. In twenty strides, he reached his overflowing floor-to-ceiling bookshelves. His books were arranged in historical order, from the cave paintings of the Upper Paleolithic on the far left, all the way to the semiotics of film and hip-hop on the right. He ran the attached ladder along its track until he reached the section dedicated to the Iron Age.

He knew an internet search might be faster. But he preferred the physicality of a book. And he knew his books well.

When he was three rungs up, a woman said, "You're salivating."

His grip on the ladder broke and he half jumped, half fell to the floor.

"Whoa, Professor," the woman said. "You'll break something that way."

He straightened and summoned his dignity. "Damn it, Di. You'll kill me one of these days, sneaking up on me."

"I wasn't sneaking. I was sitting at my desk doing the work you assigned me on the Sappho fragment when you burst in on me without so much as a *good morning, lowly minion*."

Evan straightened, tried to glare, and failed.

Diana Alanis—a brilliant and ambitious postdoc, the only American woman with a PhD in Incan *quipu*—had been his research assistant for going on eight months, and in truth, he was too fond of her to quarrel. Plus—as he admitted in his most honest moments—he worried about what she could do to him if she ever got it in her head to challenge him. The woman was well over six feet—a giantess by any standards. On top of that, she was an extraordinary athlete.

She could, if he wished to be appallingly cliché, squash him like a bug. The gods did seem to be rather fond of irony, pairing the two of them.

Fortunately, she seemed to be as fond of him as he was of her.

At the moment, she sat behind the desk in a recessed corner with her laptop and a stack of printouts that she was in the process of marking up. She had a pen behind one ear and a highlighter in her right hand. Her biceps bulged beneath the short-sleeve tee, which boasted of her participation in an Ironman competition.

Evan had no doubt she'd placed well.

"Technically, it's *my* desk," he said. "Or did you get confused about which one of us is the tenured professor?"

She rolled her eyes at him. "Well, I certainly couldn't work at the main desk. It's a disaster. Or at the table." Her Cajun accent made the words roll out like the tide. "Look at it. I leave for a week and you've buried the thing."

Evan followed the tilt of her head toward the immense library table that occupied the center of the room. He was in the middle of attempting to decipher the aforementioned Phaistos Disc, and the table reflected the chaotic state of his mind at the moment. Stacks of books on Crete and the Minoan Bronze Age were heaped next to a pair of open laptops and dangerously high stacks of writing pads. A scattering of half-empty teacups dotted the landscape, mingling with Boeotian figurines, fragments of Mycenaean pottery, and the wooden puzzles Evan was fond of using as a mental break from the harder work. In the center of the chaos, threatened by a leaning tower of bound folios, were a bottle of brandy and two snifters, only slightly dirty.

He spotted a clear space maybe seven inches wide by twelve and, with a cry of triumph, pointed it out.

"Plenty of room," he said.

She snorted and rose to her full height.

It was like watching the sun rise. Waist-length red-gold hair sheeted around Diana's shoulders; her bronze-flecked hazel eyes gleamed in her equally bronzed skin. All she needed to complete the image of the goddess Diana was a bow and a quiver of arrows.

She rounded the desk and came at him. "Now confess. You've got that cat-that-ate-the-canary look. What gives?"

He backed away, scrabbled for the ladder, and this time ascended without intervention. "A corpse."

Diana planted her feet on the woven rug near the foot of the ladder and accepted the books as he handed them down. "Go on."

He hesitated. He hadn't specifically asked Addie if he could discuss the case with anyone. But Diana had helped him on police cases before—she'd been vetted and signed the paperwork.

"Well?" she said.

"Chicago PD called." He passed down *Life and Death of a Druid Prince*. "An interesting case of posing. Now where is the Aldhouse-Green? Ah, here. Just a few more titles and that should do us."

"Us?" she asked.

"You're salivating, too."

Diana placed the books in the one open spot on the table, thus rendering invisible any clue as to the tabletop's color or construction. She read the titles aloud. "*Bog Bodies. Bodies in the Bog. Bodies from the Bog.* Am I making a leap here, or do you think we have a bog body?"

"Whatever gave you that idea?"

"Aren't bog victims a little too . . . *European* for the cornfields of America? Not to mention anachronistic."

He brushed dust from his hoodie and descended the ladder. "I *am* operating off memory. But many years ago, I spent a month in Cheshire County with my brother, who was working on a dig with a Cambridge professor. River was very much into the Iron Age then. That gave way to flashier things. Zhou dynasty relics, Moche ornaments. Treasures from Tillya Tepe. He's fully into his shallow stage now, I would say. A good mind gone astray." He shook himself. "Now, where was I? Oh, yes, at the time he was fascinated with peat bogs and humble grave goods."

"River. That's the name of your studly baby brother? The Indiana Jones guy?" Di picked up a photo from Evan's desk. "In all our time together, I don't think you've said his name before."

Evan snatched back the photo of River on horseback with a tribe of Bedouin and replaced it on the desk. "Let's stay focused. Bog bodies are corpses that have been naturally mummified in peat."

"You're saying we have a mummy?"

"Not yet. What we have is a body laid out to *look* like a bog body. Staved skull, a noose around the neck, partially shaved skull, and stakes driven into the corpse. The big question is why?"

Diana blinked at him. "I'm sorry."

He froze in the act of opening one of the books. "What? Why are you sorry?"

"About the corpse. I know you wanted to avoid getting pulled into another investigation."

"Oh. Right. Well." He opened the book. "It does help pay the rent."

"And there's Addie."

Heat rose in his face. He wondered if he was that much of an open book himself. He bent over the pages and mumbled, "Always happy to help a friend."

"One of your more endearing qualities," she said, then gave a small cry. "I almost forgot. A package came for you."

"I'll look at it later."

"It's an odd package."

He looked up from the book he was perusing. "What do you mean?"

"I'll show you." She returned to the desk, bent, picked up a white box, and brought it over. "It was sitting on the floor just inside your office."

"Inside?"

"The janitor must have brought it in." She set it on a chair. They both stared at it. "Well?" she said.

"Well, what?"

"Aren't you going to open it?"

He studied the box, sitting white and innocuous on his chair. Someone had written his name in red marker on the top of the box in a smooth, bold script that suggested confidence. There was no other writing, nothing to indicate where the box had come from or who had delivered it.

"The suspense is killing me," Diana said.

"You're impatient this morning." But he retrieved a box cutter and slit the tape holding the lid on. They peered inside.

"How . . . odd," Diana said.

Evan lifted out a wooden figure of a man riding a horse. The object was maybe eight inches high and fashioned of small twigs tightly bound together with twine. The artist had painted tiny pebbles to look like eyes and glued them onto the man's face and the horse's head. There was no other adornment.

"Do you see how small the rider is?" Diana observed. "Almost as if he has dwarfism. Maybe it's a gift from one of your students."

"Gifts from my students tend to come with a name attached in large print, to make sure I give credit where credit is due." He looked inside the box again to make sure he hadn't missed a note. "It looks like a toy from a primitive culture. Maybe it's from someone in the anthropology department."

"Then why no name?"

"It's a mystery. Anyway . . ." He returned the figure to the box, replaced the lid, and put the box on the floor near his desk. "We have work to do."

When he turned back to Diana, he was surprised to see an expression of unease on her face. It surely mirrored his own. Something about the figure was unsettling.

He pretended otherwise. "What is it?" he asked.

"Nothing." She shook herself and turned brisk. "Very well, then. Let's get to it." She opened one of the books Evan had handed down and stared at the pictures. "One common theory is that bog bodies were placed in the bog as human sacrifices."

Evan joined her at the table. "Indeed. Others theorize that they were victims of crime, with the killer attempting to hide the dastardly deed in a bog."

"Also," she said as she tapped a photo of an eerily lifelike corpse, "they might have been *perpetrators* of crime rather than victims."

"Or merely lost."

She snorted. "Too much ritual around the ancient bodies for that. Someone wanders into the bog, gets lost, and has half their head shaven and ends up with a rope around their neck?"

"The work of modern farm equipment, in the case of the shaving," Evan pointed out. "And a badly botched attempt at rescue, in the case of the rope."

"You know how ridiculous that sounds."

"We have to look at all angles, consider all evidence. Or else we aren't scientists and we're of no use to the police. But"—he held up a hand, and she closed her mouth—"I agree. Unlikely. And clearly impossible with our current case."

Diana returned to the book. "So why the elaborate presentation of the body, then?"

"That is the question of the hour. I need a list of all the bog bodies uncovered to date. Or at least the most famous ones." He considered the Anglo-Saxon runes. "Focus on England."

"Your wish is my command," Diana said, thumbing through *Bog Bodies Uncovered*. She stopped at the color plates halfway through. "Look at Lindow Man. We have everything you've mentioned, except the shaved head, which seems to be present in other bog bodies, just not Lindow. We certainly have multiple causes of death."

He leaned around her to see. "Our victim was found curled on his side."

"Bingo!" Diana said, pointing. "And he's from Cheshire. That's in—"

"Northern England." He pulled a stool out from under the table and perched on it. "Very good. Perhaps later today, you'd be kind enough to make me a map of all the English locales."

"Sounds like minion work."

"And you're a wonderful minion. We also have runes."

She set the book down. "Glad you decided to mention that."

"You young ones are always in a rush."

He moved a teacup over and opened his journal on top of a shorter stack. Together, they studied the sketches he'd made of James Talfour's runic halo.

"None of the bog bodies in the book have halos," Diana said. "Or runic inscriptions. The two elements don't fit together."

"That's only because we're not yet inside the killer's mind."

Evan grabbed a foolscap notepad and pen from the desk and copied down the runes without drawing in the wooden slats. When he finished, they had eighteen lines of runes.

ᚠ ᚲᛦᛏᛖᛏᚦᚲᛗᛁᚷᚾᛏᚨᛖᛖᛋᛁᚢᛋᛗᛖᚠᛋᚾᚢᛏᛖᛗᛖᚱᚠᛁᛋ
ᛖᛏᛗ

ᚲᚱᛋᛗᛗᛏ-ᛒᚨᛗᚠᛗᚠᛋᛁᛋᛗᚱᛋᛞᛗᛏᚾᚷᛁᛖᚱᛗᛏᚠᚱᛁᛗᚦ
ᛁ

ᚤ ᚨᛖᚾᛟᛋᚠᚠᚾᚨᛖᚠᛗᚱᛖᛗᚾᛋᛋᚹᛁᛗᛗᚱᚾᛖᛗᛁᛚᛖᛗᛗ
ᛗᛚᛁᚲᚱᛗᛈᛗᛗᚱᚨᚦᛁᚷᛋᛁᚠᛈᚱᛖᛁᚱᚱᚠᚨᚱᛖᛗᚠ   ᛃ

ᚲ ᛗᛁᚠᚨᛗᚱᚠᛋᛒᛖᚨᛏᚾᚢᛏᛋᛒᚱᛗᛚᛩᚠᛉᚱᚷᚨᛏ
ᚲᛁᚠᛗᚲᚾᛋᛗᚻᛁᛒᛏᚠᛋᛗᚾᚱᛒᛗᚻᛗᛞᚷᚠᛚᚲᛖᚱᛗᛗᛏᛈᛁᚱᛗᚠᚠ
ᛗᛩᚠ   ᛉ

ᛋ ᚠᚠᚱᛗᛁᛏᛖᛗᛁᛏᛗᛁᛏᛗᚷᛈᛏᛒᛖᚠᛗᛁᛒᛞᚱᛁᛗᛗᛒᚾᛋᛏᛗᛗᛒ
ᚨᛒᛁᚷᛒᛗᛋᛗᛋ

ᛗᛗᛒᛗᛏᛗᛋᚠᚠᛒᚨᛗᚠᛏᚱᛗᛞᚱᛚᚠᛋᛋᚱᛖᚠᛋᛗᛞᛁᚱᛚᚱ
ᚠᚠᚠ   ᛏ

ᛚ ᛁᛋᚠᚱᛗᛩᛁᚱᛗᚠᚠᚱᛗᛁᛏᛖᚾᛁᛋᛗᚾᛋᛖᚠᛈᚾᛗᚱᛩᛁᚲᚾᚱᛗ
ᛗᛗᚨᛗᚠᛗ

ᛩᛋᛁᚱᛈᛗᚤᛗᛋᛁᚱᛗᛏᛋᛁᛏᛚᛋᛋᛁᚦᛗᚷᚠᚲᛗᛏᛖᛒᛁᚠᛈᛗᛏᚾᚠᚠ
ᛗ

ᛗ ᛒᚨᛋᛚᛗᚠᚠᚠᚾᛗᛋᚠᛗᛏᛁᛚᛗᛁᛗᚾᛁᛗᛚᚠᚠᛁᚷᚾᛏᛁᛋᚾᛗᚨᛗᛋᚠ
ᚠᛏᛁᚷᚾᛏ

ᛟᛗᚠᛠᚱᛗᛒᛚᚠᚠᛚᛗᚠᛚᚷᚠᛟᛣᚠᚷᛗᚱᛈᛂᛗᛚᛈᛂᚠᚠᛚᚠ
ᛈᚱᚠᚠᛒᚠᛟᛁᚠᛒᚱᛗᛉᛣᛚᚠᛈ   ᛒ
ᚷ   ᛐᛗᛚᛈᛗᛒᛡᛗᚠᛂᛁᛂᛗᛐᛁᛐᛁᛖᛁᛂᛁᛐᚠᛁᛐᚴᚱᛁᛚᛚᛗᛗᛈᛂᛁ
ᚠᛗᛈᚠᚦᚦᛂᚠᚷᛖᚱᛂᛁᛐᚷᛁᛏᛁᛐᛗᛁᚦᛂᛚᛚᛁᛐᛂᛈᛐᛗᚱᛚᚠᚦᛚ
ᛗᛂᚠᛈᛂᚾ   ᛈᚾ
ᛚ   ᚠᛈᛗᛂᚠᛁᛚᚷᛉᛗᚠᚱᛐᛈᚠᛗᚠᛗᚱ   ᚠᚱᚱᛁᚠᛗᛟᚠᛒᛁᛗᛂᛁᚠᛂ
ᛗᚱᛗᛒᚠᛐᛗᚱᛗᚠᚱᚱᛁᛒᛂᛁᛒᚱᚠᚱᚱᛁᛈᛂᛁᛈᛂᛁᚠ   ᚠ
ᛒ   ᛈᛁᛂᚠᛐᛗᚠᛂᛈᛁᛂᚠᛐᛈᛗᚠᚠᛚᛗᛈᛚᛗᛈᛗᛁᛣᛈᚠᚱᛈ
ᛈᛗᛚᛂᛁᛂᛁᛒᚱᚠᚠᛂᛚᛐᛈᛣᛁᛈᛂᛁᛈᚠᚠᛐᛈᛣᛁᛗᚠᛗᛐᛐᛗᚠᛈᛈ
ᛣ

Diana surveyed his work. "Pretty much Greek to me. Actually, not. I know Greek."

"By the time we're done, you'll also know runes."

She beamed at him as if he'd just offered her a prettily wrapped package. "Every line of runes has one rune that is set apart from the others."

"I've had time to think about that."

She picked up a pencil and tapped it on the page. "And?"

"It could be a numbering system."

"But why would he number the slats?"

"Think about it," Evan said. "He had to have prepared them in advance. If we assume the sequence of the lines is important, and I believe it likely, then numbering the slats would ensure that he placed them in the proper order when he arranged them around the body."

"If that's the case, why not just use Arabic numerals like the rest of us? One, two, three, and so on."

"It would mess with the whole Viking aura, don't you think?"

She pursed her lips and nodded. "I suppose it would." She leaned over his journal. "Sometimes the numbers are at the beginning of the line, and sometimes they're at the end. That seems an odd choice by which to indicate sequence."

"I have a theory about that, too. But we'll come back to it."

"Fine." She huffed. "And the rest of the runes? What about them?"

"I suspect they have some significance."

She twirled a strand of hair like a bored coed. "Gee, Professor. You think?"

"Sarcasm is a fool's wit and far beneath you. Anyway, I haven't had time to interpret them."

"Well?"

"Well what?"

She tapped her foot. "What are you waiting for? Doesn't this seem like the most important thing? Start transliterating."

He cleared his throat. "Perhaps we should begin with an overview of the Anglo-Saxon rune-row."

"You don't *know* how to interpret them."

"I could use a refresher. And you, my brilliant but not wholly educated assistant, no doubt need a brief introduction."

Diana remained silent, which was as close as she ever got to letting Evan know he was right about something.

Evan went to the large wheeled blackboard and, ignoring the stepladder, clambered up to stand on a chair. He wrote six runes on the left side of the board.

ᚠ   ᚢ   ᚦ   ᚩ   ᚱ   ᚳ

"Just as our alphabet is named after the first two characters, alpha and beta," he said, "the Anglo-Saxon alphabet is named after its first six letters—*f*, *u*, *th*, *o*, *r*, and *c*, where the *th* sound is represented by a single letter. Thus this particular alphabet is called *futhorc*."

Diana rarely looked puzzled, but now her brow furrowed endearingly. "But aren't there several runic alphabets? How do you know which one the killer is using?"

He hopped down. "Through the process of elimination. When the Vikings brought their alphabet to England, they had to expand it to allow for sounds found only in the English language. Thus, the English rune-row has seven additional runes. Which our killer has used."

Diana tapped her pencil lightly against her bottom lip. "I'm impressed. You aren't exactly known for your expertise in all things Viking."

"Semioticians have very large brains. Among other things."

She arched an eyebrow.

He looked away as his face caught fire. "At least in relation to the rest of our—" He cleared his throat. "Never mind."

"Indeed," Diana said with mock sternness. "With thirty-one letters in this runic alphabet, then, it means we can't do a one-to-one mapping between the *futhorc* and our own Latin alphabet."

"Which has only twenty-six letters. That's right. Runes have characters for sounds that we don't use. That's one of the ways in which things get tricky."

"*One* of the ways?"

"Runic writing has no punctuation or capitalization. And no spaces between words. There's also some disagreement about the order of the letters in the *futhorc* and their meanings."

"A challenge." Her smile was that of a cat with a saucer of milk.

Evan's smile echoed hers. *What a pair of nerds we are,* he thought.

"Then let's get to it," he said.

CHAPTER 7

Addie pushed her way through the glass door and into the damp-wool, sizzling-bacon warmth of a crowded Mach's Deli. Gabe waved to her from a table in the back and held up a ticket slip showing he'd already ordered for them. She squeezed past the jostling breakfast line and into the booth across the table from him.

"Two eggs over easy with sausage links and hash browns?" He raised his voice above the roar of the lunch crowd. "And wheat toast, although I don't know why you bother."

"You know me like we're family. Thanks." She shrugged out of her coat and pulled off her earmuffs while Gabe poured coffee from the urn on the table. "You sure you can spare an hour away from your constituents?"

He gave his usual sleepy grin. "It'll be close to two hours with the traffic. But that's okay. My staff thinks I'm meeting with someone from the mayor's office to discuss light pollution."

"Instead of having breakfast with your cop sister. Light pollution, though? That's the best you could do?"

"Light pollution is a real issue if you care about observing the stars and planets. Or getting a good night's sleep."

"What does that look like, exactly? A good night's sleep? And stars?"

"Precisely." He tilted his head and scrutinized her in the utterly charming manner that had let him get away with metaphorical murder as a kid. "And I'm lying. I'm damn proud to have breakfast with my cop sister. Light pollution be damned."

"And I'm cool being seen schmoozing with a politician. Even from your party."

"Good. Now we've gotten the sentimental stuff out of the way, we can start prying into each other's lives."

She laughed and smiled at her handsome brother in his elegantly tailored suit. Gabe was an alderman for one of the West Side wards, the only one of the five Bisset children who'd chosen politics over policing—not that there was always the distinction between the two that one might wish for. Gabe had the jawline of a superhero and earnest, wide-set eyes that promised he'd always have your back. And it was true—Gabe knew most of her darkest secrets and had never breathed a word about them to their father or brothers. Just as she'd kept his secrets.

No question. Gabe was her favorite.

"Forty-nine!" hollered a woman behind the line.

Gabe grabbed the ticket and pushed out of the booth. "Be right back."

When he returned, they focused on the food. Gabe, always pickier than Addie about what went into his body, had chosen oatmeal with fruit and nuts, hold the brown sugar.

He ate slowly, seeming to relish every bit of walnut and apple.

She went through her meal like a lawn mower—a skill she'd learned at a young age when lunch and dinner had been battlegrounds for survival.

When she'd devoured the eggs and most of the sausage, she pushed her plate away and refilled her coffee. "It's been weeks since you managed to meet me for breakfast. How are you?"

"I'm good," he said. "Just busy. I went into Arrow Galleries the other day. So I could stare at my sister's painting on the wall."

"It's just a little gallery," she murmured. But a pleasurable blush rose in her cheeks. "You did not go."

"I did. I took Jared. He's been dying to see it."

Gabe's secrets were much harder to hold on to than hers, given his political visibility. But being gay was definitely not acceptable in Addie's rough-and-tumble, uber-macho family. And Gabe wasn't ready to upset the applecart.

Their mother, who might have mitigated the masculinity, had died when Addie was seven. As the only female on the premises, Addie had grown up in an environment so thick with testosterone that she was amazed simply breathing in the air at the dinner table hadn't put hair on her chest. Gabe had been her closest, and sometimes only, ally.

"What did Jared think?" she asked, feigning disinterest in Jared's opinion of her work by cleaning her sunglasses.

Gabe planted his elbows on the table and peered at her. "What do *you* think?"

The heat in her face deepened. "He hated it."

"Oh, Addie. You and I are always so sure that underneath our bravado, we're total fuckups. Have you heard of imposter syndrome? No? Read up on it. As for Jared, of course he loved your painting. He said your aesthetics are brilliant, with excellent contrast of light and dark and a rewarding emotionalism."

"He said that?"

"God's truth."

"That was nice of him."

"No. Jared is never nice when it comes to art. He's a snob."

Her shoulders came down. "Maybe we should have dinner. The three of us and Clayton."

"Clayton L. Hamden? *He's* your latest?"

"You don't like him. And stop saying it like I've been sleeping with a whole string of men."

"Bravo if you are."

His expression was so kind that she felt the familiar stubbornness kick in. The part of her that translated kindness into pity and wanted to mistake understanding for condescension. She didn't need anyone trying to smooth her feathers. Unlike Gabe, she didn't care what her family thought of her.

A theory that fell apart as soon as she thought of her painting—a closely guarded secret that only Gabe and Evan knew about. She wasn't ready to let Clayton L. Hamden into that part of her world.

"Forget dinner," she said.

But Gabe never dropped anything, ever. "The problem, Addie, is that you and I are living double lives, both of us pretending to the world that the other part of us doesn't exist. And right now, I think you're okay with that. You like being the detective with the secret life. And the painter with a hard edge. But until you decide it's okay for a man to see you as both an artist and a cop, you're not likely to find yourself with Mr. Right."

She squirmed miserably and attacked the only thing she could. "No one says 'Mr. Right' anymore."

He shrugged. "I'm done. That's my pop psychology for the day. But I do make my living reading people. And I read you, my beautiful Addie, like an open book."

Out of mutual agreement, they turned the conversation to idle things—how the other "boys" were doing, their dad's planned fishing trip with a group from the church, whether or not Gabe and Jared would make it to Mexico for a vacation. Addie didn't mention the Talfour case, even though she was desperate to tell Gabe before it hit the papers. Maybe when she knew more.

After a while, Gabe glanced at his phone. "I've reached my maximum allotment for a complete disappearance."

She stood. "I need to get back to work, too."

Outside, on the sidewalk, they hugged. Addie watched Gabe jog lightly across the street and down the other side toward his car. At the last moment, he turned and waved.

She smiled.

You couldn't pick your family. But sometimes you got lucky.

✗

At her desk, she checked first to see if anything had come back from ViCAP—the Violent Criminal Apprehension Program, which was the FBI's database of serial violent offenders. She'd entered the details of their case, wondering if the killer had struck elsewhere. Nothing so far.

She hung up her coat and bought a Coke from the vending machine. It was time to create a victimology and get into the nitty-gritty of police work. While Patrick coordinated interviews of Talfour's neighbors and friends, Addie focused on Talfour's store employees and the various charities he'd volunteered for. She began by building lists of people to talk to, knowing the lists would grow like spiderwebs, expanding rapidly in all directions.

People thought being a homicide cop was glamorous. But mostly it involved pounding the pavement, real or virtual.

She was dialing out to one of the employees of Finer Things when her phone beeped with a call from the Kendall County Sheriff's Department. The county was more than an hour southwest of the city but still part of metropolitan Chicago. She switched lines. A deputy explained that he'd gotten her name from the desk sergeant.

"I think I've got something you'll be interested in," he said. "I just emailed you a link to our database."

She turned to her computer and selected the link. When she opened the document uploaded by the deputy, she clicked through the contents with growing excitement.

"This is amazing," she said as she sent all of it to the printer.

He laughed. "You must be new on the job. Nothing amazes me anymore."

CHAPTER 8

"If you would," Evan said to Diana, "get R. I. Page's book on runes. It's in the section of the bookcase dealing with Old English and medieval literature. Grab the Barnes and Cragg books, too. I want to write out the entire English *futhorc* so we have something to work with."

Diana headed toward the bookcase while Evan abandoned the chair and climbed up the stepladder. Now he had access to the entire board. When she found the page listing the runes in Page's *An Introduction to English Runes*, she held up the open book so he could see.

"Keep holding it, please," Evan said as he reached for the chalk.

Twenty minutes later, he climbed back down. "Lo and behold! The thirty-one letters of the Anglo-Saxon alphabet, along with their names, meanings, and a transliteration of the runic letter into our Latin alphabet."

Order	Rune	Rune Name	Rune Meaning	Latin Letter
1	ᚹ	feoh	wealth, cattle	f
2	ᚾ	ūr	aurochs (wild ox)	u
3	Þ	þorn	thorn	th
4	ᚠ	ōs	god or mouth	o
5	ᚱ	rād	riding	r

6	ᛙ	cēn	torch	c
7	X	gyfu	gift	g
8	ᛈ	pynn	mirth	w
9	ᚺ	hægl	hail (precipitation)	h
10	ᛂ	nȳd	need/plight	n
11	I	īs	ice	i
12	᛬/ᛪ	gēr	year	j
13	ᛁ	ēoh	yew tree	ï
14	ᛖ	peorð	unknown	p
15	Y	eolhx	elk's	x
16	ᛡ	sigel	sun	s
17	↑	tīr	the god Tyr or the god Mars	t
18	ᛒ	beorc	birch tree	b
19	M	eh	steed	e
20	M	mann	man	m
21	ᚱ	lagu	lake	l
22	ᛪ	Ing	Ing (name) or goddess Freyr	ŋ
23	ᛞ	dæg	day	d
24	ᛜ	ēðel	homeland/estate	œ
25	F	āc	oak tree	a
26	F	æsc	ash tree	æ
27	ᛢ	ȳr	yew bow	y
28	ᛏ	ēar	grave soil?	ea
29	ᛤ	gar	spear	ḡ
30	ᛣ	calc	chalk? chalice? sandal?	K
31	ᛥ	unknown	unknown	k̄

Diana snapped the book closed. "So now we start transliterating the killer's runes. Should I begin with the slat on the left and go clockwise?"

"Perfect."

She picked up the chalk Evan had abandoned and wrote the transliterated letters from the leftmost wooden slat onto the chalkboard:

n listenupmightymeniundoanduntoearthisend

Underneath this line, she wrote another, breaking up the words and adding punctuation.

Listen up, mighty men. I undo and unto ear this end.

She stepped back and frowned. "Does that make any sense to you?"

"Perhaps the second half is meant to be, 'unto earth I send.'"

"Mansplainer."

"Don't feel bad. The human brain tends to insert a break as soon as it sees a sequence of letters that form a word. Thus you saw the word *ear* and stopped."

Diana erased and rewrote the words.

Listen up! Mighty men I undo and unto earth I send.

"Okay," she said. "But what, exactly, is he sending? The victim? He's sending the victim to earth?"

"As a metaphor for death and burial, it works. But . . ."

"But what?"

Evan crossed his arms. "But perhaps I was wrong with my theory about a numbering system. If the rune set off by itself is meant to indicate a number, I would expect it to be the first letter of the Anglo-Saxon alphabet. Instead, we have *n*, which is the tenth letter of the rune-row."

Diana glanced at the chart on the chalkboard. "The tenth rune means *need* or *plight*. Perhaps there's a clue in that."

"It's certainly a good word for our current situation."

"You'll figure it out." Diana returned to the board and transcribed the runes from the next row.

Pocsden-madamaisesrocdethgiewretawrieth i

"It's nonsense," she murmured. Disappointment had softened her voice. "I see *madam*. And maybe *deth* is *death*? What's the thing that looks like a hyphen?"

"I suspect it's a hyphen."

Her look dripped poison. "You said runes don't have punctuation."

"They don't, normally. So this outlier hyphen is curious. Regardless . . ." Evan scratched his beard. "It is trickier. Let's write out the rest of the lines and not worry about what they mean for now."

Diana picked up Evan's journal and copied all the runes onto the chalkboard.

n   listenupmightymeniundoanduntoearthisend
pocsden-madamaisesrocdethgiewretawrieth   I
x   youknowwhyowerthesunswimmerhomeIcame
dligrewdedrywthiwηliawroirrawyraewa   ï
p   aslayerofthebonehallsbreakη fjorgyn
liwepusdnibtahtemurbehteugalperemnewirdthaeda   j
s   forminemineminegonebowelburiedbustedbybigbosses
debmotnenwabymfotraehrekahsdrowsemircrawtath   t
l   inwardηirewardintohismouthoſhearηIpouredmymead
ηdirfoxosirennisnikssihtegacenobsithfotahw   e
m   byskollfudslaitilaidhimlowwightisheandsoonwight
Θ ethηreabllaacealgadnagerdneldnaflowrawrfludobemηkam   b
i   tellmebymanislaitilaiditoutprickmethisbut
nemnnnsagnortsthgitdlehiosllitsdlehrekamyenohsih   d
y   whenwailηthewordweawerarriwedforhisbletsian
eremoteremrorrimdidirorrimsihthiw   a

63

æ histholewasthusthathethankedthehelguard
dekciwsidrywwenkthgiwsihfothgiewehttlefeh   œ

Diana groaned. "Half the lines are gibberish. More than half." She glared at the blackboard as if it were to blame.

Evan picked out a few words of poetic imagery like *sun swimmer* and *bone hall* and *mouth of hearing* oddly mixed in with modern-day phrases like *big bosses.*

"Actually," he said, "I believe the killer is using the style of writing known as boustrophedon."

"Meaning he's writing every other line from right to left?" She lost her glare. "I believe you're right. *Daem* becomes *mead. Retawrieth* becomes *their water.* So what's that circle with a dot in it? I feel like I should know that."

"Hmm." Evan picked up R. J. M. Cragg's small blue book and flipped through it. Frowned. "I'd prefer this work be done by an actual runologist rather than by us rank amateurs. I don't suppose you know any?"

Diana gave up scowling at the board, thought for a moment, then snapped her fingers. She picked up a piece of chalk and wrote as she spoke. "Ralph Rhinehart."

"Who?" he asked even as his mind automatically categorized the name—an Americanized version of the German Reinhardt, which originally meant *clever in counsel.*

Diana said, "The guy with the podcast on mystical symbols and alphabets."

Evan set aside the Cragg book and picked up Barnes's *Runes: A Handbook.* "Never heard of him."

"That's because you live in a medieval bubble. Rhinehart was even on *Jimmy Kimmel Live!* I don't think he's a scholar, per se. Certainly not a PhD. But he seems to know his alphabets."

"Ah." A picture formed in Evan's mind of a tall man with a soft middle, a lumpy nose, and a head of tangled gray hair that resembled nothing so much as the business end of a mop. "The guy with the hair."

"Ha! You do watch television. Just as I suspected."

"Not at all. One of my students mentioned him in class. Something to do with the dark arts, I think. Rites performed in ancient temples and modern-day cornfields."

Diana had grabbed her phone, and now she showed the screen to Evan. "This is Rhinehart's website. His specialty is black magic. Not as a practitioner, he says, but as a scholar. He did some graduate work at Duke back in the day. Cultural anthropology."

Evan thumbed through the website as he considered the brutalized body of James Talfour. "Maybe a scholar of the dark arts is exactly what we need."

But something niggled at the back of his mind. Ralph Rhinehart. Had he been involved in a scandal of some kind? A forgery, maybe. And . . . a death?

"The plot thickens," Diana said. "Runes and ritual and magic. Perfect."

"It remains to be seen whether our killer is a serious runologist or a dabbler in sorcery. Either way, perhaps Rhinehart can be of help, as long as Addie and her partner agree. The posing of the body is certainly ritualistic."

"Thus we return to the bog bodies." She began pacing the floor. "Regardless of what the runes do or don't say, placing them with a bog body makes no sense. At least, not historically. Bog bodies are from the Iron Age. The Vikings came centuries later, taking center stage from 774 AD until the Norman Conquest in 1066."

He gave her an admiring look.

She kept walking. "And while Vikings often lived near bogs and no doubt burned peat on their hearths, they sent their dead into the afterlife by either burying the body or burning it on a pyre. Not shoving it into a bog."

"There are numerous variations on these themes, but yes."

She stopped. "So what gives here?"

He felt the familiar buzz that came whenever he attempted to break open a puzzle. He looked at the lines written on the chalkboard. *Listen up!*

Now that, all by itself, was interesting.

He went to the Old English and medieval literature section of the bookcase where Diana had pulled the rune books. He ran a finger along the spines, scanning the titles. But the books he wanted were missing. He must have taken them home.

He turned back to Diana. "Maybe the killer is selecting his favorite elements of the past without regard to their placement in time. Runes because they're mysterious. And bogs because they were once considered hallowed places. Or dark and secret places. Liminal areas that were neither land nor water."

"So you don't have a theory?"

"Only the barest glimmer of one." Evan returned to the table and reached absentmindedly for the brandy. "For the moment, it's a mystery."

Diana deftly interceded, plucking the bottle away.

Evan flailed, tried to grab it. "I'm still half-frozen, you know. Wandering far and wide through weather not fit for man or beast. My spirits are naturally flagging. And, if you'll recall, the Latin word for alcohol is *spiritus*. Ergo, a man's need for fortified drink."

But she only laughed. "Poor thing. I'll have you know you weren't the only one working hard before the crack of dawn. I'll make us some tea. That will lift your *spiritus*. And back to the business at hand—maybe the killer doesn't know much about history. Or doesn't care. Or it could be he or she is just sloppy."

Evan frowned at the bookcase. *Listen up!*

While she plugged in the electric kettle and hunted for clean cups, he picked up his sketch of the crime scene and held it next to the photograph of Lindow Man. "I don't think this killer is sloppy about anything. I think he knows exactly what he's doing."

"Or she." Diana rattled the lid on the sugar bowl. "Maybe *she* knows exactly what she's doing."

Evan looked up at Diana as she brought over the tea. His eyes focused on the bulging biceps of her right arm. "Is that a new tattoo?"

She deftly nudged aside a stack of books, set down the two mugs, and flexed her arm. "It's a hatchet." She kept flexing, and the ax leapt up and down. "I've been practicing down at Ragnarök Axes. There's a tournament coming up."

"Ragnarök. In reference to the Viking apocalypse, I presume." He thought of the blade that had sliced the breast of the pigeon in the park. "Do you get a lot of would-be Vikings hanging out there?"

"Thick as fleas. Some of them belong to Viking reenactment groups like members of the Vikings Vinland Society. And there are practitioners of Ásatrú at the lanes, too."

"Ásatrú. Faith in the old gods." He stared at the runes on the chalkboard. "Germanic neo-pagans."

"They call themselves heathens. But yes. And they're fine folks. Worried about the earth and trying to live good lives. At least, that's most of them. There's a far-right fringe who claim to be Ásatrú but who are nothing more than racists who admire the Vikings because they think they represent a pure white race. Their whole shtick is white supremacy prettied up as genetic purity. Come to think of it, there's quite a few of them at the lanes. Maybe the fine folks are fewer and farther between than I thought."

James Talfour, Evan thought. *A Black man with a noose around his neck.*

He narrowed his eyes at his assistant. "You rub elbows with these people?"

"I know." Diana gave a small shudder. "Sometimes you have to run with the dogs. The lunatic fringe aren't the sharpest knives in the Viking drawer, but when I'm in the mood, I enjoy handing their shit right back to them. European paganism was part of my undergraduate study, if you'll recall. Before I got detoured to the pre-Hispanic cultures of South America."

"Ah yes. Didn't you spend a summer in Denmark working Viking burials?"

"Actually, Southern England. And it was Roman burials. Very close, Professor. On almost zero counts." The corners of her mouth curled up. "The work was all right, even if I didn't get to rub elbows with anyone as drop-dead gorgeous as your brother. If I had, I might not have switched tracks."

Evan didn't want to burst her bubble by telling her that River and monogamy were like the proverbial oil and water. Constantly brushing up against each other and having a good sit-down. But never truly mixing.

Then again, Diana didn't strike him as a woman who wanted anything more than a bit of fun on the side. Like Evan and River, she was married to her work.

"Anyway," she went on. "If your killer likes runes, you should give Ragnarök a look-see. I have a lane booked for this evening. Why don't you descend from your castle and check it out? Lots of rune tattoos, now that I think about it. Medieval interlace, too, along with Valknuts and images of Thor's hammer. Maybe you'll find your killer there, shaving heads and carving mysterious messages in the walls."

Evan gave her a look of surprise. "A dwarf walks into an ax-throwing competition and asks if anyone is a killer. How could I refuse such a kind invitation? I've always felt a burning desire to be a punch line."

"Don't Vikings love dwarfs?"

"If memory serves, the *Prose Edda* refers to dwarfs as maggots festering in the flesh of the primordial being Ymir. Also sexual predators who hunger to bed goddesses."

"Oh. Sorry." She looked disappointed, then brightened. "You should check it out anyway. I'll be your bodyguard."

He made a noncommittal grunt. "Let's back up to that comment about me coming down from my castle. What are you implying?"

It was her turn to blush. "You're a man of the people, Evan. I didn't mean it that way. Just that maybe you should live a little. You know, get out once in a while."

"I get out."

"With your hawk."

"Ginny is good company. Better than most humans."

She let his words hang in the air. He glared at her.

The moment ended with Evan's phone blaring "I Am Woman." It was his ringtone for Addie.

He answered with, "I'm still working on it."

"You haven't translated the runes yet?"

"Rome wasn't built in a day."

Her sigh came over the phone. "Anyway, I'm downstairs in the lobby. I'm also kind of double-parked behind your fancy sports car."

"I wouldn't advise that. Campus police are notorious."

"I won't be there long. I need you to go on a little drive with me, Evan. We've got another murder."

CHAPTER 9

Evan broke into a half run to keep up as Addie strode toward the parking lot.

"This victim is already dead, right?" he panted.

"That's usually when I get involved," she said.

"Then slow down a bit. Or you'll have a third body on your hands."

"Sorry." She drew in a breath and slowed her pace. "The body was reported to the Kendall County Sheriff's Department a month ago. By then, the victim had already been in the field for an estimated eight weeks. Not much more than bones by the time they got on the scene."

"And now it's on your desk?" he asked. "The case, not the bones, presumably. What's the link?"

"A deputy noticed some similarities and phoned." She pulled a file folder from her immense handbag and handed it over. "Here are a few photos from the scene. Scott Desser was found naked, his decomposed body still curled on its side. There was a noose around his neck. Autopsy report indicates cut marks on the anterior aspects of cervical vertebrae."

"Meaning his throat was slashed. Was there directionality?"

"Left to right. Suggesting our killer is right-handed. Along with ninety percent of the population of Illinois. It's also likely the killer removed an eye. The Kendall County coroner noted cut marks in Desser's right zygomatic and right lacrimal bones."

"Fascinating." Evan thumbed through the photos as he walked. Even mostly decomposed, the remains were remarkably like those of James Talfour—a clear example of posing. "Was Desser a Black man?"

"No." She reeled up short and gave him a sharp look. "Why? Do you know more than you did this morning?"

"I'm just doing what you pay me to do. Thinking."

"Okay. Good." She strode forward again. "We're looking into Talfour's background. Six months ago, he had a run-in with some racist punks who targeted him as he was walking from his store to catch an Uber. He escaped with scrapes and bruises thanks to a passerby who intervened. The whole thing was caught on CCTV. But none of the attackers was ever identified."

He closed the file folder. "You think there's a link?"

"Thinking is also what *I* get paid to do."

"Back to Desser. That's a Jewish name," Evan said. "You mentioned a noose and a slit throat. Was there also a blow to the head? I can't tell from these photos."

"In a manner of speaking. He took a .22-caliber bullet to the back of the skull."

It was Evan's turn to stop walking. Addie took two more strides before she realized she'd lost him and turned back.

Evan frowned. "He was shot?"

His vision of Vikings and bog bodies vanished, replaced by the image of a thrill killer who was into the weird stuff but maybe not consciously.

Addie nodded. "From about ten feet away. Some killers prefer a .22 because it's so effective at close range. Plus, it's easy to hide. Maybe Desser got away, and the killer had to take him down."

Evan thought of Diana. "He could have done that with an ax. If he was good."

"So maybe he's not that good. Either way, it doesn't eliminate the possibility of the same perpetrator. Sometimes killers change their MO."

"Still. You're trampling on my nascent theories."

She started walking again. "I'm confident you'll reconnect the dots."

A pair of coeds strolled by. Their laughter rang like bells in the cold air, giving Evan pause. Their world was the one he preferred to occupy—one of innocent pastimes. Of open futures. Of hope. It was why he enjoyed teaching.

He hated murder. Death should be a dry and dusty thing. A thing of old tombs and archaeological digs. Not a mess of blood and mud and a man's open throat.

Addie disappeared around the corner of Cobb Hall. He hurried after her. "What about runes?"

"Crap," she said.

He rounded the corner after her. A parking ticket fluttered under the windshield wiper of her SUV. She snatched it and thrust it into Evan's hand.

"You can do something about this, right?"

"I'll see." He took the ticket and stuffed it in his coat pocket. "Back to the runes."

"No runes. Now, where are my keys?" She hunted in her purse. Frowned and kept hunting. "No wooden slats. But maybe they were scattered sometime in the two months between when Scott Desser was killed and when his body was found."

"That's why you want me there?"

She raised her keys with a cry of triumph and turned on him with a smile.

"Exactly right, Professor. We're going hunting."

ᚷ

"Scott Desser," said Deputy Templeton, his breath hanging in the cold air. "Age fifty-two, an accountant from the Loop."

Evan and Addie followed the deputy along a rutted track in open pasture toward a distant patch of trees. The deputy was an older man—late fifties, maybe—with a slight build and a tendency to run his index finger between his upper lip and his nose as if to make sure his mustache was still present and accounted for.

"We figure Desser was into something weird," Templeton went on. "Why else would he be all the way out here? Nothing for outsiders unless you're looking to buy chicken feed. Or opioids."

"You have a problem in your county with drugs?" Addie asked.

"Does a cow have teats?"

Addie kept her pace slow, forcing the deputy to slow as well. Evan, as always, appreciated her kindness. Templeton's reaction to him had been exactly like that of many people. A widening of the eyes and then a studious determination to ignore him. Which was fine by Evan. He had a lot of thinking to do.

Starting with why the killer had struck in two such different locations. A rural community and the decaying, industrialized heart of Chicago. Both locations suggested the killer's nocturnal need for privacy. And if Evan was right about the bog bodies, the killer required water as part of his tableau. But there were plenty of watery places closer to the city.

Images of the runes scrolled like a slideshow through his head. The single rune set apart from the rest. And the poetic imagery he'd managed to pick out.

All of it was too complicated for a man with his limited experience in runic writing. Interpretation was critical. For however much some of the lines looked like gibberish, Evan knew they weren't. All they needed was a proper runologist.

He'd give Rhinehart a call while Addie was driving them back to Chicago. But first he would do a Google search to see if Rhinehart had, in fact, been involved in a scandal. He always had to think ahead to a trial and how an expert witness would appear to the jury.

Addie's voice took him out of his reverie.

"Who found the body?" she asked the deputy.

Templeton pointed toward a distant farmhouse. "A teenager named Tommy Snow. He claims he was over here hunting for birds' nests. Found the body and called the owner."

"The owner, not the police?"

"That's Tommy for you. Does things his own way. I don't think he's fond of law enforcement."

"Any reason for that?"

"Nothing I ever heard."

"You used the word *claims*. That Snow *claims* he was hunting birds' nests. Is the kid a suspect?"

The deputy turned off the narrow track and plowed into tall grass. "We couldn't find any connection between him and Desser. And no motive. He's a strange kid, but he's never had any real trouble with the law. Just a couple shoplifting charges, and those ended up getting dropped."

"Who owns this land?"

"Developer by the name of Robert Wharton."

"Is he a suspect?"

"Not unless it was some murder-for-hire thing, and there's no evidence of that. Wharton lives in Connecticut. According to his real estate agent, he bought the land sight unseen six months before the murder and has never set foot in Illinois. And thanks be. We got no need for cidiots trying to put down roots here. Next thing you know, they'll be wanting to build a Walmart."

Cidiots. It took Evan just over a second to parse this into *city* and *idiots.*

He smiled. A word to add to his personal lexicon.

They approached the line of trees, and a flock of starlings flew complaining into the air, circling a few times before they settled into the trees farther along. Chin-high grasses—waist-high for Addie and the deputy—rose on either side of the trail, and Evan startled when he heard a rustling off to his right.

"Lots of pheasant around here," Templeton said. "Maybe the killer was hunting and accidentally shot Desser. You'd be surprised how often it happens."

"Perhaps not," Evan muttered, feeling very much akin to the pheasant.

"Hunting with a .22?" Addie asked. "What would he have been stalking? Mice?"

"You'd be surprised," the deputy said again. "Cidiots, like I said. 'Course a shooting accident wouldn't explain the noose."

"Or the slashed throat," Evan murmured.

"What about stakes?" Addie asked. "Had the body been pinned to the ground in any way?"

"Not by the time we got to it."

Templeton waved for Addie and Evan to follow as he took a narrow footpath into the grove of cottonwoods. A moment later, they stepped out of the woods and into a clearing. A smattering of rain pockmarked the muddy ground around them and splashed into the pond. Addie and Evan zipped their coats. Templeton looked smug in his fleece-lined hunting jacket. Only cidiots got cold out here.

"We're a long way from the road," Addie observed. "A long way to drag or carry a body, if that's what happened."

"Doubt it," Templeton said. "We had a decent amount of rain last August, but anyone with a pickup and good tires could have driven right up."

The pond lay gray and dull under the sullen sky. Cattails and reeds choked the low banks, and the remains of a wooden pier rotted in the water. When Desser was here, the place would have been quite different. Buggy, for one. But also verdantly green, the reeds filled with starlings and red-winged blackbirds, the blue sky echoing with their calls. There would have been ducks, probably. Newts. Voles and rabbits.

It would be a good place to bring Ginny to hunt.

"Body was right over there," Templeton said, pointing. "Feet in the water, the rest of him in the reeds."

Addie shot Evan a glance and arched a knowing brow. *See?* the look said. *More alike than different.*

He made the motion of firing a gun, and she scowled.

"You guys find any wooden slats around the body?" Addie pulled out her phone and showed a photo to Templeton. "Like this?"

"No, ma'am. But a lot of time went by between when he was shot and when Tommy found him. Anything could have happened." He leaned forward, squinting at the screen. "That the vic from your case?"

As if regretting having shared so much, Addie snatched back the phone. "We need to look around."

"Well, sure. Be my guest. Just watch out for copperheads and water moccasins. You run into their burrows, you'll likely rile them up." He looked at Evan. "And don't fall in. We got alligator snapping turtles out here."

"Thanks for the heads-up," Evan said.

"They're endangered. I can't shoot one. Not for any reason."

"I believe dwarfs are also protected under the Endangered Species Act."

Templeton grunted. "Uh-huh."

Addie handed Evan a few small plastic flags on wires, paper bags, and a pair of latex gloves. She waved him westward. "I'll go east. Take pictures before you touch anything and leave a marker if you find anything relevant. You know the drill. Meet you around on the far side of the pond. We turn up anything, we'll stop and the sheriff's department can reopen this area as a crime scene." She glanced at the deputy. "That okay with you?"

He looked at his watch. "Sure."

Evan eyed the tall grasses and weeds. He was glad he'd collected his wellies from his car before they left the campus. He'd offered Addie his second pair, but she'd waved away his offer. No question, she was a lot tougher than he was.

He watched her head out. He'd never tell her, but she looked damn good in jeans and a turtleneck sweater, the puff jacket sitting snugly at the top of her hips. He caught Templeton watching her as well and had to push down his possessiveness. Addie belonged to no man. Definitely not the fancy-pants attorney she was sleeping with.

And certainly not to him.

He turned and, wincing, plunged into the rustling reeds.

Make that the *sharp-bladed* reeds. He'd brought the rubber boots, but what he really should have brought was a suit of armor. Still, he plowed gamely on. It was important to be a trouper. Plus, he could never say no to anything Addie suggested.

And what philologist worth his salt could turn down a treasure hunt?

Off to his right, the water sloshed against the shore, setting the reeds asway. Rain pattered on leaves, and small things rustled through the brush. Evan thought of water moccasins and copperheads and snapping turtles and kept moving.

Focus, he told himself. *See this place the way the killer did. What led him here? Why did he choose this pond and this field to serve as a grave?*

He paused in his search and stood still. The winter-gold grass rose high on either side of him, a wind-stirred tunnel beneath a sky of hammered pewter. The water slopped faintly against the reeds, disturbed by something in the pond. Birds cackled and fussed in the cottonwoods.

They were in an oasis of nature, surrounded on all sides by hundreds—perhaps thousands—of homes. Developments ate at these old farms with the speed and hunger of the insatiable. But here . . . here he could almost imagine himself in a different place. In an utterly different world, archaic and primal.

He turned words over in his mind like a river tumbling a stone. Water. Wind. Nature. Hunger. Destruction. Death. A thought rose, glimmered on the edge of consciousness, then vanished once again into the murk, leaving behind an unexpected feeling of unease.

The thought would return in due time. He started walking again.

When he spotted what looked like the leg bone of a deer, he almost ignored it. He pushed past, wincing as yet another razor-honed edge of sedge grass sliced his face. Much more of this and he'd look like a Maasai with tribal scarring.

"Death by a thousand cuts," he muttered. "I thought that was metaphorical."

He stopped. Frowned.

Prejudice, assumption, and narrow vision were the banes of any code breaker. As soon as you think you know what you're looking for, you're doomed.

His mind flashed to the Caistor runes, the earliest writing found in England—the runes had been carved on the ankle bone of a roe deer. Disregarding the killer's anachronistic use of a .22 pistol, any serious rune carver would be happy for the chance to leave his message on bone.

He turned around. The femur—or whatever part of a deer it was— lay half-buried in the frozen muck. What was visible of the bone was surprisingly white beneath a thin layer of grime. Evan took pictures of the bone in situ, then snapped gloves on over his cold hands. He squatted and gently pried the bone free and turned it over in his palm.

A series of *futhorc* runes had been etched along the length of the bone. The very last rune, set apart from the others, was the fourth letter of the *futhorc*, *ōs*, the word for *god* or *mouth*.

Maybe he'd been right with his theory about the numbering after all.

Since Desser had died months before Talfour, it might be that the runic lines found with Talfour's body were part of a longer piece. One that had started with Desser. Lines one through nine, presumably, since Talfour's lines started with the tenth character.

Which would mean Evan now had the fourth line of what he was coming to suspect was the killer's idea of a heroic epic poem.

He slid the bone into one of Addie's paper bags, planted a flag, and continued on. But he found nothing else, and when he reached the far end of the pond, a discouraged-looking Addie stared across the water with folded arms and furrowed brow.

Deputy Templeton had remained on the other side of the pond, where he stood smoking and scrolling through something on his phone.

Evan held the bag behind him as he approached Addie.

"Nothing?" he asked.

She shook her head. "I was so sure we'd find *something*."

He grinned, held up the bag, and rattled it. "O ye of little faith."

Her expression lit, and she grabbed the bag. When she looked inside, her eyes went wide. "Runes?"

"Runes."

"I'm going to kiss you. What does it say?"

"It says to kiss the finder of this bone."

"No, really. What does it say?"

"I'll need time to do a transliteration—that is, to find the correct equivalent in our alphabet for each rune. But the rune set apart here could stand for the number four. Which suggests there should be an additional eight bones around here."

Her eyes narrowed. "How do you know?"

"I think the killer is numbering the lines of his poem. One through nine for Desser. Ten through twenty-seven for Talfour."

"So you do think it's a poem?"

"Possibly. Probably."

Thoughts came and went in Addie's eyes. Evan could almost hear sparks flying as she ran through myriad possibilities of what this meant—a poem shared by two dead men.

But all she said was, "Let's take another look."

"Don't I get a pass, since I already found a prize?"

"No."

They switched sides, and reluctantly Evan plunged once more into the reeds. Half an hour later—they both went more slowly this time, zigzagging along the shore—they regrouped with Deputy Templeton on the far side. The only thing they'd gained was more scratches.

"Nothing, huh?" Templeton asked.

Addie opened the bag and showed him the bone. "We need your men to reopen this area as a crime scene. We're looking for bone or wood that's carved like this."

The deputy whistled. "Those little marks . . . are they some kind of message from the killer?"

"Possibly. Can you get some people on it?"

"Sure."

"And widen the search. Start with"—she turned in place—"a quarter-mile radius."

"Can do. So what do those marks mean?"

"We're working on that."

"We also need to talk to the kid who found the body," Evan said. "Tommy Snow."

"Yeah?" The deputy ran a finger along his upper lip. "Good luck with that."

Addie was sealing the paper bag with tape. "Was he pretty upset over finding the body?"

"Snow?" He shook his head. "He was more excited than distressed. He's a weird one."

"You keep saying that. What do you mean?"

"Other than the fact that he's not much for hanging around people? He's . . . well . . . you'll see when you meet him. Tommy Snow likes dead things."

CHAPTER 10

Evan stood next to Addie on the porch of the Snow residence, thinking about dead things while Addie rang the bell.

Inside, a television set fell silent. A moment later, the door opened, and a frazzled-looking fortysomething woman in jeans and a sweater stared out at them through the screen.

Addie said, "Mrs. Snow?"

"Yes?"

Addie held up her badge. "I'm Detective Bisset with the Chicago police, and this is our consultant Dr. Wilding. Is Tommy home?"

The woman's pale eyes went wide. "Is Tommy in some sort of trouble?"

"Not at all, Mrs. Snow," Addie said, sliding her badge back into her purse. "We just have a few questions for him."

"Is this about that dead man he found?"

Addie gave an almost imperceptible sigh. She shifted her weight, bouncing on her toes. Evan watched as she resettled her features into a friendly expression.

Patience was not one of Addie's virtues.

"If we could speak with him, that would be helpful." Addie widened her smile. Evan, at least, found her irresistible. "Is he home?"

Mrs. Snow's eyes toggled back and forth between Addie and a space over Evan's head while her hand twitched on the door handle like a bird ready to take flight. Her nails were polished, her strawberry-blond hair cut in a fashionable bob. Diamond studs twinkled in her earlobes.

But her makeup couldn't hide the shadows around her eyes.

What Evan could see of the newish cookie-cutter house beyond her was clean and tidy—a living room decorated in a soothing palette of blues and mauves. There was a gilt-framed mirror and an artful display of magazines. On a side table, a basket overflowed with artificial gourds and pine cones surrounding a wooden turkey—a nod toward the approaching Thanksgiving holiday. A bookmarked paperback novel lay on the sofa seat. The cover showed a woman swooning in the arms of a half-naked man.

It all added up to a woman for whom appearances mattered and who perhaps needed external organization to manage inward stress. She also liked a little escapism.

At least some of this no doubt related to her son.

Addie had parked down the street and run a background check on Tommy before they approached the house. Thomas Kevin Snow was nineteen. He'd graduated from James Madison High School the previous spring and lived at home with his mother while he attended a nearby community college. A glance through Madison High's online yearbook and a quick study of Snow's meager social media presence suggested he had few hobbies and fewer friends.

A photo of the offices of the Wellness Recovery Center on his Facebook account alluded to difficulties Tommy might be suffering. The center promised medication-driven treatment for a variety of disorders.

Evan, in his capacity as a Chicago PD consultant, had leaned an elbow on the console and read along with Addie. Then, while she'd moved to a closer parking spot, he'd stared at the house for a moment before tapping quickly into his phone. When Addie asked him what he was doing, he said, "Research."

Now he gave Mrs. Snow a beatific smile. He considered his smile his best feature. After the thick curls of Wilding hair. And his emerald-bright eyes.

You had to run with what you had.

"Mrs. Snow, I noticed a dovecote in your side yard as we approached. I'm confident I saw a Luzon bleeding-heart among the ring-necked doves. Are those Tommy's birds? The bleeding-hearts can be difficult to raise."

"Oh," said Mrs. Snow. Her gaze finally met Evan's. "The bleeding-heart is Tommy's favorite. He calls her Cory, from the Latin."

"For *heart*, in the sense of courage. Tommy must be a bright young man."

She puffed a strand of hair out of her eyes. "People don't realize. They assume he's slow."

"I imagine"—Evan went out on a limb—"that Tommy's intelligence makes it both easier and harder."

"You have no idea." She opened the door a few inches. "I'm glad he's bright. But on some days, it makes him that much more of a handful. His ability to focus is both a blessing and . . . well, frankly, sometimes it feels like a curse."

An autistic savant, perhaps, Evan thought. *No wonder Deputy Templeton finds him bewildering.*

"It's exhausting," he said.

"Yes." She looked relieved that he understood. "That's exactly it. Exhausting. So if you could tell me why you're here?"

"We need only a few minutes with him," Evan went on. "We're just crossing some t's on the investigation. If he becomes agitated, we can stop and come back another time."

Addie's foot swung gently, her toes connecting with his shin. She kept her eyes and her smile on Mrs. Snow.

Evan kicked back, verbally speaking. "We absolutely don't want to upset him."

"Well." Tommy's mother wavered. "If you promise you'll back off if he gets distressed."

"It's really impor—" Addie began.

Evan cut across her. "We promise."

Mrs. Snow opened the door the rest of the way and gestured them in. "He's pretty calm today. If you start by talking to him about birds or, God knows, animals of any kind, you might learn whatever it is you're after. Come on inside."

They crowded into the entryway, and Addie and Evan wiped their shoes on the mat.

"You have a lovely home, Mrs. Snow," Addie said.

"Thank you. But you'll have to forgive the stink." She turned and led them down the blue-carpeted hall with its bland watercolor landscapes. "I've tried everything. Plants. Air fresheners. A neighbor installed a heat exchanger, and that's helped a little. But . . ." She shrugged. "I put up with it because Tommy's hobby is what keeps him calm."

Addie looked puzzled. "All I smell is pumpkin bread."

Mrs. Snow smiled. "With walnuts. Tommy's favorite. No, the smell is mostly confined to the workshop out back. But it can become quite unpleasant during the summer months when I have the windows open. Now and again, the neighbors complain."

They walked through a kitchen—clean and bright with white appliances, oak cabinets, and blue countertops—then followed Mrs. Snow out the back door and into a winter-dead yard with brown sod, the remains of a vegetable garden, and a single scraggly maple. A mournful wind rattled the tree's remaining brown leaves, tattered clouds raced by overhead, and Evan was sure the temperature had dropped in the short time they'd been inside. Against the back fence rose a single-story structure the size of a three-car garage. The door was closed tight, and blackout curtains covered the two windows.

Mrs. Snow pulled a key from the pocket of her jeans.

"This unfinished workshop is why I bought the house after the divorce," she said. "So Tommy could pursue his hobby and I could have a house that didn't smell like, well, urine and God knows what. The previous owner used it as a woodworking shop. The walls are insulated, and there's electricity and water. If I added a cot and a fridge, I'd probably never see my son."

She unlocked and opened the door. They were immediately assaulted by the smells of wild things—of feathers and earth and waste and most of all the warm, living bodies of small creatures. Hot, moist air pressed against their skin.

Addie pushed back her curls. Her smile had faded.

They stepped inside, and Mrs. Snow closed the door behind them.

"Let me tell him you're here. He doesn't like surprises." She moved away, into the gloom. "Tommy? You have visitors."

Addie glanced at Evan and crinkled her nose. *Ugh,* she mouthed.

"Don't tell me you haven't smelled worse," he whispered.

"Only when a dead body is involved."

Mrs. Snow reemerged from the semidarkness. "Come on in. Sorry about the dark, but he finds it soothing. And don't be alarmed by the rat. It's for his biology class."

"Did you say rat?" Addie's voice rose.

For the first time, Mrs. Snow seemed to take satisfaction in whatever peculiarities her son might possess. She gave Addie a small, smug smile. "You'll see."

They followed her across the concrete floor into a gloomy space illuminated here and there by pockets of light.

Unpainted drywall lined the walls. Bracketed to the studs were expensive-looking cabinets and countertops, the work surfaces strewn with microscopes, slides, stacks of petri dishes, vials, Bunsen burners, and assorted other scientific detritus. Displays of everything from the reticulated skeleton of a small alligator to a stuffed and mounted badger crowded the space along the tops of the cabinets. Potted plants, limp-leafed and pale, dotted the landscape—Mrs. Snow's attempt at odor mitigation. The forlorn philodendrons made Evan think of tiny levees mounted against a tsunami of animals and their malodourous by-products.

He turned his attention to the animals. Fifty or more cages filled an array of metal shelves, the glass or steel pens crowded with snakes, lizards, mice, and a snakelike beast that Evan was pretty sure was an enormous millipede. Creatures hissed or skittered or—in a large aquarium on the far side of the room—splashed.

The pools of light came from task lamps mounted on the underside of the cabinets. In their muted glow, Evan saw that each cage was labeled with the animal's scientific name and a date—possibly the time of acquisition. Another piece of paper the size of an index card was clipped to each cage and listed additional information handwritten in incredibly small, neat print—writing that suggested an organized mind with a great deal to say.

The only decoration came from a single poster attached to the drywall: a drawing of a man in a powdered wig. Beneath the man's ruddy visage were the words CAROLUS LINNAEUS—FATHER OF TAXONOMY.

Tommy Snow was an amateur naturalist.

The young man himself worked diligently with his back to them, hunched over something on an aluminum tray. The air reeked of formaldehyde. Silver dissecting pins glittered on the counter, and streaks of something unidentifiable spattered a nearby sink.

"Tommy," said his mother.

The boy's thin shoulders shifted, but he didn't look up.

"These people are from the Chicago police. You're not in trouble. But they want to ask you a few questions."

"I'm very busy," Tommy said.

"Remember what we talked about," Mrs. Snow said. "Priorities. One, two, and three. Right now, Detectives Bisset and Wilding are priority number one. After you answer their questions about that time you were on Mr. Wharton's property, they'll leave, and you can go on to priority number two."

"My rat."

"Yes. The rat."

Next to Evan, Addie shuddered. He threw a glance in her direction. Was it his imagination, or did she look pale?

"But I just started on the esophagus. Dr. Almadi said we had to be finished with the alimentary canal by Friday."

"Ten minutes, Mr. Snow," Addie said. "That's all we need."

"Tommy—" his mother began.

Evan cleared his throat. "Tommy, my name is Evan. And what I really want to know is if Deputy Templeton was telling the truth when he said there are alligator snapping turtles living in Mr. Wharton's pond. Because I find that hard to believe."

The boy paused. Hitched his shoulders again. He set down a scalpel and pulled off the rubber gloves one finger at a time. He picked up the scalpel again and turned to face them.

Tommy Snow had a handsome, sharp-featured face surrounded by a halo of wispy strawberry-blond hair, the same color as his mother's. But beneath pale eyebrows, his irises were as dark as his mother's eyes were light.

"You're a dwarf," he said, not meeting Evan's eyes.

"Tommy!" cried Mrs. Snow.

"The correct thing to say is that I'm a person with dwarfism. Or a little person. Or a person of short stature."

"A person with dwarfism," Tommy repeated. "Is it achondroplasia?"

"Actually, no."

"But that's the most common form of dwarfism. Seventy percent of cases."

"True. But I'm unique. One of a kind."

Tommy nodded, seeming satisfied with that. "Do people laugh at you?"

"Sometimes."

"People laugh at me."

"People can be asses."

Tommy chortled, an awkward, wheezing sound. His soft hair fluttered around the sharp planes of his pale face. His laugh died away, and faint emotions flitted across his features, his mood appearing to vacillate between humor and rage. He looked like a cherub debating whether to stay in the clouds or hurtle himself into the darkness after Lucifer.

Evan pressed his case. "Can you tell me the truth about the snapping turtles? Because aren't all our snappers in creeks in Southern Illinois? I'm pretty sure *Macrochelys temminckii* doesn't do well in a pond as small as Mr. Wharton's."

Addie mouthed at him, *WTH?*

"That's right." A spark lit in Tommy's eyes, which were still focused on the ground near Evan's feet. "I think you might be a smart guy."

"I think it takes one to know one."

Tommy laughed again. He nodded to himself as if reaching a decision and placed the scalpel down on the counter. He said, "I read that someone released an alligator snapper in the pond during the summer. Then I saw someone there from the INHS. But she said she was just checking for invasive species."

Evan recognized a test. "You're referring to the Illinois Natural History Survey."

"You know about them?"

"I do. Is that why you were on Mr. Wharton's property? You were looking for the turtle?"

"Yes." Tommy's hands fisted at his sides. "I said birds' nests because I didn't want the sheriff to know about the turtle. In case he found it first. I was looking for bones, too. For Mr. X. Deer bones and cattle bones. Mr. X likes both. He pays me twenty dollars for each femur or tibia. He likes the scapula and mandibles, too. Sometimes I have to search for miles. But sometimes I find them in the field around the pond."

Evan sensed Addie perk up.

"Why does Mr. X want the bones?" he asked.

A blank look. "Because they're interesting."

"Of course." Evan nodded agreeably. "Did you find any bones the day you found the body?"

"Yeah. Lots of bones."

Addie made a small sound. Evan ignored her.

"And did you pick them up?"

"No!" Another chortle. His hands relaxed. "That would have been wrong. They were the dead man's bones! Skeleton of *Homo sapiens*. Ha! Ha!"

Addie puffed out a sigh, but Evan pushed on. "What about other bones, Tommy? Deer or cattle bones? Did you pick up any of those for Mr. X?"

Something sly slithered into Tommy's eyes. "No."

"Do you like Sherlock Holmes, Tommy?"

He looked suspicious. "I liked *The Hound of the Baskervilles*. And *A Study in Scarlet*."

"Did you know Holmes's IQ was at least 190?"

"That's what John Radford said in his book."

"That's right." Evan was starting to figure he and the kid were twins separated at birth—both packed to the gills with mostly useless information. "It's a good thing the police had Sherlock Holmes, isn't it? Because he liked to solve murders. And he was *smart* enough to solve murders."

Tommy moved closer. His tall, thin shadow loomed on the wall beside Evan's short form.

"We need your help," Evan said. "Would you like to solve murders?"

"I think I'd like that."

"And what we need to solve this murder are the bones that were placed near Mr. Desser."

Tommy's eyes moved around the room, never lighting on his mother or the detectives. "Do you mean the bones with writing on them?"

"Yes," Evan said. "We need the bones with writing on them."

CHAPTER 11

Forty minutes later, Addie sat with Evan in her SUV, the heater running, while they munched on the peanut butter and jelly sandwiches she'd brought along. She leaned over the console toward Evan so that together they could study the photos she'd taken at Tommy's house.

Tommy had produced three bones, each etched with runes. Addie had photographed the bones and placed them in separate, labeled bags. She'd asked Tommy to sketch exactly where he'd found them. In a few short minutes, he'd produced a drawing that was remarkable for its skill. Although none of the bones was in the immediate vicinity of where Desser's corpse had been found, she assumed the map was probably accurate. Tommy seemed a stickler for detail.

Animal activity could easily explain why the bones were scattered. They were lucky to get as many as they did.

When she asked Tommy why he hadn't given the bones to the police, he shrugged and said they never asked. And until Addie and Evan showed up, he hadn't known they were related to the murder.

Now she felt a surge of her earlier excitement.

They had a serial killer.

Horrible. And wonderful. All at once. Her stomach churned with guilt.

"You should buy seedless jam," Evan said.

She straightened in her seat. "You're thinking about jelly? The great Dr. Wilding is looking at runes carved on bones by a serial killer, and he's thinking about jelly."

"We're eating peanut butter and *jam* sandwiches. Jelly is nothing but fruit juice with a little backbone. Jam is okay, but preserves would be better."

"Shut up and finish your sandwich."

"But it's the little things that matter. You shouldn't underestimate the importance of a proper sandwich spread."

"Get to work."

Evan dutifully stuffed the remainder of his sandwich into his mouth and scrolled through the photos on Addie's phone while she shifted out of park and pulled onto the street.

"This might be the word for *blessing*," he said around a mouthful of bread. He enlarged the photo. "We have the word *bless* spelled out—b-l-e-s-s. Then we have the runic character that looks like two small *X*s stacked on top of each other. In modern English, it stands for the sound *ing*." He found a napkin in her glove box and wiped his mouth. "It's possible the killer took a shortcut, and instead of spelling out the i-n-g, he used the rune. The same character appears multiple times in the bones from Talfour's crime scene."

"I thought you couldn't read runes."

He looked smug. "I'm a quick study. Plus, I have resources."

"Whatever it takes." She turned a corner and headed back toward the highway. "At least now you're talking my talk. But why would a killer use the word *blessing*?"

"It's a mystery. Just give me a few minutes."

He pulled out his journal and, using the photos Addie had taken of the bones, copied them onto a clean page. After a few moments, he said, "He once again used boustrophedon. Clever little bugger."

"What is that?" She tapped the brakes. "Bou—stro—whatever."

"It's about the order of the letters. Whether you read them from left to right or right to left. With boustrophedon, you alternate. The ancient Greeks used it quite a bit. Now, keep driving. I'm still working."

He wrote out:

2   *thus from my bothy I came, homeland's ward for cattle of riding*
3   *to sacrifice the innocent at night. She takes back her sons and daughters*
4   *who rived and tholed and peeled her flesh like ripe fruit*
9   *blessing giver my blood-feud stillbirths/still births your further crimes*

"Yes," he said after a few minutes. "Definitely the word *blessing*. A blessing giver. Not to mention a suggestion of punishment extracted for the commission of a terrible crime. Perhaps with the idea of preventing—or possibly committing—additional crimes. Impossible to know at this point. There is also a line about sacrificing the innocent."

"What kind of terrible crime are we talking about?"

"Something that involves riving and tholing and peeling, apparently. Which, in modern English, boils down to committing torture."

She frowned at him. "*Blessing* seems an odd word to leave at a murder scene."

"Depends on how knowledgeable our killer is. Our modern English word *blessing* derives from the Old English *bletsian*, which referred to an altar sacrifice. It means to mark something holy through the spilling of blood. The word *bletsian* appears in the runes from Talfour's body. So clearly it's a theme."

Her emotions hovered between excitement and distress. "You think the killer is practicing human sacrifice?"

"I think it's a definite maybe."

"The problem with you academic types is you lack a sense of commitment."

"Cops, on the other hand, want to commit everyone."

"Ha ha. What about line numbers?"

"If my theory is right about the numbering and that we're dealing with a poem, we now have lines two, three, four, and nine of the poem the killer left with Desser."

Addie mulled over the idea of sacrifice as a motive for murder. In her experience, most killings occurred because of some form of dispute. Over territory. As part of a larger rivalry. Often some asshat's belief that he wasn't getting enough respect. Sometimes even a man's dispute with his wife's cooking, although it was never really about the meatloaf.

But murder as sacrifice? Uncommon. Rarer, even, than serial killers. And human sacrifice as a punishment for both the guilty and the innocent, as the poem seemed to suggest?

Madness. A particularly evil form of madness.

She touched the brakes and executed a perfect rolling stop at an intersection before speeding through. "Who is the killer sacrificing to?"

"I need more information."

"Live dangerously, Evan."

"You want me to guess?" He rubbed his chin. "I suppose we could be looking at a Viking *blót*. And don't—"

"Clarify."

"—ask me to clarify. The word burbled up from some ancient memory. I'm not a Viking expert."

"You just told me you're a quick study. Ramp up, my friend."

He tapped in his phone, scrolled through what she assumed was a website. After a moment, he nodded and murmured, "Uh-huh."

She smacked the steering wheel and shot him a glare. "What?"

"Vikings, just like so many of us, wanted to be on good terms with their gods. A *blót* sacrifice, apparently, could go a long way toward ensuring one's continued good standing. The sacrifice was generally conducted as an exchange. I'll give you this goat if you'll give me a good tailwind for my next voyage. Or I'll donate this golden chalice in your name if you'll have my back while I pillage and burn the monastery and murder all the monks serving that newfangled monotheistic Christian god."

"Sounds a bit harsh."

"Those were harsh times. According to this Scandinavian historical website, humans and animals alike were sacrificed to Odin."

"Odin. He's a god, right?"

"The supreme being among the Viking pantheon. God of war and the dead. And interestingly, the god most associated with the runic script. His thirst for wisdom led him to allow himself to be speared in the side and hung upside down from a tree in order to be granted the knowledge of the runes. He also gave up an eye in exchange for this knowledge."

"Like Talfour."

"I very much doubt Talfour gave up anything willingly. But yes. There are parallels."

"This all sounds promising. A modern-day Viking trying to return, for whatever demented reason, to the old ways. And maybe the *she* in the poem refers to a goddess."

"Perhaps. Or a female spirit of some kind."

"But why Talfour and Desser? Why these two men?"

"If Desser is, in fact, Jewish, there could be a racial or ethnic aspect." He told her what Diana had shared with him about the Ásatrú and Viking reenactors and a possible racist element.

Addie drummed her fingers on the steering wheel. "So we've got some nutcase murdering men he believes inferior, and doing it in the name of the Viking gods?"

"The Æsir. The Viking pantheon."

"Yeah? Make a note in my phone. This guy thinks he's a modern-day Viking come to restore the world to its former white-skinned glory."

"Possibly." Evan picked up her phone and dutifully typed the information in a note-taking app. "But I'm far from convinced. You're talking about what is commonly known as a missionary killer—someone who wishes to exterminate a certain group of people."

"Come on, Evan. What else could it be? A Black man and a Jewish man walk into a Viking bar . . ."

"Hall. Vikings had mead halls. Wood-timbered buildings with trestle tables and roaring fireplaces. And a fermented honey drink known as mead."

"Mead sounds Viking-ish."

"It goes well beyond the Vikings. Mead is possibly the oldest alcoholic beverage enjoyed by mankind. Popular with the Egyptians and Mayans. The Greeks called it the nectar of the gods. But to return to my point—we might have a visionary killer. Someone who acts because he believes he is being commanded by an outside force."

"What kind of outside force?"

"It could be a group of gods. Or a single god."

"Like Odin."

"Yes."

"A visionary killer," she said. "So much better than a missionary killer."

He grunted, and she grinned at him before she sank into her thoughts and turned quiet.

⚡

Evan watched her gaze go far away. He wondered what she was thinking. He hated where his own thoughts sat. So-called religious killers were his bread and butter when it came to his consulting work. But they terrified him. Misplaced faith and passion could ignite wars.

He found himself watching Addie with the admiration she always stirred in him. He took in her dark-brown hair as it corkscrewed in soft ringlets around her face. The dimple in her chin. A scattering of freckles like tiny grains of sand across her nose and cheeks. Inwardly, he groaned. Why did love reduce its sufferers to cliché? And why could he not, like Cyrano, concoct the perfect verse that would render Addie putty in his hands?

Why could he not stop thinking in clichés?

Not that any of it mattered. Addie loved him. But only as a friend. She saved her romantic interest for the kind of man who could fold up someone like Evan and use him as a snot rag.

He forced his mind back to the matter at hand. "There's one other element we have to consider."

She jumped at the sound of his voice. "What's that?"

"Both Talfour's and Desser's bodies were arranged to resemble European burials from the Iron Age. Some of those bodies are even older—from the Neolithic. The poor victims are known by archaeologists as bog bodies."

She mouthed the words as she sped around a tractor trailer rumbling along the county road. *Bog bodies.* "And that's not a Viking thing. At least, that's what you said this morning."

"Right. Bog bodies are from a time long before the Vikings took up their marauding ways. We know about them only because, over the centuries, bog bodies have emerged from their ancient graves, usually discovered by people cutting peat and finding more than they bargained for. Or at least that was true before archaeologists got involved. We're a bit more precise in our excavation methods now."

"I heard about them. They're mummies. It was on National Geographic or something. Maybe the Discovery Channel."

"They're everywhere. Quite popular, bog bodies. And with many of them, we find garroting, a staved skull, a noose. The same postmortem positioning as with Talfour."

"A missing eye?"

"Not that. That may return us to the Vikings and Odin."

She gripped the wheel as she braked behind a large semitrailer truck. Traffic flew by in the left lane. "So . . . why?"

"There are a number of theories as to why people were buried in bogs. We have the theory of accidental—"

"I mean, why is the killer re-creating a bog body?"

"That is the question of the hour. Or one of many questions of the hour. But it's clear—given the incredible effort this kind of death and burial required—that the killer is sending a very important message."

"To who? To whom, I mean."

"Odin, perhaps. Perhaps the police. Maybe Iron Age deities. I don't know yet."

Traffic cleared, and she accelerated around the rig, cutting off the driver just as he signaled his own desire to get into the left lane. The trucker honked, and she casually flipped him off. "And what is the killer's message?"

Evan offered the trucker an apologetic smile as they whipped past. "Unknown. But if I were to live dangerously, as you suggest, I propose that he's saying this murder is either a sacrifice or a punishment. Some archaeologists speculate that the bog bodies were human sacrifices, although it's unclear to whom they were being sacrificed. Others theorize they were miscreants who had to pay for their crimes."

"We're back to that word from Talfour's poem. *Bletsian.*"

"Quite possibly."

"Why can't this be both? Maybe Talfour and Desser, already outcasts from the pure Aryan race, committed some offense against our killer." She chewed her lip. "If we can figure out their supposed crime or crimes, maybe we can use that to find him. Evan, I need those runes translated."

"I know." He held his sigh. "And I've made a pass at it. But because it isn't a straightforward process and I'm not a runologist, I suggest that you get approval from your lieutenant to bring in a professional. Someone who can lay out all the possible interpretations. Once we have that, I can use my linguistic skills to peer into the killer's mind. I can also help with the semiotics of the scene—the killer's signature, if you will. We have to consider the bog body elements, the wooden slats forming a halo. The injuries inflicted both perimortem and for a time after the victims' deaths. But for the runes themselves, Diana suggested Ralph Rhinehart."

She looked surprised. "The mystical alphabets guy?"

Everyone, it seemed, had heard of Ralph Rhinehart.

She shifted in her seat. "Do you know that he talks about how to use writing as an instrument for conducting black magic? It gets a little uncomfortable for a good Catholic girl like me."

Evan kept his voice gentle. "If Talfour and Desser were blood sacrifices, then Rhinehart might be exactly who we need."

She glanced over at him. Her freckles stood out sharply on her pale face. "You think these murders have to do with black magic?"

"By posing his victims as bog bodies, the killer is likely trying to catch the essence of those hallowed and fearsome fens. Which is to say, bogs. Just as our Iron Age ancestors did."

"A bog is fearsome?" she scoffed. "Because of the size of the mosquitoes?"

"Not at all. Think about it, Addie. Bogs are neither solid land nor true water. They're places where people wander in and never emerge, forever lost. Bogs are in-between spaces where strange mists rise, where poisonous creatures live. Where an unwary traveler can become trapped and slowly drowned. As happened to the villain in Sherlock Holmes's *The Hound of the Baskervilles*, if you'll recall. Jack Stapleton gets caught in the Grimpen Mire and suffers his just deserts."

Addie's hand flew to the cross around her neck. "Now you're the one giving me the creeps."

"Says our fearless homicide detective. Rhinehart could be useful."

"Then you go talk to him. Stay vague. Or have him sign a nondisclosure agreement. But I'm reluctant to bring in someone who isn't a

PhD or at least a recognized authority in their field. We have to consider how things will look when we go to court."

Light glimmered on the windshield from behind the scrim of clouds; Evan found his aviator sunglasses in his coat pocket and slid them on.

"We'll find someone else, then," he said. "Maybe a professor from the university's faculty. Or from another school. We could even reach across the pond and consult with someone from my alma mater."

"Now *that* is a great idea."

They fell silent, each absorbed with their own thoughts. Addie turned on the radio, flipped through the stations, and turned it off again.

"If you're right about the numbering system," she said as they approached the highway, "then I figure our mysterious Mr. X has the missing bones. I think Tommy Snow collected all of them—minus the one you found—and sold all but these three."

"Maybe."

Addie had asked Tommy a lot of questions. Who was Mr. X, how had they met, why was he supplying the man with deer and cow bones? But on the identity of Mr. X and all other questions about the mysterious man, Tommy had gone mum and refused to relent. His mother claimed this was the first she'd heard of Mr. X and Tommy's side gig collecting bones.

Evan stared out the window at the brown fields flowing past. "The bones could also have been carried off by scavengers before Tommy found the body. Or he might be hanging on to them. I can't see him giving up all of them to the police. He wants to help. But he also wants those bones for his collection."

"Because he knows they're special."

"And Tommy likes special things. It's why he wanted that turtle."

"I'll ask the sheriff to get a search warrant."

"That will be upsetting for him."

"You're awfully protective of the kid. He's a suspect, for heaven's sake."

"You see him as a killer? He shows not the slightest interest in Vikings or runes."

"He's good at dissection," she pointed out. "Handy with a scalpel."

"So is any biologist."

She turned right, onto the entrance ramp, and accelerated toward the highway. "You have to admit, his workshop was creepy."

"I do not share Tommy Snow's interests. But I understand the drive for firsthand knowledge."

"And he's clearly into death. Did you see all those animals he'd mounted?"

"Have you ever been in a taxidermist's shop?"

"What if Desser—?" She slammed on the brakes and honked as a pickup sped by without moving to the left to let them in. She shook a fist. "You jerk! Why don't you go back to driving school?"

Evan tapped her shoulder. "You were saying?"

"They'll give any jerk a driver's license." She gave a sniff and merged onto the highway. "I was saying we should look at other possibilities. What if Desser was, I don't know, hired by that developer Wharton to keep an eye on the property? And Desser told the boy the pond was off-limits? No trespassing. That might be enough to enrage a kid like Tommy, who could have been used to roaming the place at will, looking for bones. And those turtle things."

"*Macrochelys temminckii.*"

She waved a hand. "Please tell me what gives on the snapping turtle thing. *Macro*-whatchacallit. How did you know all that? And how did you know that would break through Tommy's shell?" She laughed. "Pun not intended."

"Deductive reasoning. Plus the lesson you taught me about finding something in common with a witness. I was just being prepared, like a good Boy Scout."

"You grew up in England. You were never a Boy Scout."

He sniffed. "There were Boy Scouts in Britain three years before the Boy Scouts of America opened their doors. As in so many things, we were there first."

"How do you even know that?"

"I was a Boy Scout. Mother made sure of that. It's handy having someone in the house who's always prepared." Evan adjusted the seat belt, which threatened to cut off his blood supply at the throat. It was only one of the many reasons he preferred to take his own car. "May I continue?"

"Please."

"The deputy said Tommy likes dead things. Yet the boy claimed he was there collecting birds' nests—which are biological entities but hardly dead."

"He admitted that was a lie."

"It did turn out to be false. But it carried enough of the truth to serve, and someone as smart as Tommy will create a lie that is as close to the truth as possible."

She raised an eyebrow at him. "You have a soft spot for this boy."

"As I do for all who must struggle unfairly in a world quick to judge."

"You're a softy, Dr. Wilding," she said quietly. "So you figured because he said birds' nests that he likes birds?"

"Not really. But it got me thinking. We saw that he'd been living near the pond for five years. He probably had collected all the nests he could want. So why was he really there? Then we saw the dovecote in his side yard. Getting his mom to agree to that no doubt took real effort on his part. More work for them both and probably an eyesore to her way of thinking. Plus he wanted special doves—the bleeding-hearts. He likes animals, but he especially likes rare animals. A theory that was confirmed, by the way, when I saw a tank with piranhas."

"He has flesh-eating piranhas in his workshop?"

"That's the only kind there is. But these weren't just any piranhas. A Google search identified them as the rare ruby red spilo—something I had to check after the fact, of course." He was rather pleased with how his theory had come together. It was always satisfying when a series of hypotheticals led to something solid. "Anyway, seeing the bleeding-hearts in the dovecote suggested that Tommy might have been at the pond to check out the rumor of the alligator snapping turtle. So I did my homework on the little beastie while you were working to wedge your car into a spot the size of a tricycle. I had a feeling that the turtle might be the path into Tommy's heart."

"You're a bit of a freak, Evan. And I mean that in the kindest possible way."

"Thank you. I think."

"What did you make of Mr. X?"

"People are more your specialty."

"A search warrant for the house might turn up Mr. X's identity," Addie said. "Assuming Tommy doesn't destroy all evidence in the meantime. But I'm wondering if he's even real. Why would some random dude be buying deer and cow bones? And how did he find Tommy?"

"He could be an artist. Or a middleman, reselling them to a supply company or to bone carvers."

"Then why the secrecy? More likely he's our killer."

"If our killer is a bone collector, why did he use wooden slats with Talfour?"

"I hate when you step on my theory."

Her phone buzzed. She thumbed the button to answer the call and put it through the Bluetooth. "Go ahead, partner."

Patrick's rumbling voice came through the car speakers. "You still out in the wilds of Kendall County?"

"Just heading back to home sweet home. Did you learn anything from Talfour's family or friends?"

"They all swear he wasn't into drugs or prostitution. Big surprise, right? Like they're gonna fess up to that even if it were true. Neighbors say he was courteous. Friendly. The kind of guy who would help you carry in your groceries or put together your IKEA dresser. He liked to sit on the patio in front of his condo on the weekends and shoot the breeze with passersby. What about the cold case? Scott Desser. Find any links?"

"Definitely. We've got more runes. And the body was probably positioned like Talfour's. We can't be a hundred percent sure because there was an eight-week gap between when Desser was killed and when his body was found. Speaking of which, we had an interesting conversation with a kid named Tommy Snow . . ."

While Addie filled Patrick in on what they'd learned, Evan tuned out their conversation and bent over his notebook, picking out unfamiliar words.

Like *bothy* in the line, *thus/from/my/bothy/i/came/homelands/ward.*

What, he pondered as he scratched his beard, *is a bothy?* The term seemed vaguely familiar.

Addie made a strangled sound in her throat, jerking him back to the here and now. He glanced over as she disconnected with Patrick. Her face had gone red, and there was a hard glint to her eye that would have made Evan duck if there'd been anything throwable within her reach.

He closed the journal. "What is it?"

"Criver."

"The lieutenant? What's he done?"

"He's gone and brought in Rhinehart."

"Then maybe we should take it as a sign he'll be of use."

She directed her hard gaze at him. "I don't want his help. I want *your* help. And don't give me that bullcrap about not being a runologist. I have *faith* in you, Evan."

"Does having Rhinehart in mean I'm out?"

"I don't know. I'd need a flashlight and a shovel to know what Criver's thinking. I just . . . Evan, you can't abandon me on this."

"I also can't horn in on an investigation if your lieutenant is against it."

"I'm allowed to consult with experts. Criver can't deny me that. This case calls for a semiotician. Not some guy who knows a little bit about mystical alphabets."

Evan prided himself on his ability to read subtext. "What are you so worried about, Addie?"

She startled. "It's Criver."

"The fact that he thinks women should leave the tough stuff to men?"

"All that male-superiority nonsense. I want to prove him wrong. I *need* to prove him wrong."

"I know."

"Do you? Do you know what it's like to be told all the frigging time that you're inferior just because you don't have a Y chromosome?"

"Perhaps not. But I do know what it's like for people to assume your intellect correlates to your physicality, be it gender or race or height."

She glanced at him, and her expression softened. "I know. I'm sorry."

"Humans are very good at underestimating each other."

He stared out the windshield. Chicago rose in the distance, a shimmering metropolis against a backdrop of towering nimbus clouds. In that far place resided many of the things he loved. A handful of friends. His students who, at the moment, were listening to Diana give the lecture he'd prepared. And Diana herself. His neighbor's daughter, Jo, who studied piano with him. His hawk, Ginny. And his home, which was a safe place in a world that did not look kindly on its children when those children were different.

He'd settled in Chicago almost on a whim. The job was important, of course, but he could find work anywhere. The decision had come down to a combination of the kind of classwork he'd be doing, the unscheduled hours for research, his generous office, and the fact that a professor with dwarfism and on a lengthy sabbatical had offered her home to him for the foreseeable future. Of course, there were also the city's cultural offerings. Its theaters and galleries, its restaurants and street vendors. The many places it provided to fly a hawk.

Plus, it was literally half a world away from the darker memories of his childhood.

Chicago had felt like the promised land. Aside from the traffic, of course. And the politics. Sometimes the weather.

But it had been a lonely promised land, even with all the things he enjoyed. Until the night he and Addie stumbled into each other at an art opening—quite literally, when she'd walked into him as he stood in front of a painting of a trash can that he was trying to convince himself he liked. She had crushed his toes and managed to spill both their drinks, proving herself infinitely more interesting than the trash can. They'd gone on to bond over a small exhibit of Mary Cassatt, and through the next days and weeks, they'd recognized in each other a shared yearning to do something larger with their lives, even as societal expectations held them back. Addie, a woman working in a man's world. Evan, of course, a person whose physicality kept him from being seen as a man in full.

He'd fallen in love with her immediately, right in front of the trash-can painting. Because of her clumsiness. At her insistence on replacing his spilled Manhattan. And at her snap decision to dump her date and spend the rest of the evening with him.

More than anything, at her refusal to look at him differently because of his height.

Until they met, Evan hadn't realized how much of a mask he wore. Every person who falls outside the bell curve of what is defined as "normal" has to do the same—put on seemingly indestructible armor and go out to slay the dragons, be they out-of-reach coat hooks, steep stairwells, or merely the sideways glances and uneasy giggles of the ignorant.

But Addie had slipped inside his armor. He hadn't known how much he'd needed someone who let him be vulnerable until she offered him the space to just be himself.

There wasn't anything he wouldn't do for her.

"Evan?" Addie's voice drifted through his reverie, soft as spider silk. "What are you thinking?"

He turned in his seat.

"If you think having me on the case will help you push back against Criver," he said, "then I'll do everything I can."

"What about your consulting fee?"

"We'll work it out. Or not. If you want my help, I'm not going to say no. I'll make a first pass on a profile tonight."

She reached over, gripped his hand. "You're the best."

"I'm glad you've noticed." He held his breath until she released his hand, then returned his gaze to Chicago growing larger on the horizon. His fingers tingled.

If Addie wanted him, even if it was only for his intellect, he would be there for her.

It was what friends—and if-only lovers—were for.

CHAPTER 12

Addie, her arms filled with printouts of reports and photos from both murders, followed Patrick as he rolled the whiteboard into the station house's conference room and flipped on the lights. Outside, darkness pressed against the windows, strewing raindrops that glittered in the city lights.

While Patrick sorted and stapled the printouts and slid them into folders, Addie wrote a list of facts about the two cases on the board. When she was done, she glanced at the clock. Ten minutes until the meeting started.

"I want a beer," she said. "A thick, dark stout. And a burger with all the trimmings."

Patrick had just finished setting the folders on the table, one in front of each chair. "Ach, lass, that hurts. Make do with coffee?"

"Any port in a storm."

She watched Patrick's departing reflection in the glass. Her thoughts lit on the mental image of Clayton L. Hamden, attorney to the stars. Clayton was busy with clients until later tonight. But after that, he'd be hers. They'd made plans to meet at his place for a midnight nightcap.

And whatever else followed.

She moved to the window. Outside, the rain turned heavy, lashing the panes. She leaned against the glass and watched as her breath fogged and faded on the cold surface.

Was he out there now, the killer? Prowling through the rain-whipped streets and back alleys for his next victim? Did he carry a sack full of bones that rattled and clinked and whispered to him in an ancient language about blessings and sacrifice? Was he somewhere practicing the Old English *bletsian*, the altar sacrifice? Did he seek to mark something as holy by slaughtering it on an altar of his own devising?

She jumped at the sound of voices in the hall. Lieutenant Criver and another man.

"Did you hear why they couldn't make a live-action movie of *Snow White*?" the lieutenant was asking.

"I did not," replied a low, gravelly voice. "Tell me."

"Apparently there was a dwarf *shortage*."

The two men roared with laughter, and a few seconds later, Criver waved a man into the room and followed him in. Criver's eyes locked with Addie's.

The joke had to be about Evan, and she knew she was scarlet. Her face gave her away every time. But she nodded politely.

"Good evening, Lieutenant."

"Ah, Adrianne," Criver said cheerfully. "You've obviously been working out in the field. Awful day with the weather, isn't it?"

She'd toweled the rain out of her hair but hadn't had time to do more. Her hair always went wild in the humidity, and now it probably looked like a dark-brown dandelion fluff.

"Yes, sir," she said, resisting an impulse to smooth down her curls. "Hard at work on our case."

"Good, good." Criver set a stack of papers on the table. "Adrianne, this is Ralph Rhinehart. He's an expert runologist. Perhaps you've heard his podcast or seen him on TV. Multiple networks, right, Ralph? And he's published fifteen books. We're lucky to have him."

Rhinehart was a fiftysomething man of average height with dirty spectacles, a headful of wiry gray hair circumnavigating a bald pate, and a paunch that made him look as if he'd tucked a bowling ball under his sweater. He smelled of mints and deodorant.

Addie plastered a smile on her face and stepped around the table, arm extended. "A pleasure to meet you, Mr. Rhinehart. Thank you for offering your help."

"Of course. Happy to do my part." He peered at her through the smeary lenses of his glasses. "Thomas, they just keep making them prettier every year."

Addie shoved her hands in the pockets of her suit coat and kept the smile. "I'm curious. Do you think runes are connected to sorcery? I thought I read something to that effect on your website."

He cleared his throat. "Yes, yes. It's quite common for people to associate runes with occultism."

"And you think that might have some bearing on our case?"

"I believe that's exactly what we're dealing with." Rhinehart pulled out a handkerchief and dabbed his face. Addie noticed a sheen of sweat on the man's upper lip.

"Mr. Rhinehart, are you feeling all right?" she asked.

"Of course, of course." He placed a hand on his chest. "Just need to sit down for a moment. A touch of whatever's going around."

Criver leapt into action, taking the runologist's elbow and steering him to a chair. "Coffee?"

Rhinehart nodded, and Criver raised a hand toward Addie. "Would you mind? Black for me and cream only for Ralph—is that right? Ralph and I can start going through the folders here."

Addie's chin dropped. "I beg your pardon?"

At that moment, Patrick strode into the room. Addie could tell by his darkened face that he'd heard the last part of the conversation. With false cheeriness, he set the coffees on the table. "Two more, then? I'll be right back."

"No, no, Patrick," Criver said. "Adrianne was just going. I want you to meet our runologist."

"Sir, I'm happy to do it. Change burning in my pocket."

"Detective—"

The moment broke when four of the techs from the Forensics Services Division walked in carrying cardboard trays of coffee from the local barista. Oblivious to the tension, they greeted everyone and set the lattes and a bag of biscotti on the table. Immediately after, Sergeant Billings sidled in, snagged a chair next to Criver's, and opened a laptop.

Criver cleared his throat. "Let's get started, then. Adrianne, where's Dr. Wilding?"

So Evan is still officially part of this investigation. She allowed herself a small smile.

"He just arrived, sir," she said as Evan appeared in the doorway, accompanied by a uniformed escort and sporting a plastic guest badge clipped to his woolen blazer.

Evan had cleaned up since their trip to the pond in Kendall County. When he could be bothered, Addie thought, he always cleaned up well. He'd shed his jeans and hoodie for a light-gray suit and black tie, combed the mop he proudly called a decent head of hair, and even trimmed his beard. He nodded to the others in the room and made his way to the chair next to Addie's—she'd already ratcheted up the seat. Evan set his satchel on the floor and scooted into the chair.

"Glad you could drop by, Dr. Wilding," Criver said.

"Sorry I'm late," Evan replied. "Please go on."

Criver tipped back in his chair and steepled his fingers. "Let's get started, Detectives McBrady and Bisset. What have you got?"

Patrick opened with a description of the Talfour crime scene and a summary of what he and the other detectives had learned about Talfour that day. The man had moved to Chicago six years earlier, relocating his business, a brick-and-mortar store called Finer Things, from Savannah to the Magnificent Mile. The business, specializing in high-end jewelry, furs, and a few objets d'art—Patrick pronounced it "ob-jets dart"—was successful. No outstanding debt, no suggestion of questionable activity.

Talfour paid his taxes, was well-liked by his employees, his neighbors, and his only family, an older sister, who appeared devastated by his death. His car, a black 2016 BMW sedan, was parked in the underground garage of his building.

He then went over the assault on Talfour from six months earlier.

"None of the attackers have been identified from that CCTV video," he said. "Based on the language used by his attackers, the mugging appears to be at least partly racially motivated, although Talfour was robbed of his wallet and watch. In the weeks leading up to the incident, his shop was spray-painted with racial slurs. Again, no arrests. In your folder, you'll find photos of the graffiti on his shop and several stills from the assault."

A rustling of paper filled the room.

"James Talfour was active in the community," Patrick continued. "On the board of the local chapter of a national children's charity and an occasional Big Brother. He also served on several additional boards, including his homeowners' association and an animal rights organization."

"The guy sells furs in his store and supports an animal rights group?" one of the evidence techs asked.

Patrick leaned back in his chair and lobbed his empty coffee cup in the trash can. "Go figure. He also donated generously to several police fundraising drives while marching in antipolice protests. A Google search popped up a picture of him on a website for a group that opposes the quote-unquote prison-industrial complex."

"Several points of entry for the investigation, then," Criver said, thumbing through the papers in the folder. "Did anyone look at footage from Talfour's store from before the assault?"

"He didn't install cameras until *after* the assault."

Criver's expression showed what he thought of that. Addie couldn't disagree. Nothing like closing the stable door after the horses have fled.

"Okay," Criver said. "Good work on this piece. And now I understand we have a second potential victim?"

Addie stood, smoothed her blazer, and went to the board. "We received a call this morning from a Kendall County sheriff's deputy who saw our report and believed he might have a similar case. Scott Desser was murdered approximately twelve weeks ago, although his body wasn't discovered until four weeks ago."

She launched into a description of Desser's death, emphasizing the points she'd written on the board—all the things the two murders had in common.

"And we have runes," she added. A murmur ran around the room.

"The sheriff's report didn't indicate the presence of any runes near the body," she said. "But after I read the initial report, Patrick and I agreed it was worth investigating. Given the length of time between Desser's death and when his body was found, any runic inscriptions present at the time of death could have been scattered. Dr. Wilding and I searched the nearby area and found an animal bone etched with runes."

Another murmur went around the room. Someone whispered, "Serial killer."

"Let's not get hasty," Criver said.

Addie explained how the deer bone had led them to a teenager named Tommy Snow, who'd turned over three additional bones. All the bones were carved with runes similar to those found near Talfour's body.

"In the packets on the table, you'll find photographs of the bones and the runes," she said. "It's possible that Snow has the remaining bones. The Kendall County sheriff has requested a search warrant for his home and workshop. We'll also look into someone Tommy Snow refers to as Mr. X. Snow claims he was hunting bones for this person."

Criver looked at Patrick. "Does Snow's possession of the bones make him a suspect in your opinion?"

Patrick kept his gaze on Addie.

"He's definitely a person of interest," Addie went on, swallowing her frown. "He's antisocial, obsessed with biology and anatomy. And smart."

"And this Mr. X he claims to be working for?"

"We're hoping a warrant will turn up additional information."

Billings typed something on his laptop. Criver asked, "So what do the two victims have in common? I mean, aside from the manner of their deaths. Did they know each other?"

"Unknown," Addie said. "We're still running down leads. What we've learned this afternoon since linking the two cases is that both were successful businessmen, Talfour with his store and Desser with a lucrative accounting firm. Both men lived alone in the Near North Side. Neither man was married currently or divorced. Desser was widowed. Neither had children. Talfour, as my partner mentioned, was active in the community. Desser was more private. And not as friendly as Talfour, at least according to several neighbors who were interviewed by a Kendall County deputy at the time Desser's body was discovered. Preliminary research indicates some of Desser's clients have legal issues. We're trying to gain access to his full client list along with the names of Talfour's customers, looking for commonalities outside of their geographic location. As we learn more, we'll add the information to our files."

Billings tapped on his keyboard.

Criver pointed a hand toward Rhinehart. "If that's all, why don't we hear from our expert now. Mr. Rhinehart, can you tell us about the runes?"

Addie said, "There is one more thing."

Criver raised an eyebrow.

"Talfour had dealt with racist attacks, as Patrick stated. Half an hour ago, while I was following up on a note in the sheriff's file on Desser, we learned that a month before Desser's death, an unidentified person spray-painted a swastika on his fence. Our first victim was Jewish, a cantor at his local synagogue."

"Ha!" barked Rhinehart.

Everyone swiveled to look at him. The runologist pushed back his chair and stood. His face was pale, but he was no longer sweating.

"A swastika!" he cried. He seemed to have regained his energy. "And vile graffiti. This confirms my suspicion that we're dealing with the practitioners of a dark and terrible magic. May I have the floor now?"

"I'm done," Addie said. She returned to her chair next to Evan.

Rhinehart squeezed past chairs and made his way to the whiteboard. He picked up an eraser and turned to Addie. "Do you mind?"

Her lips thinned. "Not at all."

Rhinehart wiped the board clean and wrote three words so that they formed a triangle.

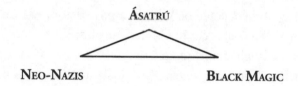

He tapped the word at the top. "Are any of you familiar with the Ásatrú?"

Silence. Addie glanced at Evan. He had folded his hands over his stomach and was watching Rhinehart with a vaguely puzzled expression.

"Very well, then." Rhinehart hoisted a dry-erase marker and adopted a professorial tone. "The Ásatrú are modern-day neo-pagans who worship the Viking gods. Many of them are Viking reenactors who re-create all aspects of Viking life, from the clothes they wear to the food they eat. And the alphabet they write with."

"Vikings are dope," someone said.

"Totally dope," Rhinehart agreed. "But most importantly for our case, the Ásatrú practice sacrifice. Animals. Crops. But also, on occasion, they sacrifice other things. Darker things . . ."

His voice trailed off as he looked around the room. Addie had to admire the man for his ability to play an audience. Everyone was rapt, even as they knew what was coming.

"They also sometimes practice *human* sacrifice," Rhinehart finished.

More murmurs. Addie found herself nodding. So far, the runologist was tracking with what Evan had told her in the car. But Evan looked dissatisfied.

Justin Wao, the evidence tech who'd been at the crime scene that morning, said, "And just to confirm, we *are* talking about the twenty-first century, right?"

"We are indeed," Rhinehart answered. "We could be discussing one of your neighbors or your mail carrier. Your grocery store clerk or your dentist. Any of them could be Viking pagans. That is, Ásatrú."

"Even"—Wao's eyes cut to Criver—"my boss?"

Everyone laughed, including Criver.

Rhinehart held up a finger. "Let's look at the next corner of my triangle." The marker squeaked as he wrote the words HATE CRIMES beneath his earlier words. "The Ásatrú believe in the superiority of the Aryan race. For some of them, this justifies taking horrible action against all non-Aryan races. Up to and including murder." He tapped the board. "I'm talking about neo-Nazism."

Wao gave a low whistle. "A *racist* serial killer."

"Damn it," Criver muttered.

Addie knew what the lieutenant was thinking. A racially motivated murder in a city like Chicago would be a spark to a fuse.

"And the third corner of your triangle?" someone asked. "Black magic?"

Rhinehart gave a doleful nod. "The Nazis were fascinated by the dark arts. They used occult ideas rooted in the so-called ancient wisdom of the Aryans to justify their persecution of the Jews. Hitler's own chief architect of the Holocaust, Heinrich Himmler, was said to dabble in the supernatural." He looked around the room. "I would bet the royalties from all fifteen of my books that if you investigate the local Ásatrú groups and the local Viking reenactors, you will find that some of them are harboring white supremacists. And that some of *them* are practicing black magic."

Criver swiveled his chair to look at Evan. "And you? What do you think of this idea?"

Evan unlaced his fingers and stretched. "I agree with Mr. Rhinehart that it's possible we're looking at ritualized hate crimes."

Rhinehart's look was cutting. "Possible?"

Evan tilted back in his chair. "Putting aside the fact that the vast majority of the Ásatrú are peaceful and productive members of society who are no more or less racist than the rest of us, I see nothing in the writing left by the killer to suggest neo-Nazism."

A flush rose in Rhinehart's face. He crossed his arms. "You're wrong. As a single example, there are forty sigel runes in the lines we have from Talfour."

Patrick spun his chair toward Evan. "What's that mean? What's a sigel rune?"

Evan leaned forward again and rested his forearms on the table. "The sigel rune is the sixteenth letter in some versions of the runic alphabet. It's used to represent the *s* sound. The sigels are sometimes called bolt runes because of their resemblance to bolts of lightning. The Nazis used two sigel runes to represent the Nazi SS, the *Schutzstaffel*. But in the case of the runic writing left with Talfour, there's only one instance in which two sigel runes appear next to each other."

Rhinehart's flush deepened. But he shook his head as if at a particularly disappointing student. "The sigel runes aside, Mr. Wilding, you might have noticed we have a symbol for the Nazi party right smack in the middle of the lines left next to Talfour's body."

A stirring in the room. Addie frowned. Evan hadn't mentioned this.

"It's *Dr.* Wilding," Evan corrected. "And you're referring to the sun cross."

"Call it what you will," Rhinehart said. "It's a version of the swastika. It's the symbol used by neo-Nazi organizations in America."

"It's also known as the Cross of Odin and—"

"Yet another reference to Vikings."

"—and a *prehistoric* solar symbol," Evan persisted. His look of dissatisfaction deepened to a frown. "Which the killer placed next to a body he posed to resemble prehistoric Iron Age burials."

Rhinehart waved a dismissive hand. "*Everyone* knows the Cross of Odin is a symbol of Nazism. It's the most logical explanation for what we're dealing with."

Evan shook his head. "It's *one* of the possible explanations for what we're dealing with. We must be aware that every sign or symbol left at a crime scene can carry a number of meanings. To our killer, this symbol could represent a Nazi emblem, yes. But it could equally stand for the sun cross, which is linked to pre-Viking burials. It's dangerous to draw conclusions too quickly and without considering *all* the signs present."

Rhinehart rapped his knuckles on the whiteboard in a steady metronome. "May I remind you, members of the Aryan Brotherhood identify as Ásatrú."

"Not only them," Billings piped up. "There are several neo-Nazi groups who reject Christianity and claim to be pagan. Groups like O9A and the RapeWaffen."

Addie had heard about both groups during a domestic terrorism class. She tried to pull up what the instructor had told them. "Don't members of O9A practice Satanism?"

"That's why they're of interest here," Billings said.

"Then how," Evan said, "does accusing our killer of being Ásatrú explain why our victims were ritualistically murdered and posed in exactly the same fashion as the ancient bog bodies?"

Rhinehart's tapping knuckles stilled. Expressions rippled across his face—confusion, anger, even alarm. "Bog bodies?"

"I feel like I missed the first half of the lecture," Patrick mumbled.

Evan smiled apologetically at the detective. "I'm probably making this needlessly complicated. And forgive me, Mr. Rhinehart. Bog bodies would naturally fall outside your area of expertise. I'm referring to the Iron Age bodies found mummified in peat bogs in Northern European countries. These bodies were placed in the swamps centuries before the Viking Age." Evan reached down to his satchel, removed two photographs, and handed them to Addie to pass around. "Here are a couple examples. The first picture shows Tollund Man, a two-thousand-year-old bog body found in Denmark in 1950. His death was relatively peaceful—he was merely hanged. But the second picture is that of Lindow Man. He suffered multiple deaths, exactly like our two victims. His killers beat him around the head, strangled him with a rope of sinew, and cut his throat."

"Holy crap, Batman," Wao said as Addie handed the pictures to him. "These guys look like Talfour."

"That's right," Evan said. "Thus, we must consider the fact that while a noose—when placed around the neck of a Black man—has a horrible and very specific meaning in twenty-first-century America, it has an entirely different connotation when looked at in context with a bog body. In a bog burial, a noose is not indicative of a racially motivated hate crime."

Patrick used a thick forefinger to scratch around his ear. "So the killer makes his victims into bog bodies. But that has nothing to do with Vikings?"

"And yet we have the runes," Evan said. "It's hard to know what message the killer is trying to send."

Rhinehart mopped his face again with his handkerchief. "This hardly seems helpful. It's just muddying the water. Bog water, to be exact."

Patrick studied the photographs when they reached him, then passed them on and stood to snag the last latte from the cardboard tray. "I'm guessing that right about now would be a good time to talk about the elephant in the room and tell us what the runes say."

Criver stood. "Agreed. Let's take a ten-minute recess to process what we've heard; then we'll move on to the runes."

As people made a beeline for the door and the bathrooms and coffee machine beyond, Addie saw a glance pass between Rhinehart and Evan.

Evan's expression had smoothed into neutrality. But Rhinehart looked like a man facing a rival—one he held in contempt. And was determined to flatten.

CHAPTER 13

Addie spent the short break writing down her thoughts. She wanted to talk to Evan, but two of the techs remained in the room, making private conversation impossible.

When everyone else had returned, Criver gestured to Rhinehart.

"If you would, Mr. Rhinehart, share with us what you've learned by translating the runes into English. I believe this is what led to your conclusions about the Ásatrú."

Rhinehart picked up the papers Criver had placed on the table and passed them around. "I haven't yet seen the runes found near Desser's body. These are from Talfour."

Addie took a stapled sheet off the stack when it reached her and then passed the stack on.

"The first page is the full poem in the runic alphabet," Rhinehart said. "The second is my initial transliteration, in which I went through and substituted letters from our alphabet for the runes. I've included these two versions purely for your reference. What I'd like to draw your attention to is the third page, which contains my actual translation."

Addie folded over the first two sheets and bent over the third.

"But before you begin," Rhinehart said, "be forewarned. The poem, if you want to call it that, is filled with nonsense words and lines that are just, frankly, garbage. There are plenty of misspelled words like *corse* for *corpse*, indicating either a lack of understanding of the runes or simple carelessness. So don't get your hopes up that we'll learn much about our killer from his writing."

Translation of Runic Characters (Anglo-Saxon Runes)
Murder Victim James Talfour
Submitted by Ralph Rhinehart

Need/plight	*Listen up mighty men. I undo and unto earth I send*
Ice	*their water weighted corses. I am adam nedscop.*
Elk's	*You know why: over the sun swimmer home I came*
Yew tree	*A weary warrior wailing with weird edwergild*
Unknown	*As layer of the bone. Halls breaking Fjorgyn.*
Year	*A death drive merely a plague. The broom that binds up evil.*
Sun	*For mine mine mine gone. Bowl buried. Busted by big bosses.*
The god Tyr	*That war crimes. Word shaker. Heart of my baw neen tombed.*
Lake	*Ire war din to his mouth of hearing, I poured my mead.*
Steed	*Making me bodulfr war wolf lend reg age claw all beari eht hw/☉*
Man	*By skull food lait I laid him low this skin sinner is u wight I she is he and so on wight*
Birch tree	*What of this bone? Cage this skin sinner is ox of riding.*
Ing	*Tell me by man is lait. I laid it out prick. Met his but.*
Day	*His honey maker held still so I held tight, strong as nnnmen.*
Yewen bow	*When wailing the word weaver arrived for his bletsian.*
Oak tree	*With his mirror I did mirror. Mere to mere.*
Ash tree	*His thole was thus. That he thanked the hell guard.*
Homeland	*He felt the weight of his wight knew weird is wicked.*

Addie read the words, disbelieving, then read them again. Disappointment tasted like bile. Was there anything here that could help them?

After a long moment, Wao broke the silence.

"This," he said, "is like some dude on magic mushrooms trying to write poetry."

"So it's not even supposed to make sense?" Patrick's voice was thick with frustration. "What the hell does something like *ire war din* mean?"

Rhinehart spread his hands. "I warned you."

"Where's the swastika?" someone else asked.

Rhinehart drew a symbol on the board: ☉ "The sun cross is denoted in runic writing by a circle with a dot in the middle. If you look online, you'll see all the iterations of the sun cross, including the version with the broken arms, which resembles a swastika. That was the version used by the Nazis. As for the rest of the words, I suspect the killer lifted some of the runes from online sites and didn't care that they didn't translate to anything meaningful. The runes are more about show than substance."

Addie's eyes met Evan's. The set of his brow suggested he didn't agree with Rhinehart's assessment.

"So he just wants to pretend he's a Viking?" Patrick asked.

Rhinehart's nod was regretful. "You must keep in mind that many people believe runes are mystical," he said. "That the letters themselves have power even without having any real meaning. It might be helpful if we focus on the word set off by itself in each line. I suggest the killer is trying to invoke something with these runes."

Patrick picked at the skin around his thumbnail. "He's invoking trees and elk? What's that supposed to mean?"

Rhinehart gazed down at the detective. "You might listen to my podcast, Detective McBrady. Episodes fourteen and fifteen, 'The Secret of the Runes.' The word *elk* doesn't refer to the animal but to a plant. Elk sedge has a sharp leaf sometimes used to slice human flesh."

"That's actually kinda cool," Wao said.

"The elk rune also stands for defense and protection. And . . ." Rhinehart paused theatrically and looked around the room. Every face was turned toward him, like upturned flowers following the sun. "And it's important to note that this elk sedge symbol, the *eolhx* rune, was called the life rune by the Nazis and appeared on the uniforms of some of their troops. Specifically, those of the *Sturmabteilung*, the original paramilitary detachment of the Nazi party that helped bring Hitler to power."

"So we're back to Nazis," Patrick said.

Rhinehart let out a breath and pressed a palm to his heart. "Exactly."

But Criver had gone rigid. "Is that a name there in the second line? Adam Nedscop?" He turned to Billings. "Run it."

Billings typed, then shook his head. "It's not a name that comes up anywhere in our system. Or the DMV's."

Rhinehart circled the name on the board. "It might be a reference to Adam, the first man. Which, in the Nazi worldview, would be the first Aryan. If the killer shares that name, he would want to emphasize it."

"And *nedscop*?"

"Perhaps a surname. Or simply nonsense. As I said, a series of runes he copied from somewhere."

Evan stirred and spoke. "You've deleted the hyphen in the name."

Rhinehart waved airily. "It was likely just a slip of the knife when he was carving. But whoever this *Adam* is, he's either current or former military."

"The weary warrior," Addie said.

Evan frowned.

"That's one mention." Rhinehart tapped the board with the marker. "I'd like to bring your attention to all the military references. There's *weary warrior* in the fourth line, as our lovely detective just pointed out. A mention of war crimes in line eight. Two lines down, we have *war wolf*. And *reg* appears in the same line, possibly a reference to regulation. We also have a suggestion of war din, meaning *noise*, in the line above."

A cacophony of voices broke across the room.

"And . . ." Rhinehart raised his hand, quieting everyone. "*And.* He ends his rantings—his poem or screed or whatever you want to call it—with the runic character for homeland, the *peorth* or *othala* rune.

Which was also used by the Nazis, this time on the uniforms of the Waffen-SS. He is, once again, drilling in the significance of war and Nazism. This rune is also linked to the idea of property. Even ancestral lands. The killer is talking about the sanctity of home."

"Which," Billings said in a voice soft as oil sliding into water, "also goes toward Nazism. The protection of the homeland against unwanted ethnicities like Blacks and Jews."

"Brilliant," Criver said. He tossed down his pen and leaned back in his chair. "Just brilliant. We know, or at least strongly suspect, we're looking for a Nazi sympathizer who served in the military and who might have the name Adam Nedscop or some variant of that. This gives us a wonderful place to start."

Beside him, Billings peeled back his lips from his teeth in what Addie finally decided was a smile.

"I have more," Rhinehart said.

The flower faces swiveled back to him.

"To emphasize my earlier point about black magic, please note the mention of *hell guards*. Someone with my experience studying the occult knows that this suggests demons. We also have the words *weird* and *wicked*. The phrase *binding up evil*, which likely refers to trapping a demon and forcing it to do your will. And we see mention of the Nordic god Tyr before the phrase *war crimes*. Tyr was the god of war. But he was also equated with the Roman god Mars, who was the receiver of sacrifices."

Criver murmured, "What kind of insanity are we dealing with?"

"I suggest your search focus on a white male," Rhinehart said. "A military man or former military. Someone of fairly low economic status and a low-level education but with an immense ego, as suggested by the repetition of *mine, mine, mine* in the middle of the poem."

"This is very helpful," Billings said. Then he turned his sly smile on Evan. "What about the professor? We have yet to hear any brilliant insights from him."

Evan sat up, cleared his throat. "I just have two small questions."

Rhinehart folded his arms, resting them on his paunch. "Go on."

"Well . . ." Evan fumbled through his notes. "Assuming the killer is using the mystic meaning of a rune to emphasize something or invoke something—perhaps the Norse gods—then why would he single out the *ethel* rune, whose meaning is unknown?"

Addie felt a stab of disappointment. Compared to what Rhinehart had just presented, Evan's complaint felt small. A technicality.

Rhinehart removed a different hankie from his pocket and blew his nose, as if in agreement with Addie's thought. He stuffed the soiled cloth back.

He said, "The *ethel* rune, because it *is* unknown, is most often linked with secrets. With mysteries. Even with the idea of luck, which the killer no doubt wished to evoke. The killer is letting us know he has his secrets. That he is a mystery to us. What else?"

"I'm curious to know if you're familiar with Old English poetry. *Beowulf.* 'The Wanderer.' 'The Battle of Maldon.' Works of that nature, many of which are about pagans from the Viking Age."

As if Evan had tipped over an inkwell, darkness spilled into Rhinehart's eyes. "Try as I might," he said, biting off his words, "I fail to see your point."

"No," Evan agreed. "I don't expect you would see the point. But a familiarity with those works would certainly clear the air around some of the killer's word choice, which you have deemed nonsense. Words like *brume*, which means *mist* or *fog*, not a cleaning tool. And *lendreg*, which you've broken into two words. I suspect it's an anagram for the monster Grendel and not a clumsy reference to military regulations. After all, the Old English poets were fond of word games like anagrams and riddles. The word you've interpreted as *weird* is actually *wyrd*, w-y-r-d, which means *fate*. And *corse* isn't a misspelling. It's an archaic form of the word *corpse*. Thus, we have their water-weighted *corpses*."

The flush returned to Rhinehart's face. His eyes glittered. "You're a *semiotician*," he said, as if Evan's profession were akin to cleaning out-houses. "Old English poetry doesn't fall within your area of expertise. You're overreaching."

"I am," Evan agreed. "But perhaps a bit less clumsily than you. A final example. I would argue that the letters you used to form Adam Nedscop don't stand for a name at all but rather mean *dam-ned scop*. *Scop* is the Old English word for *poet*. We have, not a man named Adam, but a damned poet."

The room fell silent save for Rhinehart's thick breathing. Outside, a gust slammed the building, leaving behind a glittering scatter of rain on the glass.

Well done, Evan, Addie thought.

Into the awkward silence, Evan cleared his throat. He sat forward and placed Rhinehart's pages on the table, lining up their edges with that of the folder already there. "I'm certainly not suggesting that my interpretation is the correct one. Mr. Rhinehart has made several good points. I merely suggest that at this early stage, we need to keep open minds. The motive in some murders is immediately obvious. Robbery gone wrong. A gang dispute. Hate crimes of the type mentioned by Mr. Rhinehart. But in cases such as these two deaths, where the scenes offer numerous and sometimes conflicting signs for us to consider, the truth can be an elusive thing. It would be dangerous for us to take the runes out of context from what the rest of the scene tells us."

"I see," Criver said.

"I'd like some time to study the good doctor's translation," Evan pressed, "so that I can begin creating a criminal investigative analysis."

"A profile," Billings said.

"Yes. That is what a forensic semiotician usually does," Evan said. "That's why I'm here, correct?"

Billings blinked. "Cor-rect."

"Then that's what I will do. Will tomorrow be soon enough?"

"If you need that time," Criver said, "then I suppose we'll make that work." He pushed back his chair and stood, smoothing down his tie. "Thank you, everyone. I believe we are off to a good start. We'll reconvene tomorrow at four thirty p.m. Does that work for our two experts?"

Evan and Rhinehart nodded.

"Good," Criver said. "In the meantime, I suggest we forge ahead with Mr. Rhinehart's ideas about a military connection. And do a deep dive on any local cults. Finally, let's not dismiss the possibility that Adam Nedscop is an actual name. Or that this mysterious Mr. X might be linked to our case. I'll get our computer forensics guys to hop on social media and use that data-mining software they swore would come in handy. Perhaps their time has come. Patrick, I want you full-time on this case. Shift whatever else you're working on to someone else in the department."

"Yes, sir."

"And I need a word with you and Adrianne. Sergeant Billings, I'd like you to stay as well. Everyone else is free to go."

"I'll be in the hall," Evan said to Addie.

While the others filed out, Criver hitched his trousers and perched on the edge of the table. He nodded to Billings, who typed on his keyboard, then turned the laptop around so that Addie and Patrick could see the screen, which was filled with the digital version of the *Chicago Tribune*.

Addie read the headline aloud. "'Store owner tortured, then tossed in Calumet River.' How did this get out?"

"Why don't you tell me?" Criver said.

"There's a tarp over the crime scene," Patrick said. "And media had to stay on the street. We didn't release any details. They can't have known about the torture."

"And yet they do. There's talk here about a Black man and a noose. I don't need any rioting right now. A bunch of people screaming about

Black lives." Criver tucked his head down so that his single chin became two. "What I need is an explanation."

Addie folded her arms. "We didn't leak this."

Criver turned his now-frigid gaze on her, and Addie mentally kicked herself for even opening that particular door.

"It's got your name in the article," he said.

"Really?" She leaned in toward the computer, but Billings pulled it back toward him.

"Really." Criver folded his arms. "There were certainly a lot of people there. From greenhorns right on up to Sergeant Billings and me. Adrianne, perhaps next time, you could be a bit more selective about who needs to be there."

"Sir, I—"

He waved his hand. "Anyway, our guys know not to talk. And Mr. Rhinehart signed a nondisclosure. Who I'm really wondering about is your semiotician."

"Dr. Wilding is a professional. He would never leak a story." Addie's voice rang in her own ears. It sounded cold enough to freeze mercury.

"Are you very sure he's not trying to get tenure or whatever it is those academics need? A little publicity might help his cause. Or maybe he just likes the spotlight."

"He already has tenure. And he hates media attention. If anything, the fact that the newshounds have gotten the story means he'll want to stay as far away as possible. Sir, it's just ridiculous that you'd—"

With only a slight shift in his weight, Patrick stepped hard on her foot.

She fell silent.

"I'd what?" Criver asked.

Patrick kept his foot on hers. "I think a profile would be helpful. And it always looks good when the great institutions of Chicago work together for the good of the people. Chicago PD and the University of Chicago."

Nicely played, thought Addie, although her toes were screaming.

Criver grunted and pushed to his feet, his eyes a pair of glittering rocks in the slingshot he seemed to be aiming at Addie. "Maybe. But some people can't resist spilling their guts. Get him to sign an NDA."

"He already has. It's on file with the department. Same with his assistant, Diana Alanis."

"*And* I want a list of everyone who was on scene. Sergeant Billings will follow through. I want the two of you to stick with tight protocol on this case. Nothing else, and I mean *nothing else,* gets out until I decide it's time for *me* to make a *statement* to the press. Clear as mountain spring water?"

Patrick nodded. "Clear as my conscience."

Criver rolled his eyes.

Addie curled the fingers of her right hand to keep from executing a sardonic salute. "We'll be careful as a man in cargo pants walking through a den of thieves."

"How'd I get stuck with the pair of you?" Criver opened the door and disappeared into the hall.

Sergeant Billings closed his laptop and glided through the door after the lieutenant, pausing long enough to give the two detectives an unreadable glance over his shoulder.

As soon as he disappeared, Addie bent to massage her toes through the thin leather.

"Son of a gun," she said. "That hurt!"

"Not as much as losing your job."

"*The great institutions of Chicago work together for the good of the people,*" she mimicked. "Good one, Patrick."

"Yeah, well, if there's anything Criver likes, it's looking good to everyone above him." Patrick picked up the extra folders. "Where do you think the leak came from?"

She straightened. "My money is on Rhinehart. The man's a publicity hound. All those podcasts and TV interviews he does? Who else could it be?"

But Patrick pursed his lips. "Did Criver even fill him in on the case early enough for this to hit the evening paper?"

"He could have called him as he was leaving the scene. I'd bet my job on it."

"You shouldn't tempt the fates like that, Adrianne Marie. One of these days . . ."

"You don't have to tell me," she said. "There's a target on my forehead."

CHAPTER 14

Evan walked out of the room, immediately aware that Rhinehart had followed him. The runologist waited until Wao and the others had vanished down the hall, then stretched to his full height and leaned into Evan's personal space.

"What was that about?" Rhinehart asked through gritted teeth.

Evan took a sideways step. "I believe it was two experts having a difference in opinion. As often happens in cases like this."

"It was more than that. You're trying to discredit me."

"No." Evan shook his head. "That was not my intent."

Rhinehart made a sound in his throat. "The lieutenant brought *me* in, not you. I'm the runologist. You're merely a man who thinks too much of himself. This gig is mine."

"I believe that decision belongs to the police."

The older man glared into Evan's eyes for a few moments more before he spun on his heel and quick-marched away, headed toward the stairwell. Over his shoulder, he shouted, "Stay clear."

Unsure what to make of Rhinehart's animosity and his refusal to consider facts that diverged from his neo-Nazi theory, Evan watched the other man disappear down the stairs, the heavy tread of the runologist's footsteps echoing up the shaft.

The door to the meeting room opened, and now Lieutenant Criver and Sergeant Billings emerged and headed toward the stairwell, their shoes squeaking on the rain-damp linoleum, Billings's suit coat flapping as the shorter man worked to keep up with Criver's long strides. They ignored Evan entirely.

Evan turned his back and studied the bulletin board hanging nearby while he waited for Addie to appear. The board was plastered with mug shots, notifications of changes in citation laws, and someone's handwritten plea to remember to add a quarter to the jar for every cup of coffee. Underneath that, someone else had written, WHY PAY FOR MUD? GET IT FOR FREE ANYWHERE IN THE GREAT CITY OF CHICAGO.

That last almost made Evan smile. Almost. Although he'd read everything on the board from top to bottom, he wasn't really processing any of it. Reading whatever was available—and determinedly flushing much of it before it cluttered up his short-term memory—was a habit going all the way back to a childhood spent waiting in spas and nail salons while his mother had her own natural beauty polished to a jewel-like elegance. And later in private hospital rooms, when she decided that beauty could only take a woman so far and what she really needed was medication and a *rest*. For most of those visits, Evan had been left home with the nanny. But on those occasions when Anna was on vacation or had taken a rare sick day, his mother had no choice but to bundle up her misshapen son and parade him out into the world.

It had been miserable for both of them.

Evan's eyes slid past the note about paying for coffee and turned his mind to Old English poetry and what he'd pulled up from memory earlier that day.

After Addie had dropped him back off at his car, he'd gone home to shower and change. Then he'd spent rather a long time standing in front of the immense window that overlooked the garden. There, with the clock ticking softly behind him and light falling on the floor at his feet, he'd opened the door to his memory palace. The imaginary residence where, years ago, he'd stored what he'd learned about the Old English poems in the hope of later recall. Memory palaces had been quite the thing among his fellow students at Oxford, and Evan had excelled.

That afternoon, as he'd wandered past mental images of iron breast-plates and the battle spears of long-dead Vikings, he'd remembered the lines of poetry that feted old warriors and bemoaned lost travelers.

The killer knew about these things. Evan was sure.

He turned and blinked as Addie appeared in the doorway and plowed straight for him with long strides that made him forget all about Viking warriors and ancient rhymes.

She opened her mouth, and Evan held up a hand.

"Please don't tell me that my performance in there was less than stellar," he said.

She sighed. "It was definitely . . . nuanced."

Patrick appeared behind her.

"So you really think Rhinehart is way off base?" she asked Evan. "Some of what he said made sense. That bit about the military. And the occult stuff."

"They're wonderful theories," Evan said. "They might even be right. But they're built on a house of cards."

Patrick frowned. "What do you mean?"

"Merely that I'm lukewarm on Mr. Rhinehart's interpretation of the runes. You have to go through multiple processes when converting runes to another alphabet. First transliteration, then transcription, and finally translation. It's possible at any stage to unwittingly deviate from the author's intention."

Patrick seemed to be making a mighty struggle not to look confused. "Exactly what I was thinking."

"You were not," Addie said. She was riffling through her purse for something. "Evan is being deliberately difficult. You guys up for McLeary's?"

Evan glanced at his watch. "Sure. We can discuss the case there, if you like. Just as long as I'm home before my student arrives for her music lesson."

"Before we talk about runes and whatnot, I gotta get at least one beer in me," Patrick said. "No offense, Professor, but you kind of give me a headache."

"None taken. I don't think."

"My head feels like it's been packed with more stuff than my wife takes on an overnight trip. Two suitcases, she says she needs. For one night. Plus a carry-on."

Addie's phone appeared in her hand. It was buzzing. "'Scuse me."

She turned her back and walked away. Patrick and Evan stared at each other.

Patrick unknotted his tie and stuffed it in a pocket like a man reprieved of a hanging. "There goes our dinner."

"What do you mean?"

"It's gotta be Clayton L. Hamden," Patrick said, raising his voice to mimic a woman's falsetto. "Famous attorney and pretty boy." He lowered his voice to its normal register. "Anyone else, she'd ignore it or put it on speakerphone. Addie's not much on filters. 'Cept when it comes to whoever her latest fling is."

"True," Evan agreed. He distracted himself from thoughts of the tall and manly Clayton by rereading the handwritten note on the board about the coffee. Now that he looked at it again, he saw that the writer had misspelled the word *great*, meaning *wonderful*, as *grate*, as in *to reduce something to small shreds*. *Grate* was of Germanic origin, related to the German *kratzen*, meaning *to scratch*.

Sometimes his mind would not *shut up*.

At the other end of the hallway, Addie laughed. It sounded like holiday bells.

To reduce something to small shreds, Evan thought. *Like my ego.*

"I wish she'd find a really good guy," Patrick said. "Someone stable and calm. And smart."

And tall. It hadn't slipped past Evan that Addie liked them big. Out loud he said, "I've had the same thought."

"Maybe there's some university professor you could set her up with. I mean, she'll listen to you, right? You two being so close."

Evan gave Patrick a look, and Patrick spread his hands.

"Right," he said. "When do women *ever* listen to us?"

Addie came hurrying back, beaming. "Sorry, gents. That was Clayton. His client had to cancel. Can I take a rain check on dinner?"

Patrick rolled his eyes.

Evan said, "Sure," and turned to Patrick. "How do you feel about ax-throwing?"

⚔

Outside, Addie watched the two main men in her life, not counting Clayton or her father of course, walk away together through the rain. Water misted beneath the light falling from the streetlamps, creating a halo around the two figures. Out of nowhere, she had a flash of Humphrey Bogart walking away with Claude Rains at the end of *Casablanca*, and an unexpected sadness tugged at her as she watched Evan work to lengthen his stride to keep up with the six-three Patrick McBrady.

Evan would never ask Patrick to slow down. He'd shoot himself first.

Her friend was brilliant and kind and funny and good-looking. He laughed at all her jokes and made her favorite clam chowder and sourdough bread whenever she asked, which was often. He'd held her hand and offered a shoulder through countless breakups, family frustrations, and the dark night—two months ago—when her cat, Traveling Tom, had crossed the rainbow bridge.

She stayed under the eave as the wind gusted and Evan and Patrick stopped at Evan's specially modified Jaguar convertible. Patrick walked around the ostentatious sports car, nodding in admiration. Men and their cars. And men and their dicks. Sometimes it was hard to distinguish between the two.

She snorted her disdain.

But as Patrick crouched to see whatever Evan was pointing to at the back of the car, something inside her softened. Was it possible she was yoking her horse to the wrong carriage?

Evan ducked behind the steering wheel. Patrick wedged himself in on the passenger side.

Not that it was her call. Evan had never evinced the slightest interest in her as anything other than his best friend. She knew he'd been in several serious relationships and plenty of casual ones. And that, in most cases, Evan and the woman in question eventually drifted apart without animosity. Almost all the women who floated through his orbit remained his friend. But nothing lasted. Not in a romantic sense, anyway.

Kind of like her relationships.

His laugh drifted back to her, warm and genuine as he closed the car door.

Dr. Evan Wilding.

Evan.

Was she wrong not to push?

Did it matter, in her heart of hearts, that Evan was a man who would have to stand on a stool just to reach past her shoulders?

Ruefully, she shook her head. She liked tall men. Call her shallow, but she did. Plus, she never thought it was a great idea to mix friendship and romance. One always messed up the other. She was just maudlin tonight. It was the worry about her job. And the thought of a serial killer out there in the darkness, ripping lives apart.

☒

The Ragnarök ax-throwing establishment—owned and managed, according to their website, by a man named Sten Elger—was clearly hopping when Evan and Patrick approached on the sidewalk. Light and noise spilled through the doors and the barred windows.

". . . runs like a dream," Patrick was saying to Evan. He raised his voice to a shout as he yanked open the door, then stepped aside for a chattering group of millennials as they spilled out. "I'd love to take a car like that out for a spin every Sunday. Just the missus and me. She'd be all made up. Isn't that what you Brits say? All made up?"

Evan spared him a glance. Maybe he'd underestimated Patrick. "We mostly say that if we're from Liverpool. But close enough. Aren't you from the Emerald Isle?"

"Three generations back. I'm relearning the language. And I've been watching *Downton Abbey* with the missus." The millennials ambled away in a cloud of laughter, and Patrick waved Evan inside. "What does it cost, a car like that, if you don't mind my asking?"

Evan named a figure, and Patrick's jaw dropped.

"They really pay professors that much?"

"Hard to fathom, isn't it?"

"You guys don't even have to dodge bullets." Patrick seemed to reconsider that. "Not usually, anyway."

Evan paused inside the door. Patrick nearly ran him over. They both stood in the entryway, rain dripping off their coats, and took in the scene.

Evan had been expecting the Old Norse equivalent of a bowling alley. Certainly, there were similarities. The cheerful, constant hubbub of conversation and triumphant shouts. The periodic echoes of a strike, although in this case it was that of edged steel thwacking into wood. The actual lanes were more like stubby alleyways constructed of plywood and chain-link mesh. Each lane ended with a red-and-blue bull's-eye into which energetic men and women cheerfully hurtled the kind of weapon that could take off a man's head.

A man like James Talfour. Evan looked around and spotted only one Black man among the throng. Maybe the sport hadn't caught on with the non-Nordic crowd.

Along the wall on the far left ran a bar with high stools, a few scattered tables, and a menu that included kale shakes, veggie burgers, sweet potato fries with aioli dip, and other items that Evan was confident no self-respecting Viking ever let past his lips. As if in balance, the establishment also offered half-pound cheeseburgers and turkey drumsticks.

The bar, he noted appreciatively, was well stocked.

Then again . . . alcohol and ax-throwing? Who'd come up with that combination?

A couple walked past, faux-tanned and healthy thirtysomethings dressed in fashionable athletic wear, each staring intently into their phones. The woman lifted her gaze long enough for the bright-blue orbs, set amid heavily mascaraed lashes, to land on Evan. She startled and hurried after her partner, who'd kept walking. Evan saw her lean in and say something to the man, who glanced back at Evan and grinned.

Evan considered offering him his middle finger but then decided that the canvas bag slung over the man's shoulder probably held an ax. Or perhaps two. Discretion, as he so often reminded himself, was the better part of valor.

"What's happening over there?" Patrick pointed.

Off to the right, buried deep inside the complex of lanes, a hallway with a sign for the bathrooms, and a series of what looked like whetting stones, a knot of people had begun chanting.

"Go, go, go!" the mob shouted.

The crowd swirled and broke open long enough for Evan to spot a giantess of a woman, her height crowned with copper-colored hair loosely braided. Beneath her sleeveless T-shirt, her arms rippled with muscled, tawny skin. She balanced an immense ax on her shoulder, a two-bladed monstrosity almost as long as Evan was tall, and that Evan was confident could cleave a man like him into two pieces if given the chance.

Patrick gaped. "Holy shit. Look at 'er."

"Diana," Evan said and grinned.

Now Patrick gaped at him. "You know her?"

"She's my postdoc. Come on."

Evan plowed into the crowd, using elbows and the forward thrust of his chest to muscle past legs and torsos. Patrick plunged in after him. They emerged near the front of the group, which had taken over the alleys on either side of the double-wide lane where Diana stood, and had also packed the space behind her.

It was a competition, Evan saw. Diana and another man stood side by side facing separate wooden bull's-eyes. Above the targets, a digital readout showed Diana ahead by three points, seventeen to fourteen.

Diana, Evan had to admit, looked gloriously in her element. As did her competitor, a large, well-muscled man with a shaved head and flame-red beard, who would make a perfect member of the Viking Æsir. He looked like a youthful Odin to Diana's Freya.

Ah, to have such fantastic reach. To be of such glorious height.

The man lifted his own ax over his head and transferred his weight to his back foot. He swung the ax in a high arc, shifted his weight forward, and released the blade. The ax rotated once and landed to the left of center.

The crowd roared. The man's score jumped up to nineteen. Diana nodded her acknowledgment of his throw before she lifted her own weapon.

Evan found himself jostled by the sweating, cheering, beer-raising horde of mostly young people. For an instant, among the roaring masses, Evan had the feeling he'd dropped back through the centuries, landing in the days of the gladiators.

He felt a sharp pain as someone's elbow connected with his temple and the world went briefly dark before it turned scarlet, as if everyone around him was bathed in blood.

Then a hand clamped down on his shoulder, and his vision cleared. *God's wounds,* he thought.

"Watch it," Patrick's voice growled out of the darkness.

Patrick had Evan in his grip and was glaring at someone in the crowd, a man in a Chicago Bears T-shirt who barely spared them a glance before looking back at the competition.

"Little shit," Patrick muttered.

"Excuse me?" Evan said.

Patrick turned scarlet. "Not you. Mr. Chicago Bears. He almost knocked you out."

Evan raised a hand to his temple. *He certainly gave me a headache.*

With her ax raised, Diana turned, as if with a sixth sense. She spotted Evan and beamed at him. As one, the crowd swiveled to see who had earned Diana's smile. Heat rose in Evan's face.

"In my next life," Patrick said, releasing Evan to clasp his hands to his heart, "I'm going to be a professor."

"Sorry, man," said the man in the Bears T-shirt, looking down at Evan. "Didn't see you."

He moved over, leaving a more comfortable gap for Evan and Patrick.

It helped to have friends in high places.

Diana's brilliant smile faded as she spotted something beyond Evan. When he looked over his shoulder, all he saw were hairy chests and some spectacular cleavage. He returned his attention to the competition. Diana was facing the bull's-eye. She shifted her weight to her front foot, raised the ax, and released it, leaning forward into the throw.

The ax thunked into the red center of the bull's-eye and stayed there. The crowd cheered. The digital readout on her side went up by seven more points.

Her competitor grinned ruefully and turned to Diana with his hand extended. But she enveloped him in a hug that caused Patrick to again smack his hands to his chest.

The redheaded man emerged from the hug, beaming.

"One of these days, Diana," he said.

"Just not this day, Sten," she answered.

Evan presumed this man must be Sten Elger, the owner of the club.

Diana and Sten retrieved their axes; then Diana curled her fingers around Sten's. "Come on, I want you to meet my friend."

ᚢ

Ten minutes later, settled at one of the tables with four pints of frothy dark-ruby-red Guinness stout and a platter of fries, Diana and the three men raised their glasses.

"Diana and I have been competing for a year now," Sten said. "Early on, I could take her every time."

"That lasted maybe a week," Diana said, laughing. "Here's to a good rivalry."

They clinked glasses and drank.

"I feel like I've wandered into the old country," Patrick said. "Diana, are you sure you aren't descended from Celtic chieftains?"

"I'm pure Cajun, boy," she said. "And don't forget it. *Laissez les bon temps rouler.*"

"What did she say?" Patrick asked Evan.

"Something about all the drinks being on her."

Diana ribbed him. "As soon as I'm tenured, my noble adviser."

She pulled a hand towel from her bag and rubbed the sheen of sweat from her face and arms. Evan recalled the words of his favorite undergraduate English professor at Oxford. *Women don't sweat,* the prof had told them. *They glow.* Yet another thing to enjoy about the fairer sex.

Their hamburgers arrived, and silence descended on the table for a few minutes. Diana finished first, pushing away her empty plate with a contented sigh.

"Thanks, Sten."

"Next time it's on you. I have a business to run." But he didn't sound grumpy.

She waved a hand that encompassed Evan and Patrick. "So, Sten, these boys are here to learn about some of your riffraff."

Sten replaced his half-eaten burger on the plate and licked his fingers. "You talking about the minor riffraff or the serious jerks?"

"The neo-Nazis."

"The serious jerks, then." Sten half rose out of his seat and glanced around but then sank back in his chair and shook his head. "Helskin and his crew were here earlier. Don't see 'em now."

"I saw them. Maybe they slunk home with their tails between their legs." Diana raised her glass in a mock salute. To Evan and Patrick, she said, "Hank Helskin is the kind of hard-core guy you'd expect to see driving his car into a crowd of antiracist protestors. Except he's also a coward. Sticks close to his mates. Talks the talk and struts his stuff, but I think he's actually pretty harmless. And maybe too lazy to mount anything like a real campaign."

Sten signaled for another round of Guinness. "That's why I don't bounce him out on his ass whenever he shows up. That and the fact this is America. I'm a big believer in the First Amendment."

"Are these guys Viking reenactors?" Evan asked. "Or Ásatrú?"

"Both?" Sten frowned and tugged on his beard. "Sort of. They call themselves Ásatrú, and they really go for the look. Full beards, shaved heads, Viking tattoos."

"Kind of like you," Diana said.

His grin was sheepish. "I'm no reenactor. But if I'm going to run a place like Ragnarök, I have to look the part. Anyway, Helskin and his crew are probably no more serious about Ásatrú than anyone sitting at this table. And they definitely don't care much about true Viking traditions. The *real* reenactors are hard-core when they're in character. No plastic cups. No phones. No sunglasses. They bring in axes they've made themselves. I think the only modern thing they allow when they're doing full-on Viking are prescription eyeglasses. Probably 'cause they'd look like dumbasses if they walked into the walls."

"So these men," Evan said. "Helskin and the others, they don't stick to traditional dress and tools?"

"Nah. They're always on their phones. Half the time, they got earbuds in. Probably listening to Wagner. Or Megadeth."

"What's wrong with Wagner?" Patrick asked. "Didn't he write that song they're always using in movies? The opera one?"

"You're probably thinking of 'Ride of the Valkyries,'" Diana said. "Which is brilliant. But Wagner was anti-Semitic. Hitler was a big fan."

"No shit?"

"I shit you not."

"Do you like opera?" Patrick asked.

"I do. Although my Italian isn't what it could be."

Patrick's face lit up with a goofy smile. "Whose is?"

Evan took another bite of his burger. Juices dripped onto his plate. He thought he detected garlic in the mix. And maybe coriander. It was very good. "Where do these guys fall on the intelligence scale?" He was thinking of *lendreg* and *brume* and *corse*. Of *Beowulf* and "The Wanderer."

"Helskin is somewhere between Neanderthal and Cro-Magnon. The rest have about as much going on as a bowl of mixed nuts."

The new mugs of Guinness arrived. Evan waited until the server had moved on before he asked, "Do you know what their day jobs are?"

"Not a clue."

"But they strike you as guys who might get their history mixed up," Patrick said.

"I'd pretty much count on that."

"Is this Helskin fellow the person you were frowning at earlier?" Evan asked Diana.

"When?"

"During the match."

"Who? Oh, him. That was Raven. One of Helskin's henchmen. He's definitely not one of the mixed nuts."

"Who are you talking about?" Sten asked.

"Raven. That's the name he goes by. He's dark-haired and squinty-eyed, and he has a raven tattoo on his forehead. You know who I mean?"

"Yeah, maybe." Sten squirted more ketchup onto the plate of fries. "I've more noticed the group. Like a pack of wolfhounds."

Diana snorted. "That's being unkind to wolfhounds the world over. The guy makes me think of the Nazgûl in Tolkien's books. You know, the Ringwraiths."

"The who-what?" said Sten.

"Servants of the Dark Lord. Sten, how can you run a Nordic establishment and not know Tolkien?"

"Note to self," Sten said. "Read up on Ringwraiths."

"Otherwise known as the Nine," Evan murmured, picturing the nine slats arranged around Talfour's head.

He caught the faintest tremor ripple across Diana's shoulders. It surprised him—he'd never known Diana to be afraid of anything, except maybe learning they didn't hold the mayo on her BLT.

He tapped the back of his assistant's hand. "You think we should be looking at Raven in relation to this case?"

"What case?" Sten asked. "Wait, are you guys working the guy who was offed by the river? 'Cause I heard it was a hinky one."

"A purely scholarly interest," Diana said, then turned to Evan. "No idea. I just don't like him because of the aforementioned servant-of-evil aura. He all but radiates wickedness. Intelligent wickedness, unlike the rest of the group."

"Inking a giant raven on your forehead doesn't seem like the smartest thing to do," Patrick said.

"Maybe not," Diana agreed. "It probably signals his devotion to Odin. He seems more serious about the Viking culture than the rest of them. Regardless, I don't like how he lurks. And stares."

Evan reached for his glass. "Everyone stares at you, Di."

"Not like that."

"Like what?"

She grew pensive. "When a guy stares, it's usually because he wants to ask me out to dinner. Often in the hope that dinner will lead to other things. But this guy looks at me like he'd rather put me *on* the menu."

"Why didn't you tell me?" Sten asked.

She slitted her eyes. "You think I can't hold my own?"

"Point taken."

"You have cameras?" Patrick asked Sten.

"You *are* working that case!" Sten cried. "And yeah, sure. We got five. Two outside—front and back. One just inside the front door and two overlooking the lanes."

Patrick said, "I'd like to take a look at the footage."

Sten licked ketchup and salt off his fingers. "You think you'll know a Ringwraith if you see one? What do Ringwraiths look like, exactly?"

Another swat from Diana.

Sten rubbed his shoulder. "I'll tell Marty to pull tonight's footage from the lanes and send it to you."

"We can't look now?" Patrick asked.

Sten shook his head. "Sorry. We run everything through a third party. Our footage is uploaded to their cloud. It usually gets taped over every twenty-four hours because we don't pay for a lot of space. But I'll have them pull the footage and send it to me; then I'll upload it and send you an access link. I'll send the link to Diana, too, if you want her pointing out her Ringwraith. Will that work?"

"Perfect. Send everything starting from when you opened business today." Patrick pulled a business card from his wallet and slid it across the table to Sten.

Sten wiped his hands on his napkin and pocketed the business card in his flannel shirt. With his fingers still in the pocket, he gave a look of surprise. "I almost forgot."

He fished out something and handed it to Diana. "I found this little figure outside the front door today. You ever see anything like it?"

Diana cupped the wooden figurine in her palm. Her eyes met Evan's. Although it was only a couple of inches tall, the figure was undoubtedly like the one someone had left for Evan at his office, right down to the painted eyes.

"It's odd," she said, handing it back. "Creepy, even. But I don't know what it means."

"Maybe it's a voodoo curse." Sten laughed and stood. "I need to get back to work." He shook hands with Evan and Patrick, mumbled "nice to meet you," accepted Diana's hug, and vanished into the throng.

Diana watched him go, then turned to Evan. "That was weird."

"Aw, that little doll?" Patrick asked. "I thought it was kind of cute."

"Someone gifted Evan with one of those just this morning," Diana told him.

Evan shrugged. "I'm always open to voodoo curses."

"I'm sure it's nothing." Diana waved a hand. "Someone's weird idea of spreading a little cheer. Anyway, aside from Ringwraiths and voodoo dolls, what do you guys think of the place? Evan, I don't believe you were assaulted as a maggot by a single person."

"A maggot?" Patrick asked.

Evan pointed to his left temple. "I did take an elbow to the head."

Diana ran warm fingers along his hairline. "I think there's a lump there," she said, her voice suddenly filled with concern. "I'll get some ice."

"Please don't. I have a hard skull."

"I can't argue with that." But she still looked concerned.

"How'd the cryptology class go today?" Evan asked, to change the subject.

"Fine." She withdrew her hand, and Evan sighed. "They missed you. They seem to have you confused with a minor deity."

"Minor?"

Patrick looked wistfully at his empty beer glass, then pushed back his chair. "Well, that'll do it. I gotta get home to the missus. Dr. Wilding, you mind giving me a ride back to my car?"

"Not at all."

"Let me get my things, and I'll walk out with you," Diana said. "I'll meet you at the front door."

"She's something, isn't she?" Patrick said as Diana headed toward the locker rooms. "I'd like the missus to meet her."

"I thought you were developing a crush."

"Oh, sure. The missus gets crushes, too. You should see her when George Clooney comes on the screen. Don't mean a thing." Patrick held up two tightly crossed fingers. "We're like this, the missus and me."

"So these crushes are just a form of window shopping?"

The detective grinned. "Right-o. We can look at the menu from time to time. Just as long as we eat at home."

ᛪ

A block from Ragnarök, standing on the sidewalk, Evan hesitated as he reached for the door handle of the Jaguar.

Diana was already a distant shape in the rain, hotfooting it toward her car, a graceful if admittedly large gazelle disappearing and reappearing in the soft cones of light from the streetlamps. Evan watched until she reached her Jeep and the lights flashed as she unlocked it. On the other side of his car, Patrick was groaning about his knees as he gripped the doorframe and lowered himself in.

Evan frowned. The rain had already soaked his hair and shoulders and was working on the hem of his pants. Diana had started her car, exhaust spilling into the night.

But still he paused.

Something . . .

The hair rose on the back of his neck. Ice formed between his shoulder blades. He did a slow one-eighty, blinking the rain out of his eyes.

Pools of darkness filled the spaces between the lights. Nothing stirred but the drizzling rain, a thin fog, and the holiday lights blinking from a few of the closed shops.

No blood. No pigeon killers. Not even a little wooden figure.

You are the victim, he chided himself, *of an overactive imagination.*

But he had in his mind's eye the image of Raven, a man he'd never seen but could picture perfectly. The dark hair; the sharp, narrow gaze; the feral hunger. Diana had a high tolerance for all things human. She was a firm believer in live and let live and keep your nose out of everyone else's business.

If Raven made her uneasy, then there was something to the man.

In Norse mythology, Odin had sent a pair of ravens into the world to gather news and report back to their master, the king of the Æsir. The ravens represented the mind of man himself. Thought and memory. They were Odin's spies.

Odin, the god of wisdom and death.

The god of the gallows. The god of runes.

Odin, with his missing right eye.

Just like James Talfour. And probably Scott Desser, whose orbital socket had been scraped with a knife.

"You coming?" Patrick said.

Evan shook himself and opened the door. He all but threw himself inside, pulled the door closed, and started the engine.

Patrick was staring out the passenger-side window. "Look at all that mist. Spooky, isn't it? Puts me in mind of our killer. What do you imagine he's doing right now?"

"I shudder to think."

Evan punched the gas and accelerated down the street, hoping to leave his disquiet behind.

But the dark pressed close against the windows as the world kept watch.

CHAPTER 15

Evan's rented house—which the owner had named the Aerie—sat atop a hill amid gardens and a rolling lawn that descended from the house like green waves flowing in all directions.

In times of stress or agitation—like now, when his brain was filled with thoughts of murderers and Ringwraiths—the Aerie was one place in the sprawling metropolis of Chicagoland where Evan felt safe. As he drove through his neighborhood, he turned off the car stereo and enjoyed the view.

He had rented the home two years ago on an indefinite lease from the erstwhile director of graduate studies at Northwestern University, now emeritus director, who'd lived in the house for more than twenty years and modified it to accommodate her own height of four foot nine. She'd installed low countertops and provided plenty of low-level cabinets. Bathrooms and the kitchen had been scaled down. For everything out of reach, there was the wizardry of electronics. The Tudor-style home was small compared to others in the neighborhood, which left more room for the gardens and spared Evan the feeling he was rattling around in a home meant to accommodate a family of giants.

His preferred style was cozy and intimate, and the house provided exactly that.

Once you passed through the wrought-iron gate, wound your way up between the pines, and pulled into the curved driveway, you slipped backward in time—outwardly at least—to Elizabethan England. The Aerie's exterior consisted of warm brick, exposed half timbers, a steeply pitched roof, and what the leasing agent had called rubblework masonry. Inside, lustrous flooring and paneling, overhead beams, and long rows of mullioned windows made the space inviting. Every window in the house boasted a view of either the gardens or the stately trees in front. The kitchen was gourmet, with a large and airy side room that had once been a dining room but that now served as indoor accommodations for Ginny and provided the hawk with both a view out the windows and into the kitchen where Evan spent much of his time. There were two bedrooms up, one down. A basement with a wine cellar and an entertainment room and uncountable closets for storage.

At the very center of the house, like a glittering jewel nestled in a velvet box, lay a two-story library, which the original builder had modeled as a scaled-down version of the Morgan Library in New York City. More than a hundred shelves, generous display cabinets for his archaeological collection, and a fireplace he could stand in should he ever feel the urge to contemplate life as kindling. Lots of comfortable sofas and chairs, including a padded window seat that overlooked the back garden.

Of everything in the house, the library—and its collection—was his pride and joy.

A professor's salary wouldn't have made the lease possible. It was the fees from consulting that paid for it. With the house and car taken care of, Evan had enough to pay the bills and see to his regular charities. And to allow himself the occasional treasure—an illuminated Armenian gospel book, perhaps, or an early Iron Age amphora.

As he drove through the gates, a gust of wind slapped the car, slapping him equally out of his reverie. He cranked up the windshield wipers until they lashed back and forth; then he sped up the long drive toward the distant lights. He smiled as the house came into view, the windows offering a warm glow from the lamps he'd set on timers. He wanted to see Ginny. And tonight was young Jo's piano lesson, always a highlight of the week. The two of them would share a light dinner, *very* light for him, and after she left, he'd make himself a post-meal cocktail—or three—and get to work on the profile of the man he'd come to think of as the Viking Poet.

Whoever this killer was, he promised to be a formidable foe. Addie had been right—this was one of the strange ones.

His specialty.

The garage sensed the Jaguar's approach and opened obligingly, revealing the battered pickup truck he drove when he and Ginny went hunting. Rain washed in with the car, along with a bad case of nerves, and Evan admitted to a certain relief when he shut off the engine and the garage door lowered behind him, automatically resetting the alarm.

In the mudroom, he shed his raincoat, his suit jacket, his shoes and socks, and the rain-soaked pants. He padded down the hall into the kitchen in his underwear and shirtsleeves.

Ginny called to him in her high voice and rustled her feathers as he flipped on the kitchen lights and peered in.

"My beautiful lady," he said. "How did you do today?"

She squeaked, happy to see him.

"I'll be right back. A man can't have his dignity without his pants."

Once he'd slipped into sweatpants and a turtleneck sweater, Evan pulled a plastic container from a drawer in the immense refrigerator and returned to Ginny's room to feed her tidbits of rabbit procured during one of their hunts. She flew to his gloved hand to devour her meal, and he walked about the house with her for a bit so that they could enjoy each other's company. Once she seemed satisfied, he resettled her on the perch so she could watch him as he started dinner.

He told the virtual assistant to play a Chopin nocturne—it selected "No. 21 in C-minor"—then set about making omelets. He wasn't hungry after the burger at Ragnarök. But his neighbor's daughter, Jo, would arrive soon, and she always ate every bit of food he set out. As if her parents didn't feed her enough. Jo was a bottomless pit.

On a wooden board, he sliced onions, mushrooms, and mild red peppers, then sautéed them in a saucepan on the Wolf gas stove. He cracked six eggs into a glass bowl, added salt and pepper, and whipped them to a froth. It was a mistake, in his opinion, to add cream. It only diluted the flavor of the eggs. He placed two large pats of butter in a pan over medium-low heat, then sliced thick pieces of French-style country bread and placed them on a baking sheet to go in the oven.

He was just sliding the omelets onto plates when the wall-mounted screen—installed by the owner for reasons of her own—lit up and showed him a BMW at the gate, followed a few minutes later by Jo at the front door. She wore a pink rain jacket and matching hat and looked like she was humming to herself as she waved her parents off and then punched in the security code. He pulled the bread from the oven as she walked into the room in her stockinged feet, having shed her wet things near the door.

"It smells awesome in here," she said and dashed through the kitchen toward Ginny.

"Easy!" Evan cried.

The hawk fluttered for a moment before resettling as Jo came to a halt.

"Remember what I said about approaching her slowly," Evan said. "She doesn't like to be startled any more than the rest of us."

"I know. I'm sorry. Can I give her something?"

"She's eaten. But after dinner, we'll spend a little time with her before your lesson."

Her face fell. "My mom says I need to be done early tonight. I have a history test tomorrow. I'm sorry, Ginny. But"—she turned back to Evan with a wide smile—"I've been practicing my whistles. Pretty soon, I'll be able to call her as well as you."

"That's good. Maybe you can go out with us this weekend."

"That'd be . . . what is it you say?"

"Brilliant."

"Brilliant. I wish I didn't have a test tomorrow."

"We'd best get down to business, then," Evan said. "Grab the marmalade from the fridge, please."

Once everything was on the table, Jo perched on a chair across the table from him, and for a few minutes, they contented themselves with the food. Evan enjoyed watching the girl eat. She was as skinny as a rail, as the saying went. Jo herself joked that she had to run around in the rain to get wet. Her parents had told Evan that Jo's thinness was the only remaining trace of a childhood illness that had nearly killed her and from which she was now completely cured.

Death comes for us all, he thought. *But it should not come for the young.*

Jo spoke around the last bite of her omelet. "Why are you playing the nocturnes tonight?"

"Nocturnes are obviously perfect for nighttime listening. And I thought it might inspire you. How are you doing on the waltz?"

Jo ignored the question. "Ginny likes the nocturnes, too."

"A Chopin-loving goshawk," Evan said. "Who would have figured?"

"Why not?" Jo asked. "Animals like music just as much as we do."

"I believe you're right. Shall we have tea now?"

"The English breakfast kind. With milk and sugar."

"The only proper way to drink tea, milady."

Jo giggled. He went to fill the kettle with water while she cleared the table.

These kinds of quiet moments were among Evan's favorites. In a different life, he would have married and raised an entire passel of children. But the universe had had other plans for him. Having Jo here was as close as he was likely to get to that form of domesticity, and he was grateful that her parents had decided he was trustworthy. He'd hoped for nieces and nephews, but River seemed disinclined.

Speaking of River . . . Evan excused himself and went back into the bedroom for his phone. He was terrible about carrying the wretched albatross around, even when he'd been hired to consult on a case. But earlier, he'd managed to leave a voice message for River, asking him to call so they could discuss bog bodies. River was on a dig in Mesopotamia, where cell phone service was spotty.

Now Evan scrolled through a handful of texts and messages.

Nothing from his brother. It was three in the morning in the city of Urfa. He'd try again tomorrow.

Evan found Jo at the baby grand piano in the front room. She'd turned off the stereo and was warming up with the harmonic minor scales. He eased in beside her on the bench and watched her rapid fingers fly up and down the keyboard.

Evan's small hands would never allow him to play as he wished. He managed passably well. The only reason Jo was his student was because she'd begged him for lessons when she and her parents came by to welcome Evan to the neighborhood and Jo had spotted the piano. Now he taught her through a combination of demonstration and music videos. Thank God for YouTube.

Half an hour later, the intercom buzzed from the gate. Evan told Jo to restart the B section of the waltz, then went to the speaker.

"It's Officer Blakesley," a male voice boomed through the speaker. "Sorry to bother you, but I found a couple things I think you might have left in the woods."

The camera mounted above the gate showed a blue pickup truck. A man in street clothes and a down jacket stood in front of the intercom, apparently unbothered by the rain.

As if sensing Evan's gaze, the man looked up. Evan recognized one of the two mounted patrol officers who'd found him in the woods that morning. Officer Blakesley raised his hand to show the camera a delicate silver bell.

"Is this yours?" he asked.

Ginny's bell. It was one of the best he owned—an elegant piece designed by a master of the craft. It must have fallen out of his bag when he was reaching for Ginny's hood. "It *is* mine, Officer. Or rather, my hawk's. Thank you."

He buzzed the gate. It swung open as Blakesley returned to his truck. A few minutes later, the front bell rang. In the sitting room, the piano fell silent.

"Keep going, Jo!" Evan called as he went to open the door.

She dutifully started the waltz again.

Blakesley stood on the porch. In his T-shirt and jeans, he looked like a cheerful hockey player. The kind who would check you into the boards during the game, then rush to buy you the first postgame beer. Now he smiled genially at Evan and held out the bell.

"I know it's late, Professor. My partner found this and was going to bring it by. But I was in the neighborhood. Friend of mine lives a few blocks over. I wanted to get it to you."

Evan waved the officer in and took a moment to peer out into the gloom. Mist had swallowed the distant topiaries and now twined like pythons among the boles of the trees. Damp dripped off everything.

"Something got you concerned?" Blakesley asked.

Evan startled at Blakesley's voice, unable to explain his unease with the night. "Not in the least." He closed the door and turned to face the officer's crotch.

Actually, more like the man's stomach. But it was always an awkward moment when a dwarf meets a giant. Today seemed to be the day for rubbing elbows, in a manner of speaking, with big men. First Patrick and now Officer Blakesley.

Blakesley seemed unaware of Evan's discomfort. He was studying the David Roberts Egyptian lithographs that marched down the hall. "Nice place you got. My pal Taylor loves the neighborhood."

"What's not to love?" Evan stepped back a few paces and looked up into Blakesley's face. "Taylor who?"

"Ketzsky. Taylor Ketzsky. There's a group of us gets together every month to play poker and talk issues. Ergo the T-shirt."

He held open his parka, and Evan looked at Blakesley's printed tee—LGPA–GOAL—then riffled through his mental library of acronyms. The letters stood for Lesbian and Gay Police Association–Gay Officers Action League.

Blakesley let his hands drop. "I have to admit, I'm more of a South Side guy. My Brooklyn upbringing, I guess. Plus years in military housing. Don't feel comfortable when folks are spread too far apart."

The Chopin waltz came to a tinkling stop, and seconds later, Jo slid into the hallway. "I'm Jo. Would you like some tea? It's English breakfast."

"Nice to meet you, Jo. But nah, thanks. Early day tomorrow." He reached into his pocket. "After you mentioned the birds, Sal and I thought we'd take another look around. We didn't find any more pigeons. But we kept poking around, and that's when Sally found your bell. And this."

His hand reemerged from his pocket, and he passed a man's heavy gold ring over to Evan. Evan set Ginny's bell on the console table near the door and took the piece of jewelry.

The ring was clearly designed for a large hand. Carved all the way around the band was a series of runes. At the center of the ring, where the diamond would be set in an engagement ring, the metal had been crafted to a point. Two runes sat beneath the point. The rune for *god*. And the rune for *spear*.

God's spear.

How odd that a Viking ring had shown up twelve miles from where the body of a man had been placed, surrounded by runes.

As if Blakesley had read his mind, the officer said, "Those are runic letters, right? Maybe the birds are part of some weird Viking thing?"

"Maybe," Evan said. "I'd like to hang on to it, if that's all right. I want to show it to Detective Bisset."

The officer hesitated, then said, "Sure. Not like any crime was committed. If someone calls looking for it, I'll let you know. Looks like an expensive bit of bling. And now"—he turned to Jo—"I'd better make like a tree and leave."

Jo rewarded him with a giggle.

Evan opened the door once again, and Blakesley pushed open the screen. Halfway out, he paused and turned.

"I heard a little about this case you're working on," he said.

"Yes?"

"Just . . ." Blakesley tapped his hand lightly on the doorframe. "Seems like it's one of the bad ones. Be careful out there."

Startled, Evan said, "I will."

Blakesley hurried down the brick walkway toward his truck. There came the flash of headlights, and a minute later, the night swallowed him and his truck.

Evan closed the door. Locked it. Wondered what had prompted Blakesley's advice. Whatever it was, it gave him a bad feeling. Another bad feeling to add to the night's count.

When he turned around, Jo was watching him. Her thin arms were folded over her chest. "What are you scared of?"

That was a very good question. Where to begin? Reading about bog bodies and seeing a man who'd been tortured to death had gotten under his skin, apparently.

He radiates wickedness, Diana had said about the man who called himself Raven.

Which didn't mean he went about chasing after dwarfs. Or little girls. Or anyone at all. Evan shoved the ring in his pocket.

Jo was still watching him. "Mr. Evan?"

Evan pushed off from the door and approached Jo, his arms up and fingers hooked like an imaginary monster's. "It's true that I'm scared."

She squealed. "Of what?"

"I'm terrified"—he drew closer—"that Miss Josephine"—and closer—"will never"—Jo pressed against the wall—"nail the last"—he pretended to pounce—"movement of the waltz!"

She stuck out her tongue.

Evan laughed.

Outside, the wind screeched like an unkindness of ravens.

Chapter 16

A few miles away from Evan, Addie dropped her phone onto the passenger seat.

She frowned.

Okay. She had perhaps, more accurately, *slammed* the phone onto the passenger seat.

Now she fumed, rapping her fingers on the top of the steering wheel and glaring out at the wind and the rain.

She took a few deep breaths, the way a meditation coach had taught everyone in the department. Most of the guys had laughed when human resources brought in a meditation teacher and offered a yoga class as a way of handling the dreaded "thin blue line" stress. But Addie had always been a good student. She *liked* learning things. And what the teacher said made sense—that in order to relax the mind and be at our sharpest, we first need to relax our body.

She'd been practicing yoga and meditation on and off in the months since.

Okay. She'd sat in meditation exactly twice. And done a few sun salutations. But it was a start. The teacher had talked a lot about intentions.

Right now, hers bordered on the criminal. Or at least uncharitable.

She picked up her phone, reread Clayton's text.

Sorry gorgeous. Client is back on. Hate this job. Love u. Hope ur case is going well. Breakfast at Wildberry?

First, he'd delayed their meeting. Which was fine. She'd had time to go home and shower, change into something that made her feel like a woman instead of a street-hardened cop, right down to her lacy under-things. She'd even dabbed perfume behind her ears. The bottle was a few years old, a gift from a past love whose name she couldn't recall. But the perfume still smelled nice.

She'd been halfway to Clayton's home, feeling sexy and soft and more than ready to put murder aside for the night, when she got his text. Now she sat in her SUV on a deserted side street, decked in all her ridiculous finery, the engine of her Jeep Cherokee sadly the only thing that was going to do any purring tonight.

So, okay. Tomorrow was fine. Wildberry Café was good. In the meantime, she had a case to handle. A serial killer case. With cryptic writing and strange posing. What more did a murder cop want?

She blinked. Two dead men. Why should she have a life when they didn't?

She dialed the Chicago PD digital forensics department to see if they'd pulled anything from the six-months-old video of the assault on Talfour.

Stringer answered in his usual terse way. "I got 'em," he said in his raspy voice. "They're in an envelope on your desk."

She shifted the Jeep into drive. "Anything good?"

A grunt. "Define good. I got some decent close-ups. But the guys who went after Talfour must have known where the camera was. They kept their backs turned the entire time they were beating up the poor shmuck. Most I got were some side angles."

"If the attackers knew about the camera, maybe we can catch them scoping out the area earlier that day. Or earlier that week."

"You been smoking something, right? You know that footage would be long gone. We only got this little bit from the store because someone thought to grab it right after the assault."

"We have thirty thousand government cameras in this city, and not one of them caught these guys?"

Stringer sighed. "It's not a targeted area."

"What about banks? Any nearby?" Banks tended to keep video footage longer than most businesses—typically six months.

"There's a Chase Bank ATM. I already put a call in with them, but don't hold your breath. Talfour's assault was more than six months ago."

"Six months, four days, one hour, and"—she looked at her watch—"seventeen minutes ago. Roughly."

"Addie." Stringer sounded disappointed. "And here I thought you had a life."

Not much of one, apparently. "Thanks for doing this, Stringer. I'm on my way in."

"I guess that answers that," he said and hung up.

She considered going home to change before walking into the station house. But that would waste time sending her in the opposite direction. And without Clayton in her immediate future, a sudden weariness had descended.

She'd just button up her coat and hope no one noticed the green sparkly stilettos.

Right.

⚔

The first thing Addie spotted on her desk was a stack of pink While You Were Out message slips. Hopefully at least some of them were because of the calls she'd made right after her breakfast with Gabe when she'd tried to reach the employees of James Talfour's store.

She set the messages aside for the moment and picked up the envelope that Stringer had left for her. She shook out half a dozen eight-by-ten photos. The photos were remarkably clear, but Stringer was right—the men's faces were in almost-profile, as if the attackers were aware of the cameras and knew to keep their backs turned. She got a general sense of the men—they had beards and wore their hair long and shaved around the ears, like the actors in that Viking series she'd watched on the History Channel. And they wore street clothes—jeans and hoodies and gloves. One wore a leather vest over his hoodie with the double lightning bolts Rhinehart had mentioned. If they were reenactors, they hadn't been playing the part that night.

She returned to the first photo. One of the men's sleeves had ridden up to reveal a few inches of flesh between his glove and the cuff of his sweatshirt. The skin bore an intricately patterned tattoo. Addie opened her desk drawer and fumbled for a magnifying lens. The glass revealed a series of geometric shapes needled in black ink on the man's forearm.

Why were they wearing gloves in May? she wondered.

The answer came hard on the thought—to cover up their tattoos.

"Bastards," she muttered.

She slid out of her coat, hung it on a nearby hook, and set aside the photos to see if she could find anything online about Tommy Snow's Mr. X. But there were no local bone collectors with an *X* in their name. In fact, there was no one advertising a need for bones at all. Apparently, the collectors of bones didn't need to advertise on the internet. So how had Tommy Snow and Mr. X found each other? Perhaps through the community college. She made a note on her phone to contact Tommy's biology professor, Dr. Almadi, at the college first thing in the morning.

Finally, with a sigh, she turned to deal with the pink message slips.

"Here we go," she said aloud. "Time for the crazies."

She picked up the slip on the top.

For: Detective Bisset

From: Anonymous

Message: Tell that detective that was in the paper
that wolves did it. I seen wolves near my house. The
end days are coming.

Addie laid aside the slip. Picked up the next one, scanned it. Set it
aside. Picked up the next, working her way through the stack. Wolves.
Some guy's neighbor was killing little boys. Another guy's mother had
served him something that looked suspiciously like eyeballs floating in
his soup.

The mention of eyeballs made Addie frown. She opened a tab on
her browser and brought up the *Chicago Tribune* article. There it was,
smack in the middle of the article—the fact that Talfour was missing an
eye. Whoever their leak was, they hadn't held much back.

Addie set this message aside as well. Some of these callers' claims
would have to be investigated. But hopefully no woman was making a
cannibal of her son.

Halfway through the stack, she stopped.

A woman named Rachel Chen had called to say she used to work
for Talfour at Finer Things and might have information related to the
murder of her former boss.

Score!

Addie crossed the fingers on her left hand and dialed the number
the sergeant had jotted down. Someone picked up on the third ring,
and a woman said hello.

"This is Detective Bisset with Chicago PD. May I speak with
Rachel Chen?"

"This is she. Thanks for getting back to me, Detective."

"Thanks for your call. You say you have information about the death of James Talfour?"

"I might. I don't know if it's really relevant. But I thought someone should know."

"Know what, Ms. Chen?"

"I used to work at Mr. Talfour's store, Finer Things. Did you know he was assaulted six months ago?"

"We're aware of the incident, yes."

"Well, even though I worked there, *I* didn't know. The day before Mr. Talfour got hurt was my last day at the store. I'd accepted a position at Nordstrom in the cosmetics department and was taking a trip to see family before I started my new job. I was on a plane the day he was attacked. But when I got back, no one from your department contacted me to ask if I'd seen anything or knew anything. Which is unforgivable, in my opinion. I just found out this afternoon what happened because the reporter mentioned it in the article about Mr. Talfour's murder."

"I'm sorry for the oversight, Ms. Chen." Addie grabbed a ballpoint pen from the mug on her desk and turned over the pink message slip. "*Did* you see something?"

"The article also says that the attack was racially motivated. Is that true?"

"I can't really respond to that at this point," Addie said. She clicked the pen on and off. "What information do you have?"

"Did you know Mr. Talfour was blind in his right eye? He probably didn't even see them coming."

Interesting, Addie thought. The killer had cut out Talfour's right eye. "Was this common knowledge?"

"We didn't talk about it around the shop, if that's what you mean. But it was obvious if you looked straight at him that something was wrong with his eye."

A child's voice sounded over the line. "Mommy? I need a drink of water in my Cookie Monster cup."

"Okay, Amy. You can fill your cup in the bathroom. Mommy will be right there." There was a pause and then Rachel said, "A man came into Finer Things on my last day there. The day before the attack. He wanted a ring made. A pewter band with Viking runes on it."

Addie sat up. Her tiredness fell away. "I'm listening."

"I didn't think anything about the order, other than that the guy didn't look like someone who'd drop a lot of money on a piece of jewelry. And Finer Things is expensive. But he didn't seem overly concerned about the estimate I drew up for him. He thanked me and said he'd be in touch. What made me remember him wasn't just the ring he wanted. It was what I noticed as he was walking out."

The child's voice again. "Mommy?"

"Two more minutes, baby," Rachel called.

"Please go on, Ms. Chen," Addie said.

"The man was wearing a brown leather vest over his hoodie. On the back were those lightning bolt symbols that you see on the news sometimes. The kind that neo-Nazis wear."

"The sigel runes? A double S for *Schutzstaffel*?"

"That's right. I looked them up just tonight."

"What else did you notice about this man?"

"Long light-brown hair. He wore it in a man bun. And intense blue eyes."

Addie kept writing. "Any scars? Tattoos?"

"He had something tattooed on the back of his right hand. I noticed it when he filled out a custom-order form. It was a circle with a smaller, solid circle inside."

The sun cross. Addie forced herself to relax her grip on the pen.

"It had lines radiating out from the center," Rachel said. "The lines were bent so that they almost looked like lightning bolts. It looked a lot like a swastika."

That description didn't quite match the symbol the killer had carved next to the runes. But it sounded similar. And Rhinehart had mentioned a version of the sun cross created by the Nazis. Addie's pulse slammed in her neck. "You have a name for this man, then? Since he filled out a form for you."

"I couldn't remember what was on it, of course. Not after all this time."

Addie waited.

"I asked one of my former coworkers to look it up for me," Rachel said. "We scan those forms and keep them online for about six months. The man never came back to order the ring. But the form was still in the file. So yes, I have a name. Hank Helskin."

"Can you have your former coworker scan and email the form to me?"

"I'm sure that won't be a problem."

"And can you make a drawing of the tattoo you saw and email that to me as well?"

"Of course."

"Maaa—meeee!" came Amy's voice in the background.

"I'm coming, sweetie. Detective, would you excuse me a moment?"

"Of course."

Addie typed on her computer keyboard, her fingers flying. She looked for Hank Helskin in the DMV records. Nothing. She tried Henry Helskin. Still nada. Maybe Mr. Helskin was a recent transplant who hadn't bothered getting an Illinois driver's license.

She opened another tab and entered HANK HELSKIN ÁSATRÚ in the search field. A Meetup group popped up—Aryan Ásatrú.

Addie smiled. *Gotcha.*

Rachel was back on the phone. "Detective Bisset, I'm afraid I need to get going."

"I understand. Just give me one more minute of your time, please. What other information is on the form?"

"An address," Rachel said. "And what he wanted etched on the ring in runic letters. He said the letters meant Odin's thane, whatever *that* means."

"No phone number?"

"He left it blank."

Addie glanced at the digital clock on her computer. The night was still young. "Ms. Chen, can you send me the address right now?"

CHAPTER 17

After Jo's parents came to take her home, Evan mixed himself an Old-Fashioned with an infusion of smoked rosemary, carried Ginny to her perch in the library, then grabbed the paperwork and books from his leather satchel and went to stand at the library table.

Evan's first step when creating a profile of a killer was to absorb all the available material. When possible, he looked at everything in situ—that is, placed exactly as the killer left it. The body. Forensic clues like footprints and weapons and injuries. And whatever signs and symbols the killer had purposefully or accidentally left behind.

He gently pushed aside the assortment of Japanese wooden puzzle boxes scattered across the table and opened the folder he'd received during the meeting at the police station. Methodically, he arranged the material across the table's surface. The police and sheriff reports. The crime-scene photos. His runic chart along with his and Rhinehart's transliterations. He opened his journal to the drawing he'd done of Talfour's body, the corpse set like a broken jewel amid the mud and reeds.

Immediately in front of him, he squared a foolscap writing pad—he liked the additional room offered by the larger pages—and next to it, a fountain pen. He stretched, turned his neck from side to side to work out the kinks, and frowned down at the table.

The most important thing to do whenever he was attempting to form a picture out of a scattering of puzzle pieces was to create some mental space between himself and the mystery. Distance was the key to finding the outside limits of the puzzle—the corners and sides, so to speak. Distance quieted the chatter of his brain and allowed the more intuitive thoughts to surface.

He had several strategies for distracting his monkey mind when he was trying to dive deep on a problem. The wooden puzzles he was so fond of. Walking the grounds around the house. Taking Ginny out to fly. And baking sweet and savory pastries; he was particularly fond of some of the baking shows from his native Britain.

Tonight, he decided that music would be his technique of choice.

He turned on the sound system and selected the chant for the dead sung during the requiem mass, "In Paradisum." The choral voices soothed both him and Ginny and felt right for the work at hand.

He nodded down at the documents laid out on the table. "And so we begin."

He pulled over a chair of a comfortable height and eased into it. He then picked up the pen and bent over the foolscap, touching ink to paper. A small dot appeared. His earlier unease vanished like a chill dropping away from his skin, leaving only a residual disquiet from the two deaths. And even that disappeared as he began to work. Solving a puzzle of any form was a balm to heart and soul. Every enigma had an answer, every riddle a response. It remained only to find the correct key to set the universe to rights.

He wrote out the runes left by the killer, getting the feel for their shapes. The lines and branches, the crosses and arcs. Although his medium was different—paper and pen versus wood and bone and a sharp-bladed tool—he could easily imagine the killer's satisfaction as the characters took shape beneath his hand, unspooling the killer's story.

Then, as Rhinehart had done, he transliterated the runic alphabet into the Latin one. Here, he referred to the chart he'd made that morning. His transliteration was very close to Rhinehart's. So despite the man's refusal to consider other aspects of the crime scene, the man at least knew his runes.

Finished with the first task, Evan sat back in his chair, sipped the Old-Fashioned, and watched as lamplight played along the cut crystal.

Now for the difficult part. Picking out the actual meaning from the string of characters.

"I'll be disappointed in you," he said to the air, addressing the killer as if the man stood before him. "Very disappointed indeed if most of what you've given us is the kind of nonsense Rhinehart proposed."

He set down the glass and began, again, to write. He scratched things out, circled around, rewrote the words, rewrote entire lines. At one point, he murmured, "It *is* a numbering system," as he scratched out and reordered some of the lines. The poet had not only used boustrophedon so that the lines had to be read in alternating directions but had also reordered his lines by moving every third line down, presumably to make the decipherment more difficult. Now and again, Evan consulted his phone to check a word or definition on the internet. Half an hour later, he laid down the pen and leaned back to survey his work.

"It's only a guess at the moment," he said again to the lurking shadows, which lay deep enough along the walls to harbor a murderer. "I've no doubt made mistakes. But still, your poem speaks its own strange language."

Ginny twitched her head left, then right, as if searching the room for another human.

"Your poem is also difficult," Evan continued. "There are words and lines I don't yet understand. You are a trickster. Exactly like any Old English poet worth his weight. But"—he picked up his glass and raised it in a mock salute—"what you gave us isn't gibberish."

He turned down the requiem mass until it was only a whisper in the background and tapped a button on his small audio recorder. He read the lines aloud. First the Desser runes and then Talfour's.

2   *Thus from my bothy I came homeland's ward for cattle of riding*

3   *to sacrifice the innocent at night she takes back her sons and daughters*

4   *who rived and tholed and peeled her flesh like ripe fruit*

9   *blessing giver my blood-feud stillbirths your further crimes*

10 *Listen up! Mighty men I undo and unto earth I send*

11 *Their water weighted corses. I am a dam-ned scop*

12 *A death driven mere plague, the brume that binds up evil.*

13 *A weary warrior wailing with wyrded wergild,*

14 *A slayer of the bone halls breaking Fjorgyn.*

15 *You know why! Over the sun swimmer home I came*

16 *For mine! Mine mine gone. Bowel buried, busted by big bosses*

17 *That war crime, sword shaker, heart of my bawn entombed.*

18 *Making me bodulfr war wolf and lendreg and ageclaa, all, bearing the ☉.*

19 *What of this bone cage? This skin sinner is ox of riding.*

20 *By Skollfud's light I laid him low. Wight is he and soon wight.*

21 *In warding I reward. Into his mouth of hearing I poured my mead.*

22 *Tell me! By Mani's lait I laid it out. Prick me this. But*

23 *His honey maker held still, so I held tight, strong as nnn men.*

24 *He felt the weight of his wight, knew wyrd is wicked.*

25 *With his mirror I did mirror mere to mere*

26 *His thole was thus that he thanked the hel guard*

27 *When wailing the word weaver arrived a bletsian.*

The word *bletsian* died away, swallowed by the chant for the dead.

The drapes stirred as the heater kicked on. Outside, the trees shook their needled robes.

"Now, to some of the more difficult phrases," Evan said, still recording so that the police would have access to his thought process if needed. "*Skollfud's light*, for example. *By Skollfud's light I laid him low.* Not, as Rhinehart suggested, *by skull food lait. Skoll* is the name of the wolf in Viking poetry who will one day devour the sun goddess. So perhaps the killer named the sun *Skoll's food.* And since we know Talfour was placed by the river just before dawn, let's assume the killer meant morning's light, not daylight or evening."

He could hear Addie pushing back, questioning him. *Why didn't he just write* morning, *then, if that's what he meant?* she'd ask.

Because, he'd answer. *Old English poets loved riddles. They performed tricks with their words. Note how cleverly the killer took something generally considered positive—a sunrise—and turned it into a violent metaphor of a wolf devouring a goddess.*

A poet? Addie would ask.

Indeed. Make no mistake . . . our killer is a poet. Perhaps an indifferent one. But a poet nonetheless.

He circled back to line eighteen, with its anagrams. Almost immediately, he cried, "Yes!"

Ginny fluttered awake. Annoyed at his outburst, she shook her wings.

Now on his feet, Evan made his way to the bookcase still carrying the recorder. "But the Old English style of this poem confirms my suspicions. *Lendreg* is most definitely an anagram for the monster Grendel."

He gazed at the shelf that held his books of medieval poetry.

"For any listeners unfamiliar with *Beowulf,* it's the tale of a Viking hero who slays a terrible monster named Grendel. Later, Beowulf kills Grendel's mother, the second monster of the saga. And at the very end of the story, he slaughters a dragon and is himself mortally wounded. Heroic and tragic, all at once."

Ginny lifted a foot, studied the razor-sharp talons like a woman admiring her pedicure.

"Important for our purposes, Grendel is an *aglaeca*, a word that also appears in the killer's poem. It means *monster*. But ironically, the word is related to the later Middle English word *egleche*, which means *brave* and *warlike*. A contradiction that is, perhaps, indicative of our killer's mindset."

Evan stopped recording and raised his gaze to the windows, vaguely aware of the mist twining through the hedges in the knot garden and banking against the dormant lavender. Had he heard something? But it was only the chant for the dead, looping through a second time.

Once again, he tapped the "Record" button.

"Moreover, we have the word *bodulfr*. This word isn't an anagram. *Bodulfr* is the Icelandic word for *war wolf*. In the interest of saving time, I'll skip over the etymological variants that lead us from *boldulfr* to Beowulf. You'll have to trust me on that linguistic point. The important thing we need to know is that the killer is telling us he is both monster and monster slayer." He paused. "What are we to make of that?"

Ginny failed to look impressed by Evan's philological prowess.

And Evan, moving from the windows to the bookcases, failed to find his copies of *Beowulf*. He owned translations from Heaney, Tolkien, and Liuzza. All of them were gone.

"God's bones," Evan said. "I must have loaned them out." Although he had no recollection of doing so. Not that it was uncommon for him to forget. As much as he loved his books, he was often careless with them, relying on those who borrowed a title to be trustworthy about returning it.

As he scanned the nearby shelves, an old medieval curse rang in his head.

> Steal not this Book my honest friend
> For fear the gallows be your end
> For when you die the Lord will say
> Where is the book you stole away.

He reached in his pocket for his mobile, found only lint, and went hunting for the phone, eventually locating the cursed thing under Rhinehart's translation of the poem as if it had fled there of its own accord. As Evan stared down at Rhinehart's name at the top of the page, the thought of a scandal once again tickled at him. What was it?

Something surfaced, a small flare from the depths of his mind. Hadn't Rhinehart's parents been involved in the rare book trade? Had he taken over the business from them?

There was one person who could perhaps help him with both his missing books and the mystery of Mr. Ralph Rhinehart. As well as, perhaps, his patchwork memory of Viking Age history and cosmology. Evan dialed the number of his old friend and rare books dealer, Simon Levair.

"Evan, my dear friend," Simon cried when he answered. "Whatever do you need from me on this gloomy night?"

Evan smiled. "You have a suspicious mind, Simon Levair."

"The fact that it's after eight in the evening suggests that you're on the hunt for something. So tell me, what can I help you with?"

"Three things. *Beowulf*, Vikings, and Ralph Rhinehart."

"The first is a brilliant Old English poem with delightful kennings and alliterations, not to mention truly astounding poetic meter. And, of course, monsters and heroes, swords and shields. Even a cranky old dragon. Delightful."

"And the second thing?"

"Vikings are not my area of expertise."

"I'm shocked to hear you admit it," Evan said. "And the third?"

"Rhinehart?" Simon snorted. "A scumbag."

So memory serves. "I need a translation of *Beowulf*. Any version will do. Plus whatever you might have on hand about Vikings."

"I have two copies of the Heaney translation and one of Tolkien's at the shop," Simon told him. "Come by in the morning and take your pick. As for Vikings, I'll need to dig around a bit to see what I might have in my Old Norse section."

"Thank you. And Rhinehart?"

"A deceitful fellow who lives under a dark cloud of suspicion. What are you doing tangled up with him?"

With guilty cheer, Evan wrote the word *scumbag* under Rhinehart's name. "I'm afraid I can't talk about it. But I'd appreciate if you'd tell me what you know about him."

"Happy to. But it's a bit of a long tale. Can we chat tomorrow? At the moment I'm"—Simon's voice dropped low—"entertaining a lady friend."

"Oh." Evan swallowed his disappointment. Far be it from him to hamper his friend's love life. Simon had been a widower for seven years. The man was overdue for good company. "I'll come by your store as soon as you open in the morning."

"I'm always there by eight," Simon said. "I'll have the tea brewing."

Simon disconnected. The requiem had finished its second loop and moved on to a new set of chants; the wind filled the sudden silence, fluting a mournful dirge down the chimney. In the far distance, something banged and clattered. Evan's neighbor was doing some remodeling. Maybe a bit of sheet metal had gone astray.

He returned to his chair and picked up the pen.

"It will no doubt offend your sensibilities," he said once more to the faceless killer whom he imagined standing nearby, listening while Evan recorded. "But allow me to put a slightly modern twist on your word choice."

2 *Thus from my cottage I came, homeland's ward, for first of five*
3 *to sacrifice the innocent at night. She takes back her sons and daughters*
4 *who ripped and tore and peeled [her] flesh like ripe fruit*
9 *Blessing giver, my blood-feud stillbirths your further crimes*

10   *Listen up! Mighty men I undo and unto earth I send*
11   *their water-weighted corpses. I am a damned poet.*
12   *A death-driven river-plague, the mist that binds up evil.*
13   *A weary warrior wailing with the fateful man-price.*
14   *A slayer of the bone-halls breaking Fjorgyn.*
15   *You know why! Over the sun-swimmer home I came*
16   *for mine. Mine, mine-gone. Bowel-buried busted by big bosses.*
17   *That war-crime, sword-shaker, heart of my dwelling entombed,*
18   *making me Bodulfr, Grendel, and Fierce Enemy, all, bearing the*
     sun cross.
19   *What of this bone-cage? This skin-sinner is second of five.*
20   *At first light I laid him low. Unlucky is he and soon a ghost.*
21   *In guarding, I regard. Into his mouth of hearing I poured my mead.*
22   *Tell me! By moonlight I laid it out: tell me this. But*
23   *he gave no answer, so I held tight, strong as thirty men.*
24   *He felt the weight of his spirit, knew fate is wicked.*
25   *With his mirror I did mirror mere to mere.*
26   *His suffering was thus that he thanked the guardian of hell*
27   *when, wailing, the word-weaver arrived, a blood sacrifice.*

Evan capped the pen and frowned at the lines. The murderer's presence—nameless, faceless—lurked below the dense poetry of his words. An evil thing, like the dragon in *Beowulf*, skulking far below the earth during daylight, emerging at night to terrorize whoever crossed his vindictive path.

Absently, Evan picked up one of the Japanese puzzles and worked the rope through the rings. After a moment, he returned the puzzle to the table and murmured the poet's nineteenth line, *This skin-sinner is second of five.*

Desser had been *cattle of riding.* Or, once Evan had replaced the rune names with numbers, *first of five.*

He stared across the room toward Ginny and beyond her, through the windows, the storm-wet darkness.

"Dear God," he said. "He intends to murder five people."

Desser had been murdered twelve weeks earlier. Perhaps the killer planned to murder the third victim after an equal amount of time.

Or he could be accelerating, as many serial killers did. Especially given the leak to the newspapers.

How much time did they have?

And what was the significance of *five* victims? Why not nine, the number of Odin? Why not three or twelve or any other multiple of three? Five was the number for humanity, with our five fingers and toes, our five senses. It sometimes served as the symbol for grace. The Bible spoke of the five great mysteries—the holy trinity, the creation, and the redemption.

Five symbolized the balance between the spiritual world and the material one.

Did the killer require five victims to restore balance to a world that in his mind had fallen from grace? Was this the *fateful man-price* he spoke of in his poem? The price that must be paid for our sins?

Evan felt a sideways tug. A sideways slip. As if the old gods were stirring below the world. Old gods, old vengeances.

He crossed the room and turned on the gas fireplace. A welcoming burst of warmth and light rolled over him in a gentle wave. Chiding himself for being superstitious, he picked up his drink and rattled the ice cubes in his glass before swallowing the remains of the Old-Fashioned. He went into the kitchen to mix another cocktail. When he returned to the library, Ginny perched softly, hunched, drowsing in the warm firelight, her feathers muted and rumpled, like worn velvet.

He looked toward the table where earlier he'd placed the ring Officer Blakesley had brought him. It glowed gently in the pool of light from the task lamp. He picked it up, ran his fingertips over the etched runes. *God's spear. God* probably referred to Odin. So the words meant *Odin's soldier.*

His mind rubbed up against the coincidence of the dead birds and this runic ring in Washington Park and the slain man a few miles away.

Was there a link?

If so, where did the pre-Viking bog bodies fit in? What dark trails had the killer pursued back through centuries of history and then forward into the present to leave his murderous mark?

Evan sat down once more at the library table and pulled on his reading glasses. He opened Aldhouse-Green's book on bog bodies, which he'd thrown in his leather satchel that morning when Addie picked him up at his office. Once again, he turned to the color plates in the middle of the book. His attention was caught by the Windeby Child, naked and shaved, and then the reconstruction of the face of Yde Girl, who'd been murdered and placed in a bog in the Netherlands.

What commonality had the bog victims shared that marked them for death? What linked Desser and Talfour in a way that brought them to the attention of the killer?

Evan skimmed through the book. Many of the bog bodies had been mutilated before death. Arms amputated. Bones crushed. Facial disfigurement. A great many others showed signs of congenital differences that would have caused them great misery in their daily life. Severe spinal curvature. Malformed hips. He paused on a page that described the Zweeloo Woman from a peat bog in the Netherlands. She'd suffered from severe limb deformities, which scientists concluded were due to dyschondrosteosis—a rare form of dwarfism.

Evan looked at his own limbs and imagined being led through the treacherous quicksand to his death. Stumbling forward in the mist, torches tossing smoky light while, all around, the trees creaked and cackled in the dark, boggy woods in which Iron Age people hid their secrets and their shame. He pictured himself standing, naked and bound, on the water's edge while the raised ax caught the flame.

He shuddered. He had a particular aversion to lakes and quicksand. How much sooner would his head sink beneath the murky depths than that of a man of average height?

He looked again at the photograph of the Yde Girl, whose spine had been so severely curved from a congenital condition that she would have spent her entire short life in constant pain. She looked no more than eight or nine. A mere child.

For a brief moment, he thought of Jo. This little girl slain in the bog, the Yde Girl, had been someone's much-loved daughter. Perhaps a sister and a friend. Then she'd been knifed, had half her hair ripped from her scalp, and strangled.

For the crime of her physical differences?

When his phone buzzed in his pocket, he jumped, sloshing his drink onto his sweater.

"Damn it," he said. Then realizing that it was now past seven in the morning in Turkey, he grabbed it.

"River?"

"Lake." It was Addie. "Are we playing a word game?"

"Addie." He removed his readers and rubbed his eyes. "Aren't you and Claymore doing something?"

"Clayton. And no. His client changed his mind and insisted they meet. Vitally important and all that. He probably thinks there's some political embarrassment looming on the horizon, and he needs Clayton to help circle the wagons." She paused. "Why do I live in Chicago? I hate politics."

"I'm sorry about the date."

"Don't be. It's nothing."

He heard the disappointment in her voice, and it made his own heart ache.

Outside, the rain turned heavy, thrumming on the roof like an orchestra of demonic drummers.

"Anyway," she said, "I'm on my way to check something out, and I thought I'd see how you were doing on the profile."

"I'm making good progress. I'll have something tomorrow."

"How about giving me the movie-trailer version?"

"My biggest discovery is that I believe the killer intends to murder five people." He told her about the phrases *cattle of riding* and *ox of riding* and how he'd replaced the nonsense words with the numbers of the runes they stood for. "Desser was the first victim, cattle of riding or first of five. And Talfour the second."

"And the third victim? He would be what?"

"They would be *thorn of riding*."

"Dear God," she whispered.

They contemplated this. Then she said, "Why five victims?"

"I don't know. At least, not yet. Why don't you come over?" Evan jiggled the Viking ring in his palm. "You'll want the rest of the details. I'll make you a drink and whip up something to eat."

"Actually, since you're still up and about, I have something else in mind," Addie said.

For a moment, his thoughts raced down R-rated paths. He shifted in his chair. "You do?"

"I do," she said. "There's a guy I really want to check out."

"You do?"

"Yup."

He smiled.

She said, "A man who is, apparently, the leader of a local group that calls itself Aryan Ásatrú."

Ah, the overeager male ego. A steel gate rolled across the trail leading to his brief fantasy.

He set down the ring, carried his drink over to the window, and watched the wind shiver and sway the densely needled white pines; the lower branches of the trees swept the ground like the skirts of nuns.

"How do you intend to, as you say, check him out?" he asked.

"I'm on my way to scope out his place now," Addie said. "Why don't you come with me? I'll swing by and get you."

"Sounds like a blast, but . . . no. Thanks," Evan said. "The weather is ghastly."

"I rather like it." She sighed. "Fair-weather friend."

"Dark and stormy isn't usually your thing."

"It is tonight." Another sigh. "What else do you have besides the number of victims?"

Evan told her what else he'd determined so far. That the killer might have some connection to archaeology, given the way he'd so closely duplicated ancient bog bodies. That he also—as Evan had suspected—must possess a decent knowledge of Old English poetry. "Certainly he understands the use of meter and alliteration. And kennings, I believe, more specifically. And that it is *Beowulf*—"

"What"—Addie's voice cut in—"is alliteration?"

"The repetition of sounds, usually beginning consonants. Thus we have phrases like *busted by big bosses* and the repetition of the *un* sound in *undo* and *unto*."

"Memories of high school English classes are trickling back."

"That's good, isn't it?"

"It's more like a headache, really. What about kennings? What are those?"

"Compound words or phrases. The Viking poets loved them. They'd use *whale-road* in place of *ocean*. Or *sea-wood* for *ship*. With our particular poet, we have *sun-swimmer* and *bone-cage*."

"What do those mean?"

"I'm still in the research phase. Now, as I was saying, I believe our killer is specifically referencing the Old English poem *Beowulf*."

"I thought *Beowulf* was a movie. Doesn't Anthony Hopkins play the king? Angelina Jolie was in it, too. She was a monster or something."

"Then at least you know the story."

"I didn't watch it."

"Stream it when you get a chance. But centuries before *Beowulf* hit the big screen, it was a blockbuster poem."

"What's it about? Tell me in five words."

"Man battles monsters and dies."

"Bravo. And was it written in runes?"

"No. But it's about Vikings."

"And our killer thinks he's, what, part of the story?"

"His poem suggests he sees himself as both Grendel and Beowulf. I should be able to tell you more tomorrow. Something seems to have happened to all three of my translations of *Beowulf*."

Addie was silent, no doubt turning all this over in her mind.

"What did you say his name was?" Evan asked. "This Ásatrú leader?"

"Sorry. It's Hank Helskin."

"Hold on. Did you say Helskin?"

"You've heard of him?"

Evan filled her in on what he'd learned about Hank Helskin and his crew at Ragnarök Axes.

"It's got to be the same man!" Addie exclaimed. "Helskin's Ásatrú and a reenactor. *And* an ax thrower. Remember that Talfour's skull was broken with a sharp instrument."

"It's almost certainly the same man," Evan agreed. "But that doesn't make him our killer. Our murderer is smart. And meticulous. Helskin's crew sound more like slipshod Viking reenactors and neo-Nazi Neanderthals. Odious. Possibly even violent. Certainly capable of co-opting the Ásatrú religion to serve their vile purposes. But I can't see them writing Old English poetry—not even mediocre Old English poetry. And I doubt they'd know a bog body if one rang the front bell."

"But Rhinehart said the killer was Ásatrú."

"He did. And maybe he's right." Evan tried to hide his skepticism. He knew Addie needed to keep an open mind. "But men like Helskin don't fit the profile. Not based on what I know of him so far, anyway.

They're too disorganized. If they're slapdash in how they portray themselves as Vikings, I doubt they'd be so painstaking with a corpse. Or be knowledgeable enough to have written the poetry. That writing suggests someone deeply immersed in Nordic culture and Old English literature. Not a casual Viking wannabe."

"He's still my top person of interest."

"I understand. And according to Diana, there is a member of the group who is perhaps smarter and more serious about the whole Viking thing. A guy they call Raven, presumably because of his tattoo. There might be something there."

"Even better."

Evan took a healthy swallow of his drink, returned to the table, and stared at the version of the poem he'd written out. *Hell.*

"Evan?"

"Give me a second."

He picked up his pen, slashed out one of the letters he'd added to line twenty-six.

"Addie," he said.

"Hmm?"

"You're not planning on doing anything rash, are you?"

"What do you mean?"

"You're just driving by Helskin's house, right? You're not going to pay a visit."

"Not unless I see him dragging a body around his front yard. Why?"

"Viking poets—or scops, as they were called in England—loved to include riddles in their poetry. A favorite type of riddle was to hide someone's true name."

"Okay," she said. "But what does this have to do with me driving by Helskin's house tonight?"

"When Rhinehart translated the poem, he wrote h-e-l-l."

"Okay."

"I did the same thing just now," Evan said. "But the proper line is as follows: *His suffering was thus that he thanked the hel guard. Hel* with one *l*. Pronounced like *heal*. Hel is the Viking underworld."

"And you think maybe the *hel* in the poem refers to Helskin? That the killer planted that as a clue?" Her voice had risen with her excitement, each word like a bird soaring into the ether. "It seems—" Her voice dropped. "It seems . . . subtle."

"Subtle is what the scops were all about. Imagine a world without movies or television or computers or smartphones. Your sole source of entertainment was stories. What made a scop's story better than your grandmother's folktales was not just the poetry of his lines. It was the riddles contained *inside* the lines. And all the inside jokes that a Viking audience would appreciate. And which we have little hope of understanding."

"Give me your best guess, Evan. Does the word *hel* refer to Helskin?"

Evan's eyes swept through the lines of the poem again, searching. There it was, in line nineteen. *Skin-sinner. This skin-sinner is second of five.* He palmed the back of his neck. Was this another possible clue? Had the killer buried his own name in his poem? Was Helskin their killer? Had someone committed an offense against the man and paid for it with his life?

"Evan? Is he naming Helskin?"

"I don't know." He was uncomfortable with the idea of Helskin or his crew as sophisticated killers. "We also have the word *skin*. But that and the poet's use of *hel* could be a coincidence. Regardless, why not wait until daylight? Go with Patrick. And backup. Arrest the man for being an offense against humanity. That's a crime, isn't it?"

"No, no, we're onto something. Helskin was in Talfour's shop. He wanted a custom ring. A ring carved with the runes for Odin's thane, whatever that means."

"Addie, I have a runic ring." He told her about the ring that the officers had found in the park. "This one says *God's spear*. Perhaps our Viking Poet killer was in Washington Park."

"The Viking Poet killer," she murmured. "It has a ring to it. So get this. When Helskin came into the shop, he was wearing a vest with the double lightning bolts that Rhinehart mentioned. The next day, one of Talfour's attackers was caught on camera wearing the same vest."

The wind hurled fistfuls of rain at the windows. Ginny shook herself awake, eyeing Evan with irises that glowed in the shadows.

"And—*and*—" Now Addie's voice was a rush, water spilling over rocks. "Helskin has a tattoo on his hand that sounds like a sun cross. The employee he talked to at the store is supposed to be sending me a sketch. I thought I'd have it by now."

"Give me a call when you do."

"How about I tell you in person? I'm just a few miles from your house. I figured you'd change your mind and want to go with me."

"What? I most certainly do not."

"It will be fun. Or at least not boring."

Evan sighed. "You are *not* considering roping me into going with you on a drive-by at midnight through what I feel confident is an unsavory neighborhood."

"Why not?"

"Because I know you well enough to realize that when you say drive-*by*, you probably mean pulling into their driveway and ringing the doorbell. Inviting yourself in for a little chin-wag. The very idea is insane."

Ginny winked one golden eye at him. Then the other.

"Sanity is overrated," Addie said. "I promise we won't ring any doorbells. And we definitely won't do any chin-wagging, whatever that is. But you're our consultant. I want your professional opinion."

"Of his *house*?" he asked. "Are you restless, Addie? Or merely bored?"

"I'm detecting," she snapped.

"It has just this instant become clear to me."

"What has?"

"You've developed a death wish because Claymore stood you up."

There came a long pause. Then Addie said, "If you're psychoanalyzing me, Professor, you might as well add that I've not only been stood up by the man of my dreams, I'm also pissed at half the men I work with, including my boss, who think women should fetch coffee and take notes at meetings and make themselves available for the occasional friendly grope."

"I didn't mean—"

"That isn't who I am."

"I know! I just wanted to—"

She stormed on. "So maybe this *is* about my ego. Maybe my ego is worth defending. Plus, we have two dead men. Two. Dead. Men. Or did you forget about them?"

With three more on the way.

He waited until he was sure she'd run out of steam, then said, "I'm sorry the world isn't fair, Addie. I'm sorry that you have to keep proving yourself when you've already proven yourself a hundred times over. You deserve better."

She growled. Then sniffed. "So do you."

"Yes, well. To borrow a trite but appropriate cliché, we do the best we can with the hand we're dealt."

"And the best hand I've got right now is Helskin and his link to Talfour. I promise I'm just going to drive by his house. See where the creep lives. What cars are parked in his driveway so I can run the plates. Maybe find some violation that lets me bring him in for questioning during business hours. I'm asking you to go with me because you're my best friend. And"—there came an audible sniff—"I could really use your company right now."

Cue the big guns and the cavalry. Addie could play him like a fiddle. And, mostly, he didn't care. What was sacrificing life and limb against the wishes of one Adrianne Marie Bisset?

"Come on, Evan," she said. "You're the one who's always telling me that you like to see suspects in their personal world. The *signs* they choose to have around them. Now's your chance. Aren't you at least a little curious? Oh!"

"Oh?"

"Rachel Chen just sent me her drawing of Helskin's tattoo. I'm forwarding it to you now. Open your email."

Evan complied. He stared at the image and, with a scholar's detached interest, noted how his body reacted to the image. The hair rose on the back of his neck. His chest muscles tightened. His mouth fell open until he forced it closed.

"Are you looking at it?" Addie said.

"It's a specific type of sun cross known as a black cross."

"Ha! Was it used by the Nazis?"

"It was certainly used by Heinrich Himmler, Hitler's head of the *Schutzstaffel* and the chief architect of the Holocaust, as Rhinehart mentioned. He incorporated the design when he remodeled the Wewelsburg castle for use by the *Schutzstaffel*, the SS. He drew the outer circle and the inner dot, then connected them with a series of the sigel runes. Just as we see here, in your witness's drawing."

"What about neo-Nazis? Do they use it?"

"The symbol is very popular with them. But—" He forced his shoulders down. Took a deep breath.

"But what?"

"Neo-Nazis aren't the only group who uses it."

"Evan," she groaned.

"It is also used by Nazi occultists."

"Like Rhinehart mentioned."

"And by the Church of Satan."

"Oh," Addie said. "That rather expands the pool of suspects."

In the library, the monks continued chanting their sacred songs. The fire hissed. The house creaked as the wind swept along the walls and over the roof, rattling windows and testing doors.

"So," Addie said after a moment. "Do you really have something better to do than go with me to Helskin's?"

He shook off his mood. "There's the profile I'm supposed to be writing."

"You can work on it in the car."

"I could also sleep. Or read. Maybe sort all the loose screws in my toolbox."

"You don't have a toolbox."

"Every man has a toolbox. It's a requirement. Like facial hair and testosterone."

"In that case," she said, "man up."

"Addie—"

His phone beeped and went silent. He stared at it, wondering if she'd hung up on him or if they'd been disconnected.

Probably the former. Addie was good at getting in the last word.

A moment later, the soothing Gregorian chants he'd been playing all evening cut off. The opening strains of "Ride of the Valkyries" poured through the in-house speakers in a rising swoop of violins. The volume rose and rose as if the speakers were possessed. Evan covered his ears.

Panicked at the noise, Ginny opened her beak and began to bate—flapping her wings and attempting to flee before the line brought her up short. She fell from her perch and hung upside down, a helpless flutter of feathers.

Evan raced toward her as the Valkyries gave full throat to their battle cry.

CHAPTER 18

"No!" Addie shouted in frustration when her phone died.

She reached into the glove box, fumbling around for the phone's car charger. When she plugged in her phone and the screen lit up, she called Evan back.

Her call went to voice mail.

"Come on, Evan."

She tapped his name again. Still voice mail.

He'd probably used the opportunity given by her dead battery to wander off in search of a drink and left his phone behind. Again. Evan and his classic absentminded-professor woolgathering that sometimes drove her so far up the cliff, she swore she could smell jet fuel. One of these days, she was going to staple his cell phone to his ear. She pulled up to the gate to his drive and jumped out into the rain. Without bothering with the intercom, she entered the code and hurried back into the cab of her Jeep as the gate swung open.

The drive along the road winding up to Evan's home was one Addie usually enjoyed. The sweeping scenery, the sense of having stepped fully away from the city and into nature. But the storm had turned the landscape eerie; an angry wind lashed the elegant trees, and broken branches littered the road.

A few moments later, the house came into view. The outdoor lights glistened in the rain; inside the house, a handful of lamps glowed softly.

She parked near the front door. As soon as she exited her SUV, her ears were assaulted by the screeching of an orchestra and the apparent death yelps of a group of women, all going at a volume well beyond what should be humanly possible.

That gave her momentary pause. What was Evan up to now? Then she hurried forward, eager to get out of the weather.

Her glittering green stilettos skidded on the damp stones, and she removed them. She didn't bother ringing the doorbell. Evan wouldn't be able to hear anything over the music. She reached up to enter the code on the pin pad that would deactivate the alarm and was startled to see the light glowing red. Had Evan forgotten to set the security system? It wouldn't be unlike him.

She bent to place her shoes on the porch and spotted a small figurine, a doll-like shape made of sticks and twine propped against the door. Its painted eyes stared blankly into the night.

That is one creepy doll. With her next thought, she wondered who could have left it there.

She moved the doll aside, set her shoes on the step, and tested the door. Locked. She entered the code, and this time, the handle turned.

Chiding herself for being paranoid, she drew her gun from her purse and hurried into the foyer.

Inside the house, the music came as a physical assault. Its battle cry rolled out from the hidden speakers like an unstoppable formation of tanks.

She ran lightly down the hall in her bare feet.

At the kitchen, she paused, pivoting from the doorway to scan the dimly lit space—she took in the opened bottle of whiskey on the counter, the crush of rosemary, and a peel of orange nearby—and then moved on into the house, clearing each room as she passed.

Other than the alcohol and a lingering scent of baked bread, there was no evidence Evan had even been here. Only the madness of the music, going on and on until her ears rang.

In the library, a fire burned. The remains of a drink sat on a table next to Evan's notes, which were laid out across the table's surface. Addie spotted Ginny's perch—empty—and a dismaying number of feathers dusting the ground below.

Her phone vibrated in her pocket. She yanked the phone free.

I've taken Ginny to the mews. If you've reached the house, you'll know why. Can't turn off the music.

She closed her eyes for an instant. He was fine. Of course he was. Sometimes the fact that she was paid to be paranoid was *not* helpful.

Be right there, she texted back.

She made her way back through the house to the french doors that opened onto the rear deck and the intricate knot garden beyond. The mews stood some distance farther, hidden by the slope that angled downward past the garden. Addie unclipped the flashlight she kept hooked to her keys, a powerful LED torch that was also, fortunately, waterproof. Because by now, the rain was coming so hard that it felt as if someone had upended Lake Michigan and shaken it out over the city.

She slipped outside, closing the door behind her. The volume of the music fell to that of a college dorm party.

She flicked on the flashlight. The wooden deck gleamed with moisture. Straight ahead, shadows leapt and slithered in the knot garden with its square hedges and blind corners. Evan loved the garden. But the tall boxwood made Addie think of the maze in Stephen King's *The Shining*; she half expected a man with an ax to leap out at her, swinging for her chest.

Now she skirted the garden on its west side, running along a narrow path between the hedges and a thick forest of winter-shorn trees. Her bare feet found every stone and root. Lower branches scratched her face, clawing for her eyes. On her right, the hedges kept a menacing pace, like a square-shouldered enemy force.

At the crest of the low hill, she hesitated, her breath coming hard. The trail led down to a large rectangular building—the mews. The mews had two rooms, a storage closet for equipment, and an outdoor weathering yard. A single door faced south. Five barred windows— designed to let Ginny enjoy the light and the view without tempting her to flee—were arranged on one end. More barred windows on the roof let in light and—when hinged opened—the elements. Evan had explained that because hawks depend on their sight more than any other sense, they need to be able to see out. But they also require a place where they can retreat and not be seen.

A single light fell through the slats on the south-side windows and patterned the dark.

She skidded down the slope, rehearsing in her mind the scolding she'd give Evan for whatever carelessness had diverted his music system into its martial assault. Not to mention what the rain had done to her dress.

A sharp sound broke her out of her reverie. The snap of a branch somewhere up ahead.

She played her light over the still-distant building. There! A form— little more than a shadow, standing by the door.

"Hey!" she shouted.

The shadow shifted, and her light caught something pale—skin or clothing—before the shadow moved away from the building and broke into a sprint, racing across the grass, heading east to where there was a small pond and more gardens and then a high fence.

She bounded the rest of the way down the wet hillside in awkward leaps, trying to keep her light trained on the fleeing figure.

"Stop!" she shouted. "Police!"

The figure kept running.

With the image of the stick-and-twine figure in her mind, she stopped and raised her gun, then just as quickly lowered it. Leaving a doll—no matter how ugly—on someone's front step was hardly a capital offense. And for all she knew, she'd be firing on the gardener. Or a neighbor.

She skidded to a halt at the building's single door, grabbed the doorknob, and twisted. The door was locked. She punched in the code on the keypad, and this time the knob turned soundlessly. She let herself inside.

Ginny was on a high perch, preening herself. Evan sat nearby, thumbing through something on his phone. He looked up as Addie came in.

"Sorry about the noise," he said. "I was just scrolling through an online edition of *Beowulf*. Not a great translation."

She closed and locked the door behind her. "Did you know you just had a visitor?"

"What do you mean?"

"Someone was standing at the door to the mews. And, Evan, there's a super-weird doll on your doorstep."

"A doll?"

"Just a bunch of twigs tied together, really. But there's something creepy about it. Did you piss off one of your students? Someone who has the code to your gate?"

A series of expressions swept across Evan's face—surprise, concern, unease. But he settled on an expression of disinterest and shrugged. "Anything is possible. Did you scare off the intruder?"

"For the moment."

"Well, I can't speak to the doll." He stood and stretched. "But that might have been Jo you saw at the door. Sometimes she comes through our properties to visit Ginny. Strictly without her parents' permission. I've told her to always call ahead, but tonight she was disappointed that—Addie, are you okay?"

Addie's heart felt like it had just flatlined. She leaned against the door as her legs went weak. She nodded at Evan, but she wasn't anything like okay. Had she really aimed her gun at a little girl? Was this what happened to a cop who spent all day hunting killers?

"Let's go back to the house," Evan said. "I'll get you a drink."

Addie looked down and saw that her hands were shaking. She shoved them in her pockets. "The music," she managed.

"That *is* a problem. I've called the company that installed the system. They've promised to get back to me."

She managed to push herself upright. The bottoms of her feet throbbed. "You run the music off an app, don't you?"

"I've tried everything. It—"

"Delete it."

"Really? You think—"

"Please." Her hands balled into fists. "Just try it. Or I'm going to go back up there and take a sledgehammer to your walls until I find the speakers and rip them out by their little wires."

"Ah, the rational approach."

Evan tapped a couple of times on his phone's screen, and a moment later, the only sound filling the night was the rain, quieter now, gentling onto the ceiling of the mews. Ginny gave a contented squeak, the shake of her feathers a soft rustle like the turning of old pages.

"And here," Evan said, "I thought I was the brain and you merely the beauty."

Addie growled.

CHAPTER 19

An hour later, and before he was entirely sure how she'd corralled him, Evan found himself yawning and shivering with Addie in the front seat of her SUV.

After Evan had locked up the mews and they'd returned to the quiet of his house, he had gone out front and retrieved the wooden figure. He'd stuck it in the entryway closet and promised Addie he would change his security codes. His thoughts had gone briefly to Officer Blakesley—the person most recently at his front door. But it was hard to imagine that a man on his way to a poker party was dropping off creepy dolls. He could dismiss the two figurines he'd received as the bizarre gesture of an irate student trying to give him a scare, someone who had been up to his house at some point for an end-of-semester party. But that wouldn't explain the figure Sten had found outside Ragnarök.

Another mystery in a day filled with them.

The doll taken care of for the moment, he and Addie changed into dry clothes—she kept an extra pair of sweats and a toothbrush at Evan's for when she crashed in the guest room—and she had helped herself to Evan's bottle of ibuprofen. She'd turned down his offer of a drink and a seat by the fire and hustled him into the front seat of her Jeep.

"We have work to do," she'd snapped over his loud protests. "Aren't you just a little spooked that your stereo was playing *Viking* music? Don't you want to know if Helskin is responsible?"

"I fail to see how driving by his house will enlighten us in that regard. That's assuming he even gave the correct address on that form."

"Shut up and fasten your seat belt." She slammed the door.

Now, a quick half hour later, they sat parked in a Southeast Side neighborhood of mostly post-WWII frame houses strung along streets of half-assed landscaping, broken streetlamps, and chain-link fences. Assorted detritus filled many of the yards—sun-faded plastic lawn furniture, cracked garden hoses, old tires. Maybe Helskin was a descendant of the people who had once worked in the mills. Maybe he was a vagrant. Maybe they were on a wild-goose chase.

Addie had killed the headlights even before she turned the corner, and now she pulled to the curb in front of a house with a foreclosure sign stuck into the front lawn. The location placed them across the street and a couple of houses down from the Helskin residence and gave them a clear view of his house.

In the front yard, despite the wet weather and the lateness of the hour, a rousing keg party was going down. Seven or eight men—it was hard to tell in the dark and the shadows—sat around a small firepit or moved in and out of the decrepit house. They were obnoxiously drunk and loud, their voices carrying in the autumn air. Nothing stirred in the rest of the neighborhood, not so much as the twitch of a curtain. If Helskin's neighbors were complaining, they were calling in their concerns to the police rather than voicing them directly.

Evan thought that wise of them.

He comforted himself with the thought that, given the amount of alcohol circulating, the men would be unlikely to notice two people sitting quietly in a dark SUV.

"Nice night for a party," he said.

"And you thought there'd be nothing to see." Addie sounded smug.

So much for the simple drive-by, he thought. When Addie turned off the engine, he said, "What are you doing? No engine, no heat."

"Can't have any exhaust showing. Not when you're running a stakeout."

"I feel obliged to point out that it's an unreasonable two degrees Celsius."

"How cold is that in Fahrenheit?"

"Not terrible if you're a polar bear. We mere humans might lose a few fingers."

"Wuss," she said in a voice that completely lacked sympathy.

"I must also point out that we won't be any use to this investigation if we're dead from pneumonia."

"Poor baby." Her voice turned slightly softer. "There's a blanket in the back seat."

Evan decided to man up, as Addie had suggested earlier in the evening, and make do with his coat and hat.

The wind and rain had stopped. A bruised-purple night pressed against the windows; the only light in the neighborhood came from Helskin's home, a split-level eyesore that even at night looked downtrodden and ill-kempt. Four trucks filled the driveway. Addie took a small pair of binoculars out of the console and ran the license plate on the nearest vehicle—a late-model black pickup with a Michigan plate. It came back registered to Helskin. She jotted down the license plate numbers of the others.

Evan peered past her shoulder. "How can you even see the plates, much less the numbers? Even with binoculars?"

"Carrots," she said. "Beta-carotene. And a lot of practice." She ran the plates, then frowned and harrumphed and frowned again.

"Not good?" Evan asked.

"Nothing but lousy traffic violations." She scrolled through the screen. "Although back in Michigan, Helskin's neighbors filed multiple noise complaints against him."

"Clearly the record of a violent psychopath," Evan said.

She sulked. "People change."

"We can only hope," Evan muttered. "Why don't you see if his name shows up in any poetry magazines?"

From outside, a roar of laughter infiltrated the Jeep's windows. At least in regard to annoying his neighbors, Helskin had decided to continue his old ways.

"Stop breathing so much," Addie said.

"I beg your pardon?"

"You're fogging the windows."

"I'm not breathing hard. I'm shivering. I forgot my long underwear and my insulated snowsuit."

"Think of the cold as a way to get inside the killer's mind. Like you do when you're creating a profile."

"I fail to see the connection."

"Vikings had to be impervious to the cold, right? Or at least used to it. And these creeps clearly aren't bothered. Now focus and tell me what you see."

"Trouble," he said. "Beyond that, I can hardly see them."

She grumbled something at him about using his God-given eyes. As she shifted in her seat, Evan noticed her high-heeled shoes—a shimmering green contrivance designed for a runway model.

"Nice shoes," he said. "They go well with the sweatpants."

Her glare could stop an army in its tracks. "Shut up."

He looked at his own shoes—sensible sneakers readily visible because his feet didn't reach the floor—and was struck by the realization that if he were a woman, he'd almost certainly spend the day tottering about on high heels, just for the pleasure of a few more inches.

And also for the fact that while stilettos were unquestionably designed as instruments of torture, they turned a woman's calves into a gentle invitation for a closer look. At least to the lecherous mind of the healthy male animal.

Call him shallow. Sometimes, it was true.

They both resumed staring through the windows.

The men visible in the firelight were heavily built. Most sported beards. Some of them had shaved heads while others wore their hair long. The amount of ink on their exposed skin—faces and necks and hands—was a tattoo artist's wet dream. Or at least a ticket to early retirement. The men reminded Evan of the toughs who'd lived in a neighborhood a mile from his childhood home. Throughout his youth, he'd had nightmares about accidentally stumbling into that stretch of streets and meeting a scarcely imaginable fate at the hands of men who were opposed to the idea that the meek—or the different—were entitled to any patch of earth whatsoever.

If those teens had caught him, they'd have eaten him as a bit of teatime pastry and used his bones to clean their teeth.

Now Evan shifted miserably in his seat. Watching the sheer brawn and coiled energy of the men in Helskin's front yard made those old nightmares feel fresh. Only the hair and the tattoos had changed. The simmering violence remained.

Focus on the matter at hand, he told himself.

The chairs pulled around the fire were a motley assortment of folding lawn chairs, kitchen stools, and beat-up recliners. Four men waved cigarettes around as they talked; two more passed a bong back and forth. Everyone held plastic cups they kept filled from a keg on the porch. A flag with the image of Thor's hammer was nailed to the front wall under a dim porch light, and the mailbox boasted what might be a Viking Valknut reflector decal.

"Do you know what's criminal about these men?" he asked Addie.

"Their very existence?"

"They give Vikings a bad name. The Viking Age culture. The Viking people. Their intricate and deeply developed spiritual beliefs. These men ruin all of it."

She nodded. "Too bad cultural misappropriation isn't an arrestable offense."

Two dogs clipped to heavy chains trotted restlessly at the edge of the firelight and now and again added their voices to the din, barking in excitement. Whenever they did, someone kicked them, evoking a yelp and a retreat to the porch.

The dogs looked to be barely smaller than well-fed cougars. Addie would be a light meal to them. Evan a mere kipper snack.

"Creeps," Addie murmured to herself.

"Are they dire wolves?" He had Odin on the brain. Or rather, Odin's wolves, Geri and Freki.

"They're American pit bulls." She let loose a puff of air. "Why are they so keyed up?"

"Because they smell human flesh?"

"Something's going on. Don't you wonder why Helskin and his creepy friends are partying in the *front* yard?"

"Because they can?"

"If it weren't for the trees around the back, we could take a look. But I'll bet you ten to one they use the backyard as a dogfighting pit. Or a place to pen the animals when they aren't fighting. The dogs are probably expecting mortal combat."

Evan frowned. Maybe it was paranoia, but one of the men seemed to be staring at them, as if he'd just noticed Addie's SUV. If they drove away right now . . . He wondered if pit bulls had the canines and jaw strength necessary to puncture tires. He looked it up on Google. The answer was *no problemo*.

"We should come back tomorrow," he said. "With agents from animal control. So we can rescue the poor dogs."

"We?"

"Well, you. And Patrick, of course. And the agents."

"You need to learn to relax."

Evan rarely pointed out the obvious, but now seemed like a good time. "One of these men might be a killer. Or even several of them. My nascent profile could be completely wrong."

"Posh."

"Tosh," Evan said. "You mean *tosh*. *Posh* is acting upper-class. Which these gentlemen definitely are not. *Tosh* means nonsense. And it isn't. Any one of them could be our killer."

"When was the last time you got a profile wrong?"

"It will come to me. Preferably as we're driving away."

"What's that guy up to?" Addie adjusted the focus on the binoculars as one of the men wandered to the side of the house.

"I shudder to think."

At least the man who'd been staring at them had relaxed in his chair and was laughing at something one of his pals said. One of the men tossed a log onto the fire, and as the flames flared, the men's faces became clearer. They all looked to be in their late teens or twenties and capable of deadlifting a cement truck.

The man on the side of the house unzipped his pants and peed into the weeds.

"Savages," Addie murmured.

"Now you're starting to see things my way."

She passed the binoculars to him. "Look closely and see if any of them look like a serial killer."

Evan studied each man's face. He saw anger and stupidity and malice. And on the face of one of the men, in the shadow of the man's hoodie, something that resembled his idea of evil incarnate. The malevolent expression flashed briefly before the man returned his attention to the fire, poking it with a stick, his folded-in posture that of a man stuck in a boring high school class.

"It's hard to be sure in the dark." He returned the binoculars. "But then, serial killers don't usually wear a T-shirt advertising their proclivities."

"Okay." She pulled up an image on her phone and showed it to him. "This is Helskin. From his DMV photo. What do you think about him?"

A man with an expression that managed to be both malicious and bland stared into the camera. Long light-brown hair braided and trimmed shorter on the sides, a thick beard, flat brown eyes. A brow like the overhang on a cliff and lips as thin as the line between confidence and arrogance. Evan recognized the man in the DMV photo as one of the men at the fire.

"I think he looks just stupid enough to believe he can kill people and get away with it," he said. "But I'd lay odds he had nothing to do with the deaths of Talfour and Desser. Sophisticated and ritualistic murders like that are way out of his wheelhouse."

"Okay." Addie lowered the binoculars halfway. "That's okay. Elimination is part of an investigation. So on to our next question. Do Helskin or any of the others look like men who sit around thinking about rhyme and meter and composing odes to the gods?"

"Given the aforementioned stupidity, I'd say they're more of the limerick-on-the-bathroom-wall type. Why don't you roll down your window and shout 'Beowulf' and see if any of them look interested?"

She reached over and smacked his knee. "Couldn't these guys be, I don't know, underlings? After all, one of them wanted a ring that sounds exactly like the ring the officers found in the park. We can't just ignore that."

"It's possible that they're minions of some sort," Evan agreed. "But we need to remember that Viking culture is hugely popular right now. Most of the people walking around Chicago could probably pick Odin and Thor out of a lineup."

"You always tell me to trust my gut. And my gut tells me these guys are linked to our case."

But Evan shook his head. "What you're most likely experiencing is the human tendency to see patterns and connections, even where none exist. It's how we simplify and manage our world. Which is perfectly understandable. But it can also obscure the truth."

"Seeing patterns and making connections is pretty much my job description. Mix it in with an appropriate level of paranoia, and presto, you have a murder cop." Addie lowered the binoculars to her lap and cupped her hands together, warming them with her breath. "These men are linked—violently linked—to Talfour. They're heavy into Viking culture. They aren't exactly upstanding citizens."

"Then arrest them for Talfour's assault," Evan said. "Helskin's obviously a neo-Nazi in love with Viking symbols. Somewhere in that house is probably a vest with the double sigel runes, which would help link him to the attack on Talfour. But he's not a poet, and he's not our murderer. We can go home now, and you can come back tomorrow to arrest Talfour's muggers with a phalanx of officers and some dog rescuers. Or at least Patrick. And speaking of Patrick, why isn't he here? Shouldn't he be part of this?"

"Patrick goes to bed at nine. Like any man from solid farmer stock."

"A wise man."

"Let's give it one more hour."

"I need my beauty rest."

"One hour." In the faint amber glow from the dash, she handed him a thermos. "Here's something to keep you awake."

"Tea?" he asked hopefully.

"We're in America."

"Coffee, then." Disappointed, he unscrewed the cap. The aroma of strong, fresh tea rose into the air.

Addie grinned at him. "Would I force my best friend into going on a stakeout with me and then serve him anything but tea? I'll admit the tea is from McDonald's—they filled the thermos for me. But there's milk in the bag on the floor behind you."

"You planned this before you even *asked* me to go?"

"I knew I'd be convincing."

She usually was. "Are there digestives?" His favorite cookie was McVitie's Digestives. Which, properly, should be McVitie's Digestive *Biscuits*. But he wasn't one to quibble.

"No cookies," Addie said. "Just my sweet self."

"That's good enough." Newly content, he poured a bit of milk into the Styrofoam cup she offered, then added the steaming ambrosia. He handed the thermos back to Addie and took a sip of the tea. The brew was perfect. Perfect enough for McDonald's, anyway.

He and Addie fell back into silence and resumed watching the party, which appeared to be quieting down as the minutes ticked by. The dogs settled under the porch. The men sat silently, nursing their beers, their faces slack. One man leaned back in a recliner and closed his eyes.

Evan finished his tea. A wave of sleepiness washed over him despite the caffeine. His eyelids lowered like a pair of shades pulled by an anchor.

"Something's happening," Addie said.

Evan's eyes popped open, and he bolted upright.

Helskin and one of the other men now leaned forward in their chairs, glaring at each other. The flames lit their faces orange and made their eyes shine. Helskin's adversary was he of the evil expression and fire-poking stick. The man's hoodie fell back, and Evan noticed a raven tattooed on his forehead, its wings outspread, its wedge-shaped tail and clawed feet clearly visible.

That has to be Diana's Raven. The one she claimed radiated evil.

He said as much to Addie.

"Doesn't everyone stare at Diana?" Addie asked. But she sat up, her shoulders tense.

The two men leapt to their feet. Both had their hands fisted. Cords stood out in their necks as they shouted, and their yells came faintly through the windows of the SUV. Addie cracked her window, but although the voices carried, they couldn't make out the words.

"Maybe something about tonight?" Addie guessed. "It's not going to happen tonight?"

Helskin cocked his left arm back, but before he could strike the other man, his friends jumped to their feet and grabbed him. All of them were shouting now. Helskin's adversary grinned and spat in the dirt. Helskin did likewise. Sides were drawn and insults hurled. It seemed mortal combat was about to break out.

Then, as with a flurry of snarls among caged dogs, the moment passed. Everyone resumed their seats and picked up their cups where they'd dropped them in the dirt, frowning down at the spilled beer.

Everyone but Helskin, who vanished into the house, slamming the door shut behind him.

Throughout it all, the dogs stayed under the porch.

Addie and Evan waited another half hour while the fire died down. One by one, the men stood, stretched, and went into the house.

"I guess that's that," Evan said.

"I guess it is." Addie started the engine, then reached over and briefly touched his hand. "Thanks for coming with me. I know I've been awful."

"Anytime. As long as there's tea. And next time, digestives would be good." He eased the seat belt under his arm and away from his neck. "Do you feel better?"

"Yes." She sounded surprised as she pulled away from the curb. "I do. I'll come back tomorrow. Bring Patrick and some uniforms. At the very least, we can question Helskin and the others about the assault on Talfour. And if they're fighting the dogs, we can stop that, too. Can I keep the ring with the runes?"

"Consider it yours."

Evan swiveled in his seat as they rolled past the other side of the house. On the far end of the porch, just inside the light cast from the weak bulb, a stack of bones rose two feet into the air.

"Addie," he began. "There are deer bones."

She slowed. "I see them."

There were probably fifty bones in the stack along with skulls and horns. Mostly there were the larger leg bones, like the ones found by Desser's body.

Hanging from the porch eave, twisting and swaying over the bones, was another flag.

This one carried the image of Himmler's black cross. Next to that, a sun cross, exactly as it appeared in the runes left by Talfour's body.

"Perhaps," Evan said, "I've been entirely wrong."

TWO

Excerpt from *Criminal Behavioral Analysis: The Viking Poet*
Semiotician: Evan Wilding, PhD, SSA, IASS

Semioticians, when analyzing the signs and symbols left at a crime scene, attempt to extrapolate the killer's emotional experience of the world and the narrative he has created to understand and explain that experience. But we must proceed with caution. Symbols are a form of shorthand that risk being ambiguous or indistinct, which allows for a wide range of interpretation. Proper analysis requires that we examine the greater picture—that is, the entirety of all the crime scenes—and interpret the killer's choice of symbology within that larger scope.

Likely characteristics of the Viking Poet:

- The killer has a high IQ: his narrative is clear and complex even under the stress of committing serial murder.
- The killer likely has a stable job that he has held for months or possibly years. He is trusted by his employer and coworkers (typical of most organized offenders).
- The killer's intricate modus operandi and signature suggests he is acting out a fantasy that originated long ago. A more recent event served as the trigger that sent him on his murderous path.
- The killer has deliberately embedded difficult and obscure meanings in his poems, requiring careful reading of the subtext. Thus, the most obvious interpretation of his writings—that he is a neo-Nazi and that the crimes are racially motivated—may be incorrect.

- The killer may believe he is compelled by an external force to commit murder and to do so in a way that is precise and replicable. The ritual surrounding the manner of death and the posing of the corpse allows no room for error. A "bad" killing or the inability to properly pose a corpse would render that murder unsuitable for the killer's purpose.

THE VIKING POET

Hear me!

I am the thwarted scop. The poet whose voice was not heeded, the hand of Odin whose hand was stayed.

I am the killer who clears the mead halls of monsters. Who buries your sins in the bogs. I am the poet who requires a blood price—fair retribution for what was taken. For myself. For the Others.

I am Odin's rage, Hel's handguard. The avenger.

I am also Draugr—*as I have been since Alex's death.*

For I am the poet whose heart was devoured by the dragon.

⚔

I throw down my pen and stalk the room as Sunna casts her dull light over the world. I walk until I'm tired, back and forth, back and forth, like Grendel pacing in his lair. At long last, I stop by the table and press the palm of my hand to one of the *Beowulf* translations—Tolkien's with its romantic language and noble heroes.

Do you know that I tried to appease the Others without blood? I *did* try. I made sacrifices of effigies as the Vikings once did. But their rage was too great, their fury a shriek in my ears I could not bear. At night, their words beat against my ears like wings as I curled in my bed, hunting sleep.

Do you remember the games we played? How you spread the runic tiles across the floor and taught me to tell stories with the Viking letters? How you read to me the old sagas and told me that I, too, could be like those heroes?

Do you remember that you told me I did not need to fear the dead?

You told me that my mother wasn't buried in the bog.

I knew that you lied. That all you wanted was for me to be okay. To be normal. To fit within your world.

But I never fit. I never will.

For I am of another time, and I see what others cannot.

Now I ask, will you sacrifice your own heart to the dragon?

And I answer for you, fate goes ever as it must.

CHAPTER 20

Morning dawned gray and sullen save for a menacing red glow on the underbellies of the clouds. Addie stared out the windshield as Patrick pulled to the curb across and down the street from Helskin's house.

The firepit was nothing but ashes. The dogs' chains still led under the porch, but there was no sign of the animals. Only one truck remained in the driveway—an ancient pickup owned by one Ryan Ruley.

Addie smacked the dashboard. "Fork it. Helskin's gone."

Patrick jerked his chin toward the remaining truck. "We still got at least one dipshit who might be persuaded to talk. You ever see a vehicle in such sorry shape as that one?"

"I should have moved in last night."

"Captain America himself wouldn't walk into a place like that without backup. Not to mention that you had a civilian with you. If you'd gone in, I'd have shot you myself."

She glanced over at her partner's sagging, morning-creased profile. She hid her smile. "You'd probably miss."

Patrick ignored that. He was frowning out the windshield. "Red sky in morning, sailors take warning," he said dourly.

"Are we back to snakes and augurs?"

"That's the problem with you kids," Patrick said glumly. "No respect for life's great mysteries."

Addie fell contentedly into their old argument. "I understand mysteries, partner. And not just when it comes to solving murders. We've got Catholicism in common, remember? But what you're talking about is just Old Country superstition."

"That's what you *don't* understand, Adrianne Marie. It's not superstition I'm talking about. It's wisdom. The lore of the ancients."

"Uh-huh."

"Wasting my breath on a nonbeliever, aren't I?"

She unbuckled her seat belt. "That's okay. I like hearing you talk."

"The missus could learn a thing or two from you."

He dropped his wrists over the top of the steering wheel and peered up and down the street, apparently absorbed in whatever folkloric concerns plagued a middle-aged cop who'd lately been telling her of his dreams of fishing expeditions and elk hunting. Perhaps he felt a twinge of warning from his future self—the desire to lay low, play it safe, make it out.

With Patrick, the mood wouldn't last. And his superstitions—for Addie firmly believed that's what they were—wouldn't slow him down. He was a cop through and through. The best. When it came time for him to punch his final time clock, they'd have to walk him to the doors and kick him out to the sidewalk.

Addie resisted an urge to pat Patrick's beefy hand and reassure him that all would be well. Because it almost certainly would. Better than well. Her excitement at the possible end of the hunt burbled under her skin like water simmering just below the boiling point. If they had to wait much longer, she'd explode.

Sensing her mood, Patrick said, "How many times I gotta tell you, a lot of this job is about patience?"

"I don't have time for patience."

After she and Evan had spotted the deer bones on Helskin's porch, Addie had dropped Evan off at his home, made sure he'd set his alarm, then had gone to her apartment and submitted a request for a warrant. She'd showered, crawled into bed, and waited for sleep.

They had their man.

Her eyes had popped open.

Maybe they had their man. Maybe he'd hired some clueless grad student to write the poetry.

After thirty minutes of pointless staring into the dark, she'd gotten up and—with a certain vengeful satisfaction—shot off a text to Clayton that she would not be breakfasting with him at Wildberry. She'd forced herself to cook eggs and toast and ate standing at the sink while she kept an eye on the clock. When the hands reached five a.m., she called Patrick and told him what Evan had learned so far and how they were going to spend their morning.

Then she'd gone into the station house, started coffee, and propped herself up in front of her computer, looking for anything that linked Talfour, Desser, and Helskin.

They were men. Beyond that, they seemed to have little in common. Talfour was the respected owner of a small business. Likewise for Desser. So there was that. Talfour was blind in one eye. Desser, too, had vision issues—his driver's license indicated he had to wear corrective lenses while driving. For whatever that was worth.

As for Helskin, he was a keen-eyed and deranged jerkwad who probably hadn't come within shouting distance of anything respectable since he was a kid.

So how had they crossed paths?

A Black man, a Jew, and a white supremacist walk into a bar.

She bounced back in her chair, tapped the ball of her foot on the tiled floor. Then she leaned forward and pulled up the morning edition of the *Tribune*. The headline raged.

Police Stymied by Serial Killer: Viking Poet Still Free

A five-paragraph report regurgitated what had been in the previous night's paper about Talfour and added a few tidbits about Desser—that a second body had been found in the water in Kendall County, also accompanied by mysterious runes. So someone had leaked that news as well.

Criver would be a trumpeting stampede of fury.

Not that she could blame him. A leak in a murder investigation was a serious thing. At best, it sent the citizens into a panic. At worst, disclosures of this kind exposed details of the investigation that were best kept under wraps—especially from the murderer.

Who was responsible? And why?

One thing, at least, was settled. The media had chosen a name for the killer. The Viking Poet. The same name Evan had suggested.

She crossed her ankles and hugged her coffee mug close.

Even with all the evidence, she found it difficult to believe that Evan's theories could be so far off the mark. But as he himself said, it was early times in the investigation, and there could be a lot of information they didn't have access to yet. It could be Helskin had hired a specialist in medieval literature, risky though that would be. Perhaps the grad student she'd envisioned in the middle of the night. Or maybe Helskin contained multitudes in his vicious little brain. Perhaps his home was lined with bookcases filled with the kinds of Nordic and Old English literature Evan had told her about—the *Prose Edda*, the *Poetic Edda*, *Beowulf*. Maybe there were leather journals and fountain pens strewn across the coffee table. All signs that beneath Helskin's Nazi exterior beat the heart of a poet. Addie had to admit that being racist didn't eliminate the capacity for art. There were plenty of examples to prove the contrary. These days, once-idolized artists were being knocked off their pedestals one by one.

To Addie, it seemed that art should belong to the virtuous. To the morally decent. To upright folk. But God obviously distributed talent equally among the deserving and the despicable.

"Addie!"

Patrick snapped his fingers, and the cold and the dull morning light and the caffeine shakes came flooding back in.

"You asleep?" Patrick asked.

"Only in my dreams," she answered. "What's taking them so long?"

They were waiting for the officers from Chicago Animal Care and Control. A patrol car was parked around the corner, the officers ready to approach Helskin's house from the rear should the need arise. The uniforms had already tried to scope out the backyard by standing on the roof of their unit so they could see over the privacy fence; trees blocked much of their view, but what they could see was a lot of flattened dirt. A scattering of metal stakes driven into the ground to which were clipped heavy chains. No sign of life, human or canine.

Patrick cleared his throat. "You heard of the Barghest?"

"The what?"

"The black dog. The hellhound that preys on innocent passersby. Just to see it is to invite doom. It is said to have terrible claws and teeth and to—"

"They're pit bulls." Addie stretched her legs as far as she could. Pointed her toes. "Not monsters. This case is getting to you, Paddy Wagon."

"And why wouldn't it?" Patrick drummed his fingers on the steering wheel. "Vikings and those whatchacallit bog bodies and ax-throwing pagans. Enough to give any good Irish Catholic the heebie-jeebies. And look at this neighborhood. Back in the day, the people who lived here were proud, God-fearing men and women who worked hard at the mills to give their kids a better life. Now the place looks like the worst cities of Northern Ireland during The Troubles. People hiding like rats in their holes."

Hiding from the effects of meth and abject despair, more likely, Addie thought. But perversely, Patrick's stubborn gloom cheered her. The edges of her mouth ticked up.

"Hangover?" she asked.

"Maybe a bit much of the devil's mouthwash." He squinted at her. "How'd you know?"

"I didn't. But you went out with Evan last night. And today you're terribly morose, even for a good Irishman. Trust me as one who knows— when it comes to the sauce, don't try to keep up with the professor."

Patrick groaned. "Don't tell me a Brit who can't reach high enough to sniff my hairy armpits can drink *you* under the table."

"No one can drink me under the table," Addie said. "But Evan gets as close as anyone."

"Well. Truth is, I can't entirely blame it on the lad. I might have cracked a few when I got home."

"Ah."

A stray bit of sunlight found its way through a chink in the clouds and flared off a chip in the windshield like the flash off a hurtling ax.

"Gonna rain soon, but this cursed sun," Patrick muttered. "It will be the death of me. Where are my shades?"

While Patrick fumbled in the console for his sunglasses, she turned her attention back to Helskin's house. It looked even more forlorn in the dull morning light. Gray boards showed where ancient blue paint had peeled away. Blank places on the roof marked missing shingles. The porch, with its ominous stack of bones, sagged along its length, punctured here and there by splintered holes where the wood had rotted and given way. The flag, and its emblem of Thor's hammer, had faded in sun and weather, the edges tattered. Not even the gods, it seemed, got any respect here.

From outside came the sound of wheels rolling on gravel.

"There's CACC." Patrick pulled on his shades. "Finally. I'm glad they're leading the charge."

A white panel truck with red lettering on the side pulled up behind them, and two men got out. They opened the side door of their van, and one of the men leaned in. They carried stun guns and five-foot snare poles. They were also likely packing heat.

Although the judge had decided a pile of bones and a black cross flag weren't probable cause for a warrant, even with the possible link between Talfour's assault and Helskin, there was nothing to stop Addie and Patrick and the CACC officers from knocking on the door and asking a few questions. At the first sign that something more was going on—evidence of dogfighting, runes carved on wood, a high-pitched squeal that just might be someone crying for help—they'd have probable cause and could force their way in.

And if all they accomplished today was rescuing the dogs under Article 48-1, Chapter 720 of the Illinois Criminal Code, it would still be a victory. The fact that Helskin had apparently hotfooted it somewhere wouldn't save him if he was putting dogs into fighting pits.

Addie retied her sneakers, double knotting the laces, and put her hand on the door.

"If there's dogfighting," Patrick said, as if he'd read her mind, "then there's probably also drugs and gambling. Firearms. A criminal mindset. We need to be on our toes."

She gave him the look he deserved, and his ruddy skin reddened further.

"I'd say the same to whoever was my partner," he said.

"I know. So let's go in and do our jobs. If we hurry, we can still be part of the search at Tommy Snow's place. Did I tell you the sheriff got the warrant?"

Patrick turned up the collar of his trench coat as a few raindrops struck the car. "I think you might have mentioned it. Twice, but third time's the charm." He didn't sound unhappy. "I just hope these guys know what they're doing. Did I tell you I almost got attacked by a dog when I was a kid?"

"A hellhound?"

"God's truth. Neighbor's mutt. Big. Had me cornered against my own house. Nightmares for years."

She started to let fly something about Irish ghost dogs and the Irish imagination when she caught sight of Patrick's expression. "Most dogs who've been trained to fight aren't aggressive toward humans," she told him.

He rolled his eyes at her.

"CACC will cover the dogs, Paddy," she said. "No worries."

"Oh, right. None at all."

Behind them, the CACC officer reemerged from the back of the van and headed toward them.

Addie and Patrick opened their doors and stepped out. Immediately, a sense of wrongness became palpable. Like a bad stench in the air. Addie glanced at Patrick—he felt it, too. His expression was grim, his mouth set in a thin line. He adjusted his coat and nervously picked at a loose thread on the collar.

"You don't look any tougher with the sunglasses," Addie said.

"Wife says I do."

"Yes, but she loves you."

She led the way down and across the street, Patrick one step behind while the CACC officers fanned out on either side. When they reached the broken sidewalk in front of Helskin's house, they regrouped and sized up the place.

Nothing and no one stirred. The bones on the porch managed to look both menacing and ludicrous in the foggy light, like a lazy man's altar to the gods of hate. A single carved pumpkin leered next to the door, a decaying nod to the holiday just passed. The smells of damp earth and damp dog and charred wood clotted the air. The dogs that Addie and Evan had spotted the night before hadn't emerged from beneath the porch. Addie searched for the end of the chains, but the leashes had been coiled near the edge of the porch, and both ends disappeared below.

The radio clipped to her belt sputtered.

"We're right outside the gate," Officer Smith said. "We'll stand by until you say otherwise."

Without probable cause, the officers weren't—strictly speaking—there as backup. They couldn't even walk onto Helskin's property. But this was their beat, and if a judge ever asked, they happened to be in the neighborhood.

"Still no dogs?" Addie asked.

"We can't see everything, but it's quiet as a grave back here."

"All right. We're approaching the front door."

"Roger that."

One of the CACC men led the way up the path to the front door. He walked with the stun gun in his left hand, a long stick with a crossbar in his right, his head swiveling from one side of the yard to the other and back. Spits of rain struck his shoulders and darkened his tan raincoat. Addie found herself braced for the dogs to come leaping out of the gloom under the porch to take them down. She kept her eyes on the chains, looking for the slightest shake.

At the front porch, the dog control agents stepped aside. Addie pressed the doorbell. A hollow buzzing came from inside the house.

The porch creaked beneath their feet. A sudden flow of water overran the choked gutter and splashed into the yard. The CACC agent on Addie's left twitched.

She rang again, then rapped the door three times with the side of her fist. "Police. Open up. We need to talk."

From somewhere deep in the bowels of the house came a low, repetitive booming.

"Dogs barking," said one of the handlers. "Wonder what took 'em so long to start up?"

Patrick twitched back his trench coat, clearing his gun.

The front door flew open with a fingernails-on-chalkboard screech, and a man who looked to be in his late teens stared at them through the screen door.

Tristan Walters. One of the men who'd been in the front yard the night before. She recognized him from his DMV photo.

The teen's hair was shaved close on the sides and long and tousled on the top—a classic undercut—the top hair pulled back into a messy bun. A short beard covered his cheeks and chin. He wore gray sweatpants but was shirtless and sported a series of intricate tattoos on his chest and arms—runes and a stylized hammer and the symbol Addie recognized as a Valknut.

"Good morning, Mr. Walters," she said.

The teen's bloodshot eyes regarded them blearily, the stink of last night's alcohol oozing from his pores. He swayed and then grinned. Still drunk. Or high. Likely both.

"Po-lice," Walters said.

She held up her badge. "I'm Detective Bisset with Chicago PD. This is Detective McBrady. We'd like to have a few words with Hank Helskin."

The teen slung an arm across his thin chest and scratched along his ribs, his fingernails leaving white trails on his tanned skin. "I don't think Hank's around. His truck's gone. You wanna talk to Ruley?"

Ryan Ruley, the man who owned the truck parked in the driveway. She pulled up a mental image of a heavily tattooed twenty-six-year-old white male from the suburb of Buffalo Grove.

"We'd love to talk to Mr. Ruley," she said.

"Um, okay." Another yawn. More scratching. The kid was off in Oz somewhere. "You wanna come in?"

Police and vampires.

All they needed was an invitation.

"Thank you," Addie said as the kid pushed open the screen.

CHAPTER 21

Freshly showered and changed after taking Ginny out that morning, Evan pushed his way through the magnificently carved door of Levair's Used and Rare Books.

He was greeted by a two-story space with cream-colored walls, dark wood trim and railings, and glassed-in twelve-foot-high bookshelves. The polished wood floors gleamed in wide stripes between thick oriental rugs, and display cases held tastefully arranged rare volumes and small archaeological relics. Lighting was discreet and recessed, and no windows opened into the room; the sun's rays were anathema to preserving ancient or even merely old texts.

This area of the shop was reserved for rare and expensive things. It was beautiful and enticing, but Evan actually preferred the basement, with its crowded wood-and-metal shelves of books that had been much loved—old tomes heavy with the knowledge and memory they held in their dog-eared pages.

The shop smelled of paper and history. And this morning, a hint of rain, tracked in on Evan's shoes.

It also, Evan was happy to note, smelled of Assam black tea and warm scones. Raspberry, if he wasn't mistaken. He found himself immediately soothed. And hungry, despite having had a decent breakfast. Chasing killers—even through their writings—required sustenance.

The sweeter the better.

He closed the door behind him, locking it as Simon had requested when he called to say he was five minutes away. Official business hours weren't until ten. He removed his Mackintosh, hung it on the coat tree just inside the door, and headed toward a library table in the center of the room.

"Simon?" he called, his voice swallowed by the bound equivalent of miles of paper.

"Coming!"

A door in the back opened, and a sixtysomething man the same faded brown color as much of his merchandise emerged carrying a tray with tea and pastries. Not tall, gently rotund, and owning a long face bracketed by drooping earlobes, Simon Levair resembled nothing so much as a contented basset hound.

"Evan, my dear friend," he said in his deep basso. "So good of you to come by."

After he relieved himself of the tray by setting it on the library table, he ignored Evan's proffered hand and pulled the semiotician into a manly hug that involved much back slapping. The two men were of similar height. Which, translated, meant that Simon had a foot on him, but in Evan's estimation, that was close enough.

The two men had known each other for the better part of a decade, having discovered each other at a book fair while wrangling over an eighteenth-century copy of the illuminated *Book of Kells*. They'd bonded quickly over their shared interest in languages and literature.

"So tell me about this lady friend," Evan said as they broke apart.

The book dealer had a definite twinkle in his eye, but he shook his head. "I'm not ready to tempt the fates by sharing her with the world. Or even with you. Ask me again in a month."

Evan unwound his scarf and draped it over a chair. "You've always been a tease," he said.

Simon laughed. "It's part and parcel of the business I'm in. Show a little leg, then close the robe until the client shows their coin. Now, do take a seat. The *Beowulf* translations are there on the table along with an assortment of books on Vikings. My apologies for the dog-eared pages and the highlighting. They're mostly old college texts."

"Okay if I take both translations of *Beowulf*?"

He waved an indifferent hand. "Be my guest. They offer rather different interpretations. Heaney has a whiff of the Old Country about his. Sturdy language and plain folk. Tolkien is all high language and soaring prose. Both a pleasure. Now, take a load off your feet. Tea? With milk, yes?"

"As always. Thank you." Evan pulled out a chair, folded his hands, and smiled at his friend. Simon's mild and gentle manner had no doubt fooled many a bookseller who walked away thinking they'd gotten the best end of whatever deal they and Simon had agreed on. But Simon always came out ahead. At least when it really mattered.

Simon poured the rich brew into china cups. "What's prompted the interest in *Beowulf*?"

"It's related to some research I'm doing." He accepted the steaming cup Simon slid across the table. "Plus a bit of nostalgia for simpler times."

"When's the last time you went home?"

It was Evan's turn to wave a hand. "Years. There's not really much of a home to go back to anymore. Mum moved here, of course. She's in DC. Not that we have much to do with each other. And River hasn't touched English soil in a decade."

"What about Anna?" Simon asked.

"Fit as a fiddle, according to both her and her daughter. She broke her hip last summer, but she's as feisty as ever. We talk every month or so."

Anna Woodstone had served as Evan's surrogate mother, nurse, playmate, and philosophy teacher for much of his childhood and teenage years. It was Anna who had taken him to the British Museum in

London at the tender age of six and launched his lifelong fascination with languages.

"What about your family?" Evan asked.

They chatted for a bit about events across the pond and touched briefly on Simon's new love interest—brilliant, beautiful, and an excellent squash player was as much as he'd allow—before he fell silent.

Evan picked up one of the books on Vikings. He thumbed through it, picked up another. "Any recommendation on where I should start?"

"I'm afraid I'm not much help in that regard. I've merely assembled a variety of tomes for your reading pleasure. Perhaps you'll find something useful. There is, of course, no literature that's actually from the Viking era. But there are later collections of stories and myths. The family sagas. The legendary sagas. And most famously, the *Prose* and *Poetic Eddas*. What most people don't realize is that all the Icelandic poems and sagas were written decades—even centuries—after the Vikings had come and gone."

"I assumed as much. It would probably behoove me to brush up on my Nordic mythology."

"Then you'll want Rudolf Simek's *Dictionary of Northern Mythology*. It's in the stack along with Neil Gaiman's *Norse Mythology*. But if you're looking for general information on Viking history and culture, I found something better than musty old books."

Evan bit into the scone. Raspberry. He sighed his pleasure. "And what is that?"

"She should be here any—ah, there she is now. Perfect timing."

A key rattled in the lock at the front door, and a woman entered the shop, chased by a gust of wind. She pushed the door closed behind her, shook raindrops off her coat, and removed it along with the scarf that covered her cropped hair.

"It is a *bitch* out there, Levair," the woman said in faintly accented English. "Damn wind. Like Loki himself trying to get into my pants."

Both men froze, but the woman laughed. She approached the table and extended a damp hand to Evan.

"You must be the famous professor, Dr. Wilding. Based on everything Simon told me when he called, I expect you to go outside and walk on the lake as soon as we're done here. I'll applaud you from the safety of the shore. Along with the rest of us mortals."

Heat rose in Evan's face. He stood and accepted the woman's proffered hand. "I'm afraid you have me at a loss."

"My apologies," Simon said. "Christina, I was just mentioning you. Dr. Christina Johansen, meet Dr. Evan Wilding."

"Distinguished service professor of Germanic Studies," she said. "I'm at the U of C, same as you. It's a shame our paths have never crossed, but here we are at last. Now, please, Simon. A scone and some tea. The smell is driving me mad."

She set her messenger bag on the floor and sank into the chair next to Evan's. The scent of damp wool drifted up from her black turtleneck sweater. She wore leggings and military-style boots and had a pleasant, sharply intelligent face decorated on the right cheek with a tattoo of green Celtic knots. Bright-red lipstick stood out on her pale face, and silver rings covered her slender fingers. Her black hair had been cut to within an inch of its life. Evan placed her in her midthirties.

"Your accent," he said. "The Swedish island of Gotland?"

She gave him an approving look. "Bravo! I've been here seven years, and my parents swear when I go home, they can't understand me anymore. Of course, they speak the Gutnish dialect. They can't understand anyone."

Simon slid a scone onto a plate and pushed it, along with a cup of tea, across the table. "Christina is my Viking expert. Thank you, Christina, for braving the weather in order to meet us."

"The weather suits me perfectly. The early-morning hour, not so much. But you promised Vikings and Dr. Wilding, so here I am, the hour be damned." She turned to Evan. "How can I help?"

His heart gave a small flutter at her smoke-gray gaze. Beautiful, intelligent women were his weakness. And what man would blame him? "I need a crash course on Vikings, if you would."

"I must first say that the term *Viking* is a bit unfortunate."

"How so?"

"The people of the Viking Age would not have called themselves Vikings. They perhaps would have known the Old Norse word *vikingr*. But they would have considered it a label for a single individual, a pirate or raider. Not as a name for an entire culture. It's thought that the word might have originally derived from the Old Norse *vik*, which means *bay people*."

"Bay people," Evan murmured. *Yet another link to the water.*

"Yes." Christina broke off a corner of her scone. "The term referred to people waiting in their ships, hiding in the bays to strike at passing mariners."

"So our whole idea of a Viking people . . ."

"Is artificial. A convenient label for a large group of people living in a particular area during a particular time. And unlike all these racists who have co-opted Viking symbolism and culture, there is every indication that the Viking Age people lived in an open society with a healthy population of immigrants who were accorded no prejudice or disdain. There was *never* a concept of a pure Aryan bloodline. The very idea probably would have bewildered them."

"So not racists."

"Definitely not racists. The Vikings were many things. Our rather limited and limiting idea that they were nothing more than bearded and blond men who took their battle-axes with them on shockingly violent raiding parties isn't—"

"An accurate summation?"

"It isn't entirely *in*accurate." She pursed her lips, puffed out some air, and eyed Evan through a newly narrowed gaze. "They *were* appallingly cruel sometimes. Practiced human and animal sacrifice. Enslaved children. Slaughtered Christians left and right. Indulged in a great deal of plunder and rape. But—" She leaned forward until her knees touched Evan's. She smiled into his eyes.

Evan swallowed. There was, he noted, nothing that looked like a wedding band among all the silver on her fingers.

"There is," she said, "rather a great deal more to them. Their mysterious cosmos, their elaborate funerary rites, the epic tales they loved. What is it you most want to know?"

Evan considered. His recall of the Viking Age and of the so-called Viking literature was a rather ragged patchwork quilt of this and that. It was probably due to his poor job, as a hormone-laden teenager, of encoding the information in his memory palace. He knew a little about Odin and the Æsir. Something of Scandinavian geography. A touch more about *Beowulf*.

What would the killer care most about?

He set down his tea. "I need to know how the Vikings saw their world and their place in it. I don't mean politically or even their social structure. But in terms of the gods and their relationship with those gods. Their spiritual beliefs. How they viewed the dead and their concept of sacrifice and appeasement. And"—he tapped his fingertips on the table—"their ideas around crime and punishment and revenge."

Christina offered a delicately arched brow. "Do you believe in spirits, Dr. Wilding?"

He cleared his throat. "The jury's out on that, I'm afraid."

"Hmm." She gave him a soft smile. "You see, the key to understanding the Vikings is exactly what you mentioned—to see the world through their eyes. They *knew*—in the same way we *know* the earth revolves around the sun—that multiple beings walked invisibly beside them. The gods. The gods' servants. Strange spirits and otherworldly creatures. Some friendly. Some most definitely not. Some of whom could be appeased only through human sacrifice. All of them traveling to and from worlds that humans could also visit, if they could find the way."

"Fascinating," he said.

"It is," she agreed. "Interesting, too, is the fact that men and women from the Viking Age didn't consider themselves to be the owners of a solitary soul. Not in the way Christians believe. They *knew* that their flesh housed many beings. And that these beings were separate and independent."

"You mean like someone with multiple personalities?" Simon asked.

Christina set down her empty cup and shook her head. "It wasn't a pathology. It was simply a recognition that there are many parts to every human being. The sense that spirits move in and out of us, that they move all around us, that they exist as surely as the things we see in daylight—earth and trees and water. The nine-world cosmos of the Vikings, based on what little we know of it, defied rationality, even physics. Yet it made perfect sense to every person living in the Viking world."

"It sounds complicated," Simon said.

Christina's silver rings caught the light. "Only to us. And only, some would say, because we've forgotten how to see and hear. When we tell ourselves we are but one being with one soul, we limit ourselves. To the Vikings, humans consisted of four entities, at least one of which wasn't really *of* us but merely inhabited our *hamr*, our physical shape. The Vikings walked about with alien beings hiding beneath their flesh."

Evan looked down at his journal. His pen had leaked, forming a long, narrow blob on the page. If this had been a Rorschach inkblot test, he'd have said the dribble resembled an overstuffed sandwich. A killer might label it a bloody knife. Or a well-fed snake.

"Go back to the strange spirits you mentioned, Dr. Johansen," he said. "The otherworldly creatures who demanded sacrifice."

She gently touched his wrist. "Christina will do."

"And call me Evan, of course."

"Then Evan it will be." Christina steepled her slender fingers beneath her chin. "You speak of the gods. And other frightful supernatural beings. Like the water spirit known as the Näcken, who sometimes appeared to the unlucky victim as a white horse."

"Let me think a moment," he said.

"Of course."

Evan bent over his journal, his thoughts running in a torrent, like a flooded river. The pigeon with its breast split. The runic ring that someone had left behind in the woods. The sabotage of Evan's sound system suddenly sending Wagner's "Ride of the Valkyries" soaring through his house. *Your system was hacked,* the tech guy had told him that morning when he called. *Reinstall the app, change your password, and let us know if anything else happens.*

Who had hacked his system to send him that particular message, assuming the choice in music was deliberate? Why the Valkyries?

Evan knew that these days, Valkyries were often depicted as beautiful, scantily clad women best known for escorting heroes into the eternal paradise of Valhöll. But that image trivialized their original purpose. During the Dark Ages, the Valkyries—powerful agents of fate who served Odin—had been terrors of the battlefield, swooping in to select those who would die during the carnage of war.

Again he felt that odd shift, as if the world had tipped ever so slightly.

When he looked up from his journal, he could swear that the lights had dimmed. That the air stirred in unnatural ways. He was vaguely aware of Simon shifting in his seat, as if the book dealer had also sensed something.

We're getting superstitious with the passing of the years.

Evan shook off the feeling. "Tell me more about these beings that shared the Viking world with the humans."

Christina leaned back in her chair and crossed her ankles. Evan's knees turned cool in the sudden departure of her warmth.

"Where do I begin?" she asked with her scarlet-lipped smile. "Some of them were truly terrifying. And the way to reach them—the way to open the paths to the Other World and compel the Others to do your bidding—was through a form of sorcery known as *seithr*. Odin's cruel magic."

"Seithr," Evan repeated.

"Yes," she said. "The most terrible magic of all."

CHAPTER 22

Tristan Walters opened wide the door, then lurched around on his heels and vanished up the stairs into the house, calling for Ruley. Addie and Patrick exchanged a glance. She couldn't believe their luck at being invited in.

She and Patrick and the two handlers crowded into a small entryway. The house was a split-level, with one flight of stairs heading up, another leading down. All the curtains were drawn, and not a single lamp shone. The only light came from the gray day filtering through the open door behind them.

A three-foot-high metal gate bolted to the walls guarded the entrance to the lower stairs. From somewhere below, the dogs continued to bark, their voices deep and wet and throaty.

"Standing on the threshold of hell," Patrick murmured.

He had pocketed the sunglasses, and Addie saw the gleam of his eyes in the gloom. The CACC agents had a tight grip on their weapons and snare poles; their knuckle bones stood out beneath their taut skin.

Looking around at what she could see of the house—at the broken-down furniture in the living room and the dinged-up walls bedecked with posters of buxom women clad in leather bikinis and winged helmets—Addie had to admit that the place hardly seemed the abode of a killer who wrote complex poetry stuffed with alliterations and kennings.

The air was suffused with the odor of marijuana. Addie spotted plastic baggies and wrapping papers on a coffee table next to a collection of black candles whose wax had pooled and hardened on the wood.

"We stand here much longer," said one of the CACC agents, "I'm gonna be as high as that kid."

They all stiffened when, from below, a man shouted something, and the dogs fell silent.

There came the rattle of a chain and heavy breath, and then a brindle pit bull came surging up out of the darkness and threw itself against the gate.

Patrick made a small sound and fell back. The younger of the two CACC officers swung his snare pole around, missing the detective's head by inches. The pit fell silent, regarding them through the gate with alert eyes. His neck, shoulders, and muzzle were crisscrossed with old scars, and a recent wound on the top of his head seeped blood.

"Poor baby," the older CACC officer said.

Addie inwardly echoed the thought. What kind of abuses had this dog endured?

A line of drool strung from the dog's mouth and struck on the floor.

"Hellhound," Patrick muttered under his breath.

A light popped on overhead, illuminating the entryway, and then a man appeared, climbing the stairs toward them. He wore black jeans and a red T-shirt with the words VIKINGS RULE across the chest and sported tattoos along his arms and curling up from the neck of his tee toward his jaw. He stopped on the other side of the gate and shoved his fingers beneath the pit's wide collar. In his other hand, he held a cell phone.

"Good morning, Mr. Ruley," Addie said pleasantly.

Ruley looked at each of them one by one, probably smelling authority on them the same way a pickpocket sniffed out the rich and distracted.

"The police," he snarled. He raised his voice loud enough to reach the upper level and probably set the curtains swaying. "Tristan, you stupid dick hair ball, you didn't tell me it was the police."

No response from upstairs.

Uncomfortable now with having the teen's location unknown, Addie raised her own voice. "Mr. Walters, can you come down here, please?"

Echoing silence.

"Keep an eye out for Walters," she told the CACC agent closest to the stairs.

He nodded.

"We're not doing anything illegal." Ruley scratched along his jaw. "Neighbors are full of shit."

"That's always a promising opening," Patrick said.

"All the dogs got licenses," Ruley went on.

Addie returned her attention to the man on the lower stairs. He was more fit than the teen who'd answered the door and much larger—over six feet and two-hundred-plus pounds of muscle. Like the teen, Ruley had shaved the sides of his head, leaving a thick thatch of hair on top. But in place of the teen's man bun, Ruley wore an intricate braid, dyed strands of blue interwoven with his own blond locks.

The man slid the cell phone into the back pocket of his black jeans. The jeans, like his Viking tee, were covered with dog hair.

Addie held up her badge again. "We're Detectives Bisset and McBrady. What dogs are you talking about, Mr. Ruley?"

"I don't have to answer your questions."

She had to give him that. "We're not here to cause any trouble. We just want to chat with Mr. Helskin."

"He's not here."

"Any idea where he's gone? Work, maybe?"

"No idea."

"What about when he'll return?"

"I look like his mother? Now, if it's all the same to you, I got work to do. Come back later. Or maybe never." He yanked the dog's collar as if to drag it down the stairs. The dog whined.

"You've got a lot of dogs down there," one of the CACC officers said.

Ruley sneered. "Real genius, huh? Now, get out of here."

Addie decided it was time to provoke. "Hey, Ruley. You want to tell me why you guys decided to go after James Talfour?"

Ruley stared at her. His recognition at Talfour's name snapped into place. Addie could see it happening, like watching a square peg suddenly morph and slide into a round hole.

But Ruley's gaze remained steady. "Who the hell is James Talfour? And why should I give a fuck?"

The dog, picking up on the man's anger, growled. Ruley yanked on the collar, and the pit fell silent. A strand of Ruley's hair had worked its way free of the braid and now fell forward across his face. He lifted an arm to sweep it back.

A streak of fresh blood stood out on the paler, untattooed skin of the inside of his forearm.

"What's that?" Addie asked.

He followed her gaze to his arm.

"It's from feeding the dogs," Ruley said. "They're carnivores."

"How many dogs you have down there?" the CACC officer asked.

"Let's see," the man said. "I got Fuck Off, Not Happening, and Go Away Dickwad. Is that three?"

"How'd this animal get hurt?" the officer persisted. "These wounds appear to be injuries from fighting. I need to take a look around."

"Oh yeah? And the Jews need Christ to make an appearance and save their worthless asses. You wanna see the dogs, get a warrant. And if you wanna talk to Helskin, come back tonight. Maybe he'll be here. Now, I got work to do."

The man spun and started back down the stairs, dragging the dog with him. As he turned, Addie caught a glimpse of his profile. And the intricate weaving of his braid. The series of turquoise and black beads knotted into the strands.

Exactly like in the footage from Talfour's attack.

On the back of his bulging triceps was a tattoo of the black cross.

"Stop!" she yelled in her best you-are-*so*-screwed-if-you-don't-listen voice. "Ryan Ruley, you are under arrest for the assault of James Talfour."

Ruley's shoulders came up, and Addie watched the tension in his neck. She could all but read his mind: *Stay and face the music? Or run away?*

"There are officers in the back, Ruley," she said. "Don't even think about it."

From upstairs came the sound of a sliding door slamming open and then footsteps. Someone moving fast.

"Here comes the kid," said the CACC agent by the stairs. He had his gun out.

Walters appeared at the top of the stairs. Addie could see the kid's pulse beating in his throat. His skin was pale, his pupils large in the blue irises.

"Ruley?" the kid screeched.

"Kick it, kid," Ruley snapped. "I'm right here. With the *police*."

Walters looked close to tears. "He's out back. Oh, God. It's so bad. His head."

Addie kept her eyes on Ruley. The guy had edged down another step.

"Stay right there," Patrick told him.

Ruley blinked at Patrick, then shouted up the stairwell. "Who the hell are you talking about?"

"It's Hank," said the kid. "He's all fucked up."

"Mr. Walters," Addie said firmly, pulling the teen's attention. Her own heart slammed in her ears so that she could hardly hear. "Is Mr. Helskin hurt?"

The teen's chin dropped toward his chest. A weird, high-pitched laugh emerged. Spots of color appeared in his pale face. "Hurt?" The laugh turned into a giggle as he sank onto the filthy carpet and hugged his shins. Addie noticed for the first time that the kid's feet were bare and dirty where they thrust out of sagging gray sweats. He was shivering even in the olive-drab parka he'd put on since the last time they saw him.

Addie and Patrick exchanged glances. Patrick gave a slight nod and turned his attention back to Ruley, while she moved toward the stairs. It was the way they typically worked—Addie handled the women and kids because they saw her as less threatening.

She went halfway up the stairs and knelt so that she was eye to eye with the kid. "Mr. Walters? Are you all right? Can you tell us what happened? Is someone hurt?"

He lifted his chin so that their gazes met. Another giggle, this one as sudden and shrill as if he'd just been pinched by an invisible hand.

"You could say that." His gaze slipped past her. "Oh, Jesus, God, and Odin's wolves. You could totally say that. Hank is . . ."

"Hank is what?" Addie pressed.

"Dead! He's dead!" The kid buried his face into his crossed arms. "Oh, God, what someone did to him."

Chapter 23

"What do you know about the god Odin?" Christina asked Evan. "And *seithr*?"

"About *seithr* I know nothing. As for Odin . . ." Evan drew a box around the word *Odin* in his notebook. "He was the leader of the Norse gods, the Æsir. He was the god of poetry, wisdom, and death. He also revered wisdom and was willing to make great sacrifices in order to attain it. He hung upside down for nine days with a spear in his side *and* gave up an eye so that he could learn the secret of the runes."

"Excellent, Evan. Then you can see why Odin, a god of both death and knowledge, would also command *seithr*."

"What need would a god have for sorcery?"

Beside him, Simon leaned forward. "What indeed?"

"Oh, there was a great deal that a god could do with *seithr* magic. For one, he could see the future and perhaps even alter it. But *seithr* was even more important to humans. A sorceress could bewilder her enemies or heal the land or lure a beautiful man or woman to her bed. She could strike a man down in a cruel rage. Or she could raise him from the dead."

Evan wrote furiously. "You said *sorceress*. The magicians were women?"

"Women and *ergi* men."

Evan looked up. "*Ergi* men?"

"Men considered unmasculine. As in, homosexuals. Viking sorcery was likely sexual in nature and was very much the province of women. Or of men who had the characteristics of women."

"Interesting." Evan made another note. "Please continue."

Christina arched her back and stretched. "The otherworldly beings in the Viking universe used the gaps among the worlds, the seams where worlds were pulled together, in order to travel. And while everyone knew of these so-called *Others*, it was the sorceresses who knew how to find them."

Simon stood. "You two keep chatting. But we're completely out of tea. I'll make another pot. And see if I can rustle up a few more scones."

He disappeared through the door to the back.

"He doesn't care for all this talk of sorcery," Christina said.

Evan looked up from his journal. "These sorceresses, they could find the places where different worlds came together? Where the Others lived?"

"Yes. That was one of their powers. And so they chose those places as the locations where the Vikings held their rituals—of appeasement mainly, making sure the gods and the spirits were happy."

"Sacrificial rites?"

"Sometimes. The Vikings sacrificed humans and animals. Probably even children, although not all scholars agree. But often a ritual consisted of simple prayer. Or the burial of an object with special significance, such as ice crampons as a request for a safe journey."

Evan set his pen crosswise on the open journal and folded his hands in his lap. "Tell me about these places where they held their rituals."

Using one delicate finger, Christina tapped a crumb on her plate and put it on her tongue. "The Vikings had their own equivalent of Christian churches or Jewish synagogues or Hindu temples. They called these enclosures *högr*. The *högr* were often next to the great mead halls, much as you might find a chapel attached to a rich man's manor home in later centuries. Archaeologists have found oath rings in some of them."

Evan flashed to the ring Blakesley had brought him. *God's spear.* And the ring Helskin had requested from the jewelry store—*Odin's thane.* "What are oath rings?"

"Finger rings or armbands, used to swear someone to a sacred vow. Usually an oath of fealty, as a thane promised his lord. You're familiar with the term *thane?*"

"A guardian or servant."

"That's correct. So perhaps oaths of fealty were given and received in these small buildings."

Evan recalled lines from the killer's poems: *By moonlight I laid it out: tell me this. But he gave no answer.*

Had the killer been asking for an oath of loyalty? Or was it, as he suspected, a demand for an answer to the killer's riddle?

Christina continued. "In addition to the *högr*, there were also open-air sites that utilized stone platforms and an area in which to bury sacrifices—chemical analysis from those sites indicate that rather a lot of blood was spilled. And, of course, the Vikings also used whatever natural areas of sanctuary appealed to them. Marshes. Groves. Bogs."

Evan stopped writing. "Bogs?"

"Oh, most especially bogs. You see, Viking sanctuaries were places of some kind of natural significance. And any place that existed between one thing and another, such as between earth and water, neither one nor the other, was considered to be of spiritual importance. Sacred, even. A place where the Others could pass into our world or we into theirs. In these betwixt and between spaces like bogs, the Vikings built platforms on which they performed their sacrifices."

There it is, thought Evan with a melancholy jubilation. *The link between Vikings and the bog bodies.*

Christina said, "They were especially fond of sacrificing birds."

Evan glanced up, his pen faltering on the page. He recalled the pigeon lying in the woods, its breast split open. "Birds?"

"Killing birds of all kinds was very common. Birds of prey—hawks and falcons—appear in the most elaborate of the Viking graves. One theory is that the Viking people believed that creatures who could fly could also open a path into other worlds. Especially, it is said, for the dead."

Evan pictured Ginny in her mews and was glad he'd had the lock and keypad installed sometime back. Maybe he'd move her over to a friend's house until all of this was over. He'd also told Jo's mom to make sure Jo didn't slip over when no one was around. He'd offered no explanation, and Jo's mother hadn't asked for one.

Christina uncrossed and recrossed her shapely legs. "A lot of ceramic vessels have been found in these bog sites, with holes drilled into the bottom. Presumably, these were used to hold blood, as at any *blót* sacrifice. The blood would pour through the hole and disappear into the waters of the bog, as if the gods and spirits had ingested it. That must have provided great satisfaction to the Vikings, to see their sacrifices so eagerly consumed."

He said, "So a *blót* sacrifice—"

"*Sacrifice* isn't quite the right word, even though we would certainly label their actions sacrificial. They would have considered it an offering. A gift, even. A blessing consecrated by blood."

"A *bletsian*?" he asked.

She rewarded him with a smile. "You're going to get an A in my class."

"Offerings, then." He made another note. "How were the animals and humans killed?"

"Sometimes hanging. Often with a blow to the neck with the goal of creating as great a spray of arterial blood as possible. Very dramatic for the observers. But it wasn't always so violent. Or even violent at all. Sometimes the Vikings left wooden figures in the bogs, the size and shape of men. These figures might have been representations of the gods. But I believe they served as substitutes for human offerings."

Each hair on the back of Evan's neck suddenly stood at attention. Could this be in any way related to the wooden figures left for him and Sten Elger? He frowned. Were the figurines someone's idea of a joke? Or something more sinister?

Question piled on question. Who had made it through his gate and to his doorstep? Was it the same person who had hacked his sound system? Was it really just an irate student who also threw axes and had something against Sten Elger?

Simon reemerged with a fresh pot of tea and another plate of scones. "More for everyone?"

"Please," Evan said, grateful for the normalcy, while Christina murmured, "You're a peach, Simon."

Simon blushed. "Just don't tell my clients that. I prefer they think of me as a shrewd and ruthless businessman, not a purveyor of raspberry scones."

While Simon poured, Christina went on. "Do you remember those wooden figures that appeared around Chicago last spring?"

A coolness brushed the length of Evan's spine, the faintest touch of intuition. "I was in the Middle East then. I seem to have missed them."

"I remember." Simon put down the scone he'd just picked up. "Four of them, weren't there? Curious things. Human-size stick people made out of branches. Some of them were rather sexually evocative, as I recall."

"You recall correctly," Christina said. "Large branches were used to suggest the male phallus. Knotholes indicative of female breasts. Very much like the Viking Age wooden figures that have been found in bogs."

"They stayed around for a few days, didn't they?" Simon said. "Then disappeared as mysteriously as they'd arrived."

Christina reached for a scone. "I always thought it might have been some of my students having a bit of fun, since I often include a mention of the figures in my lectures. But no one ever came forward."

Evan wrote in his journal. *Could the killer have started with wooden sacrifices before turning to humans? Definitely an unusual form of escalation for a serial killer. Indeed, unique. Check w/Addie re: police have any knowledge? Any suspects?* He hesitated a moment, then wrote, *Any link to the figures left for Sten and me? Is it a message?*

"Two more questions," he said when he'd finished writing.

"Please."

He was thinking of Officer Blakesley, a member of the Lesbian and Gay Police Association. The last person he knew who had been at his front door before Addie arrived.

"You mentioned *ergi* men as possessing magical powers," he said. "So I assume the Vikings were favorable toward homosexuality."

"Not at all. They viewed homosexuals with both disgust and horror and, in the words of one expert, considered them cowards without honor."

"Why would a despised person be granted magical power?"

"It was a trade-off. The power that came with sorcery was apparently enough of a lure for these men to risk the ridicule of being labeled effeminate."

"Magic often exists at the edges of society."

She nodded. "A talent considered necessary for the good of society. But also despised."

Thoughts of despised magic made Evan think of Rhinehart's interest in occultism and its link to the Nazis. "The Nazis also loathed homosexuality."

"Lovely people, weren't they?" Christina asked with a sardonic edge in her voice. "They also went after the Roma and Sinti, the so-called Gypsy nuisance. Jehovah's Witnesses. Those they considered subhuman like the Poles or Soviet prisoners of war. People who were disabled in some way. Those who couldn't walk, for example."

Evan thought of the bog bodies with their twisted spines and broken hips. "And people with dwarfism?"

"Yes. Although a family of dwarfs survived Auschwitz because Josef Mengele was fascinated by them—they were literally pulled from the gas chambers before they breathed their last. We're appalled, but the Nazis saw themselves as moral crusaders intent on purging any deviation from their concept of the ideal. You can thank the occultist Walter Nauhaus for raising the ghastly specter of racism in post–World War One Germany—he of the Germanic Order of the Holy Grail and the Thule Society."

"If I recall, the Thule Society is the group that sponsored the political organization that ultimately became Hitler's party," Evan said.

"And who counted Rudolf Hess among their number. They're considered by many to be the occult force behind the Nazi Party."

The three were silent for a time, save for the scratching of Evan's pen across paper. After a few contemplative minutes, Simon said, "More tea?" to which Evan replied, "Thank you, no," and Christina disappeared to use the bathroom. By the time she returned, Evan had finished writing and closed his journal.

Christina resumed her seat and picked up Tolkien's translation of *Beowulf* from the table.

"Does your curiosity stem from a newfound interest in *Beowulf*?" she asked.

"In part. I took a course on Old English poetry as an undergraduate. I was fascinated, no doubt. But I missed the *Beowulf* unit. Plus, I was a teen with raging hormones. Which, translated, means I was frequently distracted by things having nothing to do with old parchment."

"And now?"

"Now I'm no longer a teenager. Hopefully, my interests have matured along with the rest of me. Also, recent events have required me to take a deeper look."

Christina's look was penetrating. Even though Evan's name hadn't appeared in the news—at least, not yet—she might have put two and two together. But if so, she was tactful enough not to question him directly.

"Maybe I can help with that, too," she said. "Anything in particular you're looking for?"

Evan glanced at his watch. He had forty minutes before he needed to leave for class. Whatever Simon had to tell him about Rhinehart could wait for a conversation later in the day—he needed to know as much as possible about the saga of *Beowulf* to see if he could gather additional insights from the killer's poems.

He opened his journal again, turning it to the page where he'd copied out the poem found near Talfour's body. "Any thoughts about *Beowulf* you care to offer would be wonderful."

"*Beowulf* is actually a hot topic right now in the scholarly world," she said. "And not because of the great eponymous warrior or even the monster Grendel."

"Then what?"

"Grendel's mother. Also known as the hell-bride or hell-dam. The terror-monger. The so-called swamp thing from hell. She is far more interesting than her son, who appears to be little more than a blood-thirsty monster. Interestingly, given our discussion today, it was likely *seithr* magic that Grendel's mother used to melt Beowulf's sword when he first came after her."

"Is that what makes her so different?" Simon asked as he poured out the last of the tea. "I thought she was simply the second monster slain by Beowulf. Between his killing of Grendel and the death of the dragon. Part of a trifecta of evil."

"Most nonscholars would agree, Simon. A trinity of monsters through which Beowulf makes his bones as a warrior. But Grendel's mother is interesting for two reasons. The first is that she is very clearly defined as a woman. We are told she is a *brymwulf*—a she-wolf who has the likeness of a woman. She is introduced with the words *ides* and *aglæcwif*."

Aglæc *appears in the killer's poem,* Evan thought.

Simon asked, "What do those words mean?"

"They are words for *lady* and *monster-wife*. But bear in mind that *aglæc* is also used to refer to our hero, Beowulf. Some scholars have suggested that the word *aglæc* simply means someone who is more than human, like our studly Beowulf."

"Fascinating," Simon murmured.

Evan stopped writing. "You mentioned two things that make her interesting."

"Indeed. Grendel's mother, unlike her son and the dragon, appears to be playing by the rules of combat. She stays away from men and does not engage in battle with them until they murder her son and initiate a blood feud. Then she slips into the hall, murders a single warrior as the blood price, and retreats to her home beneath the sea to guard the body of her slain son. It's important to note that she responds as any Viking warrior would—by seeking vengeance. This makes her less a monster and more a noble warrior."

"You're saying Beowulf was wrong in exacting revenge for her revenge?"

"If we're playing by the rules of a blood feud, yes," Christina said. "Once Grendel's mother had taken the blood price for her son's death, the feud should have been over."

Evan flipped through his journal to his rough transliteration of the lines carved on the bones Tommy had found near Desser's body.

blessing giver my blood-feud stillbirths your further crimes

His skin rose in goose bumps as if electricity suddenly filled the air. The killer was taking revenge for something. Talfour and Desser, perhaps unwittingly, had begun a blood feud with the killer.

This was useful information, of course. But he had nowhere to slot it. Not yet. The killer had not only gone to prodigious lengths to seek vengeance but had also invested a great deal of time in his poems. Which remained mostly mysteries. If he couldn't reach the person lurking beneath the words, he'd have nothing to offer Addie and the police.

He went back to his page of notes. "Talk to me first about the form of the poem, if you would. If someone were, say, trying to emulate Old English poetry, what would they need to be aware of?"

Christina tapped her black-painted fingernails on the arm of the chair. "I'm a historian, not a professor of literature. But what I can tell you is that Old Norse and Old English poetry use a complex rhythmic structure known as *dróttkvætt*, which most translators of *Beowulf* don't even try to emulate. In addition to this difficult meter, skaldic or scoldic poetry—the name depends on what country the poet lives in—is especially known for embracing obscurity by using metaphors and wordplay and any number of riddles. In fact, I've heard it said that J. R. R. Tolkien got his idea for Gollum's riddle game from the Nordic sagas."

Evan felt something building inside him. Like a faint arrow beginning to glow, pointing him down the killer's path. He looked at the line *By Skollfud's light I laid him low.*

"You're familiar with kennings, yes?" he asked.

"Of course. The metaphors known as kennings are one of the most fun aspects of medieval poetry."

He tore a piece of paper out of his journal and wrote on it before pushing it across the table. "What do you make of *Skollfud's light*? Would that simply mean *daylight*?"

She picked up the sheet. Her brow wrinkled. "It could be a kenning to mean the sun, yes. *Skoll* is the wolf who daily chases the sun, which he will one day devour."

Evan nodded—he had earlier surmised as much.

But then she added, "To refer to the sun in this way suggests something else. Something beyond merely saying *the sun* or *sunrise*. A poet would use this very carefully, to mean something quite specific. Not merely an ordinary day."

Both Evan and Simon leaned forward.

"What else could it mean?" Simon asked, apparently as curious as Evan.

"During Ragnarök, the wolf Skoll will devour the sun. Then will come the end days, when all the earth-dead denizens of Hel and all those who drowned in the oceans of the world will come together to ride the great ship *Naglfar* into battle. And thus will begin the age of wolves."

The front door rattled while outside, a faint howling sounded. All three jumped and glanced toward the door.

"Speaking of wolves," Simon said. "It's just the wind. At the door and at the eaves. But it does sound like animals sometimes."

"Perhaps," Christina said with raised eyebrow, "the end times are upon us."

Simon gave a small shudder. "Oh, I do hope not. I've got a man coming in this afternoon with some signed first editions of Sigmund Freud's lectures on psychoanalysis. Still in their original wrappers, or so the man says. I'd hate to miss an opportunity like that."

Christina laughed, then looked at her watch and gave a small cry. "I have overstayed myself." She rose quickly and thrust out a hand to Evan. "A delight. Any more questions, please don't hesitate. Here's my business card. Do call."

She pressed her card in his hand as they shook.

Simon stood. She kissed his cheeks in the European fashion, then pulled on her coat and scarf. "Stay warm!" she cried cheerily and vanished through the door.

"What did I tell you?" Simon said. "Better than any book."

"Much better. I can't believe our paths haven't crossed before now."

"The university is really more of a city than a village, though, isn't it? And now, shall we move on to our mutual friend Ralph Rhinehart?"

Evan glanced at his watch. "I've got class soon. Let me see if Diana can cover. May I borrow your phone? I forgot mine at home."

But Diana didn't pick up either in their shared office or on her cell. Disappointed, he tucked his journal inside his coat pocket and stood. "I've got to go and earn my keep. Can we talk in the early afternoon? How about over New York Sours at a nearby watering hole?"

Simon sighed. "Unfortunately, no. Big, important client dropping by after lunch. Those aforementioned first editions of Sigmund Freud's lectures. Going through the volumes will take the afternoon. Why don't I give you a call after that? We can meet for happy hour. Especially if you're buying."

Evan laughed. "Always the dealmaker."

"I promise," Simon told him, "that if you're interested in Ralph Rhinehart, what I have to share will be worth both your money and your time."

CHAPTER 24

Whatever Hank Helskin might have been in life, whatever crimes he'd committed, Addie felt sure he'd met an ending no one deserved.

The man lay sprawled in the center of an immense concrete patio, his skull crushed, his sightless eyes open to the tin-colored sky, his light-brown hair arranged like a halo around his head. Blood-spattered fingers curled softly toward his palms.

On his bare chest, someone had scratched, NOT Þ.

Thorn—Þ. She recalled from Evan's chart that *thorn* was the third rune of the runic alphabet.

Before she saw the marks on his chest, Addie's first thought was that one of the dogs had gotten to him. That Helskin had been bending over or kneeling when a dog lunged, snapped its powerful jaws together, and then took off for parts unknown.

But there was the message, NOT Þ. Helskin was not their killer. And, if Evan was correct, then the killer was telling them that Helskin didn't even count as the third victim. Which maybe meant they were wrong about Helskin's name being buried in the poem—skin sinner and the guardian of the Viking underworld, Hel.

Addie rocked back on her heels. This case was like hunting an invisible tiger with a butterfly net and wishful thinking.

Right now, they had nothing.

From behind her, near the house, Walters's soft sobbing rose and fell like ocean waves. One of the patrolmen stood next to him, looking unsure whether to console or accuse. The other cop had already taken a dazed-seeming Ryan Ruley out to their squad car.

Was one of these two men the Viking Poet? The distraught Walters or the suddenly subdued Ruley? Or had the poet—as she suspected— escaped into the dark? Just like that invisible tiger.

"Addie," Patrick said.

She glanced at him, and he nodded toward a point beyond the body. Addie followed his gaze and saw the bone.

"That's the leg bone of a deer," Patrick said. "Looks like the killer was kind enough to leave behind his weapon."

The bone was long and thick. Blood and tissue discolored one knobby end.

"Helskin and another man got in an argument last night," she said. "When Evan and I were here. I couldn't hear what they were saying, but the other men had to pull them apart before it came to blows."

Patrick scratched his chin. "Yeah?"

"Yeah."

"Looks like it came to blows after all."

"Guess so." She pushed her hair back from her face. "The man had a raven tattoo on his forehead."

"Who doesn't? Except mine's on my—"

"Get some filters, Paddy Wagon."

But Patrick looked suddenly cheerful. "Assuming there hasn't been a run on raven tattoos, likely he's the guy I told you about from the ax-throwing place. The one Diana said radiated evil. We should have a picture of him soon." He grinned. "Forget all those bad feelings I was having earlier. This just might be our lucky break."

She looked at the dead man. "For us, maybe."

"I'm right. I can feel it." He pointed at the body. "You see those two spots on his right arm? Near the inside of his wrist."

She stretched her neck. "Little red marks. They look like the burns from a stun gun."

"That they do."

"Meaning whoever killed him might have tased him first."

"Might have." Patrick tugged on his ear. "Maybe the killer hit him with the electricity, then used the bone when the guy kept coming."

"He'd be pretty tough, then. Get hit hard enough with a stun gun to leave burns, but not fall down. At least not until he got his skull smashed."

Patrick gave another thoughtful scratch of his jaw. "Doesn't sound right, does it?"

"It might work if he were high on meth or another stimulant." She sent a text to the medical examiner, asking that he look specifically for taser burns on Talfour or any other indication of how he had been subdued.

Patrick continued musing. "Maybe if the killer whacked him with the bone *after* he was down. To make sure he stayed down."

Addie walked outside an invisible perimeter, careful not to get too close to the victim. A few feet from the bone, she knelt and leaned in.

"Paddy Wagon?"

He came and crouched next to her.

She pointed, but he squinted and shook his head.

"My eyes aren't what they used to be," he said. "What do you see?"

"Look on the underside." She pulled out her key-ring flashlight and flicked it on, playing the light along the length of the bone.

He stretched out his own neck. "Are those—?"

"Yup," she said. "Runes."

He slapped her back. "What'd I say? Faith and begorra. It's our lucky day."

She jotted down the runes on a sheet of paper, then pulled out her phone and brought up the chart of runic characters Evan had sent her along with their Latin alphabet equivalents. She did a quick one-to-one transliteration, noting the use of the *-ing* character to create the word *riding*. When she'd finished, she rocked back on her heels, trying to find her breath.

ᚠᛗᚢᛈᚠᚱᚱᚠᛈᛁᚢᚱᛁᚾᚷᚠᚤᚱᛁᚾᚷ

Patrick had gotten to his feet, but now he saw her expression and leaned down again. "You're white as a sheet, lass. What is it? What does it say?"

She shoved the paper at Patrick, and he read her translation aloud. "'The sparrow is riding of riding.' What the heck does that mean?"

She was already trying to reach Evan on her phone. "*Sparrow* is Evan's nickname. And the fifth rune means *riding*. I kind of glossed over that earlier this morning. But based on Talfour's poem, Evan thinks there will be five victims. Desser was cattle of riding, or first out of five. Talfour was ox of riding, or second out of five. The killer is telling us that Evan is going to be his fifth. Fifth out of five."

"Mary Mother of God," Patrick said. "You think it's because he's consulting on the case? How does the killer even know he's involved?"

"That is a very good question." She pressed the icon for Evan's number again. Waited while it rang through. Tried again. "He's not answering his damn phone. I'm going over there."

She reached out a hand, and Patrick pulled her to her feet. Her legs felt boneless.

"Hold on, partner," he said. "Evan lives in the suburban equivalent of Fort Knox. And if he's fifth in line, it probably means we've got a little time. It was weeks between Desser and Talfour. And as far as we know, numbers three and four are still walking around, living and breathing."

She turned on him in a fury. "Do you really want to take that chance?"

"We'll arrange to send patrol out ASAP, no worries. We'll find our professor and stash him in a safe house. I promise."

Addie looked down at her hands. They were shaking. She curled them into fists. "He doesn't live in Fort Knox. He lives in the country-club version of minimum security. We've got to find him."

"Not arguing with that," Patrick said. "All I'm saying, Adrianne Marie, is let others do their jobs. I need you here. The smartest thing we can do for Evan is find this Viking Poet before he gets to his third and fourth victims. Whoever those poor souls may be."

ᛉ

She kept trying. Evan didn't answer his phone. Not his cell phone or his office phone. Addie called for patrol to go by his house and for campus security to check his classroom and office. She requested the phone number of his assistant, Diana Alanis. But Diana wasn't answering, either.

With a heart torn between rage and worry, she stared around the yard. The concrete pad, the dying trees along the fence. An old shed in complete collapse. Only the fence and the dog chains looked cared for. She eyeballed the metal stakes driven into the hard-packed earth. No water bowls. No shade.

Fury overcame worry as she watched the CACC officers bring up the skinny, howling dogs from the basement fighting pit—"some of the worst abuse I've seen," said one of the men—and Patrick got on his phone to orchestrate the three-ring circus in blue to deal with Helskin's murder.

Addie squared her shoulders and reminded herself that Patrick was right—the best way to help Evan right now was to focus on finding the killer. She was a cop.

It was time to do cop stuff.

She walked back to the house where Tristan Walters sat on the stairs leading up to the deck, watched over by the patrol cop. She studied the kid. His man bun was lank and greasy, his cuticles ragged. On his left wrist, he wore a banged-up fitness tracker, and around his neck hung a plain silver chain with a pendant shaped like a downward-pointing arrow. The kid was as thin as a flagpole. She knew from her brothers how much a young man could eat and wondered if Hank had been feeding him anything more substantial than chicken nuggets and fries from McDonald's—she'd seen the wrappers balled up among beer bottles when they walked through the kitchen.

Walters was still weeping, but now the tears flowed in a silent, steady stream. His gaze showed the blankness of shock, his skin the color of day-old snow. He looked like a pitcher of glass that was seconds away from shattering. She reminded herself that this kid might be the killer. *Never assume anything* was Patrick's motto and hers. But she thought it unlikely. Walters seemed genuinely distressed. More tellingly, there wasn't a speck of blood visible anywhere on him. And he clearly hadn't showered recently. She could smell pot and woodsmoke from last night's party rising from his clothes and hair and grimy skin.

She turned her head and took a few deep breaths, then propped one foot on the splintered wooden step where Walters sat. She wanted to rip him apart, verbally speaking. But acting rough might make him turtle up. It was time to play the good cop.

She'd give it ten minutes, anyway.

Her face was expressionless as she stared down at him.

"You okay?" she asked.

He wiped his eyes on the sleeve of his parka. "Whaddaya think?"

"I know. Foolish question. You want some water?"

His eyes met hers briefly before he looked away. "Yeah."

Addie nodded at the patrolman, who squeezed past Walters and lumbered up the stairs toward the door that led into the house.

"Look," she said. "It's going to get crazy around here real soon. Lots of cops. Crime-scene investigators. The medical examiner. Probably someone from the DA's office. Just nuts."

He shrugged. "Okay."

"Most of them are going to want a piece of you. Do you understand?"

He dragged his eyes up to hers again. "I didn't do anything."

"I believe you. But they won't. They'll arrest you, haul you in hand-cuffs down to headquarters. Best thing for you is to tell me right now what you know."

His lips thinned, and his face went sullen. "I'm not a rat."

She held her sigh. "Not even against whoever killed your friend?"

Silence. His gaze went away again, lost and distant. She'd give her left pinkie to know what he was thinking.

The cop returned with a glass of water. Walters gulped it down.

"You live here most of the time, Mr. Walters?" she asked.

He set the glass on the stair. "Sometimes, yeah. When Hank wants me to."

"And the rest of the time?"

He shifted restlessly, picked at the skin on his bare feet. "With my parents up in Rogers Park. I work at my dad's hardware store."

"You want me to call your parents for you, Mr. Walters?"

His eyes went wide. "No! No. That wouldn't be good. My dad—he . . . no."

"He doesn't know about Hank? Or maybe he doesn't know about this whole Viking white supremacist thing you guys got going? Is that it? Does he know about any of it?"

A miserable shake of the head.

"Okay," she said. "For the moment, no phone calls. But we can't keep playing pretend, Tristan. Can I call you Tristan? My partner over there, he's pretty sure you're good for this."

"Good for—?" He stared up at her. "For killing Hank? Ah, no way, dude."

"Then talk me out of it, Tristan," Addie said. "Give me *something*."

He looked up at her, his eyes red and wet. "What do you mean?"

Patrick walked up just then. He moved the water glass to a higher step and planted one boot on the other side of Walters.

"Hi," he said to Walters.

Walters blinked up at him. "Hi."

Patrick leaned in. "What she means, Mr. Walters, is why don't you explain to us why your buddy Hank is lying dead a few feet away from where you're sitting."

Walters flinched. "I don't know, dude. I don't know. I just came out to—" He stopped abruptly.

"Came out to what?" Patrick asked.

Walters's eyes flicked around the yard. Confusion drifted into his eyes like slow-rolling fog. "I came out to take a piss and check the dogs while you guys were inside talking to Ruley. But they're all gone now."

"The dogs are all gone," Addie clarified.

"Yeah. The six that were back here. They musta got out somehow. The gate's closed."

Patrick rolled his eyes. "And the toilets? Those gone, too?"

"Someone clogged the one in the hall." Now he sounded like a sullen teenager. "And the other one is off Hank's bedroom. No one is allowed in there."

"Why can't anyone go into Hank's room?" Addie asked.

"Just what Hank said." The kid smirked. "But I've been in there a couple times."

"And?"

"And what? It's a room."

But the kid's face shone with something like adoration. She wondered if there was more to their relationship than that of mentor and apprentice. Either way, the kid had clearly drunk the Hank Helskin Kool-Aid.

Patrick showed Addie his phone. "The photo is from Sten Elger," he told her. "The owner of the ax-throwing place where Helskin and his pals liked to go. The one called Ragnarök."

Was it Addie's imagination, or had Walters cringed when Patrick said the word *Ragnarök*? Did the kid think the end days were coming? Or was it just the memory of going ax-throwing with Hank?

She focused on the photo. The image showed a handsome, narrow-faced man with a dark gaze and a raven tattoo on his forehead.

"That the guy arguing with Helskin last night?" Patrick asked her. She nodded, and he turned the phone toward Walters. "This one of your friends?"

Walters dragged his gaze up to the phone as if his eyeballs were lifting hundred-pound weights. He stared and then shook his head and mumbled something.

Patrick cupped an ear. "What was that?"

Walters shook his head again.

"Tristan," Addie said. "Look at me."

He met her gaze, and she went on. "If this man killed your friend and you don't tell us everything you know? Then he won't be the only one going to jail."

The kid licked his lips. "Raven," he whispered. "That's Raven."

"Raven." Patrick's eyes sparked. "He got a real name?"

The kid looked like he might cry. "David Hayne. But we mostly just call him Mr. X."

Addie and Patrick exchanged glances. Patrick's eyebrows shot up to his hairline.

"Why is that, Tristan?" Addie asked. "Why do you call him Mr. X?"

A loose-boned shrug, like the kid was running out of energy. "I thought it was because he likes axes." A hiccuping laugh. "I thought it was Mr. *Ax*. But he told me it's something to do with black magic. Same reason he collects all those bones. His Viking self is Raven. But he has a darker self, too. Mr. X."

Patrick pushed up from the stair and backed off a few paces, as if to get a better look at Walters. "The bones on the front porch. Those belong to Raven? To David Hayne?"

"Not all of 'em. Some of 'em are Hank's."

Patrick shook his big bull head. "And what in the name of all that's holy are they doing with all those bones?"

"Raven uses 'em for some ritual he does. With the other guys. I don't know what the ritual is. Hank says it's all a big secret until I prove myself. But Raven believes in the old ways. The ways of the Æsir. He says he can open the gates between our world and other worlds."

Addie flashed to the flag at the front of the house, the black cross hanging over the pile of bones. "Are you talking about black magic?"

"I guess." He wiped his nose with the back of his hand, then touched the neck of his coat before shoving his hands back in his pockets. "We *are* the Thule people."

Addie saw for the first time what was clipped to his parka. A gold swastika pin mounted atop two small crossed spears, also of gold. The entire thing was only an inch in diameter.

"The Thule people," she echoed. She needed Evan to explain *Thule people*. Where the hell was he?

Walters's thin shoulders came up. "Yup."

Patrick said, "What about Hank? He into the, whaddaya call it, this occult crap?"

"Nah. Hank's not much about being Thule. I mean, he says it's fine, but mostly he doesn't really care all that much one way or the other. He is"—his eyes cut toward the body—"he *was*—he was just using the bones to make jewelry."

Addie almost laughed. After the talk about black magic, jewelry-making sounded too banal for a group of white supremacists and Viking wannabes. Then again, what did she know about Vikings?

Patrick's assessment was even harsher. "Jewelry? That a little girlie for someone like Hank?"

"It's *Viking* jewelry. *Mjölnir* pendants—"

"What's that, me-ol-nair?"

Walters rolled his eyes. The message was clear: cops were *so* dumb. "Thor's hammer." He smacked the pendant that hung around his neck, the one Addie had thought was an arrow. "He makes wolf heads, too. Ravens. Runes. Sometimes he makes bigger art—sculpture. People eat it up, dude. Hank makes a shitload of money selling his stuff."

"Okay," Patrick said. "We get it. What about this ritual Mr. X does with his buddies? Any idea what that's about?"

The kid's eyes went sly, his gaze sliding off somewhere Addie couldn't follow. "Dunno."

"Does it involve sacrifice?" Patrick leaned in. "The neighbor's cat, maybe? One of those dogs you got locked up downstairs? Or something worse?"

"You watch too much TV," Walters said, probably parroting something he'd been accused of. But his expression remained cunning. His glance cut to the metal stakes driven into the earth.

Special place in hell, she thought.

"Where can we find Mr. David Hayne?" she asked. His name hadn't come up the night before when she'd run the plates.

"I dunno. Hank picked him up last night and brought him here. Now Hank's truck is gone. Raven must have taken it. Did he—did Raven . . . ?" Walters's fists clenched inside his pockets. "Did Raven kill Hank?"

"What do you think about that, Tristan?" Addie asked. "Do you think Raven killed Hank?"

"They were arguing last night. They argue a lot, and usually it's because Raven thinks he's better than the rest of us."

"Why does he think that?"

"Because he went to college. He says he's smarter than all of us put together."

Not that smart if he's hanging around here, Addie thought.

"Anyway, I mostly don't listen when they fight. Plus"—Walters's voice dropped—"I was pretty stoned."

Patrick said, "So where can we find this guy?"

"You're the police. You figure it out. It's not like Raven tells me anything."

"Do you know where he lives?" Addie asked.

"Somewhere."

"How about where he works?"

"No idea." The kid was sullen again, glaring up at Patrick.

"Or maybe he's with one of the other guys?" Addie went on. "You know where any of them are?"

He folded his arms. "I don't care about Raven. He's an asshole. But I'm not gonna rat out my Viking brethren. That's against the code."

"Ah, for Pete's sake." Patrick reached out a paw and grabbed Walters by the front of his parka and pulled the kid to his feet. "I'm done. Let's go to the station. We'll call your mommy and your daddy, and we'll all have a little sit-down. I'm thinking accessory to murder, if not something worse."

The kid raised his arms, covering his face with his hands as if he thought Patrick was going to hit him. The sleeves of his parka fell back, and Addie again noticed the fitness tracker on his wrist.

"Hold on," she said to Patrick. "Tristan, do you guys buddy up with your trackers?"

He glanced at his wrist. "Hank and I do. Did."

"What's that mean?" Patrick let go of Walters's parka. "Buddying up?"

Walters lowered his hands. "It means we track each other's runs. So we can challenge each other on how many miles we get each day. We haven't really gotten started on the running thing. But I still use it to meet up with him. As long as he's got Wi-Fi, the app uploads his data, and I can see where he is—or pretty close, anyway. We were gonna start running this week." His eyes filled with tears again.

Addie's excitement felt almost like nausea. "What about Raven?"

But Walters shook his head. "I don't buddy with *him*."

"Bloody hell," Addie said.

Walters stared past Addie and Patrick toward the gate where, not long ago, the patrol officer had marched Ryan Ruley out to a squad car. He chewed his lip for a moment and seemed to come to a decision.

"I don't buddy with Raven," Walters told them. "But Ruley does."

CHAPTER 25

"Thus we see," Evan said to the sea of young faces in his class Semiotics of Death, "that rites of burial are one of the earliest indications of man's belief in a soul. From Africa and Asia through Europe, across the Pacific and into the Americas, every culture has signifiers around death and burial. We have always cared for our dead."

Forty heads lowered toward forty desks. Pens scratched, and laptop keyboards clacked.

"Every human is a semiotician," Evan went on. "That is, a reader of signs. All of us, every single day, interpret—or decode—the signs around us. Traffic lights. Road signs. The silhouette of a man or woman outside our bathroom doors. We're constantly interpreting the man-made world around us." He thrust his middle finger into the air. The students who'd looked up gave a collective gasp. Quickly, he flipped his hand so that his palm was turned to the students and raised his index finger, forming a V. "What does this mean?"

"Peace out," someone said.

"Victory," offered another student.

Evan turned his hand again so that the back of his hand was toward the audience, still with two fingers raised. "And this?"

Silence.

"Two?" one of the students ventured. "Like my score on the last exam."

Evan waited until the laughter quieted. "In most English-speaking countries—England, Ireland, South Africa, Australia—this gesture means the same thing as my original one-finger salute. The subtlety of whether my palm is turned toward you or away creates a completely different meaning. Peace out versus eff off."

Outside the windows, the day brightened as the wind picked up and clouds scuddled past. A pair of students on the sidewalk struggled against the gale, their long hair whipping around their heads.

Evan rested his palms on his desk and leaned forward. From his place on the raised dais, he could see eye to eye with the students in the middle rows of the amphitheater-style classroom. "The signs with which we communicate don't remain static. Why? Because our culture isn't static. Our ideas of death change. So what does it say about Americans' relationship with death that we are changing its signifiers? For our next class"—the heads bowed down again—"read chapters five and seven from the textbook. And talk to your family about how they have marked the passing of loved ones. Use your training in anthropology to analyze what your parents and grandparents say regarding loss. Ask yourself what our death signifiers say about our society. Cremation versus burial. Memorial service versus graveside rites. Is death in Western culture an openly acknowledged fact? Or a carefully guarded secret?"

"Are you talking about the funeral industrial complex?" asked a young woman in the back.

"Excellent question," Evan said. "Why don't you do a little digging and share your answer on Thursday?"

The student groaned.

The door to the classroom opened, and Diana peered in. Evan closed his book with a solid thump and told the students they were dismissed. He felt cheered as he watched Diana approach his desk. Nothing like a visit from a goddess to liven up a discussion of death on a blustery day.

The students streamed out, breaking around Diana as if she were Moses wielding a staff instead of mere faculty holding aloft a messenger bag. She waited until the surge passed, then made her way to Evan's desk. She picked up a miniature replica of a Japanese *haniwa*, a funerary figure from the Kofun era.

"I've never understood your obsession with death," she said.

The same complaint he'd once made to Addie. "It starts with the fact that greater minds than mine pay me to teach this class," he said. "If they want me to talk about death, I'm happy to oblige."

"But it's morbid."

"Says the woman who spent the summers of her youth digging up Roman bodies."

"And look at me now."

"Gladly." He pretended to leer.

She looked down her nose at him with what he'd come to think of as quintessential Diana. A look that mingled exasperation with mild amusement. She replaced the *haniwa* on his desk. "Are you curious why I'm here?"

"Desperately."

"Addie has been trying to reach you. She left a message on my phone that ran something along the lines of, *Why doesn't that idiot ever carry his damn phone?* I knew immediately she meant you. She also said it was urgent and something about getting the campus police involved. And that the four thirty meeting at the police station has been delayed, but she still wants your profile ASAP. So." Diana beamed. "I figured I'd better find you before the cops did."

"She must have learned something," he said. Perhaps that his theories about the killer were all wet. He shrugged on his coat and tucked the *haniwa* in an inside pocket.

"I'll walk you out," Diana said. "I have something to give you, actually. And I've accepted a lunch invitation. You want to guess with whom?"

"Prince William. Or, no, surely Harry. He's more your style. And I'm shocked. Do you not see a man's marriage as an impediment to a casual fling?"

"You are amusing, Professor, but not in the way you might think."

"Amusement of any kind is better than the alternative."

He picked up a manila folder holding his students' homework, and they walked out of the room together and into the crowded hallway.

"Okay," he said to Diana. "I wave the white flag. Who asked you to lunch?"

"Our dear runologist, Rhinehart. Although he insists that I call him Ralph."

"Wait." Evan stopped walking.

Behind him, a student yelped as he course corrected to veer around the professor. Diana steered Evan toward the wall, out of the foot traffic.

Evan stared up at her. "Rhinehart called you?"

"Yes."

"To go to lunch?"

"It happens from time to time," Diana said. "I'm considered mildly entertaining."

"But Rhinehart is working for the other side. He thinks the murderer is a neo-Nazi Ásatrú. He also thinks a sun cross is a swastika. Plus, he threatened me."

Her eyes turned to slits. "He did?"

Evan had a sudden image of Diana with an ax, bent on defending his honor. "Don't do anything hasty. It was a mildish threat. He just wants the case for himself. Probably thinks it will help him sell books."

Her smile was thin. "This is going to be even more fun than I thought."

Evan flattened himself against the brick as the stream of students turned into a roaring river. "Where does fun come into having lunch with a Satanist? He could turn your spaghetti into worms or something."

"This keeps getting better."

"Besides," he said above the noise. "Lunching with Rhinehart would be like eating with the enemy. Is this how you pay me back for taking the time to fill you in on the case?"

"I'll be doing classic HUMINT. You can thank me later."

"You're practicing human intelligence? That's nice for a change."

Another one of those quintessential Diana looks. "That was beneath you, Professor. I'll get Rhinehart to tell me everything he knows."

"At least it will be a short conversation. And what does Rhinehart think he'll get out of it?"

"Aside from the pleasure of my company, you mean?"

"Aside from that."

"The answers. He plans to pick my brain for everything you know, then pretend he came up with it himself. Now, enough of that. I have something for you." She reached into her messenger bag and whipped out a piece of paper. "Here's the map you asked for. The English bog bodies."

He tucked the manila folder under his arm and accepted the paper. He'd forgotten all about it. Diana had drawn a map of the British Isles and penciled in small dots, clustered mainly in the central part of England, with a few outliers.

"That's where all the bodies are buried," she told him. "You really think it will prove useful?"

To be honest, he couldn't see how, exactly. But he gave her an appreciative smile. And then his smile widened as he mentally pulled up line twenty-five of the Talfour poem.

With his mirror I did mirror mere to mere.

"That's it, Diana!" he cried.

"That's what?"

"Do you remember the killer saying in line fifteen that he'd come here from across the sun-swimmer home?"

She nodded. "Followed by the words *for mine, mine, mine gone.*"

"Yes. I'm still working on that. But *sun-swimmer* is, I believe, a simple kenning for the sunfish, which dwells in the Atlantic Ocean, among other places, suggesting that the killer may have come here from England. In addition, we have the killer's comment about mirroring *mere to mere*. That is, from one lake to another."

Diana's face lit up. "The killer is re-creating the English graves of bog bodies here, in Chicago."

"It works, doesn't it? In its own odd way. We aren't an island, obviously. But we do sit alongside a rather large body of water."

She snatched back her map. "So the killer is . . . God, that's an awful thought. There are nine bog bodies in the British Isles."

"I believe our killer is intending a total of five victims." He explained his theory to her. "The number five surprised me, since nine is a number of great significance to Odin and the Vikings."

"Maybe our killer is modest and believes he shouldn't overreach."

"It clearly signifies something." He snapped his fingers. "The wooden figures."

"Explain."

"Christina—Dr. Johansen—told me this morning that four wooden figures were found in Chicago last spring, near bodies of water. If we map all four of them, I'll bet their locations correspond to four of the bog body locales you've indicated on your map."

"Which means whichever spots haven't been taken—"

"Are where his next victims will go. I'd better call Addie. Diana, you are a genius."

"I'm glad you finally noticed." Her gaze turned pensive. "You think there's any link between those wooden figures and the little man sitting in a box in our office?"

"It's crossed my mind."

"But what would it mean? That you're—" Horror filled her eyes.

He held up a hand. "If anything, the presence of the figure suggests that if I'm to be sacrificed, it will be only in effigy. Which is vastly how

I prefer to be sacrificed." But he made a mental note to pass along this theory to Addie. And to Sten Elger, who had also received a figurine.

Diana didn't look convinced. But a glance at her watch set her in motion. "I have to run. Promise you'll call Addie. And that you won't do anything rash. I'll check in with you tonight and fill you in on my lunch with Rhinehart. And by the way, I found Raven on the closed-circuit video from Ragnarök. Sten sent his picture to Patrick. It won't surprise me at all if the killer turns out to be our Ringwraith."

She sped away from him down the hall. At the doors, she turned back and gave him a wave before disappearing into the sunlight and wind.

ᛪ

Upstairs, a member of the campus police was just exiting Evan's office.

"There you are," he said when he saw Evan. "You've got Chicago PD in an uproar looking for you. I didn't see you in your classroom just now, so I thought I'd better make sure you weren't down for the count in your office—hurt or something."

"Thank you, Officer." Evan ignored the way his stomach flipped at whatever had driven Addie to call out campus security. Diana hadn't been exaggerating. "Any idea what this is about?"

The officer pulled a note out of his pocket. "It was something about riding of riding?" He winced. "Jeez, that makes no sense now that I say it out loud. I must have heard it wrong. Anyway, you'd better call that detective from Chicago PD. Is it Basset?"

"Detective Bisset." *Riding of riding.* The heat in his stomach intensified. What had happened while he'd been out of pocket? Had they already found the third, fourth, and fifth victims? "I'll give her a ring." He edged past the man still standing in his doorway.

"And call security when you're ready to leave, Professor. We'll walk you to your car. Or over to another building, if that's where you want to go. Just don't leave Harper without us."

"Got it."

The officer gave him a wave and headed toward the stairs. Evan hurried into the sanctuary of his office, closing the door and turning the dead bolt. It made sense that campus security would have keys to all the rooms. He just hadn't thought about it. And now that he had, he didn't like it. Which was rather unkind of him; they were only trying to help.

The phone started ringing as he approached his desk. He snatched it up.

"Addie? I'm so sorry!"

"Bothering the women again, are we?" asked a deep, cheerful voice that carried only a trace of a British accent.

Holding the phone, Evan sank into his chair. "River. I'm glad you called. I need to pick your brain about bog bodies."

"I'm doing well, thank you. Although it's hotter than hell here, even at whatever time of the night it is right now. How are you, brother?"

"Sorry. I'm in the middle of a particularly troublesome case."

"Aren't all your cases particularly troublesome? But this one is about bog bodies, I take it. That, at least, sounds promising."

"It is. About bog bodies, I mean. And it's a bit urgent, if you don't mind."

"Then we'll save the pleasantries for another day. How can I help?"

Evan felt a twinge of guilt. "I *should* ask how Mother is, I suppose."

"You do know that she's closer to you than to me."

"Only if we're speaking geographically. But never mind. I'll gird my loins and call her in a few days. What I want to know is if there have been any recent bog body discoveries. Say, in the last twenty to thirty years. I'm looking especially for something odd. Maybe something unusual or disturbing that happened when the body was excavated."

River's low whistle came through the line. "It's been eons since I've been knee-deep in bogs, poking around for dead bodies. I'm not sure I can pull up anything useful."

"I thought perhaps you could ring up your old Cambridge professor. Dr. Valtos. He's Mr. Bog Body himself, isn't he?"

River laughed. "Did you know that *Valtos* means *swamp* in Greek?"

"I did, actually. Can you give him a call?"

"Happy to. Bog bodies, last twenty to thirty years, something weird. Does that cover it?"

"Pretty much. I'd especially like to know of any potentially traumatic situations where a child was involved. Something that would have made a lasting impression."

"Now you've got me curious. If anyone would know of a case like that, it would be Valtos. Although he retired six or seven years back. I've heard he spends a lot of time fly-fishing in Scotland."

"Then let's hope he's better than I am at carrying his phone around."

"Guess we'll find out." The line went quiet for a moment. Then River said, "You doing okay, big brother? You sound a tad . . . frantic. Which isn't like you."

Evan picked up the photo of River from his desk. The one that showed his younger brother on horseback, tall and rakish among the Bedouins. It was the photo Diana had drooled over.

There had been a time when Evan hated his baby brother. For being of average size. For being charming. For being, more than anything, the apple of their mother's eye. River had been Olivia's do-over. A chance to set things right by proving she could pop out a perfect child.

But despite everything, Evan had fallen in love with the kid. And River, bless his heart, had continued to look up to Evan long after he could no longer do so literally. They'd had a lot of adventures together. Some intellectually rewarding. Some hair-raising.

With luck, they'd have many more.

"It's just this case," Evan said. "I'm doing fine. And you?"

"Bloody hot, like I said. But we're finding amazing stuff, Evan. Amazing. You should come out, take a look. Keep me company for a few months. What's holding you in Chicago?"

A very good question. With one or two good answers and a few more on the fringe.

Were those answers enough?

Outside the windows, storm clouds had regathered. The shadows in the room stretched to fill the space until Evan and the furniture were swallowed by the gloom.

He flicked on the desk lamp. The shadows retreated. But not by much.

"It would be nice to keep you company," he said. "Maybe I'll do that."

"I'll count on it. It's been ages. And we're family. We should see each other now and again." A yawn. "I'd better get a little shut-eye while it's dark. It'll be a hundred and twenty in the shade before I know it. But first I'll try Dr. Valtos. I'll keep you posted."

They said their goodbyes, and River rang off.

Evan pressed the "Off" button, but before he could dial out, the phone squawked in his hand. *This is why I don't carry a phone around,* he thought.

"Addie?"

"Sorry, my friend," Simon said without preamble. "I'm going to have to give you a rain check on happy hour. The work is taking longer than I expected. It's a marvelous trove. Just wonderful."

Evan found himself unexpectedly grumpy. Everyone but him was finding great things. All he was looking for were answers, and he was finding bloody few of those.

In the meantime, the killer was still out there. Or so he assumed. He hadn't even had a chance to listen to the messages on his office phone. He had no doubt Addie had left one or two. Or, more likely, fifty.

Simon was still talking. ". . . client stepped outside to have a ciga-rette. I thought I'd call you and fill you in on Ralph Rhinehart."

"I'm all ears," Evan said. He reached into his desk drawer and pulled out the wooden figurine someone had delivered to his office. The stick man on his stick horse. He set it on his desk, in the pool of light.

Simon said, "You are probably aware that Ralph Rhinehart's parents were quite respected in the rare-book industry, yes?"

"I do remember that."

"Bill and Nancy Rhinehart were some of the best in the biz. Noses like bloodhounds and with unimpeachable respectability. They always played fair, were known for being scrupulously honest. Because of that, people took their finds and treasures to them. Those two got some of the best books and manuscripts in the business."

"Didn't they acquire that original broadside of the Declaration of Independence back in the eighties?"

"They did indeed. Favored by the gods, those two. The document was tucked inside a garage sale picture frame and very nearly consigned to the dust heap. They brokered the Sotheby's auction. Anyway, every-one was both happy and a bit envious when Ralph followed his parents into the business. He showed every sign of being as honest, if not as sharp-eyed, as his parents."

"I sense the turning of the story."

"You are so correct. After Bill and Nancy were killed—"

"A car crash, if I remember."

"Yes. Terrible, the way life can turn on a dime. After they passed, young Ralph decided he wanted nothing to do with the rare-book world. He sold the business to an up-and-comer in the field for what I'm sure was a tidy profit. And then he vanished."

"Vanished?"

"Completely. Old business acquaintances didn't hear from him. If he had friends, they ran in other circles. We only got the story later."

Evan stood and walked over to the table where the brandy bottle and snifters still sat, glowing softly in the storm's false dusk. "And what was the story?"

"He up and hauled off to England, went to work for a construction firm there called Osborn-Kleinberger. Moved very quickly to the top, we heard."

Evan lowered the hand that had been reaching for the brandy. "England."

"He apparently settled in quite nicely there. Married the American daughter of the owner of the firm, started a family. But then tragedy struck again. His wife passed away while still young, and Rhinehart pulled stakes again. He went into the rare-book business once more, focusing on items from the early Middle Ages. That's when things turn sordid."

Evan grabbed the bottle and one of the snifters and returned to his desk. "How sordid?"

"He began working with less reputable dealers, or so we heard. According to the rumor mill, he was deliberating purchasing forgeries and passing them along to clients. The turning point came when he went into partnership with a decidedly unsavory young man who brought in family money and offered to do Rhinehart's footwork for him, traveling the world looking for rare manuscripts. Ultimately, this man was accused of almost pulling off an incredible coup."

Evan wiped out the snifter with the hem of his sweater and poured a splash of brandy. "You're very good at building suspense, Simon."

"Thank you."

"This isn't the time for suspense."

Simon cleared his throat. "Of course. This young man claimed to have found a companion poem to the *Beowulf* epic. As you can imagine, the announcement caused quite a stir. Old English died out as a spoken language long before the invention of the printing press, so manuscripts from that time are handwritten and quite rare. Rhinehart verified the provenance of the document and took it to an auction house. The firm initially confirmed the find, and things were looking quite wonderful for our dear Mr. Rhinehart. But then a few questions arose, other experts were brought in, and eventually the manuscript was declared a fraud. The finding destroyed what was left of Rhinehart's reputation."

Evan swallowed the brandy and poured another splash. "And with no reputation to preserve, he turned to occultism and mysterious alphabets?"

"Apparently. But not before the last nails were hammered into his coffin, in a manner of speaking. The young man who claimed to have found the poem is also believed—according to the rumor mill—to have died under mysterious circumstances before he could be brought up on charges. Something about bad brakes and a curving cliffside road. Classic cinema stuff."

"Are you suggesting Rhinehart had something to do with it?"

"That's what was rattling around the grapevine, my dear Evan. I checked back with a friend who believes Rhinehart was brought in for questioning by the police. If that's true, nothing came of it. Given that, you can hardly blame him for retreating to America and focusing his interest in other areas."

"What was the timing on all this? The pseudo-*Beowulf* manuscript, the young man's alleged death?"

"Early part of the millennium, I suppose. Rhinehart returned to the States around 2006 or 2007. Ah, here's my client back now. I've got to run. I hope that was helpful."

"Very much so. Thank you, Simon."

"Always happy to be of service. Just be careful around Rhinehart. I've heard from book dealers who specialize in the occult that he's a much darker man than he used to be. And a bit desperate, apparently, for whatever reason. Maybe finances." He cupped a hand over the phone and called "be right there" to someone. He came back on the line. "Do take care, my friend."

And he was gone.

Evan immediately dialed Diana, but his call went straight to voice mail. He left her a message to call him back as soon as possible, that he had the details on Rhinehart, that the man was considered both desperate and shady. That it was even possible he was linked to a murder. He babbled on for a minute before reluctantly disconnecting.

He leaned back in his chair and eyeballed the wooden figurine.

Diana would be fine. It was lunch, for Pete's sake. Not a midnight meeting in the woods. And if it came to it, she could disembowel a man like Rhinehart and hang him up by his own intestines, all without raising a sweat.

His phone rang. Wiser this time, he answered with a professional, "Dr. Wilding."

"As soon as we hang up, I need you to go to a police station," Addie said.

He listened while she explained what they'd found at Hank Helskin's house. The man's murder. The fact that Mr. X was almost certainly a Viking wannabe named David Hayne, aka Raven. That the men had been abusing dogs—forcing them to fight and possibly engaging in sacrifice. And that a search of Tommy Snow's house hadn't turned up any more bones, but the kid himself had gone missing.

"Where does the police station fit in?" Evan asked.

"We found a bone carved with runes next to Helskin's body," she said. "It said, *the sparrow is riding of riding*. I don't suppose I need to spell that out for you?"

"No. It's quite clear." He felt a flash of panic, then calm returned. "I just don't understand why. Any idea who victims three and four are?"

"No. I'm going to send a squad car for you."

"Please don't. I'm of more use to the investigation if I remain safely ensconced in my office, working on my profile under the watchful eyes of the campus police."

"Turn here," she said to someone else, then came back to the phone. "You promise to stay put? With the door locked?"

"I promise."

"You won't leave."

"That's generally what *staying put* entails."

"Okay. I have to go. Raven is our top suspect right now, and we're running him down. You'll stay in your office?"

"I won't move an inch. Stay safe, Addie."

"You too, my friend."

He sat for a moment, wondering at this latest development and the whereabouts of Tommy Snow. Then he called Ragnarök and asked for Sten Elger. A woman told him to hold on, and a moment later, Sten's cheery voice boomed across the ether.

"You want to try your hand at ax-throwing?" Sten asked.

Evan couldn't hold back a laugh. "That would be something, wouldn't it?"

"Don't dis it. A skill like that could come in handy. So how can I help you?"

Evan told him that it was possible the figurine left by Ragnarök's front door had something to do with the case he and Patrick were working on. "It might be a good idea to stick close to home until this is settled. Ask patrol to swing by now and again. And keep your ax handy."

"Wow," Sten said after a moment's silence. "This is crazy. But sure. I'm not going anywhere. When I'm at the club, I've always got at least ten or twelve heavily armed patrons standing around. Maybe I'll hang out here until you give me the all clear."

Reassured, Evan promised to keep Sten informed and said his goodbyes.

He unlocked the bottom drawer of his desk and pulled out the gun he kept stashed there, strictly against university policy. He didn't like guns; he was a man of mind, not muscle. The weapon was a left-over from his times traipsing around the globe with River, when things could, in a matter of seconds, go from wonderful to very, very bad. He popped the magazine, retrieved the bullets from a small safe, loaded it, jammed it back in, then set the gun on his desk.

"Ready for bear," he said. The room swallowed his words.

In the lamplight, the figurine regarded him balefully. If he was, in fact, in danger, he wondered what he'd done to draw the killer's ire. Perhaps it was nothing more than his size. Dwarfs appeared hundreds of times in the Viking sagas. When Addie pulled him into the case, the killer must have seen targeting Evan as foreordained.

He stood and hunted around until he found a map of Chicago rolled up and rubber-banded in a corner. He cleared a place on the library table and laid out the map, using books to hold the corners. Then he placed Diana's map next to it.

Assuming the most basic facts about serial killers—that they were usually white males between the ages of twenty-five and thirty-four, charismatic, intelligent, impulsive, and manipulative—then that standard profile still left a lot of room for interpretation.

Evan had told River he was looking for someone who'd suffered a childhood trauma. Because Talfour's and Desser's ritualistic deaths weren't thrill kills. The killer was salving some wound. If he was in his midtwenties to midthirties, then twenty to thirty years ago or so, something had happened that so horrified a little boy that the boy, once grown, had been driven to reenact the trauma. To purge the pain by taking it from inside himself, turning it into a story, and re-creating it.

Also, equally certain, a more recent event had served as a trigger, bringing up all the killer's horror and compelling him to at last visit his anguish on others.

For if we ever come to believe that the world reflects our childhood terrors, then something must break. Ourselves. Or the world.

He eyed the dull glint of the gun on his desk, then opened his journal to the sketches he'd made of Talfour's body, bruised and battered, naked and fetal, staked down in the watery weeds.

The scene of a murder carried many signs. Most obvious were the forensic signs, such as blood spatter and fingerprints. But there were often other, less certain signs that could be difficult to interpret. Patterns and symbols, rituals enacted or reenacted, victims posed. In cases where the killer was driven by religious intentions, versions of extreme killing weren't unusual. Perhaps the gods that demanded these deaths could only be appeased if the deaths were both brutal and prolonged.

He zeroed in on the wooden stakes he'd drawn, the ones holding down Talfour's body. The Vikings had a term for the unquiet dead—*draugar*, or *draugr* in the singular form. *Draugar* were essentially zombies—the reanimated corpses of people who, in life, had been ill-doers of one kind or another. Often, they returned as creatures much larger than humans, with superhuman strength. The Vikings had responded to this threat by sometimes mutilating their dead or holding them down with stones inside the grave. You did not want to meet the *draugar* on your way home across the fields.

This fear of encountering the dead—was that their killer's secret terror?

The answer lay somewhere in the signs he'd left behind.

As Evan bent over the maps, his mind made an all-too-familiar shift, moving into a darker and more lethal place. A place where he was no longer the detective or the semiotician. A place that had its roots deep in the ancient recesses of his brain.

He became the hunter.

CHAPTER 26

"Turn here," Addie said.

Patrick released a sigh as he pulled into the parking lot of a large chain store in Bridgeport.

"Seems so American, doesn't it?" he said. "Collaring a serial killer in a big-box discount store smack-dab next to an expressway."

For the last hour, they'd driven around the city while Addie directed Patrick. Raven's location had pinged on a map every ten minutes, whenever the signal from his tracker uploaded to the mobile app.

For the last twenty-three minutes, his location had held steady.

She placed Ryan Ruley's phone in the console and glanced across the street from the store at what looked like acres of asphalt. Several dozen 18-wheelers sat in gleaming white and chrome rows.

"We sure are a long way from Vikings and bog bodies," she said.

Patrick followed her gaze. "A freight shipping company. You know, it used to be pretty down here, once upon a time. Now, let's see if we can find Helskin's vehicle."

He drove to the east side of the store's parking lot and then went slowly up and down the lanes until Addie spotted Helskin's truck—a late-model Ford—parked near the entrance.

"He's here," she said. "Or somewhere close by. The tracker puts him within a hundred yards. Plus or minus."

Patrick gave a noncommittal grunt. He pulled the sedan into an empty space in a far corner of the lot so that they had a good visual of the area. Rain spattered the sedan's windows, and he flipped on the wipers. "Temperature keeps dropping, we're gonna get snow."

Addie unbuckled and stretched her legs as far as she could and watched as hordes of shoppers darted in and out through the automatic doors, holding their coats tight against the wind. What did all these people do for a living that left them free to shop on a Tuesday afternoon?

Was Raven—aka David Hayne—among them?

"He must have no idea we're onto him," she said. "Probably doesn't even know Helskin's death has been reported."

"I hate to pop your balloon, partner, but the signal could also mean that he's dumped the tracker and the pickup and beat feet out of here."

"Not funny, Paddy Wagon."

"Don't make it not true. It's what I would have done. There are friggin' hundreds of cars all around this area to hot-wire. He could have his pick. Heck, there's even a railroad right on the other side of the expressway if he had a mind to head out for parts unknown."

Addie's heart was pounding hard enough for her to feel it in her ears. "I need him to be here. *Evan* needs him to be here."

"I know." Patrick pulled a handkerchief out of his pocket and dabbed his nose. "Maybe he is. Even murderers need potato chips and toilet paper."

"So how do you want to play this, oh wise and experienced partner? The full-on circus in blue? With all these civilians here, I'm thinking quick and quiet."

Patrick stuffed the handkerchief back in his pocket. "I'm thinking you're right."

"Let's case the interior, then call for backup as soon as we have eyes on him."

"Sounds like a plan." He started the engine. "You take the west side of the store. I'll start on the east. You spot him, text me whatever aisle you're in. I'll do likewise. We'll call for backup, then follow him out, wait until he's fumbling bags and keys, and make our move."

"You don't really think he's in there, do you?"

"The truth? I think he's long gone. But what else we got at the moment?"

Her right foot tapped a rhythm of its own on the floor mat. "If he's not here . . ."

Patrick patted her arm. "I've been known to be wrong every blue moon or so."

☒

Inside the store, Addie snatched up a shopping basket and made a quick turn to the left, heading down the aisle behind the checkout lanes with her phone in her hand. She glanced in the coffee shop, took in the line at the in-store pizza place, then let her gaze skim over the patrons waiting in line. *Head on a swivel,* an army friend had once told her. *What you do when you need to take in everything all at once.*

When Addie reached the far side of the store, she turned right again and started down the first aisle. She maneuvered around a family—a mom and three kids—then an elderly man examining LED bulbs. She went around the corner and down the next aisle, trying to look like an afternoon shopper in a bit of a hurry.

No one paid her any mind.

Not until the fourth aisle. This one held camping gear—stoves, camp chairs, cook pots, and ignitors. And a man with the hood of his sweatshirt pulled up, standing with his back to her. He held a folded-up tarp in plastic wrapping. She was sure she'd also seen him slip something into his pocket.

She edged past him. He jumped when he sensed her presence and angled away from her, keeping his face hidden. *Just like Talfour's attackers,* she thought. She removed a heavy-duty flashlight from the shelf and pretended to read the fine print on the package.

The man fit Raven's height and build, roughly speaking. He wore jeans and sneakers and a dirty ski jacket pulled over the hoodie. Gloves covered his hands. She couldn't see his face. If he were Raven, he'd be careful to avoid being seen—by customers and by cameras.

The man tucked the tarp under his arm and headed away from her, toward the back of the store. She returned the flashlight to the shelf and followed at a discreet distance, tapping out a text for Patrick: possible suspect aisle 17

The man shot a glance over his shoulder as he turned the corner into the aisle that ran along the back of the store. Was that a tattoo on his forehead?

She set her shopping basket on a nearby shelf, unzipped her jacket, and placed a hand close to her hip and the gun holstered there. Patrick was now approaching from the other direction, moving toward them in a studiously casual way. He seemed to be raptly focused on the board games that filled the shelves on the back wall.

The man picked up his pace. Addie did the same.

Suddenly he spun on the balls of his feet and pushed through a door. Addie took off after him, vaguely aware that Patrick was now also running. She caught a glimpse of a sign declaring the area was for employees only; then she was through the door and in a cavernous space filled with shelves of overstock.

She paused. The target was nowhere in sight.

Patrick came through the door behind her. She held up a hand for silence.

They caught the sound of footsteps thudding on the concrete floor, moving away.

Addie broke into a run, darting down an aisle, Patrick right behind her. A pair of employees looked at them in surprise and jumped out of the way. There came a gust of cold air and a flare of daylight; then she heard a door slam shut.

"He's outside," she said.

Patrick skidded to a stop. "I'll call for backup."

She kept running, slapping the door handle and bursting into the open air. Rain spattered on her face. She was standing on a raised platform—a loading dock. The target was racing down a set of stairs toward the lane that ran between the store and a high stone wall. She spotted a gap in the wall and knew if the man made it there, he'd melt into the surrounding area where there were a million places to hide.

She leapt down the stairs, taking them three at a time and landing smoothly at the bottom. The man was halfway to the gap in the wall.

She whipped out her gun.

"Police! Stop!"

To her surprise, he did.

"Hands up!" she shouted.

He dropped the tarp and raised his hands.

"Now turn around. Slowly!"

When the man complied, Addie's disappointment hit her like a fist. The man wasn't Raven. He wasn't in his twenties or even vaguely Viking-like. He was a middle-aged white man, breathing hard from the run and looking utterly miserable.

On his face was a tattoo of a tiger.

She hadn't found a serial killer. She'd caught a petty thief.

⚔

The evidence techs found Raven's fitness tracker half an hour later, tossed under a dirty T-shirt on the floor of Helskin's pickup. Thirty minutes after that, Lieutenant Criver arrived—no doubt alerted by

Dispatch that they might have found the Viking Poet. He'd parked a short distance away and was now striding across the parking lot in their direction, for once missing his oily sidekick, Billings.

His face looked like a thunderclap.

"Ah, Saint Jude spare me," Patrick muttered. "You think he's here to praise our ingenuity?"

"And to thank us for our hard work," Addie said darkly. "Right after he eviscerates us for the latest leak to the press."

She was watching the evidence techs, who were carefully sifting through the rest of the truck's contents. They'd cleared out the parking area immediately adjacent to the vehicle and set up a perimeter. Outside the tape, a small crowd had gathered. Two patrol officers kept watch.

The wind was a constant slap, but the rain had fizzled out. At least they had that.

"A shoplifter?" Criver said when he drew close.

Patrick glanced at her, and she gave him a small nod. Since the lieutenant preferred to work with a man, she decided to let Patrick handle it. She was too worried to deal with misogynist jerkwads.

While Patrick began to fill Criver in on the latest developments, Addie turned her back and kept her attention on the truck and the techs.

The seats and footwells of Helskin's vehicle were filled with the detritus of a life lived without any care for the usual borders between one's home and one's vehicle—maybe Helskin spent a lot of time in his truck. Dirty shirts and socks, wadded-up food wrappers, two sets of work boots, twenty-three empty plastic bottles bearing the logo of a sports drink company. Two empty bottles of rotgut whiskey. An unused pair of running shoes still in the box. What looked like a month's worth of mail—nothing but bills and advertisements. In the bed of the truck, a bolted-on toolbox held a shovel, garbage bags, a hammer, and assorted other tools.

"Give us *something*," she muttered under her breath.

Behind her, the lieutenant said, "Detective Bisset."

She turned. Criver's stormy eyes were fixed on her.

"Sir?"

His jaw worked. Finally, he said, "Good work."

She gaped. "Sir?"

"Patrick told me about the fitness tracker. That was good thinking."

"It hasn't exactly paid off," she said, then mentally kicked herself. Why couldn't she just say *thanks* and shut up?

Now one of the techs called her name. She spun back around. He stood next to the open driver's door. He looked sick to his stomach.

"We found something," he said.

CHAPTER 27

Evan looked away from the computer screen, made a few more notes in his journal, and set down his pen.

He'd found twelve areas that roughly corresponded with the bog burial sites in England. Cemeteries, waterfronts, sketchy industrial sites. He'd then narrowed it down to seven locations based on a set of criteria: the presence of water, sufficient isolation, and—critically but also more subjectively—areas with an air of forlornness and mystery. Even abandonment. Places the killer might consider in-between spaces, like the European bogs. Neither city nor country. Neither civilized nor completely wild. Neither fully land nor entirely water.

Places where the Others gathered, demanding sacrifice.

He typed up his findings in an email, attached the maps, and sent it all to Addie. He'd follow up shortly with a phone call. For the moment, he forced himself to put aside the brandy and instead made a cup of tea, strong and mind clearing. He found an unopened packet of chocolate digestives in the cupboard under the electric kettle. Newly content, or reasonably so, he settled back in his chair and opened his journal to the killer's poems.

Christina had talked about blood feuds, and trying to find the source of a feud seemed a good avenue for his approach. He dug out a voice recorder from the depths of a desk drawer and hit "Record."

"Talfour and Desser weren't men living on the outskirts of society," he said. "They were deeply involved in their communities. Talfour with his store and his volunteer activities; Desser with his accounting business and service to his synagogue. The killer took great risk in selecting them. They are the *mighty men* of his poem."

He glanced down at his journal. *Mighty men I undo and unto earth I send their water-weighted corpses.*

"What was it about these men that made it worth the risk?" he continued. "What sins had they—wittingly or otherwise—committed against the killer to ignite a blood feud?"

He returned to the idea of a *skin-sinner* in Talfour's poem. He'd first thought it might be a reference to the fact that Talfour was a Black man. That the killer was a racist.

But what if it meant something else entirely?

How do you sin against skin?

Ideas rolled through his mind. He spoke them out loud. "Human trafficking. Indentured servitude. Prostitution." He paused, took a sip of tea. "It's certainly possible that Talfour engaged a prostitute and paid for it with his life. But it doesn't fit with the lines from Desser's poem that hint *his* sin was something very different."

He reread the line. *She takes back her sons and daughters who rived and tholed and peeled her flesh like ripe fruit.*

Translation—*She takes back the children who hurt her.*

But who was the *she* of the poem? And what had her children done to her?

Helskin's dogs, he recalled, had suffered terrible abuse. Perhaps even sacrifice.

He sat up. At the station house meeting, someone had mentioned that Talfour carried furs in his store. And that he also, ironically, supported an animal rights organization.

Evan reached for the computer keyboard and pulled up the website for Talfour's store. He clicked on the "Shop" icon. And there it was. A wide selection of furs carried by Finer Things. Fox, sable, mink. Coyote and chinchilla.

Furs. Which was to say pelts or skins. A furrier could be a skin-sinner. Especially to a poet writing in kennings.

He did some online digging about Scott Desser. A scan of newspaper articles showed the accountant's name was linked to development firms whose projects included building homes over marshes and knocking down forests to raise multifamily housing. One of the firms had purchased a Superfund site right here in Chicago, promising to clean it up. But then, months later, the head of the firm had walked out on the deal after pocketing the federal funds. A lawsuit was pending. A third firm whose books Desser had apparently handled was a mining company that boasted some of the largest bauxite and coal strip mines in the world. Here in the United States, they were best known for gold and silver mining.

His gaze returned to his journal. *Her sons and daughters who peeled her flesh like ripe fruit.*

And another line, *Thus from my cottage I came, homeland's ward.*

Speaking into the recorder, he said, "*Homeland's ward.* Which we could interpret as earth's guardian. Is the killer punishing those who hurt the earth and her creatures? In line fourteen of his poem, he mentions *Fjorgyn*, saying, *A slayer of the bone-halls breaking Fjorgyn. Bone-halls* is a kenning for humans. And *Fjorgyn* is the personification of the earth in Norse mythology. Humans breaking the earth."

That was what his mind had been groping for when he stood beneath the pewter sky at the pond where Desser had died. Some ancient part of himself had recognized the place as one where the spirits of nature still dwelled, crouched and feral before the encroaching onslaught of humanity.

Before long, the *cidiots* would be everywhere.

He typed in EARTH LAW and was rewarded with a series of articles arguing that Nature with a capital *N* should be allowed to defend itself in a court of law, or at least its proxies should. That ecosystems, like humans, have the right to exist without being violated or abused.

He tried Diana once again—still voice mail—then dug Christina's business card out of his pocket and dialed her number. When she answered, he thanked her again for her help.

"I just have one more question," he said. Then added, "At least for the moment."

"Fire away, Evan. It's nice to hear your voice again so soon."

His neck grew hot. *Stay focused. Ask her out for a drink when this is all over.* "Did the Vikings ever sacrifice directly to the earth?"

"Hmm. Good question. But I'd have to say no. Not in the way, say, the Greeks sacrificed to their earth deity, Gaea. The Vikings didn't see the Earth herself as an entity."

"I see." Nothing like having a bucket of ice water dumped on his theory.

"But," she continued, "they certainly sacrificed to those spirits we talked about. Many of the so-called Others were spirits of the land."

He perked up. "Meaning if you inflict some kind of injury against the land, it might be considered an insult against these spirits?"

"Oh, it most definitely would. And the spirits would not be happy about it."

He stood and went to a window. He stepped onto the footstool he kept on the floor in front of the panes. Outside, the clouds had bunched themselves in dark clots. A few flakes of snow drifted down. His breath misted the glass.

"What does it look like when the spirits are unhappy?" he asked.

"Any number of things could happen. It depends on the spirit. Tidal waves, tornadoes, ice storms. A great many people could be swept up by the spirit's fury. Or it could be far more personal. A direct attack against the sinner."

"What would happen to them?"

"A lone man or woman who offended the spirits? God help them. Death, most likely. And not an easy one."

Chapter 28

Addie held her hands steady as she studied the photographs. Five pictures showed the torture that James Talfour had suffered before his death. Five more revealed Desser's agony.

The full-color glossies had been in a manila envelope the evidence tech found partially concealed beneath the driver's seat. Written on the envelope in red marker was her name.

To: Detective Bisset

From: The Viking Poet

Feeling faint, she looked around the parking lot as if Raven would suddenly leap out from behind a car. She scrutinized the crowd gathered behind the police tape. No Raven. No tattooed Viking reenactors. Just a mix of curious Black and Asian teenagers along with a few alarmed white middle-aged women who were probably wondering what criminal had decided to stake out territory in the parking lot of their neighborhood store.

Still, she felt watched.

More than that. She felt naked and exposed.

Rustle up some anger, Addie, she told herself. *You are* so *going to take this guy down.*

Patrick was suddenly at her elbow. "The hell is that?" he asked, pointing at the envelope she held in her gloved fingers. "He wrote your *name* on there?"

She summoned a smile. "Feeling left out?"

But he stared at her, aghast.

"We'll need to get our digital specialists to look at these," she said. "Maybe they can pull something out of the background."

Almost instantly, Patrick's horror turned to rage at the implied threat against his partner. She watched it happen, as if someone had changed the set design in the middle of a play.

And just as suddenly, with a boil and snap in her blood, there it was: her own anger.

"We'll find something in these photos, partner," Patrick growled. "Not to worry. We're gonna get this guy. I promise you that."

"Damn right we are," she agreed.

She waited until Patrick and Criver had put on gloves, then passed the photos over to them. Her phone buzzed, and she glanced at the screen. Evan.

"I'll be right back," she said to Patrick.

She felt his eyes on her as she stripped off her gloves and walked away, chin held high, heading toward his car. She let the phone keep buzzing until she'd slid into the passenger seat and closed the door. Then she answered with, "Are you okay?"

"I'm perfectly fine. Check your email."

"What is it?"

"Locations. Take a look and call me back. I'm still working."

"Wait—"

But he was gone.

She scrolled through her email in-box until she found Evan's note. She read it with growing excitement, then opened the attachments and scanned the series of maps. She dug around in Patrick's car until she found his spiral-bound city map stuffed into a pocket behind the front seat and spread it open on her lap. Then she rang Evan.

When he answered, she said, "Tell me what I'm looking at."

"Diana put together a map of the bog body sites in England. Right now, all I have is a theory, but I believe the killer is doing a one-to-one mapping of his victims and intended victims with those graves in England," he told her. "The maps I sent are my best guesses, so don't read too much into them. But it's a place to start. Or rather, *places* to start."

Hope rose in Addie like a balloon lifting into the sky. "You're amazing."

"That remains to be seen. Don't get excited until you check out these locations. My experience with them is purely virtual."

While Addie used a pen to mark the locations on Patrick's map, Evan filled her in on his new theory—that the victims were people who had committed crimes against nature. She listened in growing astonishment while he explained the concept of Earth Laws and then told her about Talfour's and Desser's supposed crimes—taking the pelts of animals, accepting money from those who ripped open the earth for treasure.

"Helskin's abuse of the dogs would certainly qualify him," he said.

"But he wasn't the target."

"Maybe he was."

"What do you mean?"

"Based on the lines of the poem," he went on, "it's quite possible that Helskin *was* the killer's intended victim. But something went wrong. Maybe Helskin fought back and the killer had to strike quickly. Thus forgoing the torture and special burial he requires to fulfill his fantasy."

"Helskin was tased first," she said. "We thought that his killer might have tried to subdue him, then resorted to smashing in his skull when Helskin kept coming."

"Being tased wouldn't keep you down for long."

"Maybe a few minutes."

"Which brings us back to one of our original questions of how—"

"How the killer is capturing his victims and getting them to wherever he's torturing them," she finished for him.

Evan let loose a sigh that carried over the ether. "If Helskin was his target, then it means that he has to select a new victim to be his *thorn*, his number three. For whatever reason, having five victims is important to him. He won't allow his plan to be diverted."

She pictured her name written neatly on the manila envelope. But she couldn't be one of the intended victims, could she? The worst thing she'd done against Mother Earth was buy nonorganic produce.

Maybe that was enough.

She'd finished marking up Patrick's map. Now, with rising excitement, she closed the atlas, tucked it under her arm, and stepped back outside, facing into the wind.

"This second area you mention in your email," she said, the wind cutting across the mic of her phone. "The Damen Silos near the Canalport Riverwalk. That's a half mile from the store where we found Raven's fitness tracker. It looks like a person can take a bridge to the 29th Street ramp and waltz right on over. The silos are abandoned, if I recall."

"Ever since an explosion back in the seventies," Evan said. "Which makes the site particularly interesting. You have water and isolation and—presumably—nature striving to take back her own."

Addie strode to the edge of the parking lot and looked west. On the far side of the expressway were the tops of a series of concrete structures—the silos.

The anger and fear seething in her gut melted away, replaced by a hard fist of certainty. Raven was close by. She was sure of it.

"I've got to go." She paused. "You haven't left your office, right?"

"I haven't so much as left my desk."

"You're awfully calm about all this."

"I had a panic attack earlier."

"Promise me you'll stay right where you are until I come and get you."

"Addie. We've been through all this." His voice was gentle. "I do have to go home at some point."

"You have food, water, and a bathroom. Probably tea and alcohol, too, if I know you. You have everything you need in that office palace of yours."

"Except Ginny. I have to feed her."

"Have someone else do it. Or she can wait. You've let her go hungry before."

"Only when she needed to cut weight in order to—" He stopped. Sighed.

"Evan?"

"Okay. You win. I'll stay right here."

Suspicious, she said, "Promise?"

"Of course."

"Say it. Say *I promise.*"

"I promise."

"Good." She allowed herself a small, fierce smile. "I love you, my wise friend. I'll see you soon."

CHAPTER 29

A gust of wind shoved against the car as Addie and Patrick pushed open their doors and stepped out into the gale. Immediately, her hair whipped into her eyes. She reached back into the vehicle and searched around until she found an old rubber band on the floor.

Squad cars pulled in behind them. Patrol cops and detectives emerged and moved aside for two up-armored Hummers, which drove down the paved lane that led to the silos. The drivers parked, and eight members of the SWAT unit emerged wearing tactical gear.

Now her familiar three-ring circus in blue was poised to operate like the tip of a spear, with SWAT leading the charge.

Around the city, additional groups were descending on the other sites Evan had mapped, looking for victims, for evidence, perhaps for the killer himself.

Addie zipped her jacket and found the gloves she'd shoved in a pocket. No rain, thank heavens. It was too cold now. But a few flakes of snow whipped past.

She lifted her binoculars. Across the water, the Chicago skyline rose in a jumbled silhouette against a blustery sky. Closer by, the fifteen-story Damen Silos loomed like industrial castles, lording over the twenty-four-acre lot, their rounded bases covered in brilliant graffiti—gang signs and pleas for peace along with advice to fuck the police, praise Jesus, say no to drugs, and eat vegan. Outlying buildings—warehouses and structures that might have served as administrative offices—were little more than ruins with gaping holes and empty windows. The Chicago River flowed indifferently past all of it, a silky gray-green current.

If Raven was here, he'd picked himself quite a fortress.

Patrick snugged on a hat and wound a thin wool scarf around the lower half of his face before joining Addie on the passenger side of the vehicle.

"You think he's in there somewhere?" she asked.

"Now that we pulled up like Alexander's army?" He snorted. "I'll tell you one thing. If he's still here, he's watching us with joy in his black little heart. Probably happy as a mouse in a cracker box because he's made us jump through all these hoops for him. But as soon as we get close"—Patrick snapped his fingers—"guaranteed he's got some hellhole where he can pull the dirt in after him and disappear."

"We have a good perimeter in place," she pointed out.

"That we do." He glanced sideways at her. "You think it's enough?"

She didn't answer.

They'd closed off all access points to both vehicular and pedestrian traffic, including South Damen Avenue, South Ashland Avenue, and the Canalport Riverwalk. If Raven bolted for freedom in any direction but the river, patrol would see him. And grab him.

But if he had river access, their plan fell apart.

"I don't see the K-9s," she said. "We're going to need the dogs."

"They're on the way."

The SWAT teams had broken into two groups of four, each group headed toward one of the two immense structures, walking in tight phalanxes along the gravel path that ran between the silos. To Addie, they appeared to be moving with all the forward momentum of glaciers as they hugged the concrete walls and watched for any movement.

Addie bounced on her toes, and Patrick patted her shoulder.

"Easy, partner. It's a lot of space to clear."

She nodded. "I know."

"Plus, you gotta figure there are homeless people living around here. Can't be shooting at everything that pops up."

The teams came to a halt. Addie walked out onto the gravel rut, staring down the lane with her binoculars, trying to see what was happening.

She passed the glasses to Patrick, who peered through them and said, "Speak of the devil."

An old woman had appeared suddenly next to one of the silos, almost as if she'd sprung from the ground. Her spine was bent and twisted, her steps slow and uncertain. Someone on the first SWAT team shouted something that the wind carried away, and the woman came to a shuffling halt. There was another shout, and a few seconds later, she raised her hands.

One of the SWAT members moved toward her, stopping a few feet away. The woman lowered her hands, and the two seemed to confer. She pointed toward the base of one of the curving silos. The man nodded, then motioned for one of the patrol officers to come forward and escort the woman away from the area. The man jogged back to his group, and the two SWAT teams reconverged.

A minute later, six men broke away and ran toward the silo where the woman had emerged and stopped at the base. They appeared to be studying the ground.

"Looks like with all the doors bricked up, the squatters have dug their way into the place," Patrick said.

She grabbed the binoculars back from Patrick.

The SWAT guys drew back, and a moment later, there came a boom and a flare of light. A flash-bang grenade. Addie raised the binoculars again, and now, with the men standing distant and smoke rising, she could make out a pile of excavated rubble and a hole leading into the dark.

The men regrouped and dropped one by one into the hole and vanished. For a time, there was only the sound of the wind howling around the towers and the hushed breath of thirty men and women, waiting. Through the binoculars, Addie watched the two SWAT team leads, who were in radio communication with the men inside. Their faces gave away nothing.

Forty minutes went by. Then another twenty. Lieutenant Criver arrived and told Addie and Patrick that—according to the incident commander—the men were still searching the underground area.

"Our guys say there are so many tunnels down there, it looks like a rabbit burrow," he said. "Miles of them."

Patrick kicked the gravel. "Hellfire and damnation."

Addie remained silent; her throat was closed as if with metal wire. Raven was little more than a needle in an industrial haystack.

She flashed to the photos left in Helskin's truck. If Raven was in the silos, if he was, in fact, the Viking Poet, was he already at work on his third victim?

Fifteen minutes later, one of the men who'd gone into the silos finally emerged. He spoke to the team leads, then gestured for Addie and Patrick and the lieutenant to join him.

"Sergeant Ray Trujillo," he said, shaking their hands. Beneath his green helmet, his expression was tight. "There's a hell of a lot of territory down there. But we did find where someone's set up a permanent home. He's got a generator running power to a pair of light bulbs. Plenty of bottled water and nonperishables. Even got himself a cot and a table. Nice and cozy."

Patrick tucked his hands under his arms. "Any personal items?"

"Nothing lying around. We made sure the place wasn't boo-by-rigged but otherwise left it alone. Outside of that, there's not much. Remnants of old campfires, a lot of trash and human feces. And a shitload of dead pigeons."

Addie's thoughts raced back to the previous day. Evan had mentioned a bird. A dead pigeon sliced open in the field. She found her voice. "How many pigeons?"

"Maybe a hundred. They must have flown in and couldn't figure out how to get back out. There's another access point at the far end. And a nasty-looking metal staircase heading toward the upper floors."

"No other squatters?" Patrick asked.

"According to the old woman, the man who has homesteaded in there drove off everyone else."

"How'd he manage that?"

"The old lady, she's *muy loca*. But she says when the man came, so did the *others*." Trujillo curled his fingers into air quotes for the word *others*. "Everyone else was afraid of these *others*, so they left."

The others. Did she mean Raven's fellow neo-Nazis? She said, "Did you go up the stairs?"

"We went up two flights, and then I pulled my men back. Sections have torn away from the wall, and it looks like most of the landings are missing. It was probably damaged during the explosion that shut this place down." His eyes met hers. "I guarantee you, no one has gone up those stairs in decades."

Addie doubted that. If there were stairs to climb, someone would manage to get up.

"What about the woman?" she asked. "Why did she stay here after everyone else left?"

"She said she isn't afraid of the others. But when she says *others*, I don't think she's talking about people."

At a sound, Trujillo glanced over his shoulder toward the dark gloom of the river. A board had worked its way loose from the rotting pier and been caught by the wind. He turned back.

"I think she's talking about spirits," he said. "Or ghosts. I dunno, invisible people. She says the man comes and goes a lot. But when he's around, he talks to these ghosts and sacrifices things to them. Rabbits. Stray dogs. That's what scared off everyone else. He's not a nice man, she says. But sometimes he leaves granola bars along with the dead animals, and she takes those. And he gives her canned beans and potato chips every couple weeks. That's probably all she's eating."

"I'll be damned." Patrick's voice was muffled behind his scarf. "Everyone else beat feet, but this little old lady stayed."

"Probably she's got nowhere to go. And like I said"—the sergeant tapped his temple—"she's *muy loca*."

Addie's stomach had started doing swan dives from her throat to her belly button. "Did she mention a name? Or what he looks like?"

"Just that he's got a bird tattooed on his forehead."

"That's our guy," Patrick said.

Trujillo nodded. "According to the old woman, he was here earlier today, but he left hours ago. We checked out as much as we could in there, and we'll keep pushing through. But the place feels empty. All the machinery has been stripped, and except for that access point I mentioned, plus the staircase and a few windows, everything has been boarded over."

Addie's stomach dropped one more time and stayed there.

"Well," Patrick said. "I suspect our bird has flown the coop. But let's go take a look at his hidey-hole."

She nodded.

"You coming, Lieutenant?" Patrick asked.

"Wouldn't miss it," Criver said. "You'll take us in, Sergeant Trujillo?"

Trujillo said, "Of course, sir."

The three men started down the gravel path.

Addie's phone buzzed. It was a text from the medical examiner.

Just emailed my report. Detectives Bishop and Hohn were in attendance. Answer to your main question: Talfour was hit w a stun gun and injected with ketamine.

Well, Addie thought. *That explains that.* Doctors and veterinarians used ketamine as an anesthetic, although it was more commonly known as a date rape drug. The killer could hit a victim with a stun gun from a safe distance, then, while his target was momentarily helpless, inject the ketamine. The sedative took effect in one to two minutes and could be topped off as needed. By the time the target regained consciousness, he'd be tied up and in a world of hurt.

After that, it would get worse.

Patrick stopped on the path and turned back. "You coming, partner?"

"Be right there."

But she waited a moment longer. She tilted her head back and stared up at the concrete monolith. More snowflakes skittered past. The afternoon was waning; the clouds had already devoured the sun, and it would be full-on dark before they reemerged.

"Where are you?" she whispered as the wind flattened the grasses and whipped her hair about her face.

We're everywhere, she imagined a thousand voices whispering.

She hurried after the men.

⚔

In his office, Evan checked caller ID and grabbed his ringing phone from the desk.

"Diana!" he cried.

"Why, Professor," she said. "You sound surprised. I told you I'd call."

He sat down. "And you're a woman of your word. How was lunch?"

"It was a bit awkward, honestly."

"He's a Satanist. What did you expect?"

"Well, he didn't do anything to my food. And actually, he was quite pleasant. Not the least bit sleazy."

Evan turned grouchy in exactly the way a big brother did when he didn't like who his sister was dating. "You sound like you had a good time."

"Hmm. I wouldn't call him charming, exactly. But he bought me a very nice lunch with sparkly wine even if he did push rather hard for information about the investigation. When I told him I had nothing to share, he turned distracted. As if I were not the topmost thing on his mind."

He could hear the pout in her voice. "Perish the thought."

"He was also quite sweaty."

"You have that effect on men."

"Only when I'm trying to frighten them. Or seduce them. Which I most certainly was not. On either count. Ralph—"

"Now it's Ralph?"

"After I proved useless, *Ralph* seemed in rather a hurry to end our lunch. I don't think that's ever happened to me on a first date."

"*First* date? I feel obligated at this point to remind you of the man's arrogance. The fact that he smells like a pair of gym socks buried in a litter box. Did you even bother looking at his *hair?*"

"Don't be shallow," Diana scolded. "But I'm kidding. He referred to it as a date, and if that's what it was, it was most certainly our last. All that aside, I don't know why he bothers asking a woman out. He's still horribly torn up about his wife, even though she died years ago. Back when he worked as a big-kahuna developer for a firm in England. It struck me as an odd career choice for a man who went on to become an occultist."

"Maybe grief drove him to the dark arts the way it drives others to drink. I heard his wife died quite young."

"Lung cancer. Ralph said she withered away to nothing. Exposure to coal tar."

"Coal tar *is* an environmental carcinogen," Evan said, thinking out loud.

"Apparently."

Evan made a note in his journal, then fingered back his hair, which had fallen into his eyes. "So in the end, Mr. Ralph Rhinehart didn't strike you as dark and desperate?"

"Distracted, as I said. But perhaps *desperate* is also a good word. With all the sweating and whatnot. Still, for a man who claims to be fascinated by occultism, he didn't seem particularly dark. Just gloomy. A rather sad Satanist, all in all."

"A grieving necromancer," Evan murmured. "Not how one normally pictures practitioners of the dark arts. Where's the evil laugh and the sinister gaze?"

"Maybe the poor man spends too much time alone with his grief. He's got a stepchild as well as two kids of his own, but they stayed behind in England. If I were him, I would have bought myself a nice flat somewhere near the kids and become a proper British mystic."

Diana had more than once lamented the fact that she was, for all intents and purposes, alone in the world. Her parents had died within six months of each other when she was a teenager, and her only sibling, a brother, had vanished during a fishing trip. Maybe that was why she felt sorry for Rhinehart.

Her voice broke into his thoughts. "What are you doing right now? Did you talk to Addie?"

Evan filled her in on the latest, omitting anything about a possible threat against him. "I don't expect to hear from Addie again for a while, unless the Damen Silos are a bust and she's on to the next site. I'm going to do a little more work here, then head home. By the time I get there, Ginny will be absolutely mad with hunger."

He felt guilty about lying to Addie. But in all fairness, she hadn't asked him if his fingers were crossed. He would be fine, and she'd get over it.

"Would you like company?" Diana asked. "Lunch was so good, I bought extra to share with you."

He smiled into the phone. "I'd love your company. You can help me continue my work on the poem."

"Exactly what every minion hopes to hear. I have to run a few errands. I'll see you in a couple hours. Start planning the cocktails."

Evan gave her the new security code for the house and told her to pull into the garage, and they hung up. Rhinehart might once have been a big kahuna, as Diana put it. But at the station house, he'd seemed almost desperate to prove the worth of his insight. How the mighty can fall.

Outside his door, the floor creaked. Faintly from the levels below came the scrape of chairs, the rattle of voices, the clink of cutlery from the café, all filtered by distance and masonry.

Up here, the hush of centuries had descended.

Another creak. Evan eyed the dead bolt. Then he reached out and picked up the gun on his desk.

He waited.

The moment of terror he'd felt when Addie told him he was the killer's fifth target had torn through his body like the sizzling tail of a comet. Then calm had descended. River had taught him that panicking accomplished nothing. And after a few brushes with death in remote archaeological sites, Evan's body had ceded control to the logic of his mind.

Whatever will be will be, River had told him.

Fate goes ever as it must.

In the hallway, silence reigned again. Evan thought he detected the sound of footsteps retreating down the stairs. He counted to sixty, then returned the gun to the desk and his mind to his work.

He stared down at his drawing of Talfour.

This case was like the jigsaw puzzles he used to work while he sat in hospital waiting rooms as a child. Pieces missing. Pieces from other puzzles mixed in. Half the time, the lid was gone, so you didn't even know what picture you were trying to create.

You had to fill in the blanks using your imagination.

And imagination, as Sherlock Holmes told Dr. Watson, was the mother of truth.

Evan flipped the pages until he came to his translation of the killer's poem.

Over the sun-swimmer home I came for mine.
Mine, mine-gone. Bowel-buried busted by big bosses.
That war-crime, sword-shaker, heart of my dwelling entombed.

He underlined the words *bowel-buried* and *entombed*. References to an actual death and burial? Or another riddle, another kenning for him to uncypher?

Mine, mine-gone.

Could this refer to an actual, literal mine? As in, a hole in the ground? Scott Desser had paid the ultimate price for his sin of working for mining companies. Could a mining accident be the recent trigger that started the killer on his deadly path?

Mine-gone could be a kenning for someone who had been killed in a mining accident. People certainly died in mines. From falls. Explosions. Flying debris.

He frowned.

Sometimes ideas came leaping out of the void like lightning, illuminating everything, sparking connections that made the world—for an instant at least—stand clear and dazzling.

Other times, all one could do was light a single candle and gaze in awe and terror at the immensity of the night.

He bent his head and returned to his work, praying for lightning.

Chapter 30

The warren of tunnels beneath the Damen Silos made Addie think more of rats' nests than rabbit burrows. Which was unfortunate, given her current state of mind. The instant she'd slipped into the hole that led underground, she'd broken out in a panicked sweat.

The concrete alleyways went on endlessly, swallowing light and voices. A dank cold rose from the walls and floors, pressed down from the ceiling. Soon the sheen of sweat on Addie's skin raised gooseflesh on her arms, and she started to shiver. Now and again, someone's headlamp flared off a graffiti artist's painting of a woman or a few lines of poetry. Such beauty in this place made everything else seem that much more surreal.

She stopped for a moment, pretending to adjust her gloves.

When she was nine, she had spent a few hours one afternoon hiding from her brothers in a series of drainage tunnels. Unable to hear the outside world or see anything other than distant circles of daylight as she crouched in warm trails of water, she'd suddenly realized the game had become terrifying.

That was her introduction to claustrophobia.

And rats.

Breathe, she reminded herself.

Just breathe.

She sucked in air and kept walking.

Sergeant Trujillo led them to a place in a side tunnel where a blanket had been fixed over an opening into what, in the past, must have served as an office or storage area. One of Trujillo's men held back the blanket while they peered in.

The room was as Trujillo had told them—a space designed for comfortable, if spartan, living. It was also designed for the long haul; the shelves lining the walls were loaded with jugged water and nonperishables. The apocalypse, apparently, would feature a lot of tinned meat and ramen noodles.

Addie decided she'd rather go in the first wave of casualties.

"The evidence techs are on their way," she said to Patrick. "Let's keep moving."

"Sounds good," he said.

Lieutenant Criver, who'd crowded into the wide doorway with them, said nothing. His presence here—and his silence—made Addie uneasy.

As they turned away, she shone her light on the floor, wondering with morbid curiosity if rats had been inside. The light flared on a square of plastic.

"Hold on," she said.

She took off her winter gloves and slid on disposable ones, then stepped lightly into the room to retrieve the plastic from the floor. She stared at it for a moment.

"Addie?"

She turned and held up the driver's license with its photo of a dark-haired, tattooed man.

David L. Hayne.

Otherwise known as Raven.

She should feel satisfaction at the confirmation that Raven, aka David Hayne, was in fact the silo man.

But something nagged at her. A different discarded driver's license.

Patrick's uneasy gaze rose from the driver's license to meet Addie's eyes. Maybe his mind, too, had returned to Talfour's body, bludgeoned and garroted and beaten on the banks of the river.

And the cast-off wallet in the river.

"It doesn't change anything," Patrick said. "He's still our top suspect."

She nodded. But she and Patrick both knew: detectives should never get too attached to their theories.

"I want to check out the stairs," she said to Trujillo.

To his credit, the sergeant didn't shrug or roll his eyes. "Yes, ma'am."

⚔

The staircase was located in the center of the tons of concrete that loomed around and above them. Standing at the base of the stairs, Addie imagined the weight of all that concrete and darkness pressing down on them.

That, and the presence of nimble-footed rats who liked high places.

Not to mention the dead pigeons they'd walked by. She'd counted twenty on their way here from Raven's hideout, all of them broken bundles of feathers, as if they'd flown into the walls in their panic.

Patrick gave the stairs a shake. The metal reverberated, sending metallic shock waves up the stairwell. He shook his head, but when he turned to face Addie, she sensed in him a willingness for her to call the shots. She was primary. He would follow her.

And beneath that, plainly visible on his face, was his worry that she would insist on climbing the stairs. Which meant, Patrick being Patrick, that he would insist on going with her. She felt a pang of empathy. If this place was giving her the creeps, she could imagine what it was doing to her superstitious partner.

She shone her flashlight up the stairwell as it rose into the gloom far beyond the reach of her light. The black metal stairs were eaten through

312

in places; the landings—from what she could see—were entirely gone. Despite that, Addie believed it possible that Raven had managed to flee up the steps to higher floors, where he would think himself safe from all pursuit.

They could, she supposed, wait him out, a siege army camped outside his castle.

But the presence of the driver's license was weighing on her. That and the barely audible creaking that came from far, far above.

Just the wind rattling around something loose up there, she told herself.

Her thoughts returned to the driver's license. Raven might have left it behind out of carelessness. Or if he'd been in a hurry. Perhaps he'd even left it as a way of marking his territory, and someone had knocked it to the floor.

But where her brain kept getting hung up was on the idea that maybe he hadn't left it at all. Someone else had.

Still turning things over in her mind, she went to Patrick, who had retreated a few yards from the staircase, as if putting distance between him and it would serve as a permanent separation. Her flashlight swept the walls to either side of him and caught on a single word.

SESSRÚMNIR.

Next to the word was an arrow, pointing up the stairs.

SESSRÚMNIR.

By now, thanks to Evan, she at least had a feel for Scandinavian words. This certainly looked like one. She pulled out her phone but found she couldn't get a strong enough signal to either call out or use the internet.

She shone her light on the word and asked the others to try accessing the internet on their phones. But other than Patrick and the lieutenant, none of the men carried phones. And Patrick and Criver had no better luck than she did.

Trujillo gestured toward the wall. "You want to know if that word means something? I can try sending your question over the radio. Not that I'm getting a good signal, either."

But Addie shook her head. She needed fresh air. She was starting to feel as if she were trapped in the catacombs, and if she didn't take a break, she'd start imagining bones and skulls slithering from the walls and roiling up from the floor.

Plus, she had a theory she needed to explore. Taking a page from Evan's book, she'd been reading up on grain elevators while she and Patrick had been outside, waiting on SWAT.

"I'll be right back," she said.

Patrick zipped up his coat. "I'll go with you."

Criver waved them on; he was still trying to get a signal on his phone. The SWAT teams had finished searching the silos and now stood at the ready for whatever came next. Their posture was loose—maybe they'd been told to stand down. Every single one of them looked as if they'd be quite comfortable waiting down here through the second coming and beyond.

Addie heard the wind before she and Patrick reached the exit. She scrambled up the rock pile with relief, not caring that the gale had become the howl of a beast. Dusk had rolled in from the west, and clouds raced by overhead like horses trying to outrun the lash. A delicate crescent of moon gleamed briefly to the east, caught like a jewel in a cloudy gap that closed almost as soon as she glimpsed it.

She turned right, taking the gravel path to the end of the silo, where she turned right again and followed the beam of her flashlight toward the river. She made her way to the aging pier that ran along the shoreline.

"Careful there, partner," Patrick called as he hurried to catch up. "That wharf's gotta be as rickety as the rest of this place."

She slowed and shone her light along the weathered boards. "It looks all right." But she tested her weight on it before venturing farther out along the waterfront.

Patrick followed. The wood creaked and shifted but held. "You're cooking up something."

"I'm trying. I'll know more in a minute."

She continued to shine her light down the wharf. The water surged and slapped the boards to her left. On her right, the Damen Silos rose like ancient cliffs, blotting out the sky.

While Patrick stood next to her, his scarf furling and unfurling in the wind and his head tipped back as if he were surveying the heavens, Addie pulled out her phone again and typed in the word SESSRÚMNIR. She clicked on one of the articles suggested by Google and scanned its length. She nodded to herself, lowered her phone, and stared out over the water.

Across the river, downtown Chicago glittered like a fantastical city perched on a faraway world. In the near distance, the just-visible figure of a patrol officer stood watch over one of the possible access points. The other police, she knew, had fanned out across the site.

Closer by, in the grasses, something squealed, then fell quiet.

Patrick brought his gaze back to earth. "Even though it's turning dark and a storm is trying to settle itself right on top of us? And even though my eyes haven't been young for decades? I will swear on my great-grandmother's grave back in County Clare that you've got that look in your eye, Adrianne Marie. The one that always gives me the shivers. The one that says, *Damn the torpedoes, full speed ahead.* So tell me, what does that *Sessr*-whatever word mean?"

She put away her phone. "When Viking heroes die, they're carried by the Valkyries up to Odin's Valhalla. The great mead hall in the sky."

"I'm tracking."

"But apparently half of them don't go there. They're taken instead to *Sessrúmnir*, which is another giant mead hall in the sky. Or wherever in the cosmos the Vikings placed their heaven. *Sessrúmnir* is the mead hall located in the meadow of *Fólkvangr*, and it is every bit as good a place as Valhöll. But *this* hall is overseen by Freya, Odin's wife. Who, for what it's worth, brought *seithr* magic—dark magic—to the gods." She was thinking of the ritualism of the murders and the black cross in front of Helskin's house.

Patrick caught his billowing scarf. His breath hung in the air. "You think that word and the arrow mean he's up at the top. Addie, you saw those stairs. He can't *fly*."

"He didn't have to. Look."

She shone her light once again down the pier. The beam picked out a thick rope, which was tied, ten feet up, to a set of stairs that climbed up the outside of the silos.

"It's a fire escape," she said.

"Ah, Jesus. Addie, no. We are not going up there in the dark and this wind. Put that out of your mind." He placed a hand on her arm. "You may be primary on this, but I've got seniority. Have you already forgotten that the killer wrote your name on that envelope? That he probably *wanted* you to sniff him out here and climb those damn stairs?"

Before she could let fear overwhelm her, Addie shrugged off his hand and walked down the pier to the rope. She gave it a good yank. The stairs groaned, but nothing swayed or pulled loose.

She turned back to Patrick.

He stood watching her, his body stiff. She wondered if he was thinking of hellhounds and Irish ghouls. Or merely of narrow, rickety stairs climbing toward the heavens above empty space.

"If you look carefully," she said, "you can see graffiti all the way near the top. But all the windows are boarded up. People must be climbing this ladder."

He shook his head. "How would he get a victim up there?"

316

But she'd thought it through. "It was someone who trusted him. Who thought it was safe to go with him. The victim walked up willingly."

"And what about the return trip? Assuming the killer wanted to arrange the guy in a pond or a river like he did the first two. What does he do once his victim is beaten and drugged and all cut up?"

"The killer would have gravity working for him. He could use a sled to drag his victim down the stairs. Or he could lower him on a cable for part of the way."

She could see Patrick's mind humming through the possibilities.

"We have to check," she pressed.

Reluctantly, he nodded, and she released the rope leading to the bottom stair.

"We need two volunteers from SWAT," she said. "One of them should be a medic. In case someone is still alive up there."

He puffed out a breath loud enough for her to hear. "Now you're making sense."

"But," she said. "I'm going, too."

CHAPTER 31

Lightning had most definitely not struck.

Evan pushed aside the *Beowulf* translations and the stack of Viking books Simon had loaned him and leaned back in his chair, his hands folded atop his stomach.

What, he asked himself, had he learned so far? That the killer was smart, knowledgeable—most especially when it came to Old English poetry—as well as strong, ruthless, and determined. Persuasive, given that he'd managed to lure out men like Talfour and Desser.

The list continued. The killer had selected a heroic saga, *Beowulf*, as his narrative. But he was also aware that his actions were sinful—he'd called himself *monster* as well as *hero*. He would blame his sins on external forces—the spirits of the land whispering in his head, compelling him to slay those who offended them.

Evan stared at the wood-and-twine figurine on his desk. The painted eyes stared back. After a moment, he returned the figure to its cardboard box and pushed it into a corner.

He checked in with his subconscious to see if it had come up with anything useful. But lightning hadn't struck there, either.

He glanced toward the window. Addie and Patrick were out in the cold and the dark, hunting down David Hayne. What if Rhinehart had been right all along with his theory about Nazi occultism? It wasn't impossible that Raven was their killer.

Then again, surely the clues in the poem pointing to Nazism were *too* evident, *too* obvious. No scop worth his name would lay things out so clearly. What was the saying? Poets were those who never meant only one thing with their words.

Evan rapped out a beat on the desk with his palms. He recalled the pile of bones on Helskin's porch. Diana's comment about Raven and Ringwraiths.

Could he have been as blind as Rhinehart by insisting on bog bodies and *Beowulf*? Had he been blind to the signs that might have led them to Raven sooner?

He turned the pages of his journal to the notes he'd taken during his conversation with Christina. She'd talked of blood feuds and blood sacrifice. Grendel and his mother.

Seithr magic, practiced by sorceresses.

And also, Christina had told him, by *ergi* men.

He sat up.

Officer Blakesley definitely qualified as an *ergi* man. Indeed, he'd called Evan's attention to the fact. And the wooden figure had appeared on Evan's porch right after Blakesley's visit.

But a cop as killer?

Cops were about defending the public. About justice. True, sometimes that sense of justice got warped. And being a cop would make it easy to lure out a victim. And to leak details of the investigation to the press if you wanted to ensure your narrative was read by as wide an audience as possible.

Blakesley was the name of a village in Northamptonshire. Evan had surmised that much the first time he'd met the officer. But he hadn't taken the etymology far enough. Now he opened a tab on his computer and entered BLAKESLEY VILLAGE. There it was: the Old English nickname for the village was *Blæcwulf's meadow*.

Blæcwulf meant *black wolf*.

If this was right, Blakesley had plastered his name all over his poems.

Still, the thought of the patrol officer as their poet seemed crazy. Cops had to pass a battery of psychological tests. Surely a killer couldn't slip through that net.

Unless the triggering incident happened *after* Blakesley joined the force.

Evan pressed his fingertips together and stared at the ceiling.

When the phone rang, he lunged across the desk to grab it.

"Well, big brother," River said when he picked up. "I might have something for you."

"Please, God," Evan said.

"Dr. Valtos managed an archaeological find back in the nineties outside London. Or he thinks it was the nineties. The good professor was a little vague on some things. Except trout. He had a lot to tell me about trout. He informed me that it's a month past fishing season in the rivers of Scotland, but he received special dispensation from the earl to angle for not brown trout—as one would expect—but sea trout, which apparently—"

"River."

"Just baiting you, brother, with your own game. The dig Valtos recalled started when a backhoe operator struck a bog body while leveling a hill for one of those loathsome bedroom communities. The find caused quite a stir among the local populace, who were probably wondering if they'd done the right thing, selling their ancestral land to developers. I asked about children who'd visited. Valtos does remember that one of the company's owners brought his kids by two or three times. He couldn't recall if the children seemed traumatized in any way. Then again, he probably wouldn't notice a traumatized child if it were screaming in his lap. Now, here's the interesting part."

"Please don't feel obligated to keep me in suspense."

River laughed. "Valtos heard rumors years later that the burial find had been ill-fated. A curse-of-the-pharaohs sort of thing. Two people associated with the site died under odd circumstances—one of the archaeologists and a foreman. In addition, one of the owners was positively plagued by tragedy. His wife died of cancer not long after the bog body was discovered. Then an associate died in an automobile accident a few years later. And a long time after that, in America, his grandson died in a different kind of accident. Valtos wasn't sure what kind, exactly. Just that he didn't think it involved automobiles."

Mine, mine-gone. Bowel-buried busted by big bosses.

"Did Valtos remember a name?"

"I'm afraid not."

Evan pondered. Rhinehart had held a high-level position in a construction firm in England. His wife had died of cancer. His assistant had died in a car crash.

The timeline worked, based on what Simon had told him.

But there was the whole issue of bog bodies. If Rhinehart was the owner *plagued by tragedy*, as River had put it, why had he feigned ignorance of Iron Age burials? In the meeting at the station house, he'd been determined to convince everyone that he was the smartest man in the room. Why would he have been reluctant to add bog bodies to his repertoire?

Had his ignorance been a smoke screen? Could Rhinehart have had a role in the murders? Could he be the brain behind the brawn required to torture a man and drag him to water and slay him there, perhaps as an occult rite?

Or could the killer be one of his children, traumatized as a child? If Evan considered the typical characteristics of serial killers, Rhinehart's children would be the right age and race. They had suffered early trauma due to the death of their mother, a trauma compounded by the fact of another body—crushed and withered—discovered in the bog.

And then came the death of the grandson. Had that been the trigger? Had the boy been buried in a rockfall? Become lost underground?

"You still there, brother?" River asked.

"Did the professor mention anything else?"

"That's all that Old Man Valtos could come up with until he started in on the trout again. Is it not helpful?"

Evan laid out Diana's drawing again and placed it next to the map of Chicago. "You said outside London. Can you narrow it down?"

"Southeast. Heading toward Canterbury."

It took only a moment for the two maps to merge in Evan's mind. If his theory was correct and if his map-reading skills were halfway decent—which they were—then there was a solid correlation between the construction firm's site in England and his own beloved woods where he took Ginny hunting.

So why hadn't Diana listed this site on the map she gave him? Most likely she'd been working from a pre-1990s map.

"You've gone quiet again," River said.

"Thinking." He picked up his pen and drew a quick sketch of the woods in his journal, adding it to the list of sites he'd noted earlier. He labeled it WASHPK, SOUTH END, LAGOON. "This is helpful, River. Thank you. I believe I'm just missing one or two key pieces of information."

"Which are?"

"I'm not entirely sure."

"Then I wish I had more to offer."

They chatted a moment longer before disconnecting. Evan stared up at the shadowed ceiling, thinking about ill-fated archaeological digs.

He turned to his computer. He searched for information about Rhinehart's kids and the dead assistant. It was easy enough to locate people with the surname Rhinehart living in the UK and in the States. There was even a handful in Chicago. Some of the listings included relatives, but none with the name of Ralph Rhinehart. Deeper digging would require skills he didn't possess along with access to databases beyond his reach.

He stared at the ceiling again.

What if Blakesley was Rhinehart's son? The stepchild with a different surname?

Back to the computer. But he couldn't find anything that linked the two men. Rhinehart hadn't made mention of his personal life on his website. And as for Blakesley, there was almost no information. Most police didn't have social media profiles and tended to be publicity shy, for understandable reasons. He found a two-year-old article about the cop's heroic actions stopping a would-be carjacker. But nothing else.

He also looked for a connection between Raven and Blakesley. Or Raven and Rhinehart. Another strikeout. He might be a decent scholar. But he was also, he feared, something of a Luddite.

He picked up his tea mug. Empty. He set it back down.

He was close. He could sense the answer buried somewhere in everything he'd learned and studied since he'd stood next to Talfour's body and considered the eeriness of death amid the water and reeds and mist. What was it in the human heart that—over the centuries—continually linked the sacred and the violent? The same part that worshipped gods as superior beings but also believed that honoring them required the blood sacrifice of animals and people.

At some point in the killer's life, violence and sacrifice had become so intertwined in the killer's mind that they could no longer be unwoven.

Once again, Evan opened Heaney's translation of *Beowulf*.

Fate goes ever as it must.

After a moment, he returned the book to the stack. If he was playing the role of the hunter, it was a good thing no one was waiting dinner on him.

He stood. He needed to give his brain time to chew on things. Plus, it was way past time for him to feed Ginny.

He called Addie on the landline and left a message expressing his concerns regarding Officer Blakesley. Then he casually mentioned that he was heading home. When she learned he'd violated her wishes, she'd be livid. But he'd find a way to make it up to her. Maybe with tickets to *Hamilton*. And if Blakesley *was* their killer, she'd have no choice but to forgive him.

Next, he dialed the campus police and let them know he was ready to head out. They agreed to meet him near the main doors.

He tucked the gun in his coat pocket, picked up his satchel, then flipped off the desk lamp and made his way to the door through the semidarkness, his path lit by the university lights shining through the windows.

He lifted his coat from the hook and opened the door.

In the hall—hands clenched, breathing hard—stood Tommy Snow.

THREE

Excerpt from _Criminal Behavioral Analysis: The Viking Poet_
Semiotician: Evan Wilding, PhD, SSA, IASS

The fantasy the killer is fulfilling—given its complexity—likely began in childhood. A child who is troubled or traumatized will look outside himself for an acceptable narrative. He (or she) will turn to the stories of others in order to give meaning and shape to his own life.

The narrative chosen by the Viking Poet is the epic saga _Beowulf._ He casts himself as a tragic hero who does not intend to survive his own narrative. Just as the hero Beowulf was slain by the dragon at the end of his story, so, too, does our killer intend to die in battle after he has murdered the monsters of this world—five monsters, according to his poem.

We know that the killer has a safe place in which to hold and torture his victims. Bearing in mind the _Beowulf_ narrative, this is likely an underground area near water, similar to the lair of the monster Grendel.

Of interest, too, given the killer's knowledge of OE poetry: the folktales and poems of Northern Europe often center on a search for someone's secret name. We know that the Viking Poet embedded the name of at least one of his victims in his poetry. Likewise, I suspect a clue to his own identity will also be found there.

THE VIKING POET

Attend my words!

The first time I died was when she died. But I was reborn.

Then I died when Alex died.

Yet even then, I was reborn.

Then, a year ago, I held an unknown child in my hands in the street and watched her blood run on the pavement, and I became someone else. I became something else.

Killer, avenger, sacrificer. Hel's handguard, Odin's spear.

Now it is time for the hero-monster to walk out from the ælwihta eard—the land of monsters.

This time when I die, I will not come back.

CHAPTER 32

The heavens shook out a steady fall of snow as two guys from SWAT led the way up the fire escape. The plan was to go all the way to the roof, then find a way inside and work their way down.

If that was even possible.

Addie followed a decent distance behind so that they spread out their weight, her sneakers squeaking on the damp metal. An equal distance behind her came the stalwart figure of Lieutenant Criver, who looked, in the beam of her borrowed headlamp, as if he'd rediscovered his calling after years behind a desk. As soon as Addie had swung herself onto the fire escape, he'd handed his wool overcoat to an astonished Patrick and climbed after her.

A third member of SWAT would wait at the bottom, ready to go at a moment's notice.

Somewhere around the third floor, the wind coming off the river turned unforgiving. The snow came at them sideways, and Addie's gloved hands quickly turned numb, just like her feet in her damp sneakers. Snow crystals formed on her woolen gloves and coat. She followed the lights of the two men above her and, after that first glimpse at Criver when he came after her, she didn't look down.

She didn't *dare* look down. Suddenly rabbit warrens and drainage ditches seemed cozy and safe.

She kept climbing. Fifteen stories. No worries.

Each stair ratcheted up the coiling spring in her gut, and her breath came in terrified wheezes. The first time her foot slipped and she went down on a knee, her heart burst free from her chest to roar in her ears. But she quickly recovered and pressed forward.

She was, to her astonishment, fiercely jubilant. Maybe she was an adrenaline junkie.

Around the tenth floor, the lights of the police above her slowed and then stopped. One of the men called down.

"Stair—miss—here." His voice came apart in the wind, and he called again. "Stair missing!"

"Got it!" Addie yelled back. She stopped and looked over her shoulder. "A stair is missing up where SWAT is standing."

Criver's voice boomed back. "Understood."

The lights above her began to move again. After a moment, she, too, restarted her ascent. This time, she quickly found her rhythm, and her heart ceased its clamoring. Her gut quieted along with her mind.

After several long minutes, a shout came from up above. The lights of both the SWAT men had disappeared; the top two floors of the silo still hung above her and Criver.

She picked up her pace, gripping the railings hard, setting each foot solidly on each step before moving on to the next one. She reached the missing stair and pointed it out to Criver before stepping over it. She could almost feel the suck of gravity as she cleared the empty space.

Near the top, one of the lights reappeared, and the man waved her forward. When she reached the top, he offered a hand as she stepped away from the staircase and walked onto the roof.

"Beats all, don't it?" the man said as she looked around.

Her hand flew to the cross around her neck.

A minute later, Criver's head and shoulders appeared above the roofline; then he swung himself up to stand beside her.

"My God," he said.

CHAPTER 33

Evan watched Tommy devour a ham-and-cheese sandwich, a platter of fries, and start on an almond croissant in the time it would have taken him to tuck his napkin in his lap and pick up a fork.

The two of them sat at a corner table in the Common Knowledge Café in the Harper Memorial Library, on the building's third floor. At this time of night, the space was mostly empty—a scattering of students talked or read while a lone barista wiped down tables. Soft jazz played over the speakers. The aroma of someone's late-night pizza wafted from the kitchen.

Evan had told the campus police where he was and asked them to meet him downstairs in half an hour—long enough, he hoped, to hear Tommy's story.

When he'd spotted the kid standing in the hallway, his first impulse had been to slam shut the door and turn the dead bolt. Then he'd caught sight of Tommy's face. Determined. Worried. Probably scared.

"You're here to see me?" he'd asked.

The kid had nodded. "Because of the bones. And the dead men."

It was, Evan had to admit, a good hook. Definitely worth a sandwich and fries.

Now he sipped his mint tea—the café's specialty—and asked, "Does your mom know you're here?"

"No."

"You need to call her. She must be worried."

"I will. I rode the bus here. I don't like the bus."

"Understandable. But thank you for coming to see me. If you wish, and if it's all right with your mom, I'll drive you home."

Tommy popped the last bit of croissant in his mouth and nodded as he looked around the café.

"This place is nicer than my school," he said in his flat voice. "Do you think we're safe?"

Startled, Evan nodded. "I think we're very safe here. Why?"

Tommy offered a shrug, the universal teenage gesture that could mean anything from *I don't know* to *I don't want to talk about it.*

Evan sipped his tea, telling himself to take it slow. Talking to someone like Tommy was a little like training a hawk—patience was its own reward.

But Tommy, it turned out, was ready to get to the matter at hand. "Is Mr. X a bad guy?"

"What do *you* think?"

"I think he's a really bad guy." Tommy looked over his shoulder again at the nearly empty room, then swung back to Evan. "Because of why he wanted the bones with runes on them."

"He bought the bones you found by the pond?"

"All but the ones you and Detective Bisset took. I hid those from him. He gave me two hundred and fifty dollars for five bones. I bought a new reptile cage and a heat lamp for my emerald basilisk."

Questions sparked in Evan's brain faster than his tongue could move. But he knew he needed to proceed slowly. "I hope your new basilisk isn't like the basilisks of myth."

Tommy's eyes lit up. "That'd be cool. The king of serpents who could kill you just by looking at you. I'd like to have one of those in my pocket. For mean people."

"I imagine there would be laws against that."

"There should be laws against mean people."

No argument there. "And Mr. X, he's one of these mean people?"

Tommy took a moment of reflection. "Mr. X could be a basilisk. He told me he was a sorcerer."

"Mr. X sounds mysterious. Does he have another name?"

Surprisingly, the kid offered a slow, sleepy grin. "Yeah. He wouldn't tell me, but I heard him talking with his friends. They call him Dave." The grin turned wide. "That's not a scary name."

"No. It isn't." This matched with what Addie had told him—that Mr. X, aka Raven, was actually David Hayne.

"He has one more name. Raven." Tommy hunched his shoulders. "He hurts people."

"Have you seen him hurt people?"

An emphatic headshake no. "But he said he wanted the bones for his next sacrifice. I didn't want to sell them, but I was scared not to. And I needed the reptile cage."

"But now you're worried that Mr. X—Dave—might hurt you?"

"Yes. Because I quit selling bones to him, and he got mad. He might have followed me here."

The memory of Addie's desperate warning sent up a small flare. Evan looked around the room. If a killer sat among them, he was doing a damn good job blending in. As serial killers were wont to do.

"Did you see Dave follow you?" Evan asked.

"No."

"Did you notice *anyone* following you?"

"No."

"Tommy, no one is going to hurt you. When we're ready to leave, the campus police will walk us out to my car. Or, if you'd rather, we can have an officer from Chicago PD come and get you and take you home. Or we can wait for your mom, and you guys can—"

"My mom doesn't drive at night."

"Okay, that's fine. We'll figure it out." He slipped his hand into his pocket and touched his fingers to the warm metal of the gun. "Right now, you're completely safe."

"Okay." Tommy's eyes met his for the first time. "I trust a smart person with dwarfism."

Evan fervently hoped Tommy's trust wasn't misplaced. But he'd worry in a few minutes how to get Tommy someplace safe, whether or not the danger was real. He leaned forward. "Right now, what would be helpful is if you could tell me what was on the bones that Mr. X bought from you. Did you take pictures?"

"No."

Evan felt a french kiss of disappointment followed by a small lick of panic. "Do you remember what the runes looked like?"

Tommy tapped his forehead. "You aren't the only smart person."

The kid took a piece of paper from an inside coat pocket, unfolded it, and set it on the table. There were nine lines of runes printed on it in pencil; presumably this included the runes from the four bones Evan and Addie had taken.

"I wrote this down on the bus," Tommy said.

"From memory?"

"My biology teacher, Dr. Almadi, says I have the mind of a steel-jaw trap."

Evan pulled the paper close and began mentally transliterating the runes into modern English.

Tommy must have read Evan's silence for confusion. "Do you want to know what they say?"

Evan looked up, surprised. "Do you know? In English, I mean?"

Another grin, this one sly. "It's not hard, Dr. Wilding. I can show you. Some of the lines were backward. But I turned everything around so that the runes that were off by themselves lined up. Then I saw that they must be numbers, and even though five of the lines were upside down when I did that, I put everything back together."

"Amazing!" Evan doffed an imaginary hat, humbled by the straight-forward brilliance of this kid. "What do the runes say?"

Tommy pulled out another piece of paper and placed it on top of the first one. Evan scanned Tommy's transliteration, did a quick cross-check with the runes Tommy had written down, then pulled his journal from his satchel and recopied the lines, adding punctuation, trying to make sense of the poem.

He wrote:

1   *O! This hoarder caused my fall with his fall, his fall caused by the fallen.*
2   *Thus from my bothy I came, homeland's ward for first of five*
3   *to sacrifice the innocent at night. She takes back her sons and daughters*
4   *who rived and tholed and peeled her flesh like ripe fruit.*
5   *No tall tale this, for he will be mine. One day, hawk will take sparrow*
6   *to be born in a new place. Then I will have vengeance against*
7   *the evil horde-guard who shaped this shaper*
8   *and fashioned this long-clawed wolf into the*
9   *blessing giver. My blood-feud stillbirths your further crimes*

Evan leaned back and frowned. Then leaned forward again. Scowled.

"Is it supposed to mean something?" Tommy asked.

"I believe so, yes."

"Then, what?"

"That," Evan said as he scratched his chin, "is a very good question."

ᚷ

Addie stared, her eyes struggling to understand what she was seeing.

This part of the vast roof of the old silos was scattered with dead birds—most of them pigeons or starlings, although some of the birds were so desiccated, she couldn't be sure. Others looked as fresh as the day they'd first taken wing. As she and the lieutenant walked forward, stepping gingerly, the beam of her headlamp picked out what might be a pair of mute swans.

All of them had been affixed to the roof in some fashion. Tied to cables, pinned under cinderblocks, caught in nets. The cables were the source of the creaking she'd heard all the way in the basement.

Their feathers fluttered in the wind, as if the birds longed to rise as one and burst into the heavens. Addie's heart tore at the sight of so many helpless feathered things, forever kept from the sky.

In the center of the slaughter, a man lay spread-eagle. The SWAT officers had already approached the corpse before returning to inform Addie and the lieutenant that the man was, most definitely, dead.

As they drew nearer, she fanned her light quickly over the body, then zeroed in on the face.

The tattoo of a raven darkened the man's forehead.

"It's almost certainly David Hayne," she told the lieutenant. "Our suspect."

He frowned. "But not our killer."

"Not unless he did this to himself as some kind of final performance. His swan song, in a manner of speaking."

Next to the body, the feathers of a crow trembled in the wind sheeting across the rooftop.

Beyond the corpse was a wheeled metal hand truck, the kind used to move appliances. She pointed it out to Criver. "At least we know how he relocated his victims. He'd get them compliant through drugs, then strap them to that."

Criver nodded. "That's why he raked over the mud on the path leading to Talfour's corpse."

She knelt a few feet from the corpse and trained her light down along Hayne's face and naked body. His right eye was gone. A noose had been tightened around his neck. Carved on his chest were the words NOT Þ.

Not third. Not thorn of riding.

Lieutenant Criver crouched beside her. He reached out a hand, as if to offer solace or reprieve to the dead man.

Raven's eyes snapped open.

Addie and the lieutenant yanked back. One of the SWAT guys cried out, "Shit!" at the same time the other yelled, "I checked his vitals! The dude was dead."

Raven blinked and opened his mouth, sucking in a breath. His single eye searched wildly about.

"*Draugr,*" he whispered in a cavernous voice.

"What's that mean?" asked Criver. "Drow-gur?"

She shook her head. "David, who did this to you?"

He coughed. His tongue licked out and wetted his lips. "*Draugr.* Killer is . . . *Draugr.*"

Addie yanked out her phone, typed in DROWGUR. Google helpfully responded, DID YOU MEAN DRAUGR? "He's saying that the killer is an undead Viking. A Viking zombie."

The coughing grew worse, then stopped abruptly. His single eye rolled back in his head. Addie grabbed his wrist, feeling for a pulse. Nothing. She backed away as one of the SWAT men knelt next to Raven and began CPR.

"Damn," Criver said. "Was that our only suspect, Detective?"

Addie turned toward the distant city, brilliant in the darkness.

"I've lost him," said the medic.

Criver got on the radio. "The guy's still out there."

Evan, she thought.

Tommy had lost interest in the poem and sat hunkered in his chair, scrolling through something on his phone.

Evan finished the last of his mint tea. The barista came by to clear their table.

"Anything else?" she asked Tommy. She was smiling.

He didn't look up or speak. She glanced at Evan, who shrugged.

"That's it, thank you," he said.

He returned to the poem and its enigmatic tangle of words. There was the reference to a wolf in line eight, adding to his theory that their killer was Blakesley: *the evil horde-guard who . . . fashioned this long-clawed wolf into the blessing giver.*

What of the sparrow in the poem? Did the sparrow refer to him? It seemed likely. So perhaps the words *hawk will take sparrow* meant that a hawk would guide his soul to another world after his death—very much in the Viking manner. At least, if it came to that, Ginny would not serve as his sacrificial guide—she was safely locked away in her mews.

He was surer still of the *evil horde-guard* mentioned in line seven—that was a kenning for a dragon, lifted straight out of *Beowulf.*

The pounding of feet disturbed his thoughts as a herd of students stampeded into the café, shedding cold air and filling the room with laughter. Tommy studied them while Evan returned to his musings.

The Viking Poet had also embedded Talfour's name: *No tall tale this, for he will be mine.* Tall-for. Talfour.

Evan's thoughts circled back to line seven of the poem: *The evil horde-guard who shaped this shaper.*

That is, the dragon who created the poet. He looked up.

"Tommy?"

The kid tore his eyes away from the students, who were now at the bar calling orders.

"Yeah?"

Dr. Valtos had told River of a child who died in an accident in America. "Can you look online for a mining company in the United States that uses a dragon as its logo?"

"Okay." A few minutes later, he said, "There's one. Epic Mining. They mine mostly gold."

"Excellent. Please look for any death-related lawsuits that have been brought against the company. Either pending or settled. And . . ." He glanced down at the first line of Desser's poem: *This hoarder caused my fall with his fall, his fall caused by the fallen.* "Look especially for any deaths related to falls."

"Okay." A moment of silence. "There's, like, four or five lawsuits? The company was accused of negligence for not sealing up old mines or putting up good barriers. Dr. Wilding, there's lots of ways to die in old mines. People get lost or crushed or fall or they asphyxiate. Maybe the last case against Epic was settled three years ago?"

That felt too long ago to have served as the killer's final trigger. But it would have played a major role. "What can you find out about that last one?"

"Ummm." Tommy used his thumb to scroll. "There's a headline: 'Five-year-old dies in gold mine.'"

A tingling started at the base of Evan's skull and raced across his skin. Five years. Five victims. With four human-size wooden figures added to reach Odin's sacred nine. "What does the article say? Is there a name? Or any details about what happened?"

"The headline's all there is on this website. I can keep looking. But the Wi-Fi here is super slow."

A motion at the entrance to the café caught Evan's eye. It was one of the campus cops, a younger man than the one who had been in his office earlier. The man waved at him and tapped his watch.

"Good work, Tommy." Evan folded up the sheets of paper. "We'll look more later. We have to go. Call your mom while we're walking, and let's decide on a plan of action. May I keep these pages?"

"I made them for you," Tommy said, standing.

At the door, the cop introduced himself as Frank Martin and said he'd been told to walk Evan to his car. "It's getting nasty out there with the snow," he said as he punched the elevator button. "Hope you don't have far to go."

Tommy was texting on his phone. "My mom asked if you would bring me home, Dr. Wilding." He looked at Officer Martin. "Dr. Wilding is a person with dwarfism."

The cop ducked his chin to try—unsuccessfully—to hide his smile. "I hadn't noticed."

Evan found he was smiling, too. "I can drive you," he told Tommy. Even if it meant that by the time he made it home, Ginny would start by eating his eyeballs and move down from there. Taking Tommy home would give him a chance to talk to Mrs. Snow about her son's concerns regarding David Hayne.

When they reached the first floor, Evan saw a uniformed patrol officer from Chicago PD standing just inside the front doors. Through the windows behind her, the flashing lights of a squad car pulsed on the street.

She stepped forward. "Dr. Wilding," she said. "We meet again. Detective Bisset sent me to escort you home."

"I know you," he said.

"Yes, sir. Officer Osborn. We met at Wash Park. I'm mounted patrol, but we've got all hands on deck tonight with the storm and the manhunt."

A shiver walked his spine. "And your partner. Officer Blakesley. Where is he?"

"He's out sick, sir. And sorry to miss the show. Anyway, my orders are to follow you home and make sure you're safely settled in. And I do appreciate the overtime, sir, if I can be honest."

Evan wondered where Addie was right now. "They haven't arrested anyone?"

She shook her head. "Not that we've heard."

"I understand the desire for overtime," he said to Officer Osborn. "But I have to get this young man home. You're welcome to tag along, if you wish, then follow me back to the city."

"Happy to do so, sir. It beats breaking up bar fights. I'm parked right outside. Do you want a ride to your car?"

Tommy gave an energetic nod.

"Sounds like we do," Evan said.

Officer Martin made his farewells. Tommy and Evan followed Osborn through the doors and into the storm. It would be a good night to be home with a thick book and a roaring fire. And a cocktail or three.

Soon enough, he thought.

Osborn waved Tommy into the back seat and walked around to the other side with Evan.

"Are you planning any more public lectures?" she asked as she opened the door. "Your talk on sacrificial rites was fascinating."

Evan paused, one foot inside the car. Thoughts jostled through his brain, demanding attention.

Lieutenant Criver's voice, saying, *Adam Nedscop, is that a name?* Followed by Evan's own clarification that it was actually *dam-ned scop,* a damned poet, and his curiosity about the only hyphen in the poem: dam-ned.

Dam was a medieval term for *woman.*

"Sir?" Osborn said. "Is everything all right?"

The pieces of the puzzle came fast now, tumbling one upon the next. He'd been right that a cop was the killer. But he'd completely missed the gender.

First: the name Beowulf in Old English meant *bee-wolf* or *bee-hunter. Bee-hunter* was a kenning for *bear.*

The name Osborn meant *divine bear.*

Second: Rhinehart had worked for a construction company and married the owner's daughter, who presumably had a child of her own, who became Rhinehart's stepchild. The name of the firm was Osborn-Kleinberger.

Third: Osborn had found the ring in the woods, or so she'd claimed. *God's spear.* An oath ring, binding the recipient of the ring to the giver.

Evan reared back. "Tommy, get—"

Tommy looked up, eyes wide.

"Get out!" Evan cried.

The kid reached for a door handle. But there wasn't one. There was never a door handle in the back of a squad car.

"Come this way!" Evan called, pushing back against Osborn as he groped for his gun. His feet slid on the snowy asphalt.

Osborn rammed him against the open door and yanked his arms behind his back. Hard plastic bit into his wrists as her voice rang out above him: "Freeze, Tommy, or I will shoot you."

Evan felt a sharp jab in the muscle of his thigh, and almost instantly, a looping darkness filled his mind. His satchel slipped from his hand, and with his last lucid thought, he kicked it so it skidded under the car. Then he found himself tipping forward onto the seat. Osborn lifted his legs and shoved him all the way in.

"Get my gun, kid," Evan said.

But he hadn't said a thing. The words stayed in his throat.

Night closed over him with the softness of bird wings.

CHAPTER 34

Addie kept her foot on the accelerator as she and Patrick followed the lights-and-siren squad car alternately nudging and darting through Chicago's late-night traffic.

Nearly two hours had passed since she'd listened to Evan's message concerning his suspicions about Officer Blakesley and his confession that he'd lied when he'd promised to stay at the university. More than enough time for him to be home and in reach of his cell phone and his landline.

But he was responding to neither. And now she and Patrick and the patrol unit risked life and limb to force their way along the snow-slick, traffic-choked streets.

When she found him, she swore she'd kill him.

If he was still alive.

In another part of the city, squad cars would shortly descend on the apartment of Officer Ed Blakesley. They'd know soon enough if the officer was home sick with the flu or if he was out there somewhere, doing his murderous work.

At Evan's gate, the squad car rolled to a stop. Addie slammed on her brakes and threw herself out of the car to punch in the code. When she got back in, she smacked her palm repeatedly on the steering wheel, waiting for the gate to swing its ponderous way open while next to them, the red and blue lights strobed in the snowfall.

Patrick touched her arm.

"We're here. We'll find him."

She knew the look she gave him was wild-eyed.

The gate opened. She punched the gas, watching in the rearview as the unit fell in behind.

Five minutes. Five eternal minutes to get up the long drive. The car's tires slipped now and again, sending the car sailing toward the grass. Each time, she corrected. Behind her, the squad car had slowed in acknowledgment of the treacherous pavement.

She crested the rise. There was Evan's house, peaceful and warm in the snowfall. A safe haven. A cottage in the woods.

She parked and reached for her door handle.

"Wait," Patrick said in a voice that didn't allow for argument. "They're almost here."

"Damn it," she said.

The squad car appeared a minute later, flashers off, and eased in behind her. Addie and Patrick, together with the two uniforms, stepped out into the snow. All four hunched low to the ground as they ran for the terrace. They pressed themselves against the wall on either side of the front door.

The night remained quiet, disturbed only by the soft ping of the engines cooling.

Addie entered the code, then stepped back. Patrick leaned over, turned the knob, and pushed the door open.

Addie swiveled into the opening, gun raised.

Diana stood in the entryway. Her upraised ax cast a dark shadow on the wall; the hatchet's metal blade shimmered in the spooling light.

CHAPTER 35

Evan blinked upward into falling snow and waited for the fog to clear from his drugged brain.

Officer Sally Osborn. The divine bear. How had he managed to screw up so badly?

Where was he?

He lay perfectly still. It was a lesson he'd first learned during a bandit attack in Luxor and again in an ambush in Timbuktu.

Locate your enemy. Locate your weapons. If injured, take stock of your wounds.

Then move.

Around him, nothing stirred. The only sound was the ancient creak of trees leaning into the cold.

He did a quick scan of his body. He was on his back, shivering with cold, the damp seeping through his pants and coat, his gloved hands going numb, his bare head chilled. A headache pulsed behind his eyes, and his thigh throbbed where the needle had gone in. After another moment's silence, he cautiously inched his hand toward the pocket where he'd tucked his gun.

Metal bit into the flesh of his right wrist.

He turned his head to follow the chain from his swollen wrist to a nearby tree.

He moved his left hand. That hand, at least, was free, even if his fingers were numb. He reached across his body for the gun, but his pocket was empty.

His next thought struck like a blow: Where was Tommy?

He sat up abruptly, scrutinizing the darkness. Nothing but woods all around. No Tommy. No one at all.

Without intending it, he lay back down.

How does it feel, Professor Evan Aiden Wilding, that you walked right into a trap and brought a young man with you?

Not good.

Above him, tree branches interlaced in delicate trellises against a sky rendered red by the reflected lights of the city. Between the branches' dark strands, occasional stars glittered coldly through gaps in the clouds. Snow drifted down, gentle and unhurried.

A deep hush held over everything.

He yanked hard on the chain, testing it. The only thing that gave was the tender flesh of his wrist. Blood seeped over his skin.

"God's wounds," he said.

Feathers fluttered nearby. He sat up again, the headache rewarding him with an intense throb, and turned around. Ginny eyed him from a short perch thrust into the earth. He scrambled along the ground, grateful that even chained to a tree, he could reach her. He ran gentle hands over her feathers, the shackle on his right wrist clinking a discordant tune as he checked her for injuries. She tolerated his hands and blinked feral golden eyes at him and the woods beyond.

He followed her gaze. Still no sign of Tommy.

Assured now that she was uninjured, he freed Ginny from the tether, lifted her on his left fist, and tried to clench her jesses between his awkward fingers. Then he followed the chain that bound his wrist to where it was linked around a tall elm and held with a padlock.

All around were the woods. *His* woods, where he and Ginny had been hunting just the day before.

And the snow, which formed a thick carpet unmarred by footprints. Enough snow had fallen since Osborn brought him here to erase her passage.

A hollow, mechanized voice spoke from somewhere nearby. "Greetings, Sparrow."

"Officer Osborn," he answered, though he didn't know if she could hear him. He looked around for a camera.

"Turn right," she said. "Go five or six paces. The chain will reach."

"Where's Tommy?" he asked as he followed her instructions, stumbling forward in the semidarkness.

"Do you see the covered shelf nailed to a large pine tree?" she asked. "There's a laptop computer sitting on it. Touch the 'Delete' button."

The "Delete" key, he noticed, was the only option. The rest of the keyboard had been slathered with epoxy.

When he pressed the button with a numb finger, the screen sprang to life, filled with the image of Osborn's face. A clock in the lower right-hand corner indicated that Evan had been unconscious for just over three hours. Which meant he had time to try to fix this.

The sacrifice, he was sure, would happen at first light.

Osborn moved aside, revealing a small room with concrete walls and a low roof. Machinery—a system of pumps and valves—filled much of the space. There was also a cot and a few jugs of water. Canned goods were stacked on the floor. A single shelf held a few books, including what looked like his three copies of *Beowulf.*

This was, almost certainly, the pump house for the nearby lagoon.

She would want to be close.

The view shifted to show two figures lying unconscious on sleeping bags spread on the floor.

"Dear God," Evan whispered. On his fist, Ginny fluttered.

"Thorn of riding and god of riding," Osborn said.

The prone figures were Tommy Snow.

And Evan's young neighbor, Jo.

Evan yanked helplessly on the chain. The metal cuff again bit into his wrist.

"Why are they here?" he asked, although he already knew the answer.

"They're going to die," Osborn said. "It is their fate. But they will die peaceably. A child's death should always be peaceful. I am not as cruel as you imagine me to be. Not as cruel, even, as the gods demand that I be. These two will simply . . ." The camera shifted again, and she pressed a hand to her cheek. "Go to sleep."

He growled.

"It will be different for you, Sparrow," she said. "That is *your* fate. That is why you are out there and they are in here. You must die in a place where the Others can find you."

Helpless fury popped in Evan's veins. "They're *children*, Osborn. *Children.* Innocent of any possible charges you could bring against them."

"Not so." Her expression turned rueful. Even sad. A Valkyrie who hated her job but would do it nonetheless. "The gods take back their broken offspring. *Demand* that they be returned to them. Thus into the bogs went the lame and the deformed. Those who are twisted and malformed or blind. Also, Sparrow, you are wrong. These two have sinned and sinned terribly. They are not like those other innocent children."

"They're only—"

"This one," she said, nudging Tommy's unconscious form, "harvested the beasts of the field. Held them prisoner. And the other . . ." Now she touched Jo. "Her illness was cured by the drugs of companies that experimented on animals. They valued her life above the earth's small creatures."

Evan brushed melting snow from his face. The most dangerous kind of serial killer was a rational one. The killer who'd built an entire world based on false beliefs that could not be disproven.

How did one launch a cannon of logic against the impenetrable fortress of insanity?

Osborn came closer to the camera. Her expression was imperial; her skin glowed in the camera's lights.

A bog goddess, Evan thought. Grendel's mother, here to claim her due.

Gods were never required to be logical.

She sighed. "These children were not my first targets. I intended to take Helskin. But Raven surprised me, and I had to act too quickly. So I took Raven instead. He came willingly, thinking we were partners. He could not see how I mocked his pathetic attempts at sorcery. How I scorned his petty sacrifices and his unbridled cruelty. He never understood *seithr* magic."

"But you do."

"I have labored long to understand the ways of Odin and the Others." She lowered her eyes for a moment, as if in respect, then lifted her gaze again. "Raven was to be thorn of riding. But the police rushed me, and I left him on a rooftop without making proper sacrifice. I also intended to sacrifice a man who works for Sten Elger at Ragnarök—a bartender who hunts for sport and leaves the carcasses of his victims rotting in the field. I warned him as I warned the others."

Understanding dawned. "By leaving a figurine guarding his front door."

"As I did with you. But you didn't understand, did you?"

"The reasoning of madness often leaves me bewildered."

She reared back as if struck. "I thought you, of all people, *would* understand. How all of us are fated, and that sometimes our fate is wicked. I learned the truth of this when they led me to Desser after someone spray-painted his fence. And to Talfour when he was assaulted. That assault led me to Raven and thence to Tommy. Although I would have let the boy go if the police hadn't forced my hand."

"And Jo?"

Osborn rested her chin on her hand. "I found her through the papers. They loved her story, the beautiful girl saved from certain death by a miracle cure. I meant from the start to take her. But after she led me to you, and your lecture on sacrifice confirmed that you were the chosen one, I decided to leave her be. Until, again, my hand was forced."

"You don't seem to have a lot of say in what you do."

She smiled. It was a terrible smile, cold and cruel. "The gods and the Others guide us along the paths we must go."

Evan found himself grasping at straws. "I've heard that these Others are amenable to persuasion. A trade, perhaps. Some form of bribery. They aren't unreasonable, these ancient ones." *Only greedy.*

She laughed. "Maybe the gods are fickle. But the Others are not. They lay down their laws, and woe to those who cross them." She glanced away from the camera, then turned back. "The night is wasting, as they say. Just before dawn, I will consign the bodies of Jo and Tommy to the pond. Then it will be your turn, Sparrow. Yours and Ginny's. Your hawk will lead your soul and the souls of Jo and Tommy into the worlds beyond this world."

"We're all rather fond of *this* one," he said. "I'm sure there's some agreement we can reach."

She turned her back on him and disappeared out of the range of the camera.

Evan turned his wrist in the manacle, testing it as pain flared up his arm. The metal held firm, the mechanism old-looking but solid. Had she dragged it out of some evidence locker, the remnant of a mafia bust from the thirties?

Osborn came back within view of the camera. She appeared to be dragging something heavy. She turned, and he saw that she held an immense sword, a Viking Age sword with a welded blade and lobed handle.

She stopped by the motionless figures of the children.

Evan's mind raced furiously down a dark river, searching for answers. Mentally, he sped past Talfour's body and the leaden pond where Desser had bled into the killer's sacred ground. He went further back in time, back and back, past medieval scribes penning the tales of the Vikings, back and back again to *blót* sacrifices and the bowls of blood lifted to the invisible Others before their contents were poured into the dank waters of the bog.

His ears roared with the tumult of ideas until the river landed him at last on a quiet island where memory and imagination found a space where they could work together.

"Wait," he whispered.

Osborn turned to face the camera again. The muscles in her arms bunched as she raised the sword.

"Wait!" he cried.

She hesitated.

"I have a proposition," he said.

The blade seemed to hang of its own accord in the air, heavy and sharp, rich with the promise of death. Then Osborn lowered it so that the tip came to rest between the sleeping forms of the children.

"A contest," he said.

She laughed. "What kind of contest do you have in mind? War hammers? Crossbows? Battle-axes?" Her laugh grew louder. "Perhaps two-handed broadswords?"

"Riddles," he answered.

She tipped her head. "What?"

"Riddles. A contest as old as the Sphinx and beloved by the ancient Greeks as well as the Vikings. A contest that any *scop* worth her words would agree to."

Her forehead creased as she considered this.

Evan said, "You asked Talfour a riddle before you killed him. In the moonlight, you said, *Prick me this.* The start of a riddle. I imagine you did the same with Desser."

"Riddles they failed to answer."

"But they had that chance. These children deserve the same."

"Then riddle me this, dwarf. How does a sleeping child answer a riddle?"

"Through a proxy. *I* claim their riddles."

She narrowed her eyes at him through the camera lens. "What would be the conditions of this contest? If I agree. *If* I agree."

"My conditions are these." He said the words loftily, as though he held all the cards.

She scrutinized him, her gaze thin and sharp.

He continued. "One riddle for each child—"

"*Three,*" she answered. "Three riddles for each child."

He nodded his agreement. "Three riddles. You ask the riddle, and if I answer all three correctly, that child goes free. It is an honorable way of settling disputes. And it will amuse the gods. And the Others."

An uncanny intelligence shone in her eyes. Intelligence and madness entwined, like the sacred bound up with violence.

She said, "If *I* win, then I take all three of you. If *you* win, then I take only your life."

Fate goes ever as it must, Beowulf had said, acknowledging that he was destined to die under the claws of the dragon. But he was also asserting that, while he lived, he would do whatever he could to protect his countrymen.

"As you wish," he said. He was shivering hard enough now from the cold that his teeth chattered.

"And," she went on, "for each wrong answer, I will take something from the child. They won't die so peaceably."

He reeled. What had he done? He reminded himself of his favorite quote from Cicero: *While there's life, there's hope.*

"I agree," he said. "But . . ."

She cocked her head.

"But," he continued, "you must come outside, come here to these woods, and face me. I know you're close. Just by the lagoon. Come here and let us meet face-to-face, as honorable opponents. It will please the Others."

And if the gods saw fit, maybe someone would come along. Someone out and about even in the weather and even though the park had been closed for hours.

Maybe they would see and call for help.

"Do not!" Osborn cried. She picked up the sword and slammed the tip against the ground. Sparks flew from the cement. Tommy stirred in his sleep. "Do not tell me what will or will not please the Others. You do not know them. You have not sacrificed man and bird to them."

Somewhere in the near distance, there came a sound. A harsh breath, as if someone labored through the snow. Hope rose in him like a leap of light. But he did not dare speak or turn his head.

Instead, he lowered his gaze humbly. "You are right. I apologize. But it does seem fitting that you emerge from your lair just as Grendel's mother emerged from hers to avenge her son's death. Those were the rules she played by."

Her face contorted with silent grief, and he knew he had her there. He didn't yet know what final blow had sent her on this path. But he knew at least two secrets to her pain. Her mother's death. And her child's—Rhinehart's grandson. No wonder Rhinehart had tried so hard to distract them from the truth. He must have been terrified the killer might be his own daughter.

She said, "I agree to your terms. It is only right that we meet in the woods, face-to-face. When we've finished, whichever of us wins, I will begin your preparation for meeting the Others. I hope you are strong, Dr. Wilding. Your journey toward death will feel like an eternity."

The camera went black.

CHAPTER 36

Addie and Patrick stood in the office of the U of C campus police while Diana paced the hallway outside. The ax-wielding postdoc had joined up in the hunt for Evan after confirming to the police that the professor was not at home.

She had a murderous glint in her eye.

It was an anger Addie shared. Both at the killer *and* at Evan. She was ready to borrow Diana's ax and start smashing things.

She'd start with the man standing in front of her.

"Go on," Addie said to the officer. Frank Martin.

"Like I explained on the phone," Martin said. "I met him upstairs in the coffee shop. I was going to give him a lift to his car. Him and the kid. But the Chicago PD officer came and offered to escort the two of them. It seemed like they knew each other."

"What kid?"

"I don't know. He seemed kind of off, if you know what I mean. I assumed he was a student."

Tommy Snow. What was his role in all this?

"It was a male officer," Patrick confirmed.

"A man?" Martin looked surprised, as if they should know. "Nah. It was a woman."

Addie's thoughts threw themselves around her skull like caged beasts. "What woman?"

"I don't know. Like I said, Chicago PD. She had a squad car. She said you'd sent her."

"That *I* sent her?" Addie turned to Patrick. "Dispatch told us Blakesley's partner is a woman."

"Right." He nodded. "Sally Osborn."

Addie dialed Dispatch.

Diana stalked by the open door.

"Hey, you can't have a weapon on university grounds," Martin called out.

"I'm faculty."

"Don't matter. The rules are clear."

She halted in her pacing. "Come and stop me, then."

Martin scowled but made no move to approach her.

Addie pocketed her phone. "Dispatch can't raise Sally Osborn. She and Blakesley were off today, but Osborn offered to help in the search. Her last check-in was two hours ago." She pressed her palms together hard enough to hurt. "What if Blakesley has killed her, too?"

Patrick sank into a chair.

Addie ran scenarios through her head.

It was unlikely Evan and Tommy had been overpowered in such a public place. Which meant Evan had trusted the officer. But the officer—presumably Osborn—had told Evan that Addie herself had sent her. So was she in cahoots with Blakesley? Or had Blakesley provided that falsehood and sent her in to fetch Evan?

And if so, where were they all now?

Police had entered Blakesley's apartment half an hour ago and found it empty. Now they were running down every one of his known acquaintances in the greater Chicago area. Friends. His mother. Associates in the Lesbian and Gay Police Association. So far, nothing.

Other police and detectives continued to check the areas on the map Evan had sent. Even using the K-9 unit, the only illegal things they'd turned up so far were a drug deal in Lincoln Park and an attempted mugging at Beaubien Woods.

Their own search of Evan's office had offered nothing. Certainly, Evan hadn't left any indication he meant to go anywhere but home.

Desolation filled Addie's belly. A heaviness she thought might never go away. "What do we do now?"

Patrick pushed to his feet. "We wait to hear something."

"You know I'm not good at waiting."

"I know." Patrick had so much compassion shining in his eyes that she had to look away.

"We have to *do* something," she said.

Patrick pinched the bridge of his nose. "How about we join in the search?"

She nodded. Diana followed them out the revolving front doors of the Department of Safety and Security. They trudged the half mile back through the snow to where they'd parked outside the Harper Memorial Library building.

Outside the doors of the library, Diana started casting around in the snow.

"What are you looking for?" Addie asked.

"A clue." She walked backward down the sidewalk leading from the doors to the street. "If he knew something was wrong, he would have left us an indication of some kind. A pointer."

"Like what?"

"I don't know."

Addie felt a flare of hope, which just as quickly vanished. "He probably didn't have many options."

"Even a hat or a glove . . ." Diana's voice trailed off.

Patrick said gently, "What would that tell us?" Both women whirled on him, and he lifted his hands. "It's but the truth. Let's put our energy somewhere useful."

He might as well have kicked her in the stomach.

"I'm going back to his house," Diana said. Her voice was flat. "In case he comes back. And to have another look around for Ginny."

The missing hawk was another oddity to add to the night's insanity—Diana had found the mews empty when she'd gone there looking for Evan.

Addie nodded and climbed behind the wheel of their sedan. She watched as Diana started her car and flipped on the lights.

When her phone rang, she snatched it out of her pocket.

It was Dispatch. "Blakesley has been located at the home of his mother. The reporting officer says he's running a fever of a hundred and three. Officer Blakesley says the last time he saw his partner was yesterday, at the end of their shift."

"And no news of her?" she asked the dispatcher.

"Nothing yet. We've issued an investigative alert. Officers will tear the city apart to find her."

In front of them, Diana pulled away from the curb. A small, sodden brown *something* lay in the slush.

"What's that?" Patrick asked.

Addie's heart began to beat again. She pushed open her door and almost threw herself out of the vehicle.

"Call Diana," she said over her shoulder. "It's Evan's satchel."

CHAPTER 37

Evan stood motionless, listening for the labored breathing he'd heard before. Ginny had remained calm on his fist during his conversation with Osborn, but now she lifted one foot, then the other, her talons biting into his damp glove. She fluttered her wings, eager for the sky. For the hunt.

"Easy, girl," he whispered.

Could Diana and Addie have already found his map? Perhaps the police crept toward him through the woods even now.

He leaned into the silence, but nothing more stirred, and he feared the sound had been merely a late-night jogger passing by, oblivious to the unfolding drama.

Now another sound alerted him. He squinted into the semidark. Ginny, much clearer-sighted than he, swiveled her head. And suddenly there she was, Officer Sally Osborn, a woman who—in her grief and madness—had become something both more and less than mortal woman.

Aglæcwif. Monster-wife. She-wolf.

She strode into the small clearing and stopped a few paces away from where he was chained.

She'd swapped the uniform for jeans and a parka. Apparently modern-day ritual sacrifice didn't require special clothing. Over one shoulder, she'd slung a messenger bag—Evan shuddered to think what was inside.

And she'd brought the sword. She drove the point hard into the ground and leaned upon the hilt.

"And so we begin," she said without preamble. "Riddle me this, little man. Of my first victims, what sin filled each man's pockets first with gold and then with earth?"

Evan wanted to cry out for her to slow down. To give him time to think. Together, they could discuss the path she'd chosen. And he could tell her that it was not too late—even now—to change the ending of her story.

Beowulf need not die beneath the dragon's terrible power.

But she was waiting.

He turned the riddle over in his mind to make sure he hadn't missed a turn or twist in her words.

She sneered. "Have I trapped you with my very first riddle?"

"Two men," he said. "Two men, two sins, and both the same sin. Scott Desser sinned against the earth by aiding the men who peeled her flesh. James Talfour bought skins peeled from animals and sold them."

He watched her face for any giveaway, but her expression was like marble.

"Gold filled their pockets," he continued, "until the Others took their due and replaced their gold with the earth of the grave."

She dipped her head in acknowledgment. "Well done. But riddles go from easy to hard. That is how the game is played."

Wait! Please wait. But he nodded. "Go on."

"Now this," she said. "I flit as I will from fish to dog, from goat to cow, from bush to tree, from lake to pond, sipping the rich nectar offered me by wise women and weak men. Who am I?"

A bead of sweat formed at the top of Evan's spine and slid with startling coolness down his back. Possible answers flicked through his mind like the fast-turning pages of a flip-book before slowing, hesitating, then settling on a single answer.

He said, "I am the spirit of the land who accepts all sacrifice—animal and human—by drinking the blood offered by *seithr* sorceresses and *ergi* men."

This time, she frowned.

Behind her, something moved in the trees, and Ginny bobbed her head. A figure, indistinct in the dark. Hope exploded in Evan's chest with a strength that almost dropped him.

He locked his eyes on Osborn lest he betray whoever approached.

"Riddle me this," she said. "I am found in the grave, but I heal all who come to me, although they need no healing."

A faint sound in the trees, which she seemed not to hear.

He breathed in. Breathed out. Focused on the riddle.

Thank God for Christina. And for Simon's Viking books.

He said, "I am Hel, goddess of the underworld, which is also called Hel. I embrace all who die unwounded by battle."

He could see by her expression that he was right. He wanted to cheer. *One child is now mine!* But he said nothing. How could he, when he held not a single card in his hand or up his sleeve? Except, perhaps, the knowledge that at least one other human was here with them. That they weren't alone in the woods.

Whether that fact would help or harm remained to be seen.

When she stayed silent, he found he no longer could. "That's three riddles," he pointed out quietly.

She clenched her fists, her body rigid. "You will not win the other child."

"Let us see."

She slung the messenger bag from her shoulder and set it on the ground, then leaned on the pommel of her sword.

From the trees, a man's voice cried, "Stop!"

Osborn pivoted in the direction of the sound, the hilt of the sword clenched in one fist.

A figure stepped clear of the trees.

Ralph Rhinehart.

Evan's disappointment struck like the flat of Osborn's sword. He stumbled back. "You!" was all he could manage. He should have known this. Expected it. Who else would know they were here? What hope had he that Addie or Diana would find his satchel? And that, if they did, they would discover his map and understand the meaning of it?

"Father," Osborn said.

Evan thought he heard plea and anger both in her voice.

Rhinehart gazed at his daughter. The man's hair was a snarl of snow-wet tangles, his light jacket surely of little use. He wore dress shoes and dress slacks and an expression of grief.

"Sally," he said, the single word filled with both love and anguish.

For an achingly long span of time, no one moved or spoke. Then Rhinehart advanced, his hands raised.

"Halt!" she cried, her voice the clang of a bell's tongue on copper.

He stopped. "Sally—"

"No!" She raised a palm toward him. "I know why you're here, Father. You think you should stop me. You think you *can* stop me." She lifted her chin. "But you've never understood the old stories. Not the way I have. You thought they were *just* stories. Scribblings. Wordplay. Entertainments. But I have grasped the truth. And I will see it out."

Evan crouched, balancing Ginny on his fist while he felt through the snow with his numb hand, searching for a stick, a branch, anything.

Rhinehart clasped his hands in front of his chest. "Those old stories aren't *our* stories, Sal. It's not our way to act like gods. Not for us to decide who lives, who dies."

"People do it all the time!" A flush rose in her face. "All. The. Time. They poison us. Lie to us. Ignore us. They tell us that their mines and their factories won't harm us. Or the animals. And all the while, they rape the earth."

Ginny screeched as if she understood and agreed.

"They found him," Rhinehart said.

Osborn shook her head. "You're lying to me."

Rhinehart took a step forward, his hands still open and beseeching, his voice soothing. "The driver who killed that little girl was an out-of-work alcoholic. They've brought him in."

Ah, thought Evan. *There is the trigger. A hit-and-run. Another lost child.* Tragedy piled on tragedy.

Osborn said, "A year almost, it took them."

"I know, I know." Another forward step. "But the important thing is they found him."

"And what will they do now?"

"That's for the court to decide."

She curled her lip. "The way they decided for Alex? Is that what you mean? A slap on the wrist. A public scolding. An exchange of money or perhaps a detox program." She swung the sword in low arcs, scarring lines in the snow at her feet. "Please, murderer, go on with your life."

"I don't understand these things," Rhinehart said. "I'm just an old man who wants his daughter back. I love you, Sally. I'm proud of you. I always knew you would be a poet. Come home with me, and we'll write poetry together."

The runologist was weeping, the arrogance he'd displayed at the station house gone.

"Let's go home." He shuffled forward.

"No closer," she said.

But he kept moving.

"Stop!" she cried. Now she, too, wept.

Evan paused in his search for a weapon, afraid to move, watching as a father reached out with shaking hands for his broken child.

"We'll go to the beach," Rhinehart said. "We'll talk to your mother. You'd like that, wouldn't you? She's been waiting to talk to you."

As if someone had severed muscle and tendon, Osborn's shoulders dropped, and she lowered her head until her chin touched her chest. The sword came to rest point-down.

Rhinehart nodded. "That's good, Sally."

Then she moved, her left hand reaching into her jacket, returning with something small and dark in her hand. She raised her head.

"No!" Evan shouted at the same time the gun fired.

Rhinehart took a step back. Then another. Red bloomed on his coat. He stared at his daughter with surprise.

"You made me do it, Father," she said. "*Step*father. I was Mother's child. An Osborn. I was never really yours."

He sank to his knees.

She fired again, and Rhinehart toppled sideways into the snow, blood reddening his clothes, the ground. The look of surprise on his face settled into softness.

He didn't move.

Osborn pivoted back to Evan, her eyes wide and dark and deep. And completely mad. He yanked desperately on the chain that held him.

"Riddle me this, dwarf," she said, as if she had not just murdered her father. "I am she who held her child, but though he lived, he could not hug me back."

"I can't—I can't—" Evan's mind gibbered with shock.

"Riddle me this," she said again, biting off each word. "I am she who held her child, but though he lived, he could not hug me back."

The trickle of sweat turned into a river. He forced his far-flung, frightened thoughts to coalesce. To focus. A child's life hung in the balance.

Was the riddle about her own child? Impossible to know. But, whispered the whirlwind in his mind, she might wish first to link herself to that long-ago mother, the one who'd gone to Hrothgar's hall seeking the blood price.

My blood-feud stillbirths your further crimes.

He uttered a silent prayer.

"I am Grendel's mother, whose son returned from King Hrothgar's hall, mortally wounded after Beowulf tore off his arm. Grendel made it home to his mother's embrace, but he lacked two arms with which to hug her back. He died there."

A growl rumbled in Osborn's throat. "Who is the one who is mine and who is mine-gone? Who is the fallen whose fall was brought by the fall of others? Who is he and how did he die?"

The words from Talfour's poem, *mine mine mine*—they weren't a shout of ego, as Rhinehart had suggested, no doubt hoping to mislead.

They were a howl of anguish.

Still, Evan knew he was now well into Sherlock Holmes's territory of the imagination. Everything here was speculation. A mining company with a dragon logo. A lawsuit. A mysterious curse. The line from her poem, *this hoarder caused my fall with his fall, his fall caused by the fallen.*

All he could do was patch together the few facts he had from River and from Tommy and hope that the cloth held.

He said, "He is your son, who fell to his death in a disused mine shaft. Whose fall was caused by carelessness or greed—or both—on the part of the big bosses who stole the riches of the earth."

She reeled back, half stumbling in the snow. Her hair tumbled from its tight coil and fell around her face. When she looked up, all he could see of her was the snarl of her mouth.

She shook back her hair. "And what is the name of the dragon that devoured my son?"

"Epic Mining." He saw the truth in her mad eyes. "That's three riddles. The children shall live."

She tossed her head so that her hair flew about her face. Canniness slithered into her eyes. "You did well, little man. But if I were to offer a final riddle, it would be to ask you, who is the trickster god?"

Odin, Evan thought but didn't say. He feared a trap.

But she sprang the trap herself. "Odin," she said. "I serve Odin. And Odin is a trickster god." She pulled the sword from the ground and held the pommel in both hands. She raised it high. "It is time."

She came at him.

Evan cast Ginny into the air and fled as far as the chain would allow him. Osborn let loose a shriek that turned Evan's skin cold. Even as he cast about again for a weapon, a detached, wry part of his brain thought, *So this is what it's like to have a Valkyrie come for you.*

In the far distance, beyond the pond and surely as far as the road, blue and red flashing lights appeared.

Evan's hand closed on a branch buried in the snow. He raised the branch awkwardly with his cold fingers, wondering how many seconds it might buy him. If any at all.

Then a loud crack broke across the night, Osborn's feet seemed to tangle, and she was suddenly falling forward, the flesh of her throat opening even as the blade of an ax bit into her ribs and her sword arced forward, now free of her hands, sailing high and clean like death until it clattered into the trees. Osborn kept falling; she fell and fell and fell as if in slow motion, and then behind her there was Diana standing in the trees and next to her Addie, with her gun raised, her face filled with something that Evan thought was surely love.

Mortally wounded, not once but twice, struck down by bullet and by blade, Osborn hit the ground. Red poured into the snow.

And for a moment—the briefest, faintest moment—Evan imagined a ghostly form bent and lapping at her blood.

Then it was gone.

CHAPTER 38

An hour after Addie's blue circus took over the scene, Evan allowed himself to be raised onto a gurney. He was too numb to insist he was perfectly fine and all he needed—now that he knew Tommy and Jo were safe—was a stiff drink or three and to sit by the fire in his library while Ginny drowsed nearby on her perch.

After the first drink, he might even stop shivering.

The gurney jolted over tree roots. An EMT, locs swaying around his face, leaned in as he and another man maneuvered the stretcher.

"Whatever you got going, man," he said to Evan, "keep it up."

Evan watched the overhanging boughs drift by above as the gurney rolled and jerked. His mind longed to drift with them.

"What was that?" he managed to say from a distant place.

They'd told him he had hypothermia. Nothing a good Old-Fashioned wouldn't fix.

The EMT leaned in again and grinned, his teeth brilliant. "Those two fine ladies you got. Not one but *two* ladies drooling over you. Making sure you're fine. Making sure you get the best treatment. They're like those Viking warrior women. What do you call them?"

"Valkyrie," Evan whispered.

"Exactly! Man, I'd like a couple Valkyries keeping me warm on a night like this. Shit, one of them has a hawk! You see that?" This last directed toward the other EMT.

"You see that *sword?*" the other man asked. "It's like King fucking Arthur around here."

The wheels slammed into a root, and metal squealed and groaned. The EMTs hoisted the gurney up and over as if it and Evan weighed nothing at all.

"Nah, it's Vikings, man. Axes and swords and Valkyries. That is some seriously cool shit. I would *love* to have a Valkyrie looking out for my ass."

Be very careful what you wish for, Evan thought.

He closed his eyes.

X

Addie stood at the edge of the crime scene and watched the lights of the ambulance strobe against the night. The siren gave a single *whoop* as the driver pulled away from the curb, and moments later, the vehicle rounded a bend and vanished from sight.

Evan, shivering so hard that his teeth chattered, had filled her in on what had happened and what he'd surmised since their last phone call—Sally Osborn as a mentally unwell child grieving for a mother who was wasting away from cancer just as the mummified remains of another tortured woman were found in the ground. She'd then grown up under the tutelage of a stepfather whose specialty had been Old English texts. No doubt Rhinehart had shared his enthusiasm for the old sagas with his stepdaughter, teaching her the runes, never realizing until it was too late that while he was trying to fashion a hero, the traumas of life had consigned her to becoming a monster.

Evan had been focused on his own failure.

I was so intent on Blakesley and the fact that 96 percent of serial killers are men, he'd said, *that I missed what was right under my nose.*

You led us here, she'd replied. *You saved Jo's and Tommy's lives.*

But she knew he would punish himself for a long time.

Now she stared at the two bodies lying cold and pale in the snow and realized she was looking at the kind of tragedy the old poets would have turned into one of their sagas. A poem to perform night after night in the flickering firelight of the mead hall while Viking warriors and their peace-weaving women looked on.

She snugged down her beanie as snow began to fall again, gathering quietly as if it would shroud the bodies.

After the children—still unconscious—had been rescued from the pump house next to the lagoon, they'd discovered a leather-bound journal on Osborn's single bookshelf. Addie had opened it to the first few pages and realized they'd found a treasure trove: a would-be hero's descent into madness, divulged by her own hand. From the trauma of her mother's death through that of her child's and finally the death of another child who'd been killed by a driver in a hit-and-run. From her childhood crush on her father's assistant, who had also died tragically, to her growing focus on Viking culture and, ultimately, her decision to punish those who sinned against the earth.

Patrick strode up to her, an unlit cigarette tucked in his mouth.

"It's going to take hours if not days to work this," he said. "I was going to offer to take over the scene so you can get to the hospital and see how our pal is doing. But the lieutenant is adamant that you stay."

Addie glanced over to where Criver stood at the edge of the clearing, the collar of his navy wool coat turned up, his hands thrust in his pockets. He would be formulating a story in his head. Something that would play well for the media. Because for an ambitious cop, good publicity trumped personal sexism.

She could imagine the headline: Brilliant Female Detective Takes Down Brilliant Female Serial Killer.

So fitting. So politically correct.

"I'll stay a couple hours," she said. "Then I'll need to take a break."

Patrick nodded.

"You were right about this case," she said. "That bad feeling you had at the first crime scene."

"You know I was just ribbing you," he said.

A smile flitted across her face. "You were scared to death of that snake. A grown man about to wet himself."

"Yeah, well." Patrick tucked his hands in his pockets and hunched his shoulders. "The Irish and snakes are none too fond of each other. And this investigation, it's . . ."

"I know."

They stood in silence for a moment. Then one of the techs raised a hand to wave them over, and Addie shrugged off thoughts of monsters and omens and forced herself back to the matter at hand.

ᛣ

When Evan woke, he found himself warm and dry in a dimly lit hospital room. Monitors beeped. Footsteps passed his open door. An elevator dinged, and someone called for a nurse.

He stared at the ceiling and decided that he really didn't want to process anything right now. His brain was tired.

Maybe he'd take River up on his offer to visit him in Turkey. The semester would be over soon. He could spend the holidays in Istanbul. Visit the Hagia Sophia museum and the Blue Mosque. Take a stroll across the Galata Bridge. Maybe pick up a rug at the Grand Bazaar.

More footsteps and then a woman entered his room—a nurse in pink scrubs with a lanyard around her neck revealing her name, Sandra Hollister, RN.

She gave him a mock frown.

"You're awake," she said. "How are you feeling?"

Evan tried and failed to push himself up on his pillow. His right wrist throbbed. He scowled. "Absolutely splendid."

The frown deepened. "Now, now, no need for sarcasm. You want me to give you a little something to help you sleep?"

Evan mustered some fighting spirit. "Any sedatives administered to my body will be dispensed by my own hand and strictly in liquid form. I don't even understand why I'm here."

"Awake and sassy. Fine. You've had a bit of a shock. Not to mention hypothermia. And you've got a nasty wound on your wrist." She scanned the monitor to which various parts of him were attached, made a tut-tutting sound, and wrote something on a dry-erase board. "You have a visitor if you're up for it."

"Is she wearing a winged helmet?"

"Just pants and a coat, I believe."

"Okay, then. How do I look?"

"Like a heartbreaker in a romance movie."

She slipped back out the door as quietly as she'd entered, and a moment later, Addie hurried in, leaned over his bed, and kissed his forehead.

She gazed down on him with tender concern. Maybe this hospital stuff wasn't so very bad.

"How do you feel?" she asked.

"Perfectly fine. I'd like to go home."

"Tomorrow. And only if you behave."

"Tell me what I've missed."

Addie pulled a chair next to the bed and filled him in. First, Ginny was safely back in her mews. Jo had been released to her parents. All the girl remembered of the entire ordeal was accepting a ride from the nice police lady and then falling asleep. Tommy had also been released to the custody of his mom.

This time, Evan did manage to sit up a little. "Tommy helped solve the mystery. He should be awarded something. A medal."

"I'll make sure it happens," Addie said, then continued.

Both Sally Osborn and Ralph Rhinehart were dead. Rhinehart's other two children—Osborn's stepbrothers—were already on their way here from the UK. Over the next days and weeks, she and Patrick—with Evan's help—would sort through both Osborn's and Rhinehart's lives, trying to fit all the pieces together.

She said, "Rhinehart thought by pushing his neo-Nazi theories, he was leading us away from his daughter."

"But she was connected to Raven," Evan finished. "All three were into sorcery, in their own fashion."

"She was our leak."

Evan nodded, then regretted it as a headache announced its presence. "Because she needed to have her story told."

"We found her journal. In the pump house."

"You *will* let me take a look."

"Of course. One thing we learned is that Osborn had not only gone to your public talks, she'd audited several of your lecture classes and likely attended one of your end-of-year parties. That would explain how she got the code to your house and stole your copies of *Beowulf*."

"It's never a good idea," Evan murmured, "to invite the monster in."

"Worse is to not change your security code after the monster has come through."

After a time, Addie's voice trailed off into silence. Evan felt inexplicably sleepy. A side effect of shock, no doubt. And the aforementioned touch of hypothermia. His eyes drifted closed.

"I should go," Addie said.

He blinked and dug his voice out of a deep recess. "Diana has never killed anyone before."

"Neither have I," Addie said softly. "We had no choice. We'll be all right."

"I know." He didn't want her to leave. "How's Claymore?"

"Who?"

"Clayton L. Hamden, attorney to the stars."

"We just caught a serial killer and you nearly died and you're asking about him?"

"Yes." A man had his priorities, after all.

"Well, Clayton and I . . . it's over. Being with him was kind of like having a silverback gorilla banging around the place, beating his chest and trying to lord the manor."

"I'm sorry," he said. But he wasn't sorry at all.

"Don't be. He wasn't anything much." She stood. "I'm going to let you sleep."

"I'll sleep better if you're here."

"Really?"

"Most definitely." He roused himself.

She sat back down and took his hand. "Then I'll stay."

"Don't you have detecting to do? Murders to attend to?"

"Friends first."

He smiled. "Valkyrie," he whispered, too softly for Addie to hear. He knew he was still smiling when sleep came.

Acknowledgments

As a child and young adult, I fell in love first with J. R. R. Tolkien's *The Hobbit* and then with his famous trilogy, The Lord of the Rings. Perhaps that is what led me to focus on medieval works of literature as an undergraduate. The power of poems like "The Wanderer" and "Dream of the Rood" wove a spell around me from which I've never recovered.

I hope those readers who are knowledgeable about the English runes will forgive my simplification of the three-step process of transliteration, transcription, and translation. In creating the runic version of the killer's poems, I'm indebted to several books, most especially *Runes: A Handbook* by Michael P. Barnes.

For Christina's explanation of skaldic poetry, I am grateful for "Skaldic Poetry: A Short Introduction" at the website https://www.asnc.cam.ac.uk/resources/mpvp/wp-content/uploads/2013/02/Introduction-to-Skaldic-Poetry_Debbie-Potts.pdf.

The character of Christina, in my novel, is correct in reporting a recent surge of scholarly interest in Grendel's mother. For those who want a modern-day rendition of the world according to this powerful woman, I recommend *The Mere Wife* by Maria Dahvana Headley. Headley's translation of *Beowulf* is equally brilliant and was only excluded from *At First Light* by dint of its 2020 publication date.

The translations of *Beowulf* mentioned in this book are those by poet and scholar Seamus Heaney and by Oxford don and writer J. R. R. Tolkien. Each translation is powerful and thrilling in its own way.

Concerning Norse mythology, you can't go wrong by picking up *Norse Mythology* by Neil Gaiman.

And for all things Vikings, I'm especially grateful for the brilliantly written and highly entertaining *Children of Ash and Elm: A History of the Vikings* by archaeologist Neil Price. This book opened up my understanding of the Viking Age people in astonishing and delightful (and sometimes horrifying) ways. At nearly six hundred pages, the book is a tome. But it is well worth the time it takes to peruse its fascinating and surprisingly cheerful pages.

Finally, for details about the work of semioticians and forensic semioticians in particular, please see *Signs of Crime* by Marcel Danesi and *Murder in Plain English* by Michael Arntfield and Marcel Danesi.

Although I've helped rehabilitate injured birds of prey and have assisted licensed falconers, I am not myself licensed. Thus, for help regarding falconry in Illinois, I am grateful to Steven Twiddy of the Great Lakes Falconers Association.

Most importantly, I want to give a shout-out to all the people who helped as I strove to write a book during a time of great personal tragedy as well as persistent and terrifying vision issues. Please know that any errors in this novel are entirely my own.

First, my beta readers and much-loved friends, who take whatever I give them without complaint and make it infinitely better: Deborah Coonts, Chris Mandeville, Cathy Noakes, Michael Shepherd, and Robert Spiller. If anyone is keeping score in Valhöll, I'll be serving the five of you mutton and mead for an eternity.

And to the Chicagoans who graciously offered their help during a pandemic: writers Tracy Clark, Lori Rader-Day, and especially Lisa Anne Rothstein. I'm also deeply appreciative of the help given by retired

Chicago cop and full-time writer Michael A. Black as well as retired Chicago cop and crime writer Dave Case.

As always, a shout-out to retired Denver detective Ron Gabel, who cheerfully answers all questions and keeps me honest.

To those who reached out often this year to offer a sympathetic (if virtual) shoulder, thank you. This list includes Michael Bateman, Jennifer Kincheloe, and Margaret Mizushima. Your kindness brings light to a sometimes dark world.

Continued thanks to my agent, Bob Diforio. To my incredibly supportive editor, Liz Pearsons, and the rest of the team at Thomas & Mercer. And my enduring gratitude to editor Charlotte Herscher, who takes my messy and convoluted manuscripts and makes them immeasurably better.

And finally, all my love to my sisterhood—Cathy, Deb, Lori, Maria, and Pat. And always, Steve and Amanda. This small cadre of friends and family got me through this year.

For a longer list of resources, for more information about my books, or to contact me directly, please visit my website at www.barbaranickless.com.

ABOUT THE AUTHOR

Photo © 2017 Trystan Photography

Barbara Nickless is the *Wall Street Journal* and Amazon Charts bestselling author of the Sydney Rose Parnell series, which includes *Blood on the Tracks*, a *Suspense Magazine* Best of 2016 selection and winner of the Daphne du Maurier Award for Excellence; *Dead Stop*; *Ambush*; and *Gone to Darkness*. *Blood on the Tracks* and *Dead Stop* won the Colorado Book Award, and *Dead Stop* was nominated for the Daphne du Maurier Award for Excellence. Her essays and short stories have appeared in *Writer's Digest* and *Criminal Element*, among other markets. She lives in Colorado, where she loves to cave, snowshoe, hike, and drink single malt Scotch—usually not at the same time. Connect with her at www.barbaranickless.com.